Platterland

More Forays into the Fantastic by Rob Hunter

I was in a Piranesi landscape—tumbled columns, grazing goats, distant shepherds and shepherdesses about their discreet businesses in a renaissance bosky dell. Giancarlo crouched before a tiny campfire, feeding it with sticks and what looked to be loose rubble. He had several weeks' growth of beard. "Signore Twain?" He turned and saw that it was me. "Ah, you are back. I had hoped you might return. Good day. Or more appropriately, l'altro ieri, the day before yesterday. Or the week after today."

I moved in to warm myself at the fire. It was cold. "Your fire is not giving out much heat," I said.

"It is not a fire; it is a picture of a fire." Giancarlo gestured toward the grazing goats. "Push one," he said.

I walked over to the little flock; no matter which way I tried to go, everything was sideways. "Push," said Giancarlo. I pushed. The goat fell over.

—Mark Twain in Milan from *Platterland*

It was a real nice laying-out—tasteful. Well, maybe not so much tasteful particularly, but neat. They'd got Ed's left arm attached to his head and not his shoulder. And they had the remaining right arm attached on the left side. To look like them, I supposed.

—Platterland from *Platterland*

Giant bumblebees prowl thick wisteria; vines knot to frame a lovers' bower. Before the foreground, hogging the floor, lies a toppled faun, his lips curled in a sneer of passion. At his side is a sawed-off fluted plaster column with a shattered capital nearby suggesting old ruins. I could not bear to throw the stuff out. Some day someone would want to be photographed with a leering, panting satyr..

—The Tirewoman Gabriel from *Platterland*

Platterland

You'll Be Happy Here

For Charlie and Jenny who know why
and Claudia who never had to ask.

❏

"Ohh, mommy, look." A mother and child studied the darkening sky. The young one was working hard at staying up later than usual, watching for a sign, hoping to stay up for another hour. A bright blossoming flared and faded past her finger's end.

"A star exploding." The woman had been a mother many times over many years. The night sky held no new wonders for her.

The child had to think quickly. "A minute more, please. I am looking for the V of the eidolons."

"Silly girl." A pause. "What is an eidolon?" Eidolon. A new word from school. The little ones were ever bringing home new things; it was hard keeping up. The mother peered into the afterglow left by an expired galaxy.

"They are the wild flying pigs of time, unwinding the stars."

—from *The Return of the Orange Virgin*

Platterland—More Forays into the Fantastic
by Rob Hunter
First published October 2010
ISBN:978-0-578-06803-9

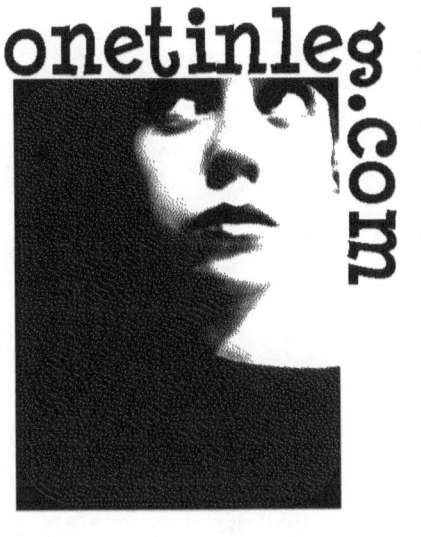

onetinleg.com

As of this writing there are as yet no Rob Hunter tote bags, umbrellas, refrigerator magnets, ties, bumper stickers, etc. The stories collected at onetinleg.com are there for free, a sad deficiency but I'm working on it—a handsome coffee mug emblazoned with the onetinleg.com logo is available at cafepress.com/onetinleg. Be the first kid on your block, etc.

Typically the afterlife of a tale consists of gathering dust until the writer's heirs and assigns shred it for packing nick-knacks and other writerly impedimenta. Not quite the half-life of linoleum. And what of the loves, lives, hopes and aspirations of its citizens? Must they float forever in a shimmering noösphere playing whist and watching the flights of eidolons? Boring. Hence onetinleg.com. I regularly record stories as they become available and copyright reverts back to me, in usually a year or so. The stories and MP3 downloads are distributed for free, under a Creative Commons license.

To misquote Walt Kelly's Pogo: "We have seen the future and it's not yet..." The call, dear reader, is yours. The gentlefolk listed in the acknowledgements —who have shown the rare taste and superior judgment to purchase my work—thank you for your support.

The tales of Platterland have appeared in print and online in the years 2005 through 2010

The house that was a city

grew and, as is the way with cities, buried its past beneath an ever-advancing present.

In the cellars of the Queen, where three corridors met to form a Y, three stone heads graced the capital of a buried pendentive. The settled dust of thousands of years had raised the level of the floor and grown hardened by the footfalls of passing errands. Lime leached from all the stories above had marbled the black granite walls and joined with the dust of the floor to form a polished cement.

The heads were malign at first glance, a dead craftsman's nightsweats and horrors: vaguely a cow, a goat, and a manticore. Each had some resemblance to the beast it portrayed—and not without an idiot twinkle—but seen through a glass cast with a ripple in it, reflected in a mirror with peeling silver. They were figments, and existed nowhere in nature.

They were the past and they were buried. They had been surrounded, enveloped and eventually forgotten in a subcellar of the great masonry sprawl as addition after addition was piled over them.

—*The Return of the Orange Virgin*

Platterland—The Entertainments

—10—

The Contrapuntal Mind

In praise of knowing some Latin—sort of an introduction.

—11—

Two of Swords

Capt. Futvoye Halfnight, F.R.S, popped his dropped eye into its socket. "Ahh." What he saw ahead was not reassuring. "Ohh..." A great gnarly man was leaning against a tree and staring at him. He was naked but for the skin of a tiger which he wore nonchalantly over one shoulder. "You pilgrims should carry rearview mirrors. You leave an inventory of lost lesions and dropped appendages all over the landscape," said the man.

—26—

The Francher

An odor of mint attracted the francher to an unpromising patch of brown scrub. It munched contentedly for some minutes then collapsed. Wide speckled eyes bulged; oval pupils stared. A pounding bright blue sky watched, thin and close, as the francher's body stiffened. Under the brilliant glare of the high, dry sun its knee joints cracked, emitting soft popping sounds. An Andean vulture circled closer.

—42—

Mark Twain in Milan

A woman popped out of thin air beside me. She was swinging a serious looking cavalry saber; She gave me the once-over and attacked. I ducked. Her pale gray eyes grew huge. "Oh, terribly sorry, old chap. I thought you were someone else," she said. "Are you still alive?" I said yes. "I say, good fun, what?" she remarked. A bullet zinged past and we dived under the desk.

—79—

Platterland

Flyin' Ed rode the rainbow, that's how he described it to the wide-eyed kids at the Elementary when he used to come to do his show and tell. "We all said someday he'd break his fool neck. And one day he did," said Pilly Hennicott. Pillsbury Hennicott, known as Pilly, was the chairman of the school board.

—90—

McMuckle Makes a Minyan

The ineffable, unnamable God of Hosts stood with a burly, bearded personage who held a bar towel draped over one arm, a symbol of his trade. The golem toyed nervously with an ear. "My people should quake at My unutterable Name, not fall on their tukhes," God sighed. The ear came off. "Bim... this is not about you. Try to stay on topic."

—103—

A Modest Proposal (the commercial)

Wherein you are invited to browse onetinleg.com's Free Reads section. These MP3 audio downloads are released under a Creative Commons license. They're free. Copy the files as much as you want, pass 'em around.

—104—

Chimaera Constant

"Sweet Jesus!" Elizabeth Profitt Pease has—for just a moment, a split second—the queer idea that there is an eyeball in her teacup. "Uh... hello, eye." The eye does not speak. She takes a swallow of Dr. Pomeroy's straight from the bottle and shakes her head to clear it. She squints; the eye in her teacup squints back—the eye is hazel and clear. It is her mother's eye.

—117—

Daphne Longhandle's Last Flight

"I am Daphne Prydferthbwytawrganawyreni. PRYD-ferth, bwy-TAW-gan, are-ANY. It's Welsh. Damned if I know how Mom got her talons on a Welsh dictionary. It's a dragon thing, I guess. I was abandoned early on. Mom went west with a crew of migrating geese." Until I met Daphne Longhandle, I figured dragons tended to eat whatever came along. The macaroni and cheese was a bewilderment.

—129—

The Tirewoman Gabriel

Giant bumblebees prowl thick wisteria, vines knot to frame a lovers' bower. Before the foreground, hogging the floor, lies a toppled faun, his lips curled in a sneer of passion. At his side is a sawed-off fluted plaster column with a shattered capital nearby suggesting old ruins. I could not bear to throw the stuff out. Some day someone would want to be photographed with a leering, panting satyr.

The Death of James A. Garfield

Short and overalled, a small figure stepped out of the roadside scrub and declaimed. "You are Lost. Lost Forever. I am Delilah," she said. "James A. Garfield has guided your feet. It's a sure thing. President Garfield never misses. After the tomatoes, of course," she said with wide-eyed innocence. This is a kid trick: getting inside your head so you trust them.

The Return of the Orange Virgin

Lechery, debauchery, total annihilation, blood and mud—the usual stuff as two prime movers contend for power. Not power to do anything in particular—threaten, coerce, destroy: illuminate a city, tighten the skeins of a siege engine, or wind up the bowels of a child's clockwork toy—just power to have around. Just in case. Just the familiar, reassuring bulge of potential, there to quiet unease was not much to ask. But who to ask?

How the Orange Virgin came to be
There's life in the old girl yet. Think of it as a hypertext puzzle box.

Orange Virgin Dramatis Personae—characters map
The citizens of the tale.

A Brief History of the Author—a short personal note

Acknowledgements

Wherein the blame is parceled out—brickbats, accolades, etc.

Legal Stuff

The Creative Commons Connection

The Contrapuntal Mind

Weird, the world of "genre fiction." For the uninitiated, that's a category, genre fiction—and within the category are labeled pigeonholes; all God's chillun got a label. Mine would appear to be "slipstream." Or "magical realism." Cool. Well, *carpe titulum*—take what you are given and be grateful. A label gets respect. This said, there's no better way to get fast respect than big words or maybe some Latin to show you finished high school. I had all four years: Caesar's Gallic Wars through Virgil, and have forgotten most of it. But back to weird.

Weird is certainly an effect I sometimes try for. Problem is: weird alone won't work for the characters as they navigate the mechanics of a fugal landscape. And note: select citizens of this book will consume many cigars, cigarettes, and otherwise smoke, chew and/or ingest tobacco products. Make of this what you will. I ceased a decades-long affair with nicotine during the course of these tales and wistful longings sometimes seep into the work.

While smoking is an unfashionable disorder, ADHD appears to be the latest in the flavor-of-the-month sweepstakes for fashionable disorders. Maybe it helps to have ADHD when approaching slippery twists in a plot line. I plead guilty on all charges. One of my kinder critics once said I had a "contrapuntal mind." For which read "slipstream."

"I never dreamed that algorithm would work," says Lady Augusta Ada Byron King, Countess of Lovelace in *Mark Twain in Milan*. "...on material human beings. This is too, too fabulous. I was stretching my intellectual muscle, showing off a bit in front of those self-important preeners." Clearly, a contrapuntal lady.

My first experience of "slipstream" was in a book, *Take Three Tenses: A Fugue in Time*, by Rumer Godden. I read it when I was 12. I was captivated.

Virginia Woolf on escaping self-absorption, quoted in the *New York Review of Books*: "...one should read; see outsiders; think more; write more logically; above all be full of work; & practice anonymity."

Ecce liber—a book peopled with stories that have been previously in print and/or online from 2005 to 2010. The characters are frequently confused and often weird. Aren't we all? Hope you like 'em.

Rob Hunter
Pembroke, Maine
October 2010

Two of Swords

The divine person is a source of danger as well as of blessing; he must not only be guarded, he must also be guarded against... thus, the practice of putting kings to death either at the end of a fixed term or whenever their health or strength began to fail.

—Sir James George Frazer, The Golden Bough

Capt. Futvoye Halfnight, F.R.S. considered his puttees.
A fleet eland had given its all in their manufacture yet he was not happy with them. His puttees were a fine suede, unborn oryx, skinned alive in its mother's womb, their extreme softness achieved by a vigorous rubbing with placental blood. This was a native practice which the captain deplored, but it did produce a grand puttee of an optimistic fawn color. He regarded an irregular blemish of smut on one freshly brushed puttee. It was not the arrival of the vagabond smut that he found disturbing, for smut happened. It was the speck's irregular shape, a portent of the unanticipated.

"I am only having a look-about," pronounced the captain for any unseen listener. "I like to know where I am," He whistled up his left eye. "Pweet! Here girl." The original eye, which had been hazel, he had lost chucking quoits with the dervishes of the Taklamakan Desert. A native healer had plucked a replacement eye from a pile of battlefield offal. It was of perhaps human origin.

"Pweet!" The eye came rolling toward him across the forest floor from where it had been investigating the nest of a spotted vole.

The captain popped the eye into its socket. "Ahh."

What he saw was not reassuring. "Ohh..." A great gnarly man was leaning against a tree and staring at him. He wore a stewpot tilted backwards on his head and was naked but for the skin of a tiger which he wore nonchalantly over one shoulder.

"You pilgrims should carry rearview mirrors. You leave an inventory of lost lesions and dropped appendages all over the landscape," said the gnarly man. He approached with the side-saddle gait of a cripple. One hip had been dislocated and poorly healed. "You are in the woods. *My* woods. Capt. Halfnight I presume?" He gave the captain's eye a speculative look. "Hullo, there, Claudia."

The eye winked.

"You know my eye's name. And while we're at it, how is it that you know *my* name?"

"Easy enough. You were yowling it all through the sacred wood. And that's a mighty handsome eye ye got there, if'n ye don't mind me saying. Should be mine. Mustn't let one's eye go poking about unsupervised."

"You presume overly much."

"I never presume anything. You haven't commented on my limp. That is polite of you."

"Uhn, sorry. I didn't notice," Halfnight lied.

"Don't give it a second thought." The man lifted the leather flap of an eyepatch to reveal an empty hollow behind. "They took my eye, too." The gnarly man looked appraisingly at Claudia. "They put me out of joint and I healed crooked; they figure I can't get far." The gnarly man winced and lowered himself to the ground. "I'm likewise missing most of my teeth."

"Odd you should mention oral hygiene. I am a diplomate of Macclesfield Dental Academy. Teeth were my bread and butter till I answered the call of King and Country. I had a flourishing dental practice in Derbyshire—genuine replacement teeth, wed inextricably to the jawbone. You would be an excellent candidate."

"A winsome smile won't save yer brisket here, laddie. The basic diet of a sacred king is oat porridge, butter and honey—hogsheads, puncheons, barrels, firkins, rundlets and tuns of butter, the fatter the better. I keep on the go so's not to pack on the pork. The girls haven't yet started sizing me up for the stewpot. But I can't leave off answering the dinner chime—goes with the job; when the girls decide, I die. And that, me laddie-buck, is where you come in." With a great greenish-black smile consisting mainly of rotten stumps, he held out his hand. "I was once called Charley Blackwell. And you?"

"Futvoye Halfnight, F.R.S, V.C., D.D.S. I am a Fellow of the Royal Society. The V.C. does not denote any particular distinction. Very Careful. I am very careful."

"Careful is as careful does," offered the gnarly man. "We all are lamed; soon it will be your turn. See, my time is approaching and if I don't come up with a surrogate, well... there will be a fight to the death for my fiefdom—a fight with the next comer, which I gather to be you."

"You are a king." Halfnight found himself wishing he had packed the ceremonial sword presented to graduates of the Macclesfield Dental Academy.

"Rex Nemorensis, the king of the sacred wood," said the gnarly man. He reached into a pouch he carried slung over one shoulder and, extracting a treacle, began ecstatically gumming away at it. "You know, all that Golden Bough mumbo-jumbo. And call me Charley."

"Sugar treats will rot your teeth, Charley." said Futvoye Halfnight. "A word to the wise. You *do* floss?"

"You are here to kill me. What care you if my death-rictus is cavity-free?" Charley Blackwell spat his treacle into the trees. "Solicitude for the well-being of a victim is unbecoming in an assassin. But I forgive you, for this is the practice in the Lady's wood."

"I have taken an oath to save life, not take it. I am an army surgeon... well, dentist. I became separated from my unit in a dust storm in the Taklamakan Desert. Now I am here."

"An eventful life," said the gnarly man as he picked his remaining teeth with a twig, trying to excise a wedged-in treacle bit.

"The Lady...?"

"You don't know, then. Well, you'll get educated right quick soon as you kill me. If you kill me. There's a world of hurt a-waiting for those as disrespect the Lady. This is her wood, actually—the sacred king's on sufferance. Unless he has True Grit," added the gnarly man.

Halfnight felt about in his pockets. "I am gritless, I fear."

"There is a chance—a slim chance, but a chance nonetheless—that we may both cash in on the Lady's good will and find favor in her eyes. And salvage our own humble flesh in the bargain."

"Eyes... again. And this Lady..."

"*The* Lady." The gnarly man grew thoughtful as he spat out a tooth. "There's a ghost in Her machine needs excising. Some says..." He drew closer. "It's the Basilisk." The gnarly man shuddered, composed himself and, extending a little finger, gave off picking his teeth to perform a vigorous excavation of an ear. "A big chicken with the tail of a serpent. Very big—spits poison draughts into the eye of an adversary: a great contentious creature big enough to gulp down a brewer's dray in a single swallow. We shall have to be prudent on our quest. And if you're so careful, Halfnight V.C., how come you lost *your* eye? Twice, I might add. Pweet! Here, Claudia." Whereupon Halfnight's stuck-on battlefield eye leapt from his head and snuffled rapturously at the very large feet of Charley Blackwell, the Rex Nemorensis.

"Hoy..." Halfnight opened his mouth as if to ask what was going on and Charley scooped up the disembodied eye from the Taklamakan Desert and popped it into the open mouth.

"Mmmm... urph!" exclaimed Halfnight. He swallowed.

"Neat toss. Huh, just having a bit o' fun, I was. You shouldn't have done that—swallowed your eye. Here..." Charley began pounding the displaced dentist vigorously on the back all to no avail. "I'll have to Heimlich, don't fight it," said Charley as he clutched him from behind and drove his massive fists deep into Halfnight's abdominal cavity.

"Urp!" Halfnight F.R.S. gave a mighty belch and the dislodged eye flew high into the air. "My ribs," choked Futvoye Halfnight, F.R.S. "I think you broke some." The gnarly man held up a hand to signal for silence. "Shhh..." said Charley, head cocked to one side. There was a great thrashing of twigs in the underbrush nearby and the flying eye was caught in an enormous, parrot-like beak.

"Basilisk?" asked Halfnight.

"Basilisk," replied the gnarly man.

"Big."

"Very. We must be close to its castle. Run like hell."

"Pardon my mentioning it, but you are a cripple."

The gnarly man came close. "I've got me an exercise regime," he whispered. "Not much good fer walkin' but I can scale me a cliff fast as a mountain goat."

Charley hobbled, bobbled and wobbled, seemingly without a labored breath. Futvoye followed, turning red from the effort and wheezing mightily. The gnarly man thrust aside an elderberry thicket with a single swipe of a massive arm. "In here. You're about having the apoplectics. You need a rest, m'boy." The dentist collapsed gratefully. From the distance came a general thrashing and laying-about that indicated the Basilisk had lost their trail. "He'll catch our scent again, never fear," said Charley as he popped a fresh treacle into his mouth. "But for the nonce I presume a riddle. Why does the Basilisk cross the road? Think it over, your very existence depends upon a proper answer."

Two of Swords

The gnarly man doffed his stewpot helmet and produced a Tarot deck from its depths. "You're a one-eyed dentist, more's the pity. I'd a been happier with a one-eyed chiropractor all be told." He held up a card. The card showed a pair of fighters, swords drawn and standing back to back, posed to repel an onslaught by superior forces. By misadventure the swordsmen had run their blades through one another. They seemed unaware of this, and stared steadfastly ahead. The taller of the two wore a large saucepan on his head.

"Uhn... one of them is you. The stewpot? You match the picture."

"Aye, laddie-buck. Look close at the other."

"Not a bad likeness. Is my nose that big..."

As Halfnight studied the card the gnarly man stood, "Break's over—on your feet."

The gnarly man set off in a sideways shuffle at surprising speed. "Follow me and keep close. Be brisk about it. We'll have to see the Lady, that's all there is to it," panted the Rex Nemorensis. He charged on ahead, seemingly oblivious to the scrapes of bramble and thornbush. "She'll sort things out." His voice grew faint in the distance.

Halfnight followed. "Ow, ow, ow..."

The brambles at last gave way on an open vista of marshland and bracken ferns where swarms of bloodsucking insects attacked them. As he swatted and squirmed, he noticed that the gnarly man was becoming shorter.

"A quaking bog!" Charley called back over his shoulder. "The mud'll suck 'ee down if you stand still for more'n a heartbeat." The King of the Wood set out in a labored forward progression that resembled a clockwork toy at the end of its windup. The place reeked of decaying vegetation.

Halfnight tried to follow, leaned forward and fell on his face grasping a tussock of witch grass which he used to pull himself out of a sinkhole. The two moved as quickly as they were able with mud pulling at their shoes with every step. After what seemed an eternity of stings, bites and clinging clods, a gentle breeze drew off the miasma of the swamp and a vista of neatly manicured parkland opened before them.

Halfnight paused to examine his feet. "I fear my puttees are ruined," he lamented.

"Ooo," said a mellifluous female voice. "Hello there. Are you here for the execution? We shall have a lovely soirée. Tomorrow night. Don't be late," the voice sighed, also mellifluously. "I'm named Dryope, by-the-bye. Oh, hiya, Charley."

While he revolved to view the voice's source with his remaining eye, Halfnight bumped into an ornamental shrubbery, driving a twig under the lid. "Damned tree." He lifted the eyelid, extracted the twig, and partial vision returned. Through a milky halo a female form became visible.

The gnarly man nodded and picked at his teeth. "Pretty little thing, isn't she? A nymph. Flat as failed omelets, most of them—naught but tits and gristle. But frisky lasses, one and all. *Hee-hee, ho-ho, harrumph, hack, whack wawarrgh...*"

Halfnight pounded the King of the Wood on the back till his spasms passed.

"Thank 'ee, lad. Got treacle up me nose."

"Hmph." Snorted the nymph. "I should have hoped it to be the memory of our last liaison taking you into a transport of rapture." Dryope was carrying an armload of knotted net bags full of a white substance. She pinched Halfnight's nose and waggled his head back and forth. "You are not lost by any chance? You are early but I am certain we can find you a place in the line."

"Uh... line?"

"The line of succession, silly. And you are devastatingly cute in your khaki pantaloons and wooly socks. We shall have jolly times together, you and I."

Halfnight found himself staring at her naked thighs. The nymph was graceful and slim, dressed in a gossamer chiton that struggled ineffectively to keep her covered. Its excess fabric had been pulled up and gathered under a sash knotted at her waist.

"Yes, I am—am I not?" Dryope said. Halfnight blushed.

"Y-y-you are..." Halfnight's blush deepened.

"Delectable. They all say so—both the contenders and the kings." At the word "king," Dryope's cupid's bow mouth pouted as though she had discovered a slug in a bowl of wild berries. "But we are getting ahead of ourselves. You must kill *him* first; for that is the way of things. Bye now."

Dryope skipped off through the forest undergrowth, humming tunelessly to herself. Charley Blackwell and Halfnight F.R.S. followed close behind. "Following me, are you?" said the nymph, and gave Charley a playful slap on the nose. "You naughty, naughty boys." The young woman stopped at a larch sapling where a net bag hung from a low-lying branch. She lifted the bag and held it to her nose. "Ugh! Quite ripe. The Lady loves to feed the birds but it has been unseasonably warm this past nonad." She tucked the smelly bag into her waistband and replaced it with a fresh one.

"Suet bags," whispered Charley Blackwell.

Dryope gave the gnarly man's midsection a poke and pouted. "Tsk, tsk. We're going to have to fatten you up, Charley. Can't have the Lady's wrens dropping from famine now can we?"

"Dryope, old cupcake, meet Futvoye Halfnight, V.C., D.D.S. He's here to fit me out with a set of dentures."

The nymph gave a look that signaled disapproval at the suggestion of false teeth. "Humph. We'll see about that." And with a twirl of her hips and a toss of her head, Dryope marched away.

"What was that all about?" asked Halfnight as he admired the play of Dryope's retreating hips.

"My predecessor. His leftovers now line the paunches of chickadees and nesting wrens." With a crunching of distressed vegetation the Rex Nemorensis plunged into the sacred woods. Beyond a hedge a pathway opened, its course delineated by two rows of squared-off granite blocks. The parallel lines diminished in one-point perspective to where a shrine of toppled pillars rose in a misty distance. "My place," he said. "The girls like to know where I'll be when they want me."

"I say, statues..."

At the base of the first stone lay two swords. "Pick up your sword." Charley Blackwell stooped to retrieve a wicked looking double-handed broadsword.

"We are supposed to go at one another with these swords?" said Halfnight. "You are bigger; you would win."

"Ahh, the only acceptable means of dispatching a king..." Here the Rex Nemorensis took a test cut with his sword, sending the blade whistling through the air a fraction of an inch from Halfnight's nose, "...or a contender are strangulation, throat cutting and drowning. Not chopping or stabbing. For now, you are safe." The explanation sounded weak to Halfnight, but he kept any misgivings to himself.

"This then would be mine, I guess." Halfnight picked up the remaining weapon, a slender-bladed rapier which he swung in imitation of Charley. It cut the air with a gentle whisper.

Charley grinned an approval, "Sounds sweet as the peeing of a butterfly," and stabbed the point of his great shining sword into the turf at his feet. "That one's *sharp*. You'll skewer me brisket right handy." He leaned casually on the pommel of his broadsword. He did not appear threatened by the dentist's rapier. "Now for dinner."

The gnarly man led the way to where the circle of ruined columns had been roofed over with a gilded dome. "The gold leaf is peeling, but be it ever so humble, etc..." said the gnarly man. In the shade of the dome was a hammock strung between two columns. Flies buzzed around a sticky-looking pottery porringer and a silver platter filled with partially rotted fruit.

"We've got us our swords; there's dinner," said the gnarly man as he flopped into the hammock.

"The swords. What for, exactly? If not fighting one another."

"To extirpate the Basilisk, o' course. 'Tis a weary task but the Lady will demand it of us."

"B-b-b-basilisk. You said the beast has a taste for human flesh..."

"Just a figure of speech; souls are their proper purview. The basiliki are not a bright tribe, and rending their victims is the only way they've discovered for getting at their insides. If you had a Swiss army knife in those capacious pockets of yours—the kind with a corkscrew and an earspoon, f'rinstance—we might make a trade with the Basilisk and he might—might, mark you—spare us. Better things for better living and all..."

Halfnight made a show of turning out his pockets. "Sorry, old chap, I'm without."

The gnarly man looked wonderingly at the contents of the pockets. "What's that 'ee got? A hazelnut bonbon?"

"I was saving that for later"

"Give it here."

"I say..." Halfnight recoiled as the gnarly man snatched the chocolate from his hand and popped it in his mouth. "Wait. You are telling me that the soul, the self-essence unique to a living being, may be removed from a chap with an earspoon?"

"Dunno, never tried it though legend has it thus. A good sharp sword is my choice for soul-extraction. Time-tested, tried and true, as they say." The gnarly man looked hopefully at Halfnight. "Chocolate is my favorite. Over earwax."

"Uhn... I only had the one."

"Earspoon, corkscrew, whatever." Charley stood and buckled on his broadsword. "Time we were going. The Lady's cavern is right under our feet." He drew Halfnight, F.R.S. after him past a midden of broken pottery and what must have been the personal belongings of previous sacred kings. It was an impressive pile. A short way on where a freshet bubbled from a cleft in the rocks, he brushed aside a barricade of thornberry and wild roses.

"Yikes!" From the branches of a dwarf cypress hung two dolls, suspended by one foot on a twisted scarlet ribbon. Each had a single eye painted in the center of its forehead. One wore a tiger skin cloak, the other khaki shorts and knee socks. "It seems that we are expected," offered Halfnight. A young woman stood guard at the entrance to a cave.

"Hullo, Electra. The Lady about?"

"Not a good time. Herself is whipping Alcyone—she giggled at vespers."

"We have official business. The underworld open for visitors?"

"For you, Rexie, any time. Who's your friend?" The young woman sidled up to Halfnight and, slipping a velvety shoulder out of her chiton. "Mmmm... you the next king? You'll be killing Charley, then." Long slim fingers stroked his face in an unhurried caress. He found himself wishing that he had stopped to shave that morning.

"Your friend is cute, Charley. We had some good times though, didn't we, you and I?" Electra wriggled her hips and pulled up the hem of her hymation to expose a length of shapely leg.

"Look but don't touch, me laddie-buck," said Charley Blackwell. "Remember Dryope's suet bags. The fauna hereabouts are easy on the eye but particularly lethal." The gnarly man made a grab for her.

Electra slapped him away. "Ah-ah-ah-ah-ah... business, you said. The pythoness is in." She crouched to pull open a grating from which mephitic vapors rose. "Yecch," she said, making a three-fingered gesture of aversion. "Better you than me." She passed her fingers under her nose, sniffed and made a dainty face. "Down you go. Be seeing you."

Rising fumes churned about their heads. Halfnight coughed and cast a wistful glance at Electra; she blew him a lingering kiss: "Remember, the

Lady is not the pythoness: she occurs, as though sprung from the ground, a keeper of the spring of mysteries."

Chiseled from the living rock there were steps. "And don't breathe if you don't have to." The Rex Nemorensis and Futvoye Halfnight, F.R.S. descended.

They found themselves in a cavern; phosphorescent mineral deposits gave an eerie greenish cast to their faces. A woman sat atop a bronze tripod that straddled a chasm cut in the living travertine; her eyes were rolled back in their sockets so that only the whites showed. In one hand she held a wine cup, in the other a green laurel switch with which she was beating a naked girl on the back.

"Uh, hullo, there," said Halfnight. "Are you the Lady?"

The woman turned at the sound of his voice. The beating stopped. "Company, then," said the woman. Empty eyes stared blindly ahead. "I am a pythoness, Her representative. You will speak to Her through me."

"Ahh..." Halfnight opened his mouth.

"When you are *told* to speak." The volcanic vent at her feet hissed and a stream of chartreuse vapor swirled about the woman on the tripod.

"Yes, ma'm," Halfnight closed his mouth.

"Call me pythoness—only pythoness. I am but an oracle, a gatekeeper. But you will have to pardon me; I am disciplining a wayward nymph."

The naked girl whimpered and looked up at them. "These are her ways, my lords; better let her get on with it." The girl looked beseechingly to the woman on the tripod. "Greek. It is a Greek silliness; that is all I said. And for saying that I am to die?"

"You will not die, my child," said the woman as she began anew with the thrashing. "You see, gentlemen—and that is you, Charley Blackwell unless I miss my mark. For you I use the term advisedly—Alcyone has incurred our wrath by her irreverence in demeaning the rites of the Lady of the Wild Things. She might have been buried in sand to the chin and left to die."

"But, but..."

"Tsk, tsk, tsk, my daughter. You blasphemed the rites of the goddess. The vestals of Rome would expect no less a punishment. I fancy myself more merciful than that gaggle of guinea broads. Why do you complain at a mere thrashing? Good for what ails you."

"Meaning no disrespect, isn't the beating a mite severe?" said Charley.

Two of Swords

"Nonsense. We'll have her back at play with the hamadryads on Mount Oeta before you can say Jack Robinson. Alcyone, you are dismissed." The chastened nymph, covering her nakedness as best she could with her hands, slipped quickly past. Through clouds of volcanic exudations Charley monitored her retreat up the stone stairway.

"Ahem. Eyes front, Charley—what eyes you have left. You want something," said the pythoness.

"Ahh, your ladyship, now that you mention it my dentist friend here would like his eye. Basilisk ate it."

"I must simply have it and that is all there is to it," said Halfnight. "Otherwise I shall have to go through life spinning like an angry woodpecker."

"Whatever, that probably won't be long. It is the way of things," said the pythoness. "It's your life or his, remember? You wish to become a mission for the Lady of the Wild Things? Perhaps. After you have dealt with the Basilisk all bets are off." The pythoness' pupils dropped into place. Her gaze was not at them but through them, as if she watched a drama projected on the walls of the cavern. She remained thus for upwards of twenty minutes. "Very well. The Lady says to bring me the Basilisk's venom sac. Then we shall talk. Go!" Her eyes came back into focus and the intensity of her gaze drove them to their knees. A vertical streamer of orange gas burst from the crevasse at her feet. "And have a nice day."

"Aye, lady." The gnarly man picked up a smooth rock to hone the edge of his sword.

❏

The mountain range of scraggly scree and boulders rose from a well-watered plain rich with wheat and barley. "High enough, I wot..." said Charley Blackwell, the Rex Nemorensis, "to keep away the idly curious. Basiliki are not the most sociable of creatures. They do love their unscalable pinnacles. Don't look down whatever you do."

Halfnight, F.R.S., looked. "Ooo... It's not far down at all. Not for all the sweat and skinned knees we have expended to climb this far."

Far below laborers bent double as they toiled in the fields; their massed voices rose to fill the sweet-smelling dawn. Flooded paddies spoke of the cultivation of rice or cranberries. Halfnight paused to wipe his brow with his military hanky. "That's it, then. Not quite the mountain fastness we have been led to believe."

"The Basiliki are subject to nosebleeds and have a morbid fear of heights," said the King of the Wood. "They are only known to come this far up in their mating season."

"You are telling me the creature is in rut." High above the two a small puffy fair-weather cloud fluttered cheerily by. "And, while we are at it, you never answered your riddle: Why *does* the Basilisk cross the road?"

"To get laid."

"Oh. *Ohhh...*"

"Well, yes. About the only time they stray off their patch. Otherwise they're busy despoiling maidens and ravaging the Lady's lettuces. Whew, I'm tired."

In the fields below all singing stopped as the morning calm was shattered by a warbling whistle. The noise was so intense it required the two men to cover their ears. "I say, sounds like a bad landing at Heathrow," said Futvoye Halfnight, V. C. as he scrambled up for a quick peek.

Chicken-legged, serpent-tailed and with the body of a winged lion, the Basilisk was gathering sticks and arranging them into an improbable nest. At its feet was a jumble of odds and ends. Ever so often it would consult the pile with the air of an artist at work, select one shiny trinket and place it lovingly into the wall. "It is building a bower," said Halfnight.

The gnarly man sat and fanned himself with his saucepan. "The Basiliki have an exhausting and complex mating ritual; this is why there are so few of them. He hopes to lure a mate to his bower by its architectural complexities."

Halfnight raised himself to peek over the edge of the barricade of wattle and daub. "Careful," hissed the gnarly man. "Inveterate magpies, Basilisks. They accumulate pretty doodads to hang on the arches of their nests." At the sound of a human voice, the Basilisk looked up.

The King of the Wood grabbed at Halfnight's shirttail and pulled him down. "The eyes, lad. Don't look 'im in the eye. Leonardo da Vinci has said the creature is so utterly cruel that when it cannot kill men by its baleful gaze, it turns upon herbs and plants, and withers them up with a glance."

"Uhn, sure." Halfnight F.R.S. scrambled up and over tearing his trousers on a tightly woven latticework of thorn, bramble and cadaverous leftovers. The Basilisk's escarpment was constructed of chance objects painstakingly fitted together: sticks entwined with what had to be human remains, gobbets of flesh still clinging to the bones, feathers and fur. And a single set of Tyrolean hiking galluses with large pearl buttons.

"A backpacker passed this way." Halfnight examined the suspenders, "42 long, just my size." He slung the galluses over his shoulder and thrust a finger into the brushworks; it had been slathered with a gummy substance. He tasted the finger. "Hmm... rather like Szechuan noodles."

"Basilisk snot," said Charley. "When it dries it'll stick tighter than a constipated hierophant."

The Basilisk's warbling whistle shattered the air, this time followed by a shrill screech. In cranberry paddies below, peasants ducked and covered their ears. "Yikes," exclaimed Halfnight—for the second time that day, if you are keeping count.

Peering back from the Basilisk's beak was a bright beady eye. Small and familiar. "Claudia?" The eye winked as the Basilisk opened its beak, dropped it, and let out an ear-piercing whistle. The creature's razor-edged beak took out a sizable patch of Halfnight's scalp and hair and, satisfied that honor had been served, it retreated back to its bower. Halfnight went somersaulting head over feet back to the cleft in the rocks. "It is angry," he said.

"You don't feel withered or anything. I mean, you didn't look it straight in the eye, did you?"

"Pro'ly so, 'magine. But it was *our* eye; the Basilisk has her captive. Am I dead?"

"You appear pretty lively for a dentist, but appearances can be deceiving." From above there emanated a massive scratching sound. "It's cleaning up the dance floor; that's one horny bugger we've got up there," Charley said. "When they're in heat they forget all else. He'll climb on top of anything that moves." The Basilisk's cooing grew in intensity.

"So?"

"Don't move."

"It's humming," said Halfnight. "And I seem to recall the tune. Hauntingly familiar."

"The beast's powers..." said Charley. "Its look can kill and its song beguiles its prey. For the object of its affections—that's you—to be receptive, it must put words to the music. You hear words, boy?"

"It's *Teddy Bears' Picnic*, my nanny had a gramophone, and played it ceaselessly to quiet the colic."

"The Basilisk's song is an evocative projection—something hypnotic, I fear. You are lost. A crazed Basilisk will think of naught else till it's had its way with a female of its species. Or whatever's handy. On the bright side it is oblivious to all but the call of the glands. You may kill it with ease."

"Me."

"As king apparent the honor is yours. You'll have to excuse me—the heights. Thin air gets me weary."

"Uhn... of course." Halfnight, F, R. S. took on a dreamy expression. His head bobbed in time with the rhythm of the Basilisk's song. Over the edge of the brushworks that defined the outer boundary of the Basilisk's mating floor—came a cooing sound. "Ahhh... sorry to cut short our little entrenous but I've got to go."

Charley sprang to his feet and caught hold of Halfnight's leg as he fought to return to join the Basilisk's dance. With his free hand the gnarly man drew his sword, "I hate having to do this to 'ee, lad. But death or chicken-rape—think about it—not much of a choice. Personally I'd choose death meself."

"That is because you are not in love." The cooing rose and fell with an increasing urgency. "Mustn't be late for my own wedding night." Halfnight drew his own sword and took a ferocious swing at Charley Blackwell's stewpot helmet, knocking him unconscious and slicing off an ear. "Cheerio, and remember me to the girls. Sorry about the ear." He clambered over the revetment to be enfolded in the coils of the waiting Basilisk. "Ohhh... Urk..." called Halfnight. From behind the palisade of sticks and bones came a frenzied yowling.

Regaining consciousness, the Rex Nemorensis raised himself on an elbow looked up with his one remaining eye. "Steady as she goes, m'boy," he shouted. "Keep him happy and you'll enjoy a long and eventful life." As he tore strips of his tiger skin cloak to bandage the stump of his severed ear, the howls and shouts gradually lessened into a subdued chorus of mutterings and moans.

"Halfnight?" There was no answering call. The Basilisk crowed once, then all went still. There was a panicked scuffling as through a hole in the gruesome wickerwork of the Basilisk's palisade the errant eye came rolling toward him.

"Oh. Hullo, Claudia. Seen too much for one day, haven't 'ee old girl?" Lifting his eyepatch, Charley popped the eye into his empty socket.

❑

"You might say that I done a bunk on poor old Halfnight. I wouldn't say that, but you might." Charley Blackwell lay with his head in the lap of the nymph Dryope while she tended to his wounded ear. "Jolly good fella and all, but a bit of a doodle-dash." He scratched Claudia. The eye quivered rapturously in its socket.

"Tell me about it," said Dryope. Charley told her about it. The nymph hummed her tuneless song as she braided an intricate design into the bandages that wrapped Charley's head. "...and that's about all there's to tell," said Charley. "I won; he lost. I gets me another year."

"Ahh... yes."

"I do. Don't I—another year? I mean the Lady's rules and all. Some fruit, if you please. Storytellin's dry work. Don't a fellow get some fruit to keep him regular after an adventure such as I've had?" Charley scratched affectionately at his eye, which had been in turn Halfnight's and the Basilisk's. "Aye, the doings we've seen."

With one pink, sandaled toe Dryope nudged forward a silver salver heaped with melons and grapes as she reached beneath their couch.

"Oh, a surprise. I loves a good surprise," said the Rex Nemorensis. The sacred king launched a grape into the air and caught it neatly between two decaying, yellow teeth. "I say, Dryope, is that what I..." His replacement eye winked at the Nymph of the Wood as she raised her axe.

The Francher

"My great-grandfather said if he built what his customers wanted, he'd build a faster horse. Now we will build what our customers want."
—Ford Chief Executive Bill Ford, January 23, 2006

An odor of mint attracted the francher

to an unpromising patch of brown scrub. It spread its fetlocks, a legacy of embedded Przewalski horse genes, and arched its neck down to feed. It munched contentedly for some minutes then collapsed. The francher's nostrils flared as it gulped at the thin unsatisfying air. Wide speckled eyes bulged; oval pupils stared. A pounding bright blue sky watched, thin and close, as the francher's body stiffened. Under the brilliant glare of the high, dry sun its knee joints cracked, emitting soft popping sounds. An Andean vulture circled closer.

The Bell L-4 LongRanger landed on a slate outcropping. The dust raised by its rotors stung the eyes and irritated any exposed skin. "Salt," said the chopper pilot. He had been here before. But not often—replacement parts were hard to come by.

James Edward Locker—Big Jim—unlatched his safety harness and undogged the helicopter's passenger hatch. On the ground he threw up, gasped for air in the thin atmosphere and leaned into the side of the chopper for a series of runner's stretches. "Cramps," he grinned to the pilot. Big Jim threw up again.

"Altitude," said the pilot.

"Fuck you," said Big Jim Locker. "Where's the franchers?"

"There's a dead one under that pile of vultures." The pilot fired off a pistol round and the feeding vultures looked up, curious but not alarmed. The Altiplano was theirs. The pilot tossed down a thermos and a bottle of pills. "Acetazolamide. Take two."

"Damn things make me pee."

"If you enjoy barfing, headaches, shortness of breath, dizziness, drowsiness, and cerebral edema, then don't take them. It's all the same with me." The pilot reached out for the pills.

"Fuck you sideways," said Big Jim Locker as he knocked back the pills.

"Burraow. Hick. Hick." A llama-like creature approached with bared teeth, its tail up. The francher stood with head and ears erect, mouth open. A split upper lip curled derisively to display its fighting teeth.

❏

Six thousand six hundred eighty-six-point-nine kilometers to the north, Dr. Ann Mari Buitrago y Francher approached the paddock at General Motors Organics in Flint, Michigan. This close to the former factory sites toxic residue in the soil precluded food use for humans even after fifty years. Harvesting parties came, carrying weapons and riding armored threshers and combines. The crops were destined for the fermentation vats to feed the Organics.

A llama came over to the chain link fence. Dr. Buitrago pushed her hard hat back and fitted a respirator over her lower face. She hummed a low-pitched warbling as if she were imitating the purring of a large cat. The Organic's ears perked up. "Burraow. Thurrump, thurrump. I am orgling. Getcha hot, Barney?" she asked as it approached.

The Organic orgled back at her. "Burraow. Hick. Hick." It pawed the ground and bared its fighting teeth.

"Wrong answer. Thurrump, thurrump, thurrump is what I wanted to hear." She drew a 9mm pistol from the holster at her side and fired three rounds in rapid succession into the animal's head.

❏

"Hi there, neighbor."

"Howdy." Claude and Ronnie looked suspiciously at the two men who came on foot leading a pack mule. They wore patched white coveralls and the brassard of the Michigan Confederation. They went unarmed in pairs, the more fools they.

"This land yours?" Behind them was a trampled path through the parched tassels of the field where corn was left out to dry on the stalk, to be harvested later.

"Most likely." It was a bright fall morning and the dust of the men's passage followed them and hung in the air when they stopped.

"Snaring rabbits?"

"Guess so. Can't deny it," Claude Ellis gave a tight laugh and nodded toward his twelve-year-old son who carried five long-eared hares slung on a string over his shoulder. Claude looked from Ronnie to the government men. "You trampled my corn."

"Mighty fine stand of corn. A man could brew up a kettle or two of liquor."

"If he had a mind. Wanna taste?" Claude pulled a flask from his rucksack.

The man looked relieved. "Don't mind if we do." The man reached for the flask and came away with the hilt of Claude's bowie knife protruding from his stomach. "Why...?"

"Not my birds, you don't," said Claude. "Ronnie. Now." There was the report of an ancient single-shot .22 and a small hole appeared between the second man's eyes. "Good shot, son." If he'd sat by and let the epidemiology crews kill off his homing pigeons, there'd be rendezvous all right, but not for him—he would never know about it.

Claude and Ronnie dragged the corpses to the pond and sunk them there weighted with stones. Claude supposed those two to be last of the lot. There were no more callers.

❑

Barry Jillson stepped into the waiting elevator and called out a floor. "Sixteen." The elevator did not reply. The expected female voice, suggestive yet aloof—omnipresent throughout the GMO campus—was silent. The bay lighting flickered, the car dropped an inch then shuddered to a stop as the automatics cut in. A growl from the sub-basement as an auxiliary generator sent the car homing back to its threshold.

The elevator spoke. "What floor, please..." languorous, almost sexual. It was a synthesized voice with a detectable mechanical edge.

"Oh, you're back. Sixteen. On a coffee break?" The doors lurched shut.

"Watch the closing doors..." The doors were already closed. Another power dip.

There was a cough from the sub-basement and an odor of diesel exhaust. The lights brightened then dimmed before flaring into full luminescence. The door opened. "Floor please?"

"Sixteen."

As the doors slid shut, partially blocking the fumes from the standby generator, a young woman made a desperate charge for the car shouting, "Hold the doors. Hold the doors!" Jillson slapped the rubber safety edges and the woman slid past. "Hey, thanks."

"Sorry. Overcapacity." The car shuddered to a stop between floors.

"You'll get used to it. New here?" The young woman smiled at Jillson. "Melanie. Melanie Gamertsfelder. What's yours?"

"Sixteen, godammit," Jillson said. The elevator did not reply. "There *is* no overcapacity. There are only two of us."

"Watch the closing doors." The elevator heaved and rose in its shaft. "Have a nice day."

Jillson turned to the woman. She seemed to be waiting for a reply. "Jillson, Barry Jillson."

"Ahh... I was afraid for a while there that I'd be calling you by a number. And you don't look sixteen. More like forty, I'd say." Freckles flickered across the bridge of Melanie's nose as she made a shy grimace. "Sixteen is Product Development." Melanie pronounced the words with distaste. "You are a biotechnician," she added.

"No, I'm from Legal." *Good-looking*, thought Jillson, *...and she knows it. I must be the first new face she's seen in three years.* "...and forty is a bit old for you is what you are thinking?"

Melanie blushed becomingly. "You're going to see the witch," she said.

Witch. "I'm here to see Dr. Francher. Is she a witch?" Jillson smiled—his best try, but then he hadn't had much practice.

"Oh, no. Though sometimes she'd like you to think so. They named them after her, you know. Here's my extension." Melanie flashed her company ID. General Motors Organics, Melanie Gamertsfelder, Marketing Liaison—followed by a number. The distant generator ground to a stop, echoing dimly in the shaft.

❑

Claude Ellis smelled burning hair and reeled back coughing. A flare-up had set off the scalplock that swung at his side. He undid its knot and let it fall to the ground. Godammit. "Helen!" The gas grill where he had been superintending a line of rabbit fillets died with a tiny blue sputter.

"Ye-esss." His wife's voice came warily over the twittering of children at play. "Did you remember to turn on the valve?"

"Uh-huh. *On.*" He thought he had. He grabbed a set of jeans off the washline and beat out the flaming hair.

"Burraow. Thurrump, thurrump, thurrump." Wide speckled eyes with oval pupils looked questioningly at him.

"Holy shit. Sweet bleeding Jesus." The creature had the severed end of a methane hose in its mouth and was chewing as if deep in thought. Claude smelled gas.

"Thurrump, thurrump." The Organic pulled back as Claude reached for the half-chewed gas line between its teeth. "Hick, hick," the beast's upper lip curled to show three pairs of fighting teeth, two upper pairs and one lower pair. There was an odor of methane as it belched.

"It's a francher," said Helen Ellis. "The things they make at GMO? They're dangerous."

A shadow, swift and low, passed between them and the sun; they ducked from reflex. The GMO chopper pilots liked to make occasional strafing runs on outlying farmsteads; they did it to no apparent schedule. Claude straightened and shielded his eyes to scan the sky: a homing pigeon circled the house. It took a tentative spin at the grill then veered around and settled on its roost as the byproducts of burnt flesh dissipated on a light afternoon breeze. The now-charred rabbit fillets gave off a rank, chemical smell.

Claude reached into the dovecote; the bird's throbbing body barely filled one of his big hands. He kissed it, mouth to beak, and removed the message cylinder tied to its leg. "Guess you want to get laid, huh? Go to it, buddy." He released the bird and it was welcomed back with appreciative cooings.

"A million and a half dead the radio said. Do the numbers..." Claude told Helen in bed that night. "...that's small change against the population. Do we know anyone ever died of the flu? Remember that rendezvous I let you come along? You got freaked and made a run for it. Missed all the fun 'cause you were afraid of catching something."

Helen remembered. Claude had followed her home with a full Mason jar of gold teeth as a peace offering. That was when he started wearing his trophy belt.

The Over-Homers—Canadians from Chateauguay and Trois-Rivières—paraded their trade talk and swaggered, but they got a hold on the gas commerce early; you had to hand it to them.

Only the Over-Homers had the secret of capturing and compressing methane and they were not about to share. The Over-Homers guaranteed peace for all who came to trade. Going for a piece of the Canadians' action, the Detroiters once tried to set up a rendezvous at the Port Huron Portage. A confrontation turned bloody and the Detroiters now wintered-over at St. Claire Shores. The Over-Homers had the bullets and the hired men to back them up. Ted Baillargeon and Claude Ellis liked that; in the woods you were anyone's game. Claude and Helen ran a whiskey still with Dotty and Ted, the neighbors. It was a profitable sideline.

In fairness to the former owner of Claude's prize scalp, a wayward Detroiter lost in the woods, he had never heard of Claude Ellis; he was just in the wrong place at the wrong time and had been dead anyway, along with a whole lot of others. The Over-Homers most likely caught them sniffing around and shot first. The Canadians were OK, not like the government men: rendezvous, free food, free whores and no trouble. The Canadians owned the lakes, downriver from Sarnia to Lake St. Clair where Grosse Pointe was an open city. Claude and Ted showed up late for the slaughter but not too late to pick over the corpses.

❑

"Shh... she'll hear you. She doesn't ah... communicate well." Harry Fenderson, General Motors Organics Product Engineer, was conducting a visitor. They didn't get many visitors on the sixteenth floor. Not lately. "With human beings—people, you know. You don't want to spend too much time with her. She talks like one of those AI programs—programmed to bust your balls. They say she named the things after herself."

"Talking about me again, Harry?" The woman was short, wide-hipped but athletic; her voice was muffled. She wore a hard hat and a self-contained positive pressure respirator.

"You are the main attraction, Doctor." The product engineer broke off his sentence with a self-conscious, embarrassed laugh.

The woman stood on tiptoe and patted Harry Fenderson on the head. "You're a good boy, Harry. Go back out front and play with your little friends." The product engineer muttered deferentially and made an awkward retreat. She patted at the pockets of her cargo pants. "Mind if I smoke? He can't help it. I'm the tour. And you are...?"

"Barry Jillson, Legal." Christ, she is short, thought Jillson, those heels must be three inches high.

Ann Mari Buitrago, Ph.D. Neuroendocrinology, Rutgers University, 2026 withdrew a green packet of cigarettes and waited—for a light, Jillson supposed. None being forthcoming she shrugged and put it back. "In here." The door opened into a research library with carrels, shelves and rows of filing cabinets. "Legal, huh? Wow! A pontifex minimus, I should feel honored. You are no more a lawyer than I am. You are a spook, a corporate snitch." She pulled a file drawer out and withdrew a bottle and two plastic cups. "You can cut the 'Legal' crap. We must have an Organic loose somewhere. Cool scenario, an Organic on the rampage. Hypothesis: an Organic makes a run for it and kills somebody. And God forbid a noseypoke TV crew with an uplink gets it. Let's see—how's about in the mountains of Wyoming? Wyoming is supposed to be beautiful this time of year, oodles of mutagenic wild plants to nibble. Our hypothetical transgenic stops for a wee nibble and is knocked flat by a long-chain protein polymer that his ancestors never met up with. I would expect a visit by the grand frommage himself on that one. Big Jim out at golf? Or has he decided to keep his head down while whatever crisis wears itself out?" She sipped appreciatively at her plastic cup. "Its corn whiskey, all we can get. Musty, an acquired taste. We trade machine parts with the hostiles for it when we're not out shooting at each another."

Jillson made an appreciative grimace and swallowed. "Doctor Buitrago, I am here as a friend. We are only exploring our options in case things get out of hand."

"So it *is* trouble, then. Not for me, for the Company. They drop the ball and I get a visit from the spooks."

"Some of your organics *do* appear to thrive in the wild. James Edward Locker—he is dead. His pilot brought the body—what was left of it—back to the field station this morning. He was shredded like lettuce at a sushi bar. No TV crew. Not Wyoming, Doctor. The Altiplano."

"Ooo." It was a small Ooo, and out of tune with the doctor's in-your-face style.

Jillson nodded sympathetically. "As we see things, Jim Locker made it by steps to the high Andes—one of our antique choppers. The place is pretty damn isolated."

"Tell that to the Incas. The Altiplano—so Big Jim went over my expense vouchers. I never credited him with the initiative to snoop. Mea Culpa. I should have cooked the books but now it's too late. For Jim Locker. Too bad. I did so enjoy getting him wound up." The woman looked up into Jillson's eyes, challenging. "I had a dream for the Organics. Big Jim Locker—and the dumb klutz never caught on that there might be a pun in his name—bought in early: freeways become the footpaths of commerce, diminishing to the horizon in single-point perspective, clogged with foot traffic—man and beast. McLife as we know it wouldn't get much better. On paper. We were lovers, did I tell you that?"

Jillson's jaw dropped as he expelled an all too graphic image of this older woman and the late CEO naked in bed. "Ahh... *McLife?*" He clutched at the nearest incongruity.

"The hamburger chains. McLife, Big Jim loved that word; he boasted a highly-developed sense of historical irony. He compressed his relationships into mini-experiences, McMoments. And I'm not that worn out, young man. It is a corporate skill to express intimacy in 15 well-chosen minutes. I was younger then; so was Jim." Ann Mari Buitrago y Francher took another slug of corn whiskey. "Alpacaburgers. My guys are too good to end up on a bun." One strand of her aerial hairdo had come loose and she brushed at it, a curiously feminine gesture.

"But they will not all die. Not all," she said.

❑

Claude Ellis and Ted Baillargeon dragged their sledge, straining against twin tumplines yoked at the shoulder. They stumbled along a bracken trace hardly well enough defined to be called a path. The 80-gallon pigs were empty but the demijohns of home-brew were a heavy haul; the sledge would be lighter going home. Coming in to the meet-up with the Over-Homers they took different routes when they could. The depth of mud or snow made the choice of a way back for them. This particular route cut across flat terrain, frozen in winter and easier to slide a sledge; they hadn't used it since late March. Ahead the bracken ferns opened onto an upland swamp where jewelweed and stinging nettles kept the idly curious at a distance.

"Shit!" Pushing through a copse of black spruce and deadfall tamarack Claude took a twig in the eye.

"Ted. Wait up." Claude peeled back the eyelid and poked around with a fingernail in case there were loose splinters left inside. He rubbed at the eye until a sort of blurry vision returned. "OK." As he stood, one of the scalps he wore at his waist snagged on a splayed limb. He gave a yank that left a red clump caught behind. The Detroiter had had long hennaed hair, worn in dreadlocks. "Shit." Claude retrieved the lost strands and plaited them back in. As they trudged ahead of the sledge, to the east the pillar of a thunderhead climbed and billowed to an overarching gray and black that filled the horizon. There was a growl of invisible turbine helicopters.

"Like the fuckers are laughing at us," said Ted.

Claude agreed and pulled a rifle from its case between the methane pigs. "In case there's a decent shot." Those GMO pilots were a quick study;

their choppers flew in low, coming over a rise before you could react. He studied the wind as he fitted a silencer and extracted a handful of parabellum loads from his belt.

From behind the tamarack copse they had just left, a Bell LongRanger rose, seemingly out of the ground. Claude got off three quick shots, jacking the cartridges as he fell, flattening himself into the swamp. There were three satisfying pings, a contact hit—cockpit or the belly tanks.

Claude shot for spite as there was nothing that could be salvaged after a crash. When they hit a ball of flame erupted, toasting the engineers, executives, private army—whatever—from the GMO tank farm. And burned up all the gas.

❏

Buitrago y Francher tamped her pack and withdrew another long brown mentholated cigarette. "Stop me if I am wrong on this, Mr. Jillson. La Paz is out of countenance at having Jim Locker's shredded remains strewn across their sphere of interest."

"I represent certain parties, let's leave things there." Jillson gulped his whiskey. "Anyway, *around* does not exist as a timely executive option. The LongRangers piss away aviation kerosene 25 gallons to the hour and eighteen choppers are all we have left; La Paz is concerned. But why South America for your private project? Executive junkets on a whim are expensive. Plus, any breakdown and a managerial scalp is swinging on some hostile's belt."

"Hostiles, friendlies. Silly me: we're out of gas. I should get out more, I know—they are all hostiles down on the ground. Only last week a chopper I hitched a ride on took three bullets in the cockpit from a war party headed for Lake St. Claire. The material as well as the spiritual world is running on empty and now it is someone else's turn."

"The franchers?"

"'Four legs good...' That's a literary reference, young man."

"I have read George Orwell, doctor."

❏

"Where do they get the fuel to fly, anyway? General Motors Organics have got to be hoarders, the bastards." Claude was home from rendezvous and feeling resentful. It was an unsatisfactory trip.

"Thurrump, thurrump." The Organic looked offended as he snatched away a half-eaten corn cob.

The Francher

"Can we keep him? Please?" From atop the animal's back three tow-headed kids determinedly stared down at their parents. The francher took a tentative nip at Claude Ellis. Helen started and jumped away, "Honey..." Claude stood his ground; wide speckled eyes with oval pupils stared curiously back at him.

Claude held the corn cob out again. As the francher bit into it, he fished a plug of chewing tobacco from his pocket and held it up with his other hand. The francher looked confused, waited a moment, then chose the tobacco.

"Dad..." The kids were pleading now.

"Well... yeah, sure." Here was protein on the hoof. Claude Ellis temporized. "But you'll have to find something else for him to eat. We need all the corn we can grow for the still. And gas and tobacco are hard come by. Try him out on the compost."

"Thurrump, thurrump." The francher thrust its nose deep into the heap of rotting corn husks and cabbage leaves. It surfaced with a mouthful of cabbage. The Ellis kids cheered.

"We'll call him Wally," said Claude. "Waldorf, get it? After the salad?" We'll fatten the thing up, thought Claude.

Rita, Ronnie and Yolanda scrambled down and off, up and on Wally's back by snatching at the thick clumps of his wooly pelt. As long as he could get his nose back in the compost pit every twenty minutes, he was theirs to command.

❏

Ann Mari Buitrago y Francher ground out her cigarette with the toe of a platform shoe. "La Paz will close the research station because that is where Big Jim Locker died, Q.E.D.: Eat raisins, shit rivets. The mossbacks at Ford wanted to get some extra mileage out of their proprietary brand. The Mustang? Cute. They are not pets."

"Cuteness sells, Doctor. Besides, you had the pilot organism was up and running at the time Ford Organics absorbed GMO."

"The Altiplano franchers are a robust strain. They are capable of taking care of themselves. Like the hair?" She shook loose her luxuriant braids and they fell down past her waist. "Took me almost as long to grow my hair back as it took for my cancer to recur. Ovarian cancer. It used to go to the floor before chemo. Strange weather we've been having."

She's leading me, thought Jillson. "The weather? It's always strange." The announcement of cancer had not been made for sympathy. She wants me to know this for her reasons, whatever they are. Jillson filed the statement.

"Laddie—that's my husband—has a cake on order. Yellow and blue icing, quite festive. You can take the girl out of the country, etc. That's a Quechua joke. You may laugh or not—your call."

"I'm not laughing, Dr. Buitrago."

"I'm not doing chemo again. My husband is a dentist, an oral surgeon: Alfonso Francher, Celebrity Dentist. He has squirreled away morphine by shortchanging deserving patients of their painkillers—not enough to matter to them but over the years it accumulates. I have one final mega-dose saved up. Watch and wait."

"Huh?"

"That's what the oncologists tell a cancer patient when they've run out of options. GMO has a problem, Barry Jillson. So hang tough, maybe it'll go away."

❑

Ted had come over to ask for help beating back a brush fire that threatened his potato patch—that was how Claude and Helen found out about the Baillargeons' secret stash of fuel. All around, at street and grade level, the shoulder-high lawns smoldered. He stood, knees flexed and gasping, trying to get the words out. "The backfire I started went the wrong way. Shake a leg; it might blow out the still." The women and the kids were set to passing buckets up while the men strung together lengths of plastic hosing. The water in the pond was near bottom after twelve weeks of drought and the bodies of the two government men had been partially exposed.

They were making some headway wetting down the dry grass where tendrils of fire crept toward the whiskey boiler when the pump coughed and stopped for good. Each time the generator stalled, the line to the pump had to be primed again. Claude and Ted checked the hoses; they had been sucked flat by the pressure and the pump was clogged with mud.

"I got tarps down cellar," Ted shouted. "We can beat the fire out with those."

They ran to Ted's bulkhead door and dived down into the earthy wintering-over smells of carrots and potatoes in the ground. Ted started feeling around in the dark, "I've got them somewhere... here."

The Francher

"Ted." As Claude's vision adjusted to the lack of light he spoke softly, every syllable carefully articulated. "What... is... *that?*"

Ted backed away, panic growing behind his eyes. "Just a little something put by. Not a lot..." Number 2 burner fuel in 55-gallon drums and half a dozen 250-gallon pressure tanks of methane lined the far wall of the cellar.

Claude's hand moved toward the pistol he wore in a shoulder holster. Ted's hand moved simultaneously in an echo of Claude's. "Careful," Helen screamed, "the gas!" Ted wore his sidearm low, at his belt. Claude's hand was closer to his pistol. The right side of Ted's face disappeared and he moaned on the floor, giving little shrill yelps. Two shots took out Ted, then Dotty. Dotty was hit full in the chest. Helen cut their throats with a hunting knife.

The discovery changed things and Claude did not like change. He had liked things the way they were. The fuel had not ignited.

❑

Ann Mari Buitrago y Francher lit up a fresh long brown cigarette.

Jillson coughed. "Are you supposed to be smoking in here?"

"Nope. I do it all the time. See?" Buitrago y Francher held up her cigarettes. "Mentholated. Doesn't bother the Organics one bit. I think they like the mint aromatics, reminds them of grazing."

"I thought the things were supposed to be docile—the perfect family Organic. With a chemical safety interlock, strepto something."

"The Andean Organics are genetically booby-trapped; the North American strain are not."

"How long does it take?"

"In the laboratory test subjects dropped like a bag of hammers. My fault, I wanted to talk with them."

"Talk."

"The recessive for aggression is manifest in their utterances, the way they talk. They don't have much to say—warning, challenge. Challenge without a threat: very human, don't you think? The franchers can tear an opponent limb from limb when they are annoyed. Some are irritable all the time."

"But if they don't eat they die anyway."

"Maybe... and with all our tinkering it turned out we made a critter that could metabolize methane. Relativity, go figure..." said Buitrago y Francher. "Clean living—that's what will kill an Organic. But you've got to get it to eat its carrots and Brussels sprouts."

"I thought..."

"Whoa, boy. You didn't pick up on the carrot reference. An extract of hemlock root was given to Socrates. The Greek philosopher? Poison hemlock belongs to Apiaceae, the carrot family. The toxic alkaloid in poison hemlock causes paralysis, asphyxia and death. Socrates was judged to be an enemy of the people in 399 B.C. He was condemned to die: Death by carrots. That's a joke."

"OK. Let's start all over again. I apologize for barging in here."

"And I conditionally apologize for blowing smoke up your ass," said the doctor. "Conditionally." Buitrago y Francher ground her cigarette out on the spotless polished terrazzo tiles of the floor.

❑

The Ellises had some spare oil drums in their cellar and number 2 burner fuel was as good as methane for firing the still. "We'll drain a tank, then move it empty for the next one," he said. The methane they'd leave where it was, pipe it out as needed. Helen nodded an assent; she was left in the cellar with the bodies of Dotty and Ted to assemble the pieces of copper tubing. "And take their hair. It'll be a lesson to them." He untied the Detroiter's scalp from his belt and threw it at her. "And comb this out."

As he trudged home Claude avoided looking back at the Baillargeons' house. Finicky and fickle, chance spared some, eliminated others. This time it was Ted and Dotty's turn.

While the kids played with Wally, Claude improvised a siphon and unkinked the lengths of plastic garden hose sucked flat when the pump failed. He trailed these behind him across the smoldering yards over to Ted and Dotty's cellar bulkhead. "Got it. You about done?" He shuffled down the bulkhead steps and froze. "What..." Where there were two mismatched sections, Helen had wrapped long red dreadlocks around the joint. "Godammit, Helen..." He crouched to unwind the Detroiter's hair. "This is *mine*." Grabbing her by the ears, he slammed her head again and again against the side of a methane tank. There must have been a leak, some static buildup, a spark.

After the explosion and the ensuing fire that took the gas, the oil and the corpses of the Baillargeons to an apocalyptic hereafter, the Ellises and

The Francher

the children were preoccupied with saving the still and the remaining house.

❑

Barry Jillson squinted through eyelids stuck fast with the mucilage of sleep. "Mr. Jillson?"

"Huh? Yes." Jillson sighed, cobwebbiness of broken sleep dissipated. *The call was to his Company number.* "Yes?" *Company business*, he had left the autopager enabled. "Yes, *yes*. Barry Jillson. And this is..."

"Laddie Francher. Sorry to call you at this hour. Your machine must have caught you at home."

"I forgot to turn it off. And I'm not at home." Jillson put his hand over the transmitter, "Melanie...?" No, she was gone, slipped away after he dozed off. He returned to the autopager. "Francher. Oh, the *doctor*, Ann Mari. She..." A remembered phrase returned, abstracted from their conversation. "...told me you are a dentist."

"Oral surgeon. Yes, a dentist." Jillson could hear the smile. "Celebrity dentist. Or was when there were celebrities. She is dead."

Jillson smelled menthol-tinged tobacco smoke. "When? How?" The doctor had spoken of a planned suicide.

"Oh, an hour ago. Right here, with me. She left a piece of cake for you. She asked me to call you, left a note with this number. Strange weather we've been having. She said you would know what that meant. I don't, if this is any comfort to you."

"To me. Comfort. You are—*were*—her husband."

"I still am—it's just that she is dead. Could I come by? With the cake: tell that to Security; it should get me through. They were quite fond of her."

Jillson met Laddie Francher at the Security desk. His crinkly gray hair worn short, Laddie Francher knew a joke, a joke he relished and that he was going to enjoy sharing slowly. "It's OK, Hank, I'll escort him myself."

Dr. Alfonso Francher was fitted out with a biometric ID badge and the two returned to Jillson's office. He accepted the offered chair and placed a cardboard box, the kind a boutique patisserie would give you with a single napoleon, in his lap.

"Do you believe in God, Mr. Jillson? Ah, I have embarrassed you; you needn't answer. If *we* have a God, well... then why not all living things?

The beans in your garden surely look to you for nurture and support in time of drought, the bringer of nitrates. Ann Mari believed the Organics had come to look upon her as a divinity, and why not, I ask you?" He handed over the crisply folded bakery box.

"Uh, thank you." Jillson opened the box. Inside was a piece of cake frosted in yellow and blue.

"She knew she would die, sooner rather than later, and provided for them, her creations. She could not save herself but had high hopes for the Organics."

"I recall there was a woman who left a baseball team to her cat," Jillson said. "Is that what we are talking here?" He felt a guilty twinge as soon as the words were out of his mouth. He again smelled the mintier-than-mint exhalations of the doctor's long, brown cigarettes. "I'm sorry, Dr. Francher."

"No problem, Mr. Jillson."

"What could she..."

"Good genes, Mr. Jillson. The Organics are quick learners and they need us. But first we have to be domesticated. Humankind are a violent tribe. Take a bite."

Jillson did as he was told. "Carrot cake. Delicious. *Oh, Jesus*."

"Nonononono. You haven't gotten the Socratic death-dose. Think of it as a farewell chuckle from my wife. She would be happy to know you got the joke. And there is a note." Laddie handed over a piece of paper torn from a spiral-ring steno pad. "It's to you."

The handwriting was small and precise, albeit with elaborate flourishes, like the doctor herself:

"Sorry I had to leave you with the problem, Mr. Jillson. You piss off one person—a single solitary nabob in the corporate food chain—and suddenly you've got them all on your ass. You are damned if you do and damned if you don't. And if that was the choice, I opted for damned if I do.

"Do not terminate the Organics. Let them live free and forgotten. They may be all we have left. Remember the Orwell quote.

"Cordially, the late Ann Mari Buitrago y Francher."

❑

"Too bad about Dotty and Ted," said Helen Ellis.

The Francher

"Too bad," said Claude.

"Burraow. Hick. Hick."

Helen and Claude, Rita, Ronnie and Yolanda looked to where Wally was savaging the now exposed corpse of one of the government men.

"Thurrump, thurrump, thurrump," Wally dropped an arm, now half eaten, and looked inquisitively at the family grouping, his head and ears erect, mouth open. A split upper lip curled derisively to display his fighting teeth. "Burraow. Hick. Hick."

Claude Ellis stooped to retrieve a thirty-ounce shingling hammer out of the bottom of a toolbox.

The Francher was first published in the March 2009 issue of *Aphelion* [www.aphelion-webzine.com]

Mark Twain in Milan

Suspended in mid-ceiling, yellow work lights
cast fitful shadows every hundred feet; a half foot of water in a concrete
channelway reflected oily rainbow ripples. There was a distant vibration
of machinery. If I had gone to Hell at least they kept up with the electric
bill.

"Mister Ivory I believe," said a tall tenuous man as he strode down the
empty tunnel toward me. He wore a large untended mustache and a red
fez in the Turkish style. I fumbled in my pockets for loose change. This
was most likely one of the legion of New York's homeless who slept
down here. The man waved me off.

"My pleasure, for the moment," said the gent. "...put aside your charity.
And your mouth is hanging open—close it, please. Ivory or Onions, one
or the other. You may choose." He extended a hand. "Samuel Langhorne
Clemens: author, adventurer, general bon vivant."

I'm not afraid of rats, or the dark, but entombment with a lunatic in one
of the silent landfills that herald municipal progress gave me the willies.
I guessed this was the 2nd Avenue subway tunnel. It is a given of
municipal affairs that if you keep a botched project under wraps long
enough, people will forget about it. Parts had been sealed off since the
late 1920s.

"No matter, I shall call you Onions," said Samuel Langhorne Clemens.
"How do you do?" He squinted and smoothed his moustache. There was
a small squeak as on the wall behind him a New York City Transit
Authority plaque slipped to hang on one remaining unrusted screw. It
cautioned against smoking or spitting.

"Sam Clemens—Mark Twain. I read your books in the sixth grade.
Aren't you dead?"

"Hogwash, if I were dead I'd be out and voting. This *is* New York. And
yes, I am better known as Mark Twain—a sad deficiency, but I'm
working on it. Although I am not one to put on airs, I do turn a handsome
phrase, my publisher demands it. I bestride the ocean like a colossus, if I
do say so myself. And there is soap on your nose."

"Uh... I was getting a shave. The last thing I remember is lying back in a
barber chair under a mound of steaming towels." Like that explained
things. "Andy Saperstein," I said as I reached out to shake hands.

"...formerly of Bay Ridge, Brooklyn." Sam Clemens looked suspiciously at the hand. "It's okay; I just washed it. And I'm not Onions."

Sam Clemens/Mark Twain produced a set of those nineteenth century eyeglasses—pince-nez they're called—and settled them on his large nose.

"Your hygiene habits are not in question here, Mr. Onions, but your hesitation—life is about choices. I name all my porters and attendants—steamship stewards, Montenegrin muleskinners, waiters at table. They nigh burst with joy that I might be on familiar terms with them. They are who I say they are." We shook hands. "You, too," he added.

I felt a minute vibration from an inside pocket—cellphone. Sam Clemens peered into my eyes. "Your shirt is singing," he said. Rimsky-Korsakov's "Flight of the Bumblebee" is my ring tone; as we talked I must have wandered into a hotspot. Cellphone signals leak into parts of many stations through the street grates.

"Hello?"

"Valerie?" A wrong number.

"Nope, sorry. No Valerie here." I rang off. Then dialed 911. The cellphone was dead; I was stuck underground with a strangely arranged person who insisted he was Mark Twain and that I was someone else. A rat scuttled across his shoe and he looked down disapprovingly.

"Rat," I pointed out.

"Yes," said Mark Twain. There was a scurry of small animals escaping. "We have surprised them."

I checked around for stragglers. "Hey, you guys, it's only me, Uncle Andy. I come in peace." I hoped the rats felt the same way. I tried to radiate nonchalance. One late diner, a disheveled two-pounder, scampered over my foot on his way to anyplace else, preferably dark. He was in so much of a hurry that he dropped the French fry he was toting. I kicked it after him. He grabbed it, waggled his ass at me and dived down the nearest drain.

"Well," I said, "it is an axiom of city life that there's never a cat around when you want one. A split second ago I was dunking a brioche, enjoying a forty-dollar shave and a haircut marked up to a hundred for the ambience and smelling of rosewater and glycerin. Then I am in an empty subway tunnel."

"I too, Mr. Onions. I likewise seem to have departed the premises of a tonsorial parlor. I am understandably on edge, having just turned up in what, on the face of it, is an ancient Greek netherworld. Death notwithstanding, I do have an aversion to rats."

Overhead, crystallized accretions from a century of seepage had turned the tunnel into a backdrop for a vampire extravaganza: beryl, quartz, calcite and tourmaline. Spray can art had over the decades gotten layered in with the mineral deposits and produced murals that glistened with an eerie iridescent life.

Samuel Langhorne Clemens joined me in trying to puzzle out the scrawls. "Ahh, you admire the graffiti," he said. "So encouraging to meet a fellow art lover."

Recessed into the tunnel walls, every fifty feet or so, were niches that retreated down the line in diminishing perspective where track workers could dive when a train came by. But there were no trains, no tracks, no workers; this was a deserted tunnel.

"Buona sera." A man stepped out of the nearest niche.

"Holy shit!" I must have jumped a foot.

"Scusi, signores. Un po' di fuori, eh? You were preoccupied and I have disturbed your reflections. Cane che abbaia non morde. This is a proverb. I am harmless, a toothless terrier; I am not begging. I will not disturb you further." He shrugged back into his niche.

"Wait. Hey, I'm sorry. Come out and let's talk. I'm Andy Saperstein and this is Sam Clemens."

The man beamed like a kid with his first chocolate sundae. "Giancarlo Pieranunzi," he said. "Formerly docent in mathematics at the Università di Torino."

Giancarlo was well-groomed and in his thirties, a decent looking gent wearing one of those tight Edwardian tweeds with the high narrow lapels that come in and go out of fashion every ten years, regular as clockwork. I noticed his buttonholes were leather-lined, custom tailoring.

"I thought the niche was an uscita d'emergenza, an escape hatch. But, alas, no. I apologize for affrightening you." He paused to groom a closely clipped military mustache. After repeating our introductions, we three sat on the cement walkway and dangled our feet above the oily slick that slithered down the middle of the tunnel.

Samuel Langhorne Clemens leaned across to offer Giancarlo a hearty, manly handclasp. "You must be Mister Ivory."

Mark Twain in Milan

"Pieranunzi, Signore Twain. And I had not planned to become a graduate assistant at the Università. I was a romantic youth and dreamed to become a shepherd. Then came Mussolini and I went. No more Università. *Eppur si muove.*"

"Shepherd..." I began. If Mussolini chased him out of Italy that made him a hundred years old. His moustache was flecked with gray. Maybe I had underestimated his age. "...welcome to America, by the way. There's always room for an extra shepherd." I confronted Sam Clemens. "...and we are *not* Ivory and Onions," I said.

"I am cut to the quick; you are a pair of ungrateful wretches. You could as well have been Obloquy and Irony. Those gems, however, I have bestowed on the Berber porters who tailed me like faithful dogs in Marrakech," said Sam Clemens.

Our male bonding was cut short by a great rush of displaced air and the overwhelming thrust of a train entering the station. No tracks, no trains... remember? There was a screech of tortured steel as brakes caught hold and slipped, steel on steel whipping up great clouds of archival dust. Discarded flotsam from the daily commuter trek battered our faces. There was no train to be seen. A newspaper flew straight at me and covered my eyes. I was blinded and pulled it away in a panic.

L'Osservatore Romano. The type face was archaic—the kind you'd see in a museum. It was in Italian and the date was July 18th, 1869. There were two photo-engravings on the front page. After reading subway ads all my life, I am pretty good at translation if I've got a picture to go with the story. A pretty girl waved from the rear platform of what might have been a train. In the other picture a beneficent looking man in liturgical costume held a hand aloft in a blessing. The caption said something about a council of bishops. This guy to be the pope. The pretty girl in the other picture was a different story. The only part of that caption I could decipher said something about an apparition.

"What's that you've got?" asked Sam Clemens. He reached out for the paper as he clamped eyeglasses on the end of his nose. "Apparition... hmmm." He studied the newspaper. He was holding it upside down. He noticed my stare and aimed his intimidating moustache in my direction.

"Harrumph. You are not yet initiated into the mysteries of the camera obscura phenomenon. I am squinting: the smaller the hole is, the clearer the picture is. Op. Cit., Qui Bono, QED and so forth."

I was forming an opinion that, however fine a writer he was—or had been, Mark Twain was a bit of a humbug. "What do you make of this, Giancarlo?" I handed the docent in mathematics the newspaper.

"The Holy Father," he said. He then kissed the picture. Not the picture of the pope, but the picture of the young woman.

The tunnel shook with a passing rumble, the uptown express on the Lexington line a couple of blocks to our east, separated from us by cubic tons of basaltic granite. As I turned around to look for the train, a reflex, Giancarlo grabbed at my sleeve. "Mi dispiace. I was afraid you might be leaving. Look. Look at the date." We looked at the date.

L'Osservatore's masthead read July 18th, 1869. "So?"

Giancarlo wept. His shoulders heaved and tears ran down his cheeks. "It is too late. She is dead in 1869. Don't you see?" He looked to Sam Clemens and me for confirmation.

"Yes, we see," we said in unison, even though neither of us had the slightest idea what he was talking about.

"I am always late. No matter how hard I try. I always miss her."

Sam Clemens held the page at arm's length. From the yellowed page a bright-eyed, attractive young woman, bustled and beribboned and in a tweedy Victorian getup waved cheerily out at us.

Giancarlo translated. "They are saying that this is a, how do you say—fakery. The photograph is not true but it has been staged by some malicious anti-Christian force. Such as the Risorgimento. It is claimed by some to be a miracle. The Church denounces her. My Ada."

"Ah-hah, the lady has a name," said Sam. "The giving of a name transcends the humdrum, the everyday, and elevates the wearer. A mother-gift, the name. Wear it humbly and reverently." He rambled on, weaving eloquent variations on this theme.

"Ada Byron, Lady Lovelace," said Giancarlo. He lifted aside a foulard silk tie and unbuttoned two buttons in his shirtfront to produce a portrait cameo attached to a gold chain.

"The face is the same as the woman in the paper," I said. The woman was drop dead gorgeous, even allowing for some artistic license by a carver who had wished to please a finicky client.

"A mighty handsome lady, that," offered Samuel Langhorne Clemens.

"You have seen her?" Giancarlo looked reproachfully at him.

"You've lost her?" Sam Clemens/Mark Twain turned the cameo over in his large hands. "Careless of you, I would say. No, I have not, more's the pity."

"Alas, I, too, have never met her." Said Giancarlo. "But I have yearned for her since I was an undergraduate. Lady Ada is—was—likewise a mathematician. She has such a well-formed formula." The woman of the cameo had a scrappy air. Her upturned nose was offset by a chinoiserie of coiled hair cascading over very creamy, very white shoulders.

Sam Clemens and I began talking at the same time. Sam Clemens/Mark Twain gave me a dark look and I shut up."Ahh, that's better," he said. "Now sir, if you are a professor, explain yourself. And the bizarre situation in which we find ourselves while you are at it."

Our new arrival quailed under the assault of the great drooping moustache. "Scuse," he stammered and walked back to his niche.

"Nononononono," said Sam Clemens. "Don't go back down your pop-hole, please. We shall be needing all the help we can muster. Three heads are better than one, even when one of the heads is mine."

Giancarlo reluctantly allowed himself to be pulled from his niche. We exchanged reminiscences and family histories. And found out that we hailed from different decades—different centuries. "Time travel," I said.

"Claptrap," offered Sam. "If there is such a thing as journeying through time, where are all the tourists?"

"Right here: us. Now," I said.

"But *which* now?" Giancarlo let out a long Mediterranean sigh and gave one of those elegant whole body shrugs that only an old world Italian could pull off. "Time travel is impossible. It appears that you and I and Signore Twain are trading places on a space-time continuum defined by the 2nd Ave. subway tunnel. Alas, I fear this is too simple an answer. There is a *hooker* as you call it," said Giancarlo. "Something which precipitates oscillations between your parallelism and ours."

I explained hookers to Giancarlo.

"Bouno, a catch, then," he said.

"So time travel is impossible? They do it all the time on TV." From Giancarlo's and Sam Clemens's expressions that remark positioned me firmly with single-celled organisms although by rights they shouldn't have even known what TV was.

"I am not from *your* past, Andréas," said Giancarlo Pieranunzi. "I am from my past. And Signore Clemens is from his past. Our pasts must differ slightly for the switching to take place without a massive release of energy."

"Ka-boom!" I said.

"As you say, Andréas—Ka-boom. This is not time-travel," said Giancarlo. "This is a randomness. There are two kinds of randomness: the wild randomness which abounds in nature, and tame randomness. This you find at the roulette table. Wild randomness has been intruded upon by tame randomness. It is as if we are an infinity of trains that speed along side by side through the fog, unaware that the others might even exist."

"Until now."

"Everytime and any time," said Sam Clemens. "There was this spiritualist at last season's Chautauqua. He spoke of the concept of simultaneity."

I figured he was getting his own back. "Is this going to be like me explaining hookers?"

"Nononono. He spoke of a mathematical concept. An algorithmic machine which once begun it is impossible to stop."

Giancarlo smiled. "You are indeed perceptive, Signore Twain."

"You are telling me that what is happening to us is foreordained," I said. "Predestination, Kismet, some new age thingybob. All we have got to do is go to the Emerald City, three scarecrows and no Dorothy." Sam Clemens grumped; I had begged to differ with him.

Another express rumbled by on the Lexington Avenue line. The noise mounted to a crescendo.

"The espresso," shouted Giancarlo as the rumbling passed. Some words do make it across the language barrier.

"The Lexington Express," I said.

"A punto. We hear the train but we do not see it. Shhh..." He held a finger to his lips. Silence, the train was suddenly gone. "I feared this. The anomaly has taken a substance from this—our—parallelism. The Lexington espresso. We may only pray that we get something in return. Though vast, infinity is a biography of finite numbers: sooner or later the displacement will arrive back where it started, and then Ka-Boom as you say. Good-bye everything. You would like me to write this out for you?"

"You're the genius. So stop this merry-go-round and let's get off. Say the magic words and get us the Lex Express back."

"Andréas, my friend, life is not that simple. I also know how pneumatic tires function but I am not prepared to stand before an onrushing taxicab

Mark Twain in Milan

just to disprove a statement in inertia and momentum. How did we get here and what happens next, these are the questions at hand... We are summoned by destiny." Giancarlo straightened and thrust out his chest.

"We have been called by a power greater than ourselves?" asked Sam Clemens.

"Which would be the New York City Transit Authority," I said. "Oops..."

There was a *thunk* at the base of my neck, a curtain of blue ozone, shimmery like the aurora borealis, and I was standing behind the head of a beefy, elegantly tailored middle-aged man straight out of a 1920s gangster movie, the black and white variety. Said head was slathered with brilliantine. Sleek, like an otter.

"Less off the top, capiche?" said the head. His tone suggested I was a service sector clone and to speak only when spoken to. This was fine with me because I was sure I was not the one he thought he was talking to.

The head was sipping an espresso—thick black coffee with a twist of lemon peel—and I could not see his face. Across the room a big moose lounged dreamily with a sharpshooter's rifle across his knees. The head was fiftyish and its attached body wore an Italian silk suit: pearl gray with wide, wide lapels and very expensive, an antique or something from a retro store. Except it's new. I thought of him as Carmine, which is what I decided to be a good name for a head with an espresso and a henchman—I had seen *The Godfather* ten times. The Moose was tilted back against the wall, balancing on the two rear legs of a wooden chair. The bodyguard stared at me, I stared at the bodyguard.

"Chi è lei?" said the Moose, nonchalantly taking aim at my head. He showed a wide, ominous grin of many black teeth. I gathered this was him asking who am I. *Pop, pop, pop!* The Moose peppered the wall past my right ear with three shots in quick succession.

The blue aurora quivered and a woman popped out of thin air beside me. She was togged out in a tweed-and-velvet something that clung agreeably as she moved and swinging a serious looking cavalry saber. A veil covered her face and head. She brushed aside the veil and peeped out. This was the face on Giancarlo's cameo. She gave me the once-over and attacked. I ducked.

The breeze of the sword's passage sounded just like in the ninja movies. I made a note of this. "Ow!" I landed on my tukhes.

Her pale gray eyes grew huge. "Oh, terribly sorry, old chap. I thought you were someone else," she said. "Are you still alive?" I said yes. "I say, good fun, what?" she remarked. A bullet zinged past and she dived under the desk. Under the desk seemed to be appropriate; I dived too. And missed the floor.

As I departed the scene, behind the Don and the Moose there was a shimmer—like on Star Trek when they use the transporter? In an electric haze stood Giancarlo Pieranunzi; he flickered and went out. I fell through the aurora borealis and was back in the tunnel.

"I was in Milan," Sam Clemens was saying.

"I am a Milanese," Giancarlo said. "I but lecture at the Università di Torino."

"Ah, Milano," posited Sam Clemens. "...vast, dreamy, bluish, snow-clad mountains—the Italy I read of in the poems of Lord Byron."

Giancarlo brightened at the name. "Byron. You *have* seen her, then. Lady Ada."

"*I* have seen her," I said. "Didn't you guys notice I was gone?"

"Lady Ada?"

"I suppose so. She nearly took my head off with a sword. You, too, Giancarlo. You were coming in as I left."

"Andréas... I have been here all the time."

"An unholy miscegenation of locations, these comings and goings," said Sam. "However, I have yet to meet myself."

"You wouldn't," I said. "We would. *Holy shit!*" There was a blast from an air horn and bumping down the tunnel came one of those red double-decker buses that used to run on Fifth Avenue years ago, a genuine historical relic. Except shiny and new and minus most of its top deck where the subway's roof beams had sheared it off. A vertical exhaust pipe remained, chugging forlorn puffs of acrid coal smoke. There was no driver in evidence and no visible passengers. All its tires were blown; I guessed from running on the cement footings of the subway tracks. What was left of its destination banner—the canvas roller where terminals and routes are listed—said *Università*. Another parallel universe. We had gotten our mass exchange that, while heavier than Sam Clemens, Giancarlo Pieranunzi and me, was still nothing to the disappeared Lex Express.

"Now we go Ka-boom! Right?" I said.

Mark Twain in Milan

"Si, Andréas. I believe so. Unless something additional that we do not know about went over to make up the negative mass the espresso left behind."

"Ivory. Onions. This can be our ticket out of here." Sam Clemens was hopeful. "All we have to do is get aboard; which one of you..."

"Close but no cigar, Sam. We're still a few tons shy of our missing train."

Ka-bunka, ka-bunka, ka-bunka, the bus named *Università* flopped to a stop on squared-off wheels right where we stood. A woman got off, descending what remained of a circular stairway to the upper deck. She could have been entering a ballroom. She carried a white sable muff, one of those 19th Century hand warmers that doubled as a lady's carryall.

"Well, *that* was exhilarating," she said. "And you gentlemen are staring. This is rude," said Lady Ada Lovelace.

"You'll have to pardon us, your grace, but you tried to kill me only two minutes ago. With a sword," I added.

"Balderdash," she replied. She eyed me speculatively as if the idea might have some merit. "The last thing I remember is being booed off the podium of a lecture hall at the University of Turin. And here I am."

"Yes. Here you are," said Sam. He eyed her appreciatively. Giancarlo glowered. Lady Ada's floor length gown was white silk trimmed with magenta velvet touches; her hair was coiled into a lacquered confection that framed a delicate oval face.

"I am sure you men find this all excruciatingly amusing, but I have things to do. You have had your fun, now if you will please..." And she was gone. No ozone, no blue aura, nothing. She was there, and then she was not. The bus steamed as it settled to one side and fell over.

There was a slithering as something tugged at my shoelaces. It was the same rat—back and begging on his hind legs, real cute—a number the Central Park squirrels use.

"Nice esquirrel," said Giancarlo as he patted the rat on its head.

"Times are hard all over, pal," I said. The rat looked disappointed and scuttled away. The bus called Università belched a final puff as its boiler went out. Hands clutched behind his back, Twain sauntered off to the end of the platform to light up a fresh cigar.

"Andréas, we are stuck in a Monte Carlo simulation," said Giancarlo Pieranunzi.

"Uhn, great. What is that?"

"A bump in nature. We have hit an anomaly in God's roulette system. We are trapped together like St. Sebastiano awaiting the flight of the arrows. Samuel Langhorne Clemens has explained this all in his estimable *Mark Twain in Milan*. You have read this?"

I had to say I had never heard of the book. "I read *Tom Sawyer* once," I said. "By Mark Twain."

"Nononono. By Samuel Langhorne Clemens. Twain was the unreliable narrator which he made up for the tale. Furthermore he meant Torino, not Milano, but dared not to speak openly of what he had seen. Samuel Langhorne Clemens also experienced the Monte Carlo Simulation."

"Use my name gently, sirs." Hands behind his back, cigar at a tilt, Sam strolled back. "...it is protected by copyright. Furthermore I never wrote the book. That's a barge-load of nimble-fingered rotgut. And if I did, I don't remember doing it." He blew a smoke ring. "Well, I am pouring if you are buying. I recognized the lady, too."

"Really?" I was surprised.

"From an illustration, actually—the frontispiece—of a book I have read. Can't recall the book. But the lady... memorable. Ask our friend the mathematician."

"Si, Andreas—Ada has explained it all. She was English, but her heart was Italian." Giancarlo kissed the cameo with the face of Lady Ada.

"Well," said Samuel Langhorne Clemens, as he adjusted the tilt of his fez, "I must be getting along. This has all been very, very... instructive. Ivory. Onions. I must return to whence I came. Whilst I should enjoy remaining here with you—exploring the future—while you rummage in your past, I have a deadline to meet. My telegraph dispatches for the New York newspapers which have underwritten my European escapade will not wait. I have *editors*," he said meaningfully.

Mark Twain/Samuel Clemens stopped for a breath of air and Giancarlo threw himself into the gap. "I have been to America," he said.

"It's not the same," said Twain. "It's already discovered. Europe was never discovered; it was merely inhabited. I am leaving. As intriguing as this all is, I want out."

"Sam is right," I said. "Thanks for the chat; let's do it again some time." I hustled down the tunnel.

Mark Twain in Milan

And then returned. "No Soap. For fifty yards in either direction both ends of our section of the tunnel have been bricked up. No way out without a sledgehammer."

Giancarlo said something in Italian that sounded like I told you so. "We may then continue our conversazione?"

I sat down again.

"I require a favor of you. I have no idea how long we will have together, Andréas, so I must be talking fast. It will be for you to identify il portiere. I have not the word for this in English, a person who stands guard at a doorway."

"Gatekeeper. Like doorman?"

"Sì, sì," said Giancarlo; he was eager and urgent.

"Why me?"

"Because you are here and I am here. We are here together." This made some sort of convoluted sense. I let it drop.

"As an environs for the remainder of Eternity, an empty subway tunnel is a mite whingy, I opine," said Sam Clemens. He cocked his head to one side, as if listening.

"Il portiere is more of a catalyst, the lost operand who points the way," said Giancarlo, "...mathematically speaking. Alas, my Darling Ada's equations were not perfect in every respect."

"Bummer. The woman on the bus—this Ada—she is not the gatekeeper?"

"No. She is but one of an infinite number of Adas. The love of the middle years is a melancholy thing; one requires assistance. You must help me to win the woman I love. Amor vincit omnia. That is Latin, not Italian." The dapper Italian slumped inside his suit, decidedly droopy and depressed. "She is a nineteenth century mathematician. In terms you will comprehend, dear Andréas, as a man of your marvelous 21st century, she is the nexus of a probability cluster. A line of code, like the "Else" of an "If, Then, Else" contingency."

"Sure. Why not?"

"Il portiere, the gatekeeper, is the catalyst who connects 1841, 1867, 1929 and today." A lung-clogging vapor of cigar smoke had glided our way from where Sam Clemens sat squatting on his heels, writing in the dust of the tunnel with a pointed stick. It stopped to hover over

Giancarlo's head. He turned red and gasped for breath, then collapsed in a coughing fit. I slapped him on the back until it passed.

"Huh? You mean all we have to do is find this person—this gatekeeper—and we'll be home free?"

"I knew you would help me. Otherwise we will spend forever with Samuel Langhorne Clemens. We will strangle on his cigars."

There was the *thunk* at the base of my neck, a curtain of blue ozone, and an invisible express train came cannonading through, right between my eyes.

❑

Everything was pitch black.

"You okay in there?" It was the voice of my barber. He hovered in a moist haze that reeked of soap and cologne as he lifted a steaming towel from my face. I was back. And the face was the face of Giancarlo Pieranunzi.

"Uh... Giancarlo?"

"Welcome back Mr. Saperstein. You must have dozed off."

"Call me Andy. What is your name if you don't mind my asking?"

"Johnny. You should know that; you've been a regular for over two years." He nodded to a framed license. New York City Dept. Health. Barber. Johnny Pieranunzi.

"Short for..."

"Giancarlo. Gianni, Johnny—they sound the same."

In the days when 65th and Lex was a palmier neighborhood, when Bloomingdale's yet flourished and the local hookers bought their bait and tackle at Abercrombie's, the place where I get my hair cut occupied the mezzanine, rightly floor number 1½, of what was once the local firehouse. Cast iron columns sought a vertical climax through neat holes drilled in designer teak genuine hardwood flooring tiles to bloom as cast Corinthian capitals eight feet off the ground. On the wall was plaque with letters incised in gilded bas relief: Parrucchiere Gianni. An oval cartouche framed a sepiatone photograph of a man with a military moustache—my Giancarlo from the 2nd Avenue tunnel.

I thought to play it cagey just in case I had dozed off in the chair and dreamed the whole thing up. "The man... a relative?"

"My great-grandfather."

"He was a barber?"

"Nope. A university professor—mathematics. I found it buried in the attic when my folks retired to Florida. There were two."

"And your family hailed from Milan and your great-grandfather was a mathematician, right? Hold on, two pictures..."

"The other was a woman; I figured her for my great-grandmother. Want to see it?" I did.

He rummaged through some drawers muttering "Be patient, I'm looking" sounds under his breath just in case my attention might have strayed. It hadn't. "Voilà." He held aloft a portrait—an oval face in a gilded ormolu frame. "A great beauty, they say." It was the face from the cameo. Cascades of auburn hair framed pale gray eyes with an elfin twinkle. I could swear the picture winked at me.

"Uh, Gianni... you ever hear any family stories about a Gatekeeper?" As this was half an hour ago, stuck in an empty tunnel with Mark Twain time, I wasn't supposed know about gatekeepers yet, as Giancarlo wouldn't have yet told me. But I *did* know. So sue me.

Gianni gave me a funny look and steered me back to the chair. "Nope. Just some recipes. I've got an uncle though who used to be a doorman at the Carlyle."

As Gianni Pieranunzi—the great-grandson of the man in the tunnel—scissored away at my hair there were tears streaming down his cheeks. What the hell, I figured—Italians emote. "My hair isn't all that much a catastrophe, is it?"

"Sorry about that." Gianni choked back a sob as he removed his scissors from the area of any vital organs. "News travels fast, Mr. Saperstein—Andy. The hairdressers' jungle telegraph, take a look." We went to the window together. Across the street scaffolding crept up the walls of a four-story townhouse and a bucket truck was horsing a large fiberglass sign into place. The renovators had moved in, hanging ferns and opening painted-shut Palladian windows to dapple highlights on freshly exposed brick walls. I noticed Gianni was jabbing his scissors into the windowsill; the competition was moving in. "BrowBeaters, a franchise. They do body waxing."

I put a consoling arm around his shoulders. "Tragic. A tragic sight. Trust me, Gianni, I've got a hunch a cut-rate hot wax joint is going to be the least of your troubles."

Ding! Parrucchiere Gianni's receptionist rang her chime to announce Gianni had a customer waiting out front. I jumped. I noticed that I was jumping a lot lately. Unannounced shifts in time and location will do that. Like jet lag. Ding! Ding! Ding! Ding! Ding! The receptionist was getting antsy.

There was a squawk from the bitch box, Parruchiere Gianni's in-house intercom, "Gianni. *Now.*"

I picked up the phone. "Gianni's tied up. This is Andy."

"Andy," said a harassed voice. "Tell him I got a live one. And tell him no crap about my spiritual work."

"I am so very happy for you, ahh..."

"Lindy. I want her the hell out of my reception area toots-sweet, if you catch my drift."

I turned to Gianni. "Lindy has a live one," I said.

"Nice for a change. She channels the dear departed in her spare time. I'm not complaining; most of the girls read magazines or do their nails." He grabbed the phone away. A high velocity stream of verbiage poured from the earpiece. Gianni's face fell. Then Lindy paused long enough for him to get a word in edgeways. "A new client... Listen, you're not in one of your altered states of consciousness are you? Good. Come in here. Alone. Give her a soy latte, a health shake, whatever." Gianni turned to me. "Business is slow. New clients—live ones—have to be coddled."

There was a businesslike rap at the door to Gianni's sanctum and it opened a crack. A woman slipped in. She was so slim she made it through with room to spare. Lindy was your basic legs job and glad to show them off, thank you. And she looked great in the indie rock T-shirt she was wearing as a dress.

"Uh... hello."

"Andy..." She made eye contact and smiled a smile of generous full lips. My pulse rate rose and my palms started to sweat.

"Hi there. You must be Lindy," I stammered.

"Lindy Earlywine..." She paused. It was my turn.

"Andy Saperstein." We were face to face in one of those epiphanies that are the bread and butter of the daytime soaps. Neither of us had moved. "Uh, you're a medium?"

Mark Twain in Milan

"I channel spirits, yes. When I'm not booking cuts and perms." Like I said, this was Lexington Avenue, no big deal.

Gianni cleared his throat. "Heads up, young lovers. Company." He squared his shoulders and stepped forward with his best floorwalker's smile as a tufted pink hairdo thrust itself around the corner. I suspected this was one of Lexington Avenue's medicated mamas. A small, determined woman shoved past Lindy and struggled into the room. She stared at me and Lindy, registered shock then delight. "I hope I am not interrupting a *moment*, but you are not Charles. It *works*." It was Lady Ada Lovelace. She gave me a hug. She was naked.

As none of us was named Charles, I felt some reply was called for. "Ada Lovelace?" I said. That was the best I could come up with.

"I fear, sir, you have the advantage. Yes. Ada Byron Lovelace. And whom do I have the pleasure..." She arched a speculative eyebrow and looked me over.

The ball was in my court. "Andy Saperstein. Bay Ridge, Brooklyn." Lindy placed herself between me and the naked Ada.

Ada Lovelace brushed a hand through her hair and let out a small squeak of dismay. She hurried to a full length mirror to inspect the damage. Her hairdo was spiked and colored day-glo pink. Not the coiled perfection of her portrait cameo. "Charles. Luigi. This is their doing. I told them to wait for my final calculations. But would they? *Men*." She turned to face me. "I seem to have a nosebleed. Ice, please."

"This happens all the time on Lexington Avenue," said Gianni. "It's our uptown ambience."

"There is something amiss in the algorithm. I think having to bleed to death because one acquires strange hair is a bit severe, don't you?" She placed a thumb and forefinger at the bridge of her nose and held it till the bleeding stopped.

Wham, Bam, etc., and Giancarlo was in the room—not his great-grandson Gianni, but the original from the 2nd Ave. tunnel in the flesh, very suave and cool as a cucumber. He bowed, "I witnessed Don Paolo's attack and I feel I must apologize for my countryman... Dio mio!" Lady Ada au naturel was probably more exposed woman than he had ever seen outside of the Uffizi Gallery. Mussolini ran a tight ship.

"Ma le dà fastidio se la fisso per un momento?" Giancarlo's eyes traveled over her. All over. He ogled.

"He has requested permission to stare at me," said Lady Ada as she clutched her hands over her heart. "Remarkable." Her nose began to run red as soon as she loosened her grip.

Lindy handed Lady Ada a Kleenex. "Where's that ice?" She turned to me, "Andy?"

Just then Sam Clemens thrust a wild-eyed head around the edge of the door casing. "Andy. You won't believe this, but..."

"Oh, I'll believe it all right. And *he's* Mark Twain," I told Lady Ada.

"Wow. Some people will believe almost anything," Lindy said.

"I don't know how I got here, but there's a man in a futuristic suit—wide lapels, snap brim fedora, the works—and he has a machine gun," said Sam. "He must have followed me through. He just appeared then disappeared. Out of nowhere."

"Nowhere is a statistical improbability, Sam. Except in a singles bar." I flopped into the client chair. The gent with the ordnance had to be our very own Moose, somehow out of his time and after us with an assortment of bigger bullets. I kept my opinion to myself; it would have required too much explanation. "He'll be back," I said.

There was a splintering and crunch of distressed construction materials as the Moose appeared, a little behind the curve. He popped into place behind Gianni's barber chair, wedged halfway into the room between framing studs, dismembered electrical wiring and what was left of Parrucchiere Gianni's drywall. He looked ready to shoot the hell out of the place.

"Oh, sweet Jesus!" Sam Clemens stared through the cloud of plaster dust at the Moose. The parts of him not stuck in the wall held a smoking tommy gun, to which device he was methodically attaching a fresh rotary magazine of ammo. I guessed he was after anything that moved. Gianni yelled something appropriately bloodthirsty in Italian and raised his scissors to strike.

Splonk! The scissors went into the padded backrest right up to their rings. Anybody sitting all the way back in the chair would have been a goner. The Moose's reloading was almost finished when he evaporated. The tommy gun fell to the floor. I was a minor casualty; Gianni's shears nicked my arm.

Gianni rolled his eyes. "That chair. Imported Italian leather. Six thousand dollars."

Mark Twain in Milan

"That's all right, Tonto. It's only a scratch. Don't worry about me." I pulled myself up, clinging to the chair. The wall, as well as a stand of potted ferns and Gianni's imported upholstery, was a total loss.

"Excuse me. I gotta make a call." Gianni headed to his office to phone the contractors.

Lady Ada stepped up to the plate. "Master Twain. I do believe I have seem you before—for a fleeting moment. You will excuse the paucity of my manners but at the time my attention was understandably elsewhere." Sam Clemens preened his moustache as he blushed beet red; Lady Ada was a distraction clothed or unclothed.

"I was watching myself about to be dispatched by that very same hired thug. I was dressed as though for an African hunting expedition and I disappeared in a hail of bullets. I was behind him and he couldn't see me. *You*," here she indicated Giancarlo Pieranunzi, "have the most delightful accent. You were also there for a split second. Then you both disappeared and the thug turned on me. 'Giancarlo,' that was what he said. So now there are three of us. I am an honorary Giancarlo."

I handed over a washcloth stuffed with ice cubes.

"Thanks. When faced with danger I often recover my equanimity by contemplating things of beauty. I looked about. The place was an obvious bachelor's haunt. And the wallpaper! I tried sweet reasonableness, but it was as though they couldn't see me. I started peeling the wallpaper. Toile de jouy, very au courant but hideous."

Giancarlo cringed. "Don Paolo Carbone's prized wallpaper. I came; you went." So the Don was not named Carmine. I filed away this tidbit in case we ever met socially.

"And the great looming lout knocked the ladder out from under me in mid-peel," said Ada Lovelace. "The last thing I recall is a brilliantined individual thumping away at the malefactor who had seized me. With an umbrella. He smelled like lavender pomade."

"Don Paolo beating Nunzio Calabrese over the head with an umbrella. Don Paolo must have been heartbroken over the wallpaper."

"Nunzio?"

"His bodyguard."

"Oh. The umbrella thumping has not improved his disposition. He must have followed you here," said Ada Byron Lovelace. "And I seem to be naked. Cover me, please." Unflappable. Breeding will tell.

His eyes large and staring, Gianni ripped down one of a pair of floor-to-ceiling draperies and wrapped her in it. Ada Lovelace looked him up and down. "You are a barber, a leech, a surgeon. You draw teeth and let blood, then. You'll do," she said. "Fix my hair."

"Your blood type, my lady? Just in case." That from me. My aplomb recovered, I was now all business.

"Jesus Christ," said Lindy, "if you guys do transfusions too, it says a lot about whatever barber college you escaped from. She's not going to bleed to death. She only whacked her nose."

Gianni fumbled with the scissors and attempted to appear professional. Lady Ada had hit him as hard as she had hit his great-grandfather.

"You are dithering," said the draperied lady. "Oh, I'll cut it by myself." She grabbed the scissors, made for the door and went tearing down the stairs to the street. I figured she'd be back because she left her drapery behind.

Five minutes later Lady Ada Lovelace was back, dripping with contrition. "Sorry, I was in a rush."

She must have used the absconded scissors on herself. Her hair was a mess. She now wore an abbreviated shingle cut, one side only, East Village casual. It was an interesting look.

"Pardon me." I nipped out to the hall and searched through my pockets; I needed a smoke. I left Lady Ada to fume unchaperoned. I hoped Sam Clemens wouldn't pop out of the woodwork and catch me: I was supposed to have quit after bitching and moaning about his own ever-present cheroot.

I extracted a crumpled pack from an inside pocket and struck a match. Ever get an electric shock? Not the sizzle and burn, but a sandbagging at the base of your skull, the paralytic pounding that announces in big, blue letters that you can't let go and you are going to die. This was heavyweight stuff, like the 600 volts DC they run through the third rail.

❑

I was in a Piranesi landscape—tumbled columns, grazing goats, distant shepherds and shepherdesses about their discreet businesses in a renaissance bosky dell. Giancarlo crouched before a tiny campfire, feeding it with sticks and what looked to be loose rubble. He had several weeks' growth of beard. "Signore Twain?" He turned and saw that it was me. "Ah, you are back. I had hoped you might return. Good day. Or more appropriately, l'altro ieri, the day before yesterday. Or the week after today."

I moved in to warm myself at the fire. It was cold. "A couple of minutes ago you said something about a gatekeeper..."

"For me that happened three weeks ago. I asked you your name. You told me Andy Saperstein." He looked me over. "You *are* Andréas?"

"Last time I checked. Your fire is not giving out much heat," I said.

"It is not a fire; it is a picture of a fire." Giancarlo gestured toward the grazing goats. "Push one," he said. I walked over to the little flock; no matter which way I tried to go, everything was sideways. "Push," said Giancarlo. I pushed. The goat fell over.

"Oops." The aurora borealis number again and both of us, Giancarlo Pieranunzi and Andy Saperstein, were back in the 2nd Avenue subway tunnel. It was still devoid of tracks, trains or passengers. The Lex express rumbled by, invisible.

"Ahh, the phenomenon is occurring with greater frequency. Someone did something." His tone was accusing.

"Well, it wasn't me. Where were we? I mean the place was so... flat."

"Wallpaper," said Giancarlo. "Wallpaper is supposed to be flat. And of a familiar pattern. I believe we were in Don Paolo Carbone's wallpaper."

"Sure." Holding a conversation with him was like playing checkers with all red squares.

"Every time is a different spatial dimension," said Giancarlo. "Wherever you are, seem to be—you are. You will always be the same you with all your memories and experiences intact. The others you may meet—and the connections are powerful: Signore Clemens, myself, Lady Ada—these will be the native population of wherever you find yourself. They will wonder that you have changed, in some small way, perhaps. I thought you understood that. The Monte Carlo occurrence will find each universe different in some minor respect."

"Like a butterfly died in Cleveland?" I asked hopefully. "Wallpaper, huh. So where's Mark Twain?"

"He went off exploring. That was three weeks ago. He had not returned." Giancarlo's eyes got a dreamy, distant—well, *Italian* look. "He will be a three-dimensional being lost in a two-dimensional probability cluster." He gestured with a subtle old world combination of hands and shoulders.

"We have a problema, you and I. We must cooperate. Our entire predicament spins on the tip of a pin. These are the people with the answer to our dilemma—Ada, Charles and Luigi."

"Well, if I could get your dream girl to stay in one place long enough to ask her a civil question... These are the people behind all this? With the slipping back and forth in time?"

"Conditional branching—this is the brilliance of the daughter of Lord Byron."

"Well, you are the mathematician. You tell it to stop."

"Alas, one must do that before one starts the apparatus and I was not yet born. This is a mathematical machine, not a physical machine. Without an algorithmic manipulator who posits the structure to tell it when to stop, it will go on forever. Lady Ada, Charles Babbage, Luigi Menabrea and Garibaldi, heroes of the Risorgimento. They had a falling out."

"Well, I am so sorry for them." I thought he was going to cry. "These folks were all jolly coeds at the University of Turin, right?"

"They met. Luigi would become the Premier of the United Italy. This was in 1841. I have read his paper on the phenomenon we are presently experiencing. Ada Lovelace, how I worship the wildflowers that spring beneath her feet! Her mathematics do indeed perform as expected. Since I first met you in this empty tunnel I have thought of nothing but discovering the mechanism to join with her in some parallel reality."

I was wondering if I was expected to run interference with these other nineteenth century suitors of Ada Lovelace, but I didn't rush him. There was a cyclonic roar behind us. If you are taking notes, "Yeoow!" is the same in English or Italian.

Giancarlo and I flattened ourselves against the wall. The train kept getting closer and closer. After some seconds, maybe minutes, its noise reached a climax and, after one last ka-whallock like a piano dropping off a truck, there was utter silence.

"You look," said Giancarlo.

"No you look." Giancarlo had his eyes shut tight. So did I.

When we looked, no train. It was Nunzio the Moose. He looked confused and he had a gun, his target rifle, a potentially lethal combination. The Moose came tearing up the empty tunnel hell bent from 1929 to some phantom future. He saw us and stopped. He was not a happy camper.

Mark Twain in Milan

"T'ta a facc' arruso!" yelled the Moose and charged."Wha'd he say?" I asked Giancarlo.

"Hard to translate, Andréas. Literally, I'll strip your face, asshole."

"Oh." The two of us ran like hell. The trackwalkers' bolt holes shot past as we hotfooted it down the tunnel. In the glare of the maintenance lamps our shadows danced around us; doppelgangers chased us through double-shadowed brownouts from light to light between puddles of sodium yellow.

Spang!

The Moose stopped to get off a couple of shots. *Spang, yang, yang, yang.* The ricochets echoed fitfully down the empty tunnel.

We must have run half a mile when I pulled Giancarlo to a stop. Hadn't the tunnel been bricked up? "Hey, wait. There was a barricade here."

"This one," said Giancarlo. He ducked into a trackwalker's niche identical to many we had raced by. But this one was not a dead end. There was a ladder leading to a tiny grated rectangle and daylight in the distance way, way above us.

"Uscita d'emergenza. What did I tell you?" said Giancarlo. We rattled up the ladder, popped the grating at street level and clambered out. Passersby paid no attention. Everyday stuff: two sweaty red-faced guys pursued by a gangland hit man scramble out of a hole in the ground. I took some comfort in the unflappability of my fellow New Yorkers. I hailed a cab.

"Step on it," I told the driver, "There's fifty bucks in it." I felt just like Philip Marlowe. Or Christopher Marlowe. I'd have to check up on that. Whichever Marlowe was the hard-boiled private eye. The driver beat all the uptown lights and Giancarlo and I were soon in his great-grandson's barber shop. There was a note from Gianni taped to the mirror:

"Grandpop—This is all too confusing. The rent is paid up through June and I'm at BrowBeaters for the duration. The place is yours; last one out please turn out the lights. Here's the security code—this was followed by a string of numbers—there's a keypad by the door."

Lindy was still there, reading a magazine. "Andy..." She threw her arms around my neck and gave me a peck on the ear. There was no Lady Ada or Mark Twain in evidence: when one of us went forward, a like mass had to go back. Rather like a square dance. Someone or a part of someone must have gone in the opposite direction. Samuel Langhorne Clemens. I thought about Mark Twain as a refugee in time scattered in bits and pieces across three centuries. A shot of blue ozone and Giancarlo was gone. Not a word, not a sound.

But there was a return package, kicking, cursing and thrashing around generally. It was Sam Clemens, returned from Don Paolo's wallpaper.

"My God, I feel flat," he said. "Where's the naked lady?" He meant Lady Ada.

Simple. "Uh, Lady Ada is dead," I said. "A hundred years at least."

"Here, but not at the loop's beginning," said Lindy. "I was channeling Ada Lovelace only last week. Or a lady in a big hat who spoke Italian and had a father who was a poet."

Lindy caught me rolling my eyes, "I can't help it; it's a gift. I am a channel for the spirit-world." But Giancarlo was more than interested.

"Mi scusi, signorina. Can you get through to her and ask for a little advice?"

"Giancarlo!"

"Si. I watched myself disappear as Signore Twain materialized. I fear my parallel self is in great danger."

Lindy rummaged in her handbag. She didn't open it, just held a plastic bottle of prescription pills close to her heart like a talisman. She went walleyed and teetered like she was in a trance. I turned to Giancarlo and cleared my throat.

Lindy glared. "This is a sensitive contact. Don't agitate while I'm out." Her head flopped to one side and back she went. Giancarlo stared at her as though he really expected something to happen.

Lindy held the pose for several minutes.

"Nope. No go," said Lindy, "the spirits are not talking today. But I do know about the tunnel. My Uncle Larry was a foreman with Vents and Drains. He used to take me down for fun when he babysat me. I was six years old and we were supposed to be watching the seals at the Central Park Zoo. And the lady in the big hat was Sarah Bernhardt. Sarah says Lady Ada told her to hold all incoming calls. Sorry."

"But Giancarlo #2 is still out there in the Great Wheresis with a gun-crazy torpedo. We've got to get him out. Any volunteers?"

"I, alas, cannot go," Giancarlo shrugged. "To send me after myself might initiate an unpredictable cascade. Zero-sum gain, I fear."

Lindy studied her nails.

Mark Twain in Milan

"It's your idea, Andy," said Sam Clemens.

"No. Not my guy." Lindy threw a protective arm around my shoulders. In some circles I am considered a prime example of reverse Darwinism. I am a slow learner but I get there, eventually. I hugged her back.

"Then I am odd man out," said Sam. "I am not your everyday have-a-go hero. My birth was attended with omens and portents with the appearance of Halley's comet; my death will come when the comet next returns." He glanced at an Ansel Adams calendar on the wall. "2061, I believe. I am damn nigh immortal." On the other hand, he had never expected to be stuck on a contingency loop with an Italian mathematician on the run from Mussolini and the Mob.

"Let's get ourselves straight. Sam, do you really want to swap times with Giancarlo #2, right? Permanently?"

"Of course not. You two'll find a way to get me back. Right as rain on all other counts, my friends."

"It will be like going on a cruise." I high-fived Lindy and Sam, to whom this was but another custom of his adopted century, exotic and intriguing.

"Sam, you will be walking into a shooting gallery," said Lindy.

Sam picked up the tommy gun from where it had rolled under a planter of ferns. "But not empty-handed, little lady."

"It's not loaded," I said.

"They don't know that," said Sam.

"So how do we get Sam back?" asked Lindy.

"I'll be here. Don't worry."

"I hope so." I walked to the scale. "Get on, and we'll find out how much mass exchange we are talking about." I weighed in at 60 pounds less than Sam Clemens. "I'm lighter," I said, relieved.

"Weight and mass are different animali," said Giancarlo #1. "Isaac Newton's Second Law of Motion."

"I am willing to take a chance. Since I am technically in motion the inertia I would exhibit at rest should not register as weight. Phew!" Sam Clemens mopped his forehead and looked pleased with himself. "Chautauqua," he explained.

Duh. Well, it worked for me. And we were ready to go.

After a quick trip to a surplus store, we got Mark Twain decked out with a camouflage fatigue jacket with his name, S. L. Clemens, stenciled on the chest; he wore a black turtleneck. He checked himself in a mirror and was pleased. "Buff, bluff and ready, SAH!" he bellowed. He snapped to and sucked in his waistline. "Oh, great galloping codswhallop, I can still do it." He winked at his reflection. The mirror winked back.

"But let's do it somewhere else and give Parrucchiere Gianni a break," I said. I sized him up. Sam Clemens was tall and angular and even with sucking in his stomach, I doubted that he was capable of standing off a determined assault by a hit man twice his size without a stand-in double. The drywall contractors were still finishing up the repairs from Nunzio Calabrese's latest visit so we headed for Bloomingdale's and the 59th Street stop.

"Why are we going there?" asked Lindy. "I told you Uncle Larry's secret way into the 2nd Avenue tunnel."

"We are going to the Lex because it's closer and safer. And easier on Sam's sensibilities—no rats."

"You think it's me, don't you?"

"The gatekeeper? Maybe, maybe not. Then again it could be the subway itself, or a scam of Donald Trump to milk the city fathers for an underground shopping mall. And I don't want to lose you." I gave her hand a squeeze.

"But Sam Clemens is your friend."

"I don't love Sam. Well, like a brother, OK? Besides, Sam is a big boy."

"Like a very big kid," she agreed. "Andy, did you just make a move on me?"

"Yes."

With no idea of how to get to 1929 on purpose, we supposed closer was better and trooped on down to the change booth where we bought four tokens and descended to the trains. Sam adjusted the line of his moustache in the mirror of a candy machine. "I am ready. If I get stuck in time, check the personals of the New York Times for 1929. I read about that in..."

And he was gone. No ozone, no blue aura, nothing. No Mark Twain, either. He had been standing on the 59th Street platform and then he was not. There was a lackadaisical "foop" as air entered the space he had occupied. Great, Giancarlo's analysis of the Monte Carlo simulation worked. Sam Clemens must have made it back to the shooting gallery.

Mark Twain in Milan

But the exchange of masses routine? Where was our return bundle of joy from 1929? We waited.

Nothing. Not even a train. Neither of us said a word for upwards of ten minutes. We went for coffee.

❑

With Sam Clemens/Mark Twain gone, Giancarlo, Lindy and I ran Parrucchiere Gianni by ourselves. Oh yes, Giancarlo #2 was there waiting for us, sitting in the six thousand dollar leather and chrome chair and looking very pleased with himself. #1 stared at #2 who shrugged and evaporated. But no Mark Twain. With the departure of the redundant Giancarlo the mass transfers, time-hopping, whatever, stopped.

On the back of Gianni's farewell note was a tip on how to run the salon: establish an appropriate artistic setting. "If the client in the chair thinks something creative is going on, she feels special. This is the psychology of a good cut. The client thinks you are consulting with the hair muse." The salon flourished but Mark Twain was stranded. We three moped between appointments.

"Lindy, remember your impromptu séance?" I asked.

"I'm sorry it was Sarah Bernhardt and not Lady Lovelace, Giancarlo." She oozed empathy in his direction.

"I am used to be disappunto, Lindy. It is not your fault," said Giancarlo.

I thought it was time for Plan B. "Your Uncle Larry's vent grates. You said something about him knowing another way in."

"Oh, sure. There's an access hatch just past Bloomingdale's."

"That's the Lex," said I, "not the 2nd Avenue. How come?"

"I don't have the slightest idea," said Lindy, "but I remember the empty tunnel. They must connect. I was only six."

Any answer is a good answer and, after all, I had asked her. "Plan B it is. We'll go train-diving with Uncle Larry." And we three were off together, headed against the uptown flow of rush hour traffic.

When we arrived at Uncle Larry's grate there was a squatter in possession: a sidewalk hawker had parked his blanket and sat cross-legged in a semicircle of assorted wares: junk jewelry and silk scarves, brown twisted cigarettes and glassine envelopes. He sized us up, then turned to hustle a passing knot of commuters, "Loose joints. Loose bags and joints," He noticed Lindy and switched his pitch. "Bracelets, lingerie, earrings..."

A voice with a Missouri twang sliced through the clamor and babble of midtown. "A sensible list of accessories for a most beautiful woman."

"Sam!" No flash, no aura, no sparks, just Sam Clemens. Albeit Sam Clemens was a formidable enough looking specimen, he had well... bulked up. He was taller, younger and considerably more muscular than the last time I'd seen him. Even in Manhattan, he attracted stares. He was six foot six in his gaiters and must have weighed in at 240. Onlookers cheered as he came sashaying, moustache first, up the street like he had just bounded out of a cavalry charge. He took a bow.

"Be right with you, kids." Sam Clemens walked over to the sidewalk vendor and lifted him off the ground. One powerful arm held him upside down while the other went through his pockets for the advertised loose joints and bags. "Cubebs, you say? We'll take eight. Four for now, four for later."

"Easy, easy. The customer is always right. No hard feelings, OK?" The man struggled in Sam's powerful grip.

"No hard feelings, Kemo Sabe," said Sam as he put the man down. "And a word to the wise—you're as obvious as a wart on a debutante; try another corner. And cut back on smoking up your inventory. If the constables catch you you're yesterday's news. Not everyone has my forbearance." He tossed a twenty-dollar gold piece to the street peddler, "Keep the change." The man dusted himself and moved off Uncle Larry's grate. He cast us a baleful glance as he spread his blanket a few yards away.

"Well?"

"Well what?"

"Where were you. Where did you go?"

"As close as I can figure—nowhere: a featureless terrain, sun always at three in the afternoon, a gray haze. Nothing ever changed; I have not the slightest idea how long I was there."

"Hmm..." Giancarlo looked wise. "Signore Twain—if you do not mind my saying—you are the same Mark Twain we last saw?"

Sam scratched his head. "Far as I can tell."

Sam was lighting up a cubeb we four dived down the iron ladder beneath the recently vacated access hatchway. At the bottom of the ladder was the same 59th Street stop we had sent Sam off from yesterday. All that work to save four fares.

Mark Twain in Milan

By the time we got past the first landing with a Rastafarian and his folding table of incense and essential oils and a Bible Lady with her sandwich board, it was just before the early rush hour.

Lindy grabbed my elbow and spun me around to face her. "Andy? What if Sam hadn't come home and *you* were stuck back there. I mean, I am here and you are there—forever?"

"Well, to be on the safe side, I could learn how to factor quadratic equations."

"No. Just look at me."

I looked at her. "Wow."

"See," said Lindy. She kissed me right there on the second landing of the 59th Street Station and I was a lost man. I held on tight and kissed her back. There were appreciative yells and a few wolf whistles as the uptown express pulled in.

"Andy. We've got Sam back. What are we waiting for?"

"Lady Ada."

We hung around for hours—then gave up and trudged back to Parrucchiere Gianni.

❑

Giancarlo revisited his theory of there being a human agency for these events. "You may be the switch that turns the phenomenon on and off. A gatekeeper. You or Ada. Or both of you. Or Lindy." I was thinking this over, playing with a set of scissors and staring out the window.

"Drop the scissors," Lindy screamed.

"Yeoow! Ouch!" The scissors were hot. I tried to shake them loose but they clung to my hand. I was being electrocuted in a shimmering of blue aurora starbursts and the smell of ozone.

"Shhh..." said Lindy. The closer she got to the scissors, the hotter they got. She slapped the scissors out of my hand. They went flying and stuck in a far wall where they caught a Tuscan shepherd right in the crotch. Said shepherd was a decorative trope on Don Paolo's toile de jouy wallpaper and one of the few left adhering to the wall. We were back at the target range cum speakeasy Ada Lovelace had vandalized.

"Ready a sinistra, ready a destra." Somebody was calling out from the other room, "Ready on the left, ready on the right." The next command would be to commence firing. I thought of stray, or not so stray, bullets. "Lindy, down," I said.

"Don't push," she said. We piled under a huge desk that filed the farthest corner of the room.

Grief-stricken, Don Paolo was sobbing over the shredded remains of his imported wallpaper—shepherds and shepherdesses about their discreet businesses in a renaissance bosky dell. As he dabbed at his eyes with a silk embroidered hanky, he spotted us. Don Paolo's face turned an apoplectic red. "Nunzio!" he screamed. The Moose lumbered into action and squeezed off a barrage of shots in our general direction.

Poppoppoppop. Click, click. The Moose was out of ammo. He had missed, probably the enthusiasm of the moment. Next time he wouldn't miss. Reverberations and ricochets died away to be replaced by silence broken only by our labored breathing. Then a rattle as the Moose fumbled in his pockets for more bullets.

As the Moose inserted a fresh clip, at the far wall an aurora borealis shimmered. It was Mark Twain. He had flaming red hair, wore a bronze-plated kilt and was younger and more muscular than the Mark Twain from the subway. Hanging onto his arm was Ada Lovelace, her hair long and flowing, held in check with a single golden circlet and dressed in body hugging spandex: a Druidic princess right off the cover of a Sci-Fi paperback. She waved. The carabinieri had arrived, a little late but we weren't complaining. We now had the numbers but the Moose had the bullets. Lady Ada sized up the situation and began closing in. Very quietly she picked up an alabaster objet d'art, a lissome lass with her arms held over her head, adjusting a laurel crown, a nymph. Clunk! Lady Ada dropped the Moose.

"I have always wanted to do that," said Ada Byron Lovelace. "It is a probability cluster. These show up as irregularities in the mathematical calculations..." She examined the Moose's unconscious form. "...sweet in the code string. Endearing I thought, but what we have here is wretched excess." She turned the Moose over with the tip of a toe and registered distaste. "Perhaps not so sweet." The Moose groaned and cautiously opened one eye. The eye registered indifference, then surprise. A hand shot out to grip Lady Ada's ankle. "Awful cheek," she said as she bonked him again with the nymph.

The Moose was down for the count and there was no discernable damage to the alabaster statuette. The thing must have been the genuine article; in antiquity they built doodads to last.

"So glad you could come," said Lindy, standing and dusting off her knees. Wham, Bam, etc. again, the heavy ozone smell of sunrise over the gas works. And...

We were back at Parrucchiere Gianni but without Lady Ada. She was left in yet another alternate 1929 at the mercy of Don Paolo and the Moose—when the Moose came to. Blue auroras danced from the ceiling and the walls as Lindy let out a shriek. Reclining in the leather and chrome chair was Ada Lovelace and leaning over her with a bundle of hot towels, me. Lindy passed out; I considered it. Lady Ada looked up, noticed us, and likewise screamed. She was disappearing as I watched. There was a minor thunderclap as air rushed in to occupy the space formerly occupied by, well... us. Lady Ada's departing scream and the pop of collapsing air brought Sam Clemens running in from his sanctum—a former utility closet, where he now spent most of the day hunched over a 2½ inch TV. He had become addicted to C-SPAN and the History Channel.

"Sam, I have this woman..."

"Good for you, Andy. Something sweaty, I trust. I wish you both many happy assignations."

"I beg your pardon; I don't mean to intrude, but..." There was a fresh arrival. Mark Twain again. This one was clean-shaven. The two Mark Twains looked at one another, stepped back for a better look and circled one another in a neat figure eight not unlike a pair of cheetahs stalking in high grass.

"Sam..." I said.

"Yes." they both answered simultaneously. "Uh, hello, Andy." Then, each pointing to the other, "...who's he?"

"You."

There was a crunch of crumbling drywall and the clearing of a manly throat as a third Mark Twain arrived, our red-headed guy in the Roman army getup. He was stuck in the wall just as the Moose had been. Mark III was carrying a standard issue Roman short sword. "But there are so many of you..." Lindy said.

"Yes." The three Mark Twains replied in unison. He—they—were very pleased with him—them—selves. "Can't have too much of a good thing," quipped my Mark Twain—the man in the red fez. Or I supposed it was him. Mark Twain, Mark Twain and Mark Twain had been keeping busy while we ducked bullets.

"I sense a pattern here," I said.

"Well, good for you," grumped Mark III. "So do I, and I'm it. Get me out of the goddamned wall."

There was a girlish giggle. "Hello, Marcus, well-met," said Ada Lovelace. This Ada wore the spiky Day-Glo hair of Ada Lovelace #3 but was dressed in skin-tight black spandex. "My stars and garters, we must have a kink in the fabric of local space-time."

Mark III, who even though stuck in the wall was absorbed with admiring himself in the mirror, flexed a bicep and grinned from ear to ear.

"Marcus Tertius Secundus," said Mark III as he gave us a clenched fist salute and hammered said fist against his chest. "Agent of Empire." He raised an admiring eyebrow at Lady Ada.

I gave a yank on the sword. It was hot to the touch. Mark III was immediately surrounded by a bluish aura. The University of Turin's time-traveling docent found this encouraging. "Ahh, Ada's theory is correct. I had hoped so. He will not be with us for long." The three of us pulled Mark III out of the wall. His aura subsided as he shook himself off.

"Would you mind telling me what this is all about. I thought... I thought bodies occupying the same space was impossible," I stammered. I was developing a nervous tic.

"Simple," Lady Ada said. "If a butterfly dies in Cleveland there will always be a superfluity of Clevelands where the butterfly did not die. And went on to procreate and flourish."

"We'll always have Cleveland," I shrugged. "Whenever."

"Pay attention, please. Cleveland is real estate—a place—and firmly positioned in its parallelisms. To quote your marvelous Stephen Hawking, the laws of physics do not allow time machines, thus keeping the world safe for historians."

"You are not supposed to know about him," I said.

"I am a woman ahead of her time; don't worry about it," said Ada Lovelace. "The more the merrier. In case of trouble, I thought to bring along a friend with military training." She nodded at Marcus Tertius Secundus. "And I am not the Ada Byron Lovelace with whom you have been associating." Here she consulted a large platinum watch. "She is due to arrive in ten minutes. Come Marcus, we have interrupted a dalliance." She winked at Lindy.

Mark Twain in Milan

"But we must be away, Marcus and I. I am totally assured that my beloved shepherd will have covered the variora satisfactorily. There is a future for him, but not with me."

❑

Uncle Larry's pop-hole took us to a network of underground passageways, and back to the 2nd Avenue tunnel. We waited.

Ka-bunka, ka-bunka, ka-bunka, the bus named *Università* flopped to a stop on squared-off wheels. A woman got off, descending what remained of a circular stairway to the upper deck. She could have been entering a ballroom. Her floor length gown was white silk trimmed with magenta velvet touches; her hair was coiled into a lacquered confection that framed a delicate oval face. She carried a white sable muff, one of those 19th Century hand warmers that doubled as a lady's carryall.

"Well, *that* was exhilarating," she said. "The last thing I remember is dodging overripe tomatoes at the University of Turin. And here I am." It was Lady Ada, another Lady Ada. And if you've got a creepy feeling that you've been here before, join the party. It was déjà-vu all over again, this time with tomatoes.

"Lady Lovelace #5, I presume?" said Lindy.

"I never dreamed that algorithm would work," said Lady Augusta Ada Byron King, Countess of Lovelace. "On material human beings—characters as they navigate the mechanics of a fugal landscape. This is too, too fabulous. I was stretching my intellectual muscle, showing off a bit in front of those self-important preeners."

"Giancarlo?" I asked.

"Sì."

"Would the faculty of the Università di Torino have been the sort of folk to throw overripe fruit at a guest lecturer?"

His eyes grew large to the point where they bulged. "No, Andréas, excitable but not violent. Atti di violenza are for football and the opera. Oh, sì. This proves my hypothesis: I am not me. I mean, I am not *your* Giancarlo; if there is a Giancarlo Pieranunzi in your timeline he probably did not escape from the Fascisti and come to New York. And he would be 115 years old, which the General Theory of Relativity forbids."

He smiled at Ada Lovelace and groomed his moustache; she smiled back coquettishly.

"Relativity? Tosh. Interesting, but a plaything. Wilmo Darndlefang of Gothenburg, a clerk at the Swedish Patent Office, wrote of it in 1839. A curious fancy, hardly the mete of serious mathematics." Lady Lovelace smiled fetchingly at me. "And mathematics is an art, not a science. Science is all steam and rivets." At this there was a hiss and a belch from the omnibus as it expelled a shower of glowing cinders. "And bitumen is so noisy," concluded Lady Lovelace.

"For you." Giancarlo handed Lady Ada his treasured cameo.

"Ohh," she held it at arm's length. The long lost carver had done her justice. "Do I really look like this?" We all nodded. She shrugged her very creamy, very white shoulders. "I wish I had known before I married William."

"It is never too late," Giancarlo made calf's eyes at her then kissed her hand. Even though she was heart stoppingly beautiful Lady Ada had to be almost two hundred years old. Albeit her husband was stranded in their home continuum, she was far along in years for this timeline. She certainly didn't look her age.

"What about 1929?" said Lindy and I simultaneously. "And if the omnibus is from 1841, where are the horses?"

Giancarlo displayed a cavalier grin. "Another train has pulled into the station. This time an omnibus. Like the trains on the tracks, the espresso and the train we could hear but not see? In the empty tunnel?"

"Yes. Yes," from all four of us.

"Lady Lovelace," he bowed in Lady Ada's direction and was rewarded with a fetching curtsey, "is from a different continuum altogether. Different from yours and different from mine. And, since I am here, she at least may leave but it is unlikely that I shall ever go home again. This pleases me. I like it here. Even the lovely Lady Lovelace," another bow and another returned curtsey—very European, these Europeans, "must obey the constraints promulgated by Relativity."

"If we wish it so. Men! Is that not correct, my dear?" Lady Lovelace asked of Lindy . "By the way," said Lady Ada, "I simply adore your little dress and your shoes. Would you allow me a small intuition?"

"Of course, your ladyship."

"You are around when these arrivals happen—these conditionals?"

"Gee, I..." Lindy gave us a questioning look. We nodded. "...yes, I guess so."

Mark Twain in Milan

"Then you are the operand. The missing factor of my most elegant equation. You are the gatekeeper."

"You mean I have a supernatural thingy?"

"No, only cute shoes. It is right that a woman have cute shoes. Because I am a woman, even dear Charles and Luigi tended to patronize me—I am but a woman. Likewise the Earth is hollow and spontaneous human combustion occurs regularly. Just look around you."

We looked around. There were no flames.

"A gatekeeper," said Lindy with an ear-to-ear grin that would have melted even Don Paolo Carbone's heart.

"Don't let it go to your head, my dear," said Ada Lovelace. "China flats do not a summer make and if I might essay an observation—and this is not a characterization of you, dear girl—in my equation the gatekeeper is more of a doorstop than a doorperson: a brick, a lump, a catalyst. If you appreciate conditionals as I do, my dear, you will know that if you are not really the missing operand, you are a flag, a pointer to where it resides. Op. Cit.: a gatekeeper. You are not a part of the phenomenon. But without you nothing happens."

"What about the scissors. They were hot," said Sam as he wistfully eyed Lady Ada's silk ball gown.

"An effect, not a cause, dear boy. Do you like it? I had it made in Paris. You have excellent taste for a man."

"200 years old. And horny," I volunteered.

"As you say," said Ada Lovelace, "Men are a testosterone time machine." Sam Clemens took a bow. He averted his eyes and shuffled his feet.

Lindy gave my hand a squeeze.

"You don't remember trying to cut off my head? With a sword?"

"Nonsense, I don't even own a sword."

I explained the goings-on with Carmine the Don, the Moose and the 2nd Ave. tunnel.

"Hmmm... a genuine bohemian demimonde," said Lady Ada. "The underworld can be so stimulating—and you have assured me that you have seen me here before, have you not?"

"I have. Three times at least, although it is hard to keep count when one is being shot at and run over by a train..."

"Understandable, albeit not helpful," she replied. "Confusing. This is a clue, I believe."

"Ahh... a clue," said Sam Clemens, trying to look wise.

"A clue. We are in a mystery, a detective story. And, like all good mysteries must have a peak, a climax and, sadly, a dénouement."

"But what about Lindy... the gatekeeper..."

"And your marvelous calculating machine, the difference engine," said Giancarlo Pieranunzi. He blushed as Lady Ada leaned forward to ruffle his hair.

"Lindy is, alas, the love interest. This is a story after all, nichts wahr? A power greater than ourselves has found us to be diverting playthings; our realities are mere hallucination. The machine is naught but a quantity of cogs and wheels held together with rivets, my darlings. Without a soul it is nothing but ingenious levers and switches. I have the key to its soul."

"Hallucination..." I gave myself a pinch. "Ouch. I seem to be real enough," I said.

"I should hope so," said Ada #5. "Dear Giancarlo, pinch me."

"Uh..."

"Go ahead."

He went ahead. He reached tentatively for an exposed earlobe. "No, something more personal. If we are Destiny's playthings, let us be more adventuresome. If I can feel your pinch, then we are both in for a surprise." She hiked up her petticoats and exposed what the High Victorians would have called "a comely thigh."

Lindy quickly put herself between me and the exposed Lady Ada. "Where you are from? I mean to say it sounds, well, *messy*. Steam omnibuses, no refrigeration and all. Your potato salads must be crawling with bacteria. Your ensemble is, of course, devastating," she added. "Coordinated."

"Coordinated... I can swim quite well, my dear, and can ride a velocipede, if that is what you are getting at," said Lady Augusta Byron King, Countess of Lovelace. "Ah-hah, you are asking me if my socks match the drapes. I am afraid not."

Lindy got that out-to-lunch glassy stare I recognized from her séance and I knew she was plotting the makeover of an entire parallel universe.

Mark Twain in Milan

The steam omnibus gave a puff, then another. The reek of coal gas was intense; my eyes watered. "Woo, the fumes," said Lindy, waving her hand in front of her nose. The omnibus gave a tentative chug then rumbled into full steam idle. Cinders rose from a ruptured vent somewhere in its innards.

A cat, scruffy with long hair, singed and with irregular bald patches, descended the steps from the bus's truncated upper deck. There was a squirming bundle in its teeth. "Oh, hello, Puss." The lady and the cat seemed to be on speaking terms. It walked over and dropped a rat at Lady Ada's feet. "Thank you Widdershins." She held the rat up by its tail, examining. It raised its head and looked at her with black, beady eyes. "No, Puss. If you won't eat it, neither will I. But thank you for your concern; I *have* missed my lunch. Well, time to go." The rat scuttled off. The cat sat and groomed itself. "Giancarlo, would you care to accompany me?"

"Ahem." Sam Clemens a/k/a Mark Twain reached down to pet the cat. He was toking on one of the sidewalk peddler's absconded joints. "I hate to be an old stick-in-the-mud, but things must be piling up back in Milan. I have a book to write."

"That aroma. Surely it is not bitumen fumes from the omnibus's boiler." said Lady Ada. Mark Twain passed her the joint.

"Ahh, the Arab weed," said Lady Ada, inhaling deeply.

"Andy?" Lindy gave my hand a hopeful squeeze. She wanted to go along and neaten up the nineteenth century.

"Uh, I think we might make them feel intruded upon. And they won't have indoors plumbing." The two sweethearts would crave solitude at their nineteenth century picnic, even with all the bacteria and botulinum toxins.

"I didn't think about that. You don't even have TV?"

"I am aware that smoking is detrimental to the lungs but, no. My mother's brother died in a sanitarium, however." Lady Ada passed the joint back to Sam Clemens. She looked hopeful but was puzzled by the reference.

"Not tuberculosis, television." Sam explained television to Lady Ada.

"No. No TV. But 'talking wallpaper,' you say? This brings to mind the wallpaper in your gangster's inner sanctum: shepherds and shepherdesses disporting themselves in a bosky dell? Such naughty business, particularly for wallpaper. I am absolutely entranced. And by-the-bye..."

She pulled a dog-eared notebook from her carryall. "And if my calculations are correct I should soon be leaving you lovely people. I can only hope poor Luigi and dear Charles are adjusting to things where they are. But then, they wouldn't have a choice, would they?" She giggled becomingly.

Giancarlo sighed and shuffled his feet. Lady Ada offered him her hand. "Shall we continue this discussion en tête-à-tête? My, won't dear Charles and Luigi be jealous."

"I have always wanted to be a shepherd," said Giancarlo Pieranunzi.

Mark Twain in Milan was first published as an online serial in *Bewildering Stories*, summer 2010, Don Webb, managing editor.

Platterland

It was a real nice laying-out—tasteful.

Well, maybe not so much tasteful particularly, but neat. They'd got Ed's left arm attached to his head and not his shoulder. And they had the remaining right arm attached on the left side. To look like them, I supposed. Ed's critters had laid him out like a guy caught in one of those exercise machines you see on late night TV, an origami fold-up man, and without the pretty girl. I noticed they'd braided his nose hair. Artistic, a nice touch. His body was covered with a dusting of early frost.

The Maine Warden Service always figured sooner or later they'd be coming back with Flyin' Ed Moholland in a body bag. I used Ed's phone to call the wardens; they'd been looking for him for three weeks. No one expected Flyin' Ed to actually die; he was a monument to time—closing in on eighty and keeping pretty much to himself.

I'm Phil LaPointe. Ask anyone about me: reliable, a sober—well, usually sober—citizen and what the summer people call "a local character." I should have checked in on Ed during the weeks he was missing but it wouldn't have mattered. I've been around and gotten pretty well insulated against the nasty surprises life throws at me but I scrambled up the stairs and threw up clutching the sides of the kitchen door and bent over double. Between spasms of half-digested home fries, I stumbled down the porch steps.

Down by the road a trio of crows squabbled on top of Ed's sign: "Platterland: Thousands more inside." Sixteen shiny hubcaps hung from the sign, all from upscale cars: Mercedes, Cadillac, Tucker, DeLorean. Flyin' Ed kept the hubcaps shined up in case he ever got a customer. When Ed was a kid, back in the 1940s, his father's hubcap sideline generated maybe fifty dollars a year at best. Ed's regular business was selling and servicing vacuum cleaners.

The crows perched on the sign watched disinterestedly as I up-chucked. "Shoo!" I clapped my hands and they flew off.

❑

It all started with an expired vacuum cleaner. That good old Electrolux that chugged away for years, even before I was janitor, finally gave up the ghost. Pilly Hennicott left me a note pinned to the door of the utility closet at the school: "Get the vacuum fixed. We clogged it up after the eighth grade dance. And for God's sake, clean up the rug in the pre-K room, it's been six months now."

I had been janitor and bus driver at the Meddybemps Elementary going on ten years. Pillsbury Hennicott was my boss and I generally did what he said. I stripped off the vacuum's chassis and got around the switch assembly with a pair of clip leads. Yep, the motor was fried. I set off up Meddybemps Hill after Flyin' Ed, the Electrolux man. I figured a new motor and a beefed-up power nozzle would fluff the rug where I couldn't get the stains out. Shirley Dilworth, our principal, suggested they were finger paint.

Anyway, I chucked the defunct vacuum cleaner in the school van and headed up to Ed's place. He was out back of the hubcap museum tinkering with one of his flying machines. He dropped his wrench and wiped his sun-blotched forehead with an oily hand.

"Hiya, Phil. Come on around to the front porch, I got some brewskis on ice." I was on school time, driving the school van, but I figured since it was summer vacation the beers wouldn't count. We passed the time of day and I finally got around to the busted Electrolux. "Bring 'er in," said Flyin' Ed. I lugged the vacuum plus a carton of loose parts I hadn't bothered to put back in up the porch steps and into the cool confines of the front room that doubled as Ed's parlor and repair shop. I plomped the disassembled vac onto his worktable. Ed sighted down the hose, gave the pile of parts the once over and looked relieved. He gestured to the refrigerator next to a large screen TV. "I got a case in there."

Now neither Ed nor I were what you would rightly call drinking men, but summer was new and fresh with another Maine winter just behind us: reason enough. "Let's pop a couple and socialize."

We sat and drank, watching Ed's TV with the sound off for fifteen, twenty minutes.

"Phil, I got things to say. Put your can back in the cooler and let's get airborne. Then we'll talk. It's been lonely since I got banned from the school." That was when I took my first and only ride with Flyin' Ed.

❑

At his visits to the Elementary Ed would stand before the whiteboard, a dashing figure for all his seventy-plus years: jump suit, safety helmet and goggles, ramrod straight. Flyin' Ed brought into that safe, snug schoolroom an element of secret, forbidden things for kids who came into town once a month, when their folks went shopping for groceries at the Pick 'N' Pay. These were country kids. But, though not yet allowed

Platterland

to cross the main road unaccompanied, they had been raised on cable TV and weren't easy believers. Ed had to promise them a ride. His trailer with the powerchute on board was parked out by the ball field.

In his late 50s Ed became addicted to flying powerchutes. Powerchutes are motorized parachutes as their name suggests, sort of a flying bicycle with a big sail up top. Flyin' Ed rode the rainbow, that's how he described it to the wide-eyed kids at the Elementary.

Word got around. The school board panicked about their insurance premiums. Pillsbury Hennicott called an executive session. Shirley Dilworth had allowed two kids to fly with Ed on the strength of a parental consent form with signatures the kids had faked themselves. The parents were steamed. Seeing as how Shirley was their teacher, I felt she should have recognized the sloppy penmanship.

It was a short meeting. Parental consent slips were not worth the paper they were written on. The school could be sued.

"Well, I think Ed Moholland is a fine law-abiding man and no threat to the children," Shirley huffed at Pilly.

Pilly Hennicott loved an attentive audience. "We are not impugning Mr. Moholland's character, Mrs. Dilworth, but we have considered any impact he may have with the children. He obeys the laws of gravity just like the rest of us."

Flyin' Ed was grounded—stuck in Platterland with his vacuum cleaners as far as the kids were concerned.

❏

Ed and I were up for about an hour on my first, last and only powerchute ride. Ed spun in to set us down, chute fluttering out behind him like neatly folded wash, and dropped the last foot or so to a landing that drove a chill right up my spine. It was a gentle hit, almost like getting out of bed but, like I said, I was not meant to fly and I was pretty shaky.

"Terra firma," said Ed, opening the fridge and extracting two fresh cans.

We relaxed.

The telephone rang. Ed ignored it. After a couple more rings Ed's recorded voice cut in, "Platterland, Flyin' Ed Vacuum and Repair. Leave a message at the beep."

Beep.

"Ed! I've got a thing in my vacuum and I can't get it out. It's dead in there." A woman, middle-aged and desperate.

Ed chugged down his can and smiled apologetically as he went to pick up the phone. "This is Flyin' Ed." There was an agitated chattering that I could hear but not understand; the caller was talking fast and loud. "Yes, Molly. Yes?" More excited babble from the earpiece. Flyin' Ed sighed and cupped his hand over the mouthpiece. "Molly Guptill." A woman we both knew. "This is the heart of the problem," Ed said. "Explaining."

He removed his hand and keyed the caller in on the speakerphone so I could listen. Ed spoke in tones of calming reassurance. "Yes, Molly, this happens... occasionally."

Full speed and full volume, Molly's voice poured out of the tiny speaker in Flyin' Ed's fax-copier-answering machine. "I tried to get the thing open. To see if there was a mouse or something...? Let me tell you... remember that moose died last winter over near Ayer's Junction? Stuck in the culvert? And no one knew until after the thaw? I mean by August you had to take a twelve mile detour."

"Yes, Molly."

Molly would not be pacified. "A jelly—gooey and the smell? Stinks to high heaven. Is there a way anything that big could get to the insides of a vacuum? Something that grows?"

"Suppose I come over this afternoon. OK?" Molly snorted assent. Even across the room I could feel the clunk as the phone slammed down at her end. Ed's shoulders heaved as he slumped back into his chair. He gave a mighty sigh. "Phil, how long have we known each other—ten, fifteen years?"

I said that sounded about right.

From the determined set of his jaw this was not going to be about the lost loves and minor regrets that decorate every man's past. I made myself comfortable. Ed started right in.

"Back from the Navy, I was; I served an eight-year hitch. That must have been '57. Mom had died three years before. Her funeral was the only time I got home in all those years. I caught the bus from Willipaq—they do that afternoon run up Meddybemps Hill?—and there was the old homestead, the house I grew up in, all gone to hell and empty, weeds up to your ass in the dooryard."

Ed scrunched his beer can in one huge hand as he reached for another. "Plowed ground gone fallow under last year's rye grass and the yard overgrown. And the Electrolux vacuum cleaner."

"What about it?" I was on my third beer and I guessed this was the hook to Ed's tale.

"It was sitting in the middle of the driveway smack dab under my dad's old Platterland sign and waving its hose at me. All frantic it was, like it had been waiting for me to come home. Like Lassie would, in those Lassie movies, when someone was in trouble. So I spoke to it, What's the matter little fella? And it turned on its wheels, ran partway towards the house, waited, then ran back to me and waved its hose.

"I said Okay, little fella, I'm coming. The vacuum gave a sort of whir from its power nozzle like it understood and headed out behind the well house.

"As it turned out, it had a companion—another Electrolux—and it was in trouble. Well really, it was dead. The poor little thing was some broken up. I sat and stroked its hose there beside the corpse until sunset thereabouts. The little one circled around—sniffed, like. Waiting for me to do some magic. When it started to stink, the dead one that is..."

"You buried it." Here I was drinking Ed's beer, and he believed he had space aliens on the old homestead. The beer made the story easier to accept.

"No, I put it in the freezer. Come along downstairs. And watch that first step." I got to my feet, not as wobbly as I thought I should be about now. "Phil? That little vacuum, the one that met me in the dooryard?" Flyin' Ed beckoned me to follow him.

"Yes?"

"Turns out she was pregnant. Sure enough, come fall, she comes out from under the barn, tentative-like, with two little ones, just like her, in tow."
Ed led; I followed.

It was a large cellar, some of its walls carved out of solid ledge, slate and granite, the way they did with those old Maine farmhouses. There must have been twenty freezers parked about in a circle. Ed had them on old wooden shipping pallets, the kind you see piled for burning out back of the forklift depots. Mostly Sears—the freezers that is. I asked Ed about his preference for Sears products.

"Sears minds its own business. Till they went local anyway. Sears used to deliver out of Bangor, different driver every time. No busybodies asking why I wanted a new freezer every two years without bitching about the old one."

"And the freezers?" I had an idea where all this was heading but I wanted to hear it from Flyin' Ed.

"Full of critters. Dead critters. They don't have a lot of little canisters, just enough to replace themselves with a few left over to cover accidents. And they age and die. And once every year they come down cellar and visit their ancestors, like. I open the freezers and we have a silent moment together."

"And what do you get out of all this?" I asked.

Ed turned, amazed that I hadn't caught on. "They run the farm. And I get paid when I rent them out, sell them and fix them. I get the regular maintenance calls—a new hose, lube job, cord and switch. I sell a line of bags and attachments. They can spray paint, too, but not too well. They're no trouble. They tend the fields—at night of course. God! If the neighbors ever got wind of that!" Ed drained his can and scrunched it. "I got a bottle somewhere," he said hopefully.

"Bottle it is," I replied.

We made it back, pretty well lubricated by now, to Ed's porcelain-topped kitchen table. He retrieved a quart of J. W. Dant from the flour hopper of his late mother's Hoosier breakfront.

"Thanks for sitting down and listening to me talk. I've been carrying the secret alone for way too long. I didn't realize what a burden it was till now. Us talking and all."

We drank and talked like two men will who are past the age of having to impress one another. This was an uncommon event—our conversation as well as Ed's space aliens—and we paused to savor it.

"Something else I got to show you. I call it the Rug Suckers' Ball." He held one finger to the side of his nose, like Santa Claus in The Night Before Christmas. This was going to be top secret stuff. I tossed back what was left in my glass. Ed's chair scraped the linoleum as he beckoned me back down the cellar steps. "I dug a tunnel out to the barn, so's I could watch without disturbing them. This is their time, their mating time." Ed fetched a lantern.

"Don't rightly know how they figure their mating season. They all answer some call and come together here, probably something to do with the moon, the tides. Like the horseshoe crabs. Watch your head." We were almost sober enough to navigate the steps.

I collided with a low ceiling beam. "Ouch!"

Ed held a finger to his lips. "I find good homes for 'em," Ed whispered. "Their real home must be far off. I figure they're just waiting for a lift. They wouldn't survive long on this world; they haven't seen all the movies we have—alien invaders, and all? 'Take me to your leader' and total destruction follows. I figured the best way for them was to go under cover, as themselves, or close to it. They don't seem to mind that I sell them. They eat dirt, stuff they suck out of folk's rugs. They don't really require plugging in but I figure all that electricity gets 'em hopped up. They sure do love a good housecleaning. And when they need some companionship, they stop working and their owner brings them back home to me. Shhhh."

An eerie dance was taking place. No music, but instead, a whir of pulleys and belts, servomotors from ecstatic power nozzles and an underscore of flap flap from their vacuum hoses as they twined, untwined, and stroked one another. And the light reflected from their chrome trim made things wild and passionate even with the silence.

"They come to Meddybemps Hill to make little baby Electroluxes?" I asked in a hoarse whisper. I had to ask even though I felt silly from the moment I opened my mouth.

"Yep. From all over the world—the universe for all I know. They just like me. Most of the year they're your normal, everyday vacuum cleaners. The canister type—a lot of folks prefer those." Ed threw an arm across my shoulder, not unlike a proud dad at his daughter's dance recital.

The dance stopped. The assembled Electroluxes pivoted towards Ed and me. There was a long moment of what I could only call respectful silence. They then turned their backs and reformed their circle, completely ignoring us.

"We'd better go," Ed said.

❏

Ed believed he had space aliens in his cellar. Well, I had seen them. And the Electrolux community seemed to appreciate Flyin' Ed. They ran his farm for him. Stranger things had happened in Willipaq. Well, no... maybe they hadn't. I took another pull at my can.

Ed bent over his workbench saying, "Tsk, tsk," as he removed a continuity checker from my old motor.

"Let me guess," I said. "You call up with a customer's vacuum all fixed up like new, but a different one actually goes back to the happy housewife."

Ed installed a rebuilt motor as he talked. "You got it," he said. "They don't mind getting separated and they're generally well-behaved away from home. That's here with me, I guess." Ed removed his Willipaq Historical Society baseball cap and wiped his speckled forehead. A trickle of sweat ran into one red-rimmed eye.

"Damn!" Ed rubbed away the salt sting. Going on eighty years in the out-of-doors had decorated his face, neck and forearms with spots, splotches and furrows.

"Have you asked about those white spots?"

"Yep. The doctor cautioned me and said it might be good if I had a biopsy. Or two. What would that change? I'd still have it. Cancer. Or not. And I'm 78 years old. Why worry?"

"But..."

"When their time comes, they die." Ed bowed his head, a slight incline, showing respect. Ed was that sort of guy.

"That woman on the phone," I said, "Molly."

"Yep."

"Molly's old vacuum will go in one of your freezers?"

"Yep." Ed snapped the vacuum shut and picked up a rag. He popped a blemish on the chrome polish of the donut-shaped cord winder that straddled its rear end. "Done. Good as new." He gave my carton of leftover parts a shake. "But it has issues." He looked thoughtful. "Now what do you think? Do you want your plain old mechanical vacuum cleaner like it came from the factory? Or would you like your very own living unit?"

He was offering the Meddybemps Elementary an organic vacuum all its very own. If Pilly Hennicott ever twigged there was a space alien living in the janitor's closet, I was going to be in for some heavy-duty explaining. I opted for what I already had: the traditional wheels, cogs and pulley unit that plugged into a wall.

Ed reached down a factory-sealed carton with a brand new power nozzle assembly. "It's yours. No living tissue inside, guaranteed. My gift to the school district."

"Sorry, Ed. Got to pay you for it." The purchase order was already made out. I handed it over.

"Bye, Phil."

"Bye, Ed."

It had been a full day. I had that all-over queasy feeling you get after a lot of beer and cut-rate bourbon on an empty stomach. I thought about hitting Ed up for dinner but saw his eyes were drooping. Nap time. With a man like Ed you tend to forget his age.

"Don't forget the vac," Ed called after me. I loaded the repaired vacuum with its brand new power nozzle in the van and drove very carefully under the Platterland sign, under its hubcaps, and down the hill. And sure enough, the Electrolux was as good as new. But I hired a commercial rug cleaner to shampoo the finger paint out of the rug in pre-K. Pilly grumped but signed the purchase order, no questions.

Summer faded into fall, and a new school session. The refurbished vacuum cleaner died yet again—Pilly had been using it to spray paint over at the fire station. I gave Ed a call but got the answering machine for three consecutive days. I figured he was off on a toodle with some of his powerchute buddies. Not wanting to take any chances with a possible dead alien in the vac, I locked it away in the closet for a few weeks. When I checked back, there was no smell. It was the genuine, factory-made variety Electrolux, gathering dust instead of sucking it.

It was Thanksgiving break, a four-day weekend and no push for immediate cleanliness at the Meddybemps Elementary, when I headed up the hill with the school van.

❑

The place reeked. And no Ed in sight. On a hunch I checked the electric meter. It was locked off and sealed. The freezers had been left to melt. The stench was appalling. I got as close to the house as I could without gagging, then headed to town. Sure enough, Eastern Maine Electric Co-op had shut off the power. Non-payment of accounts, etc. The buzz at the Co-op was Ed's powerchute had been observed hitting a power pylon in a freak upward thermal gust. The Maine Warden Service was called to pick up what was left of him. They returned empty-handed. I had the power turned back on and visited a week later when the smell was under control.

There were a few crows picking at what looked to be an Electrolux canister vacuum cleaner in the weed-clogged gravel driveway. I checked the electric meter out back behind the kitchen. The seal was removed; it was spinning at a furious pace. Service restored. I covered my face with a bandana soaked in mineral spirits and started down the cellar steps.

The smell was less powerful down among the freezers than it was upstairs. The cellar was cold and damp, the air thick with condensation. A rime of frost several inches thick spilled over the bulkheads of the open freezers. It would be a good day for the Electric Co-op's shareholders, dividend-wise, when and if I paid the bill. I did pay the bill, by the way. Sort of a tribute to Ed.

Except for one, the freezers were empty.

I had feared what I might find down there. The reality came as a welcome relief. It was a kind of spiritual moment, if that's what trips your trigger. It did for me and I stayed on for a while. Then I was dizzy and made for the stairs that promised warm air and sunlight. I sat on the porch to get my bearings, just a little sick—probably more from the mineral spirits than from the smell of death. The place had gone to weeds just as it had when Ed's mother died all those years back.

I noticed an overgrown path, Ed's route to behind the barn where he launched his powerchute up and over the tall stand of white spruce his dad had planted to celebrate his birth. Tracks criss-crossed flattened patches of chickweed and plantain. Tracks made by many tiny wheels, headed for the cow pasture where a cover crop of rye grass was on the mend from where something large and heavy had sat on it. Not long enough to obscure the rain and the sun, not long enough to kill the rye grass, but long enough to load some freight, perhaps.

I returned to the cellar to pay a final farewell to Flyin' Ed. This time I looked closely at the frozen, reassembled corpse. The Rug Suckers had got it right, by and large. The Rug Suckers he had cared for in life and in death had returned him to their own now emptied burial freezers, one last gesture, and they'd done the best they could putting him back together.

I headed back to my truck and jumped at the creak of rusty wheel bearings close behind me. It was one of Ed's critters and it was in trouble. It had lost its cord winder. A pair of eyes on stalks, like a snail's, stared intently out at me. The pupils were yellow and the irises slits, more like a goat's eyes than a cat's if you've ever looked a goat in the eye. Spooky. But these were more melancholy than spooky, all rheumy and runny at the edges. Old eyes. It had been left behind, I guessed, too sickly to make the trip. It wobbled to me on off-center wheels, got stuck in a muddy rut left by my pickup and rolled half over on its side. Its eyes were clouding over; its hose lay limp in a spring rivulet of ice melt.

I carried it back into Flyin' Ed's cellar and placed it gently beside his body. Showing respect. Ed would have liked that.

Platterland

Platterland was first published in *On the Premises,* the November 2007 issue, Tarl Roger Kudrick, editor.

McMuckle Makes a Minyan

Maven Lipchutz was banging at the piano
while a fish—an overlarge golden carp—sang. The fish wore a
shimmering gold evening gown that draped suggestively from one
shoulder. Lipchutz' guest, a fixer, winced as he pointedly fumbled in his
pockets for his earplugs. "Ah-hah..." The earplugs were inserted. The
planet whereupon they stood—circling a middling G3 sun in an
intergalactic bubble called DEM L 299—was Hyperion II, renamed
Dreidl by its latest arrivals.

"Heidi, take five. Go daven or something," said Lipchutz. Heidi gave a
dorsal shrug, adjusted the lamé drape of her shimmy, and flopped off the
piano. She belly-rolled over to the Maven's studio wall where she began
to rhythmically bob her head. "Fish have feelings, too, McMuckle. I
mean the earplugs. Heidi is capable of surprising flights of creativity. We
have brought the gift of song to Hyperion II."

"One piano and a fish on a barren planet in the Large Magellanic."

"Barren is as barren does; it will not want for music. We have now a
culture."

"So do bacteria. Bacteria don't vote. Yet." The fixer removed an earplug,
studied it, then explored his auditory channel with the tip of a little
finger. "Itch," he explained. The plug was replaced.

"Bacteria don't sing," said Lipchutz.

"Ah, a plus point. By 'sing'—you refer to this caterwauling which
requires a piano." The fixer waved an accusatory finger. "No, bacteria do
not 'sing.' They are therefore the superior species. Tush, tush, Lipchutz.
It's just that I do not believe we have a identifiable chartbuster here,"
said Ivor McMuckle. McMuckle was a fixer much respected throughout
the Large Magellanic Cloud. "What is 'daven,' by-the-bye?"

"Daven means to pray," said Lipchutz as he gazed after the departing
Heidi with the look of a love-struck teenager. "Comes from the
Latin—same as the English 'divine.' Emphasizes the One to whom
prayer is directed."

"A prayer, I dunno. A cry of angst, now—that would be good. Angst is
big: something to paralyze the soul or set the toes a-tapping, whatever. I
do not hear angst here; I do not hear the thrumming of happy feet.
Besides your fish is fat and sings in the cracks."

"You've got to get past exteriors, McMuckle," said Maven Lipchutz. "This is not about Heidi, it's about her music. Thrill My Gills is... Ouch!" Lipchutz held up a thumb from which he extracted a thumbtack. He had been leaning over his keyboard to remove the tacks from deep in the piano's mechanism. "Thrill My Gills is guaranteed to get those happy feet in motion. Plus Heidi has the cutest caudal peduncle in the LMC. Slim and trim."

"I am a fixer," said McMuckle. "I extort triumph out of tragedy to earn my humble bread. My general credo is there's no hustle too small, but for you I will make an exception. And I keep your retainer." McMuckle nodded to the bobbing Heidi. "Nice tail for a fish, but calendar art she's not," said McMuckle, patting his vest for a smoke. Sucking at his punctured thumb, Lipchutz passed him a cigarette box—genuine wood, teak—a pre-diaspora object and priceless.

As McMuckle lit up, Heidi stopped davening and began to cough. "'Nice tail for a fish,' is it? And you are staring; what am I, an eclipse?" said Heidi between bouts of phlegm brought on by the perpetual Dreidl fogs. "I... we, were giving you..." Hack. "...the first refusal." Hack. Hack.

"Thank you. I refuse," said McMuckle to the fish. "Sorry about that, kids: bottom thousand, no bullet. This baby is a non-starter. No offence intended, but Thrill My Gills doesn't have a prayer," said McMuckle.

"No offence taken, but..." Lipchutz paled and did his best to appear pious. "No sentient being doubts the efficacy of prayer."

"Come now, Lipchutz; you are a man of the world. Has anyone ever *seen* this ineffable, unnamable Supreme Being of yours? I mean, lately..." McMuckle swung his hands, making a circular motion to indicate centuries elapsing.

"Shhhh..." Lipchutz rolled his eyes apprehensively. "These are things... People *know*."

"But this praying claptrap is properly Old Earth stuff. Why should it work in the LMC? And are you seriously suggesting that we *pray* for a hit?"

"'When two or more are gathered together in my name...' If their faith is sincere?" Lipchutz looked nervously over his shoulder.

"More than two. That's three."

"Jews need ten. A minyan."

"Ten. Not two or more? Alcoholics Anonymous and the Nazarenes make it work with just a deuce. You Jews need a minivan?"

"Minyan. Nope. Prayer won't work without the full lineup on the bench. To make sure it's not a hustle. God watching and all..."

"Whatever works," said McMuckle.

❑

The ineffable, unnamable God of Hosts stood with a burly, bearded man who held a bar towel draped over one arm, a symbol of his trade. God had created Shlomo Bim from the native bedrock; He was rehearsing His golem. "Ah, Bim, Bim, Bim, our colloquium is the chit-chat of everyday life which makes one feel connected, for, without a connection, what are we? I ask you this in My name."

"'When a fish sings...' It is written, Lord.'"

"No, it's not. And if it is, I don't remember writing it. And just what shall we be when said fish vocalizes? Shall we all sprout spontoons from our heads?"

"We are running low on schnapps at the Svartze Shikse, Lord," said Bim, who had yet to be schooled in the fine points of spontoons.

God sighed. "My people should quake at My unutterable Name, not fall on their tukhes," said God. "And besides you are changing the subject. This Lipchutz is a peculiar person. He couldn't find a nice Jewish girl? I know I have a tendency to micromanage but I do not wish My people to forget. A normal girl is one thing; a fish is another, Bim. Do you follow my reasoning? He—this piano thumper—the fish thing? Seafood aside, it is time for today's lesson. My people need to be reminded."

The golem nervously toyed with an ear. The ear came off.

"And it is here to Hyperion II that I have brought my people for a Last Diaspora..." prompted the God of Hosts.

"Everybody knows that." The golem fumbled with a sheaf of notes. "A last... a last..?"

"Di-AS-por-a, a dispersal. And how would My people have heard of My Commandments?" God raised an eyebrow.

"Well... at the Svartze Shikse, the geezers carrying on like they do... and one thing leading to another..."

God sighed, "They get you drunk and you blab, a good and faithful servant. But you lose at cribbage. What about My Commandments?"

"You neglected to mention games of chance, Lord." The golem held his detached ear at arm's length like an explorer with a freshly unearthed artifact.

"Bim... this is not about you; try to stay on topic."

Bim grinned sheepishly and stuck the ear back on in the middle of his forehead.

"I have created you," said God, "to keep an eye on current affairs. This is My commandment: exercise your fabled peasant cunning. Stir things up a bit."

"Di-AS-por-a." Shlomo Bim looked pleased with himself.

"Get a move on," said God. "I have vespers with the Catholics and an evening Bible study with the Nazarenes."

❏

"Thrill my Gills..." McMuckle was speaking, "only divine intervention can save this turkey. Delicatessen aside, why the tacks on the piano felts?"

"The Honky-Tonk sound." Lipchutz patted his battered piano, a concert model pianoforte in tiger stripe maple with a mahogany box and cabriole legs. "It's a Bösendorfer. Well, a copy. Our lounge act was a hit in the boonies," said Maven Lipchutz. "Heidi and I trouped the Magellanic until she picked up that dose of blue fin on Harrigan III. Her solfeggio went all to hell and she packed on the pork."

McMuckle stubbed his cigarette out and rose to leave. Heidi snuffled and looked grateful.

"Wait. Have another." Putting himself between McMuckle and the door, Lipchutz held up the priceless teak cigarette box. "See this? Art. Came across duty-free. Likewise the piano. The tacks would have cost a year's income per dozen. I smuggled them in, one at a time, stuck in my heel."

McMuckle waited. What he expected was an offer, at least a try at negotiating down his percentage. It had been a long run between triumphs for Ivor McMuckle. Lipchutz looked desperate, a man with nowhere left to turn. But there was no offer forthcoming.

Heidi prayed, muttering in Hebrew and bobbing her head, as the two men each waited for the other to make a move. McMuckle broke the ice. "This Protojudiasm of yours. The religion with the minivans?"

"Minyans."

"We need eight more to pray for a hit, right? I'll get them. Is there some temple, tabernacle, whatever, where I can hustle us up a quickie minyan?"

Lipchutz appeared embarrassed. "Well..."

"Surely your coreligionists have erected a place of worship and contemplative study."

"There's Shlomo Bim's—the saloon." Lipchutz looked discomfited.

"A barroom. No problem. And..."

"And?"

"Sixty-forty," said Ivor McMuckle. "And win or lose, you double the retainer."

❑

At the Svartze Shikse, a Gentleman's Bar, a coal stove glowed as the Dreidl fog pressed tightly in against the windows. Aged, bearded men dozed over backgammon and cribbage. One was arguing with a bartender. McMuckle singled him out as a potential ally and extended a hand. "Ivor McMuckle, how do you do? Maven Lipchutz tells me you're the man to see about a minyan." McMuckle squinted; the sole source of light was a hanging kerosene lantern that followed any motion of the fetid air.

"Schmulka Weisbrod and it all depends." McMuckle's extended hand was ignored. Weisbrod held a thick glass tumbler of schnapps in the glow of the lantern's minimal lighting. "Bim, I said two fingers only; I got digestives." Shlomo Bim, golem and proprietor, obligingly poured most of Weisbrod's schnapps back into the bottle.

An elderly gent at a corner table stood to refill his lungs. Shadows scrambled as he doubled over with a coughing fit. "Jimmy, I told you—you got to breathe do it away from the stove," said Weisbrod. "Otherwise don't breathe. Life is about choices." Weisbrod raised one gnarled blue hand. "Bim, how's about you poke the stove? We're cold here." The heat and humidity were already unbearable. A ceiling fan rotated grudgingly. "Listen, mister, that Maven Lipchutz is one schmendrick."

McMuckle stripped off his overcoat and followed as the septuagenarian hobbled to a huge silver samovar to top off his glass with scalding dark tea. "Schmendrick, by which you mean..."

McMuckle Makes a Minyan

"Clueless—a loser. A song and dance man with a pretty fish. Unnatural." McMuckle was not inclined to argue, friendship or no.

"Fish are for pickling, not for a girlfriend," recited Weisbrod. "Not hardly human at all, though that isn't necessarily a shortcoming. If you catch my drift." Weisbrod pointed toward to the barman. Towel over an arm, Shlomo Bim shuffled over. He carried a tray with a bottle and one glass. "Bim, Bim. My friend, ahh... Sorry, name again?"

"McMuckle."

"McMuckle here, he's not drinking?"

The barman looked unconvincingly apologetic. "That's the last clean glass."

McMuckle figured this as an interaction honed by many repetitions. "Listen, I only need you and your guys for two hours. I'll pay off all your bar tabs."

"Take Shlomo here," Schmulka Weisbrod continued as he struggled creakily to his feet. "He's not human, but who's to tell?" Weisbrod brightened as he hammered the bartender over the head with his cane. Shlomo Bim placidly wiped up a spill with his bar towel as Weisbrod waled away. "God made him," said Weisbrod.

"As He did all of us," said McMuckle with uncertain piety.

"All our tabs? Retroactive?" said Weisbrod as he caught up with the conversation.

"I *said* I'll pay."

"I'll wash a glass," said Shlomo Bim. The golem shuffled back to the bar.

"You need eight, right? I'll have to check it out with the boys." With an airy wave Weisbrod indicated the habitués of the Svartze Shikse. There were seven, counting Weisbrod. It didn't look as though many would make it back alive after a session of intense prayer.

"Not to worry," said Weisbrod, anticipating McMuckle's reservations. "Sound as horses, all of us."

"Then it's a deal."

"Not so fast. There's a problem with God. The fish. This fish thing with Lipchutz is unnatural; you'll have to square it with Him."

"And how do I do that?"

"Go ask."

McMuckle got the feeling he was being sucked into a one-liner and he was the pratfall. "You want me to ask you how I find God."

Weisbrod waved to attract the bartender's attention. "No problem. He's in a tent down by the river. Upstream. Downstream you'll run into the camps of the Nazarenes. Poverty is big these days, ecclesiastically speaking; everybody's out-of-doors."

"I beg your pardon?"

"This is the umpteenth diaspora, sonny boy, and even the trappings of heaven get threadbare after a few generations. We never got up the cash for a proper temple. God's broke, even the Pentecostals are living in trailers."

"By the river, you said." McMuckle fastened his galoshes for a slog back into the sloppy Dreidl weather.

"He'll be there. Where else? And..."

"And?"

"Sixty-forty," said Schmulka Weisbrod. "Off the gross."

Dust-festooned cobwebs hung from the blades of the ceiling fan, casting eerie shadows on the walls. McMuckle sat down suddenly, one galosh dangling from his fingertips.

"Nice," said Weisbrod as a dangling web brushed his face. A dusting sometime, Bim?"

"In the fullness of time," said Bim.

An irritated voice complained from somewhere in the miasma of dust and humidity, "You could hold things down to a roar, please. People are trying to sleep here." A substantially tattered raven flopped out from behind the stove, bedraggled and black and the size of a cocker spaniel. It looked more like a drying-out drunk on a rehab day-pass than a bird.

"A buzzard," said McMuckle. "How'd it get in here?"

"The window, schmuck," squawked the bird. "It was open, now it's not. What are you, ignorant? And I am a raven. That's for identification only, not to suggest any affiliation." The Messenger grumped and probed its wings for lice. "The appointed time, Schmulka."

"He's out of some story, a reminder for me to kick the bucket." said Weisbrod, "A messenger of God, blessed be His name. Ignore him; I do."

McMuckle Makes a Minyan

"They all ignore me," said the bird. It flapped dispiritedly back behind the stove where it had been warming itself. "Ten minutes, Schmulka."

Weisbrod spoke in a hoarse whisper. "Gotta talk fast. God's people need a synagogue. You will build it." Bim arrived with two fresh glasses and a new bottle. Weisbrod held out his tumbler. "Four fingers only, Shlomo, I got digestives."

"I, I, I am going to what?"

"Found the New Jerusalem, dummy," said Weisbrod, "That's what. One choice: yes or no." Weisbrod clutched at McMuckle's sleeve and pulled him close. "Ooh." His eyes fluttered shut as a short burst of agony stiffened his body. "It's early. Damned bird." He quickly downed his drink. Weisbrod's eyes were open and staring, the pupils wide and black.

"Shmulka? Mr. Weisbrod?" McMuckle caught the old man under the arms as he slid to the sawdust and peanut shells that covered the floor.

"This is it, the Big One," said Weisbrod between gasps. "The Maven wants a top ten hit; you got to give some quid pro quo. There's a slim chance but first you got to square things with God. It's that fish. Lipchutz has snapped his wrapper. Get your ass off the table and get to work. You're gonna be one short on your minyan, McMuckle. Sorry about that. And take a spotted hare. God loves bunnies." He gave out a mighty exhalation and slumped lifeless in McMuckle's arms.

"Yitgaddal v'yitqaddash sh'meh rabba," said the Messenger from behind the stove.

"Exalted and sanctified is God's great name," said Shlomo Bim.

"Whatever," said McMuckle. "You got a defibrillator in this place?"

The Messenger ambled over, looking pleased with itself. "I told him. They never listen." He gave Schmulka Weisbrod a poke with his beak. "Kaput." The scraggly bird went grubbing under a wing with its long shiny beak. "Not that it hasn't been a pleasure, and believe me it hasn't, present company included," said the bird as it excised a louse, cracked its shell and swallowed it. "But my work here is done." The bird flapped, trying for a takeoff, rose a few feet from the floor and crashed into a window. Shlomo Bim picked it up and threw it into the street.

McMuckle knelt by expired septuagenarian and looked up to the bartender. With might have been tears in his gravely eyes the bartender took the newly-dead corpse from McMuckle and laid it on the pool table where he covered the face with a bar towel. "Mourners' Kaddish tomorrow afternoon at three," said Bim. "He has gone home to God. You know where that is, right?"

"I've got the directions," said Ivor McMuckle.

❏

As Shlomo Bim threw back the tent flap an icy wind scattered glowing coals from a brazier, the only source of heat in the tent of the Almighty. Bim cleared his throat with a sound of pebbles rattling deep in his viscera. "A visitor. A special pleader, Lord."

"Close the door; that would be nice," said God, rising to stamp out a smoldering spot on the rug. "A visitor... well."

"Emissary of Lipchutz. The fish guy? He's a fixer, a song plugger." Shlomo Bim thrust a finger down his throat and made a gagging noise. "He would like a resurrection thingy."

"He has an offering?"

"A spotted hare, Lord."

"Show him in." The ineffable, unnamable Supreme Being snuggled up to the brazier and arranged His robe so as to have the patched area at the rear. Ivor McMuckle strode into the tent. He wiped his feet on the rug. God grimaced. Schmulka Weisbrod stood just behind the Throne of the Almighty, where he averted his eyes. He had been prepared to be embarrassed.

"Weisbrod," said McMuckle. "You are up and walking around. I thought..."

"You thought I was dead. I am dead—so sue me. You want to hold a mirror under my nose to see if it steams up? Watch this..." Weisbrod vaulted up onto the brazier of the Almighty and wriggled his rear end over the glowing coals. "Dead is not all that bad. I haven't felt this spry in years. You try it, McMuckle: you'd fricassé your tukhes for sure."

"Schmulka, Schmulka," said the Almighty. "You are showing off."

"Sorry Lord." Weisbrod jumped down from the brazier, scattering coals on the rug. McMuckle stepped on a small breakout as the smell of burning wool filled the tent.

"Thanks for the gesture but the rug is ruined. That rug was the gift of Jehonadab the Rechabite. A good, solid man—a teetotaler." The Almighty glanced meaningfully at Schmulka Weisbrod. "You would appear to be known to My servant Weisbrod. Name?" asked God.

"McMuckle. Ivor. I thought you were all-knowing."

"I was observing the niceties. You, too—a bissel more respect, please. And in the future take your shoes off at the door. Thanks for the spotted hare, though. Thoughtfulness, I appreciate that. You Jewish? McMuckle, that doesn't sound Jewish to me. Whatever, I keep the spotted hare."

"Consider it yours. I'm not Jewish, but my partner is if that helps out. We need a favor."

"Then you need a minyan. This is My law. *McMuckle*..."

"No, not a Jewish name. Scots. Old Earth. Presbyterian. "Uh, your worship..."

"You may call me Lord God of Hosts, fixer."

"I need Schmulka back among the living for a minyan—to glorify Your Name." McMuckle pulled a handkerchief from an inside pocket and, spitting into it, began fluffing up the rug's nap to hide one badly charred place.

"You want something; they all want something. Enough," said the Almighty, shifting uncomfortably in His seat. "A comb-over the rug doesn't need. You may have him until Kaddish starts. Shake a leg, McMuckle." The Lord God of Hosts turned to Weisbrod. "Sorry, Schmulka, I realize you were getting settled in."

"Whatever is Your will," said Weisbrod. "I can take the arthritis for another day. Lord...?"

"Yes, yes, yes, yes. The drinks will be on the house. Now get out of here and take the shaygitz with you. But you'll still need a minyan, McMuckle." God stroked the spotted hare. "Ten percent."

"Come again?"

"My portion—the Lord's tenth. Dismissed." Shlomo Bim ushered Weisbrod and McMuckle out into the slush and rain.

"Bim."

"Lord?"

"I want to be alone."

❑

In the hours past early midnight, God—ineffable, unnamable—watched as the skies cleared, familiar stars in strange arrangements. There was the Harper, the Cat, the Whale. Time was of a piece: all time in glorious simultaneity. Geological ages flashed by on God's whim. When the ice was in the yard, blue and green dazzled the eye from the miles-high cliffs of frozen torrent stretching away to the mountains. Time to think.

When the morning star brushed the crescent moon in the first watch before false dawn and an orange and violet curtain descended, God lay on His back under the sky, its solitary beholder.

"Lipchutz and the fish." God breathed in the oxygen-rich air from a wandering polar massif and delighted in a concert by the aurora borealis. "A little interspecies hanky-panky, what of it? There are worse things." The spotted hare hopped up to have its ears scratched. The hare was shivering and wet. He'd have to do something about the weather if McMuckle made a minyan.

❑

From inside the Svartze Shikse came a high, fine baritone voice. It sounded like Weisbrod. There followed a repetitive murmur of group response accompanied by the occasional punctuation of a breaking glass. Weisbrod's voice rose above the group at regular intervals. The voice was rusty from lack of use; it had been a trained voice.

The front door of the Svartze Shikse had warped shut in the constant downpour. McMuckle kneed it open and entered. He slipped quietly inside and sat to remove his galoshes. The prayers stopped and Weisbrod's congregation made a determined run on the bar with much flourishing of canes and walkers. "OK guys, take five," Weisbrod announced belatedly. "McMuckle. Don't be shy." Weisbrod greeted him with a cheery wave. "You brought Lipchutz and the fish?"

"They're outside. In the rain. You look very, uh... *lifelike* if you don't mind my saying."

"I'm a loaner, remember? And I got a kink from twelve hours stiff on the pool table. Tell the fish to wait. The rain shouldn't bother her considering. Listen, we only got nine; I counted Shlomo."

"So?"

"He's not a human being. We're still one short of a minyan."

McMuckle slumped into his upturned collar. "So this is it? It's all over?"

"Not till the fat lady sings. You circumcised?"

"Uh, well... yes."

"Presbyterians. Go figure. Join the congregation, McMuckle.

"I don't speak Hebrew."

"Have a schnapps. We'll have you talking in tongues better than those Nazarenes camped downriver. Shlomo!"

The bartender arrived looking apologetic. "Schmulka, this is the last case of schnapps."

"Well then, Bim, we'll just have to cut another deal with the Almighty." Weisbrod tipped his glass and coughed. "Mmm, smooth. Just remember this, McMuckle: you don't ever, ever, pray *for* something. You pray to glorify God. You may pray to be worthy of a desirable outcome. Just in case."

❏

Lipchutz, Heidi and McMuckle were gathered round Lipchutz' piano, the Bösendorfer concert model copy with cabriole legs. "Every star system that boasts sentient beings," said Ivor McMuckle. "Top ten everywhere. We are comfortable if not wildly wealthy."

"Considering that you bargained away 120 percent of something we didn't even have at the time," said Heidi. She dipped a carrot stick into her yogurt. She had taken Weisbrod's fat lady remark to heart.

"Plus the ten percent tithe. Even playing it honest which, considering our partners it would be difficult not to do, the postclassical trio Zirconium Blond have a tera-platinum monster with Thrill My Gills. As their managers, we are fat and happy. Present company excepted," said McMuckle to the fish. "Time to break out the champagne and caviar," he chortled.

"Abortionist," said Heidi.

Meanwhile, elsewhere on the planet Hyperion II, known as Dreidl, from outside the tent of the Almighty came the prefatory clearing of a throat.

"Bim?"

"We have a problem, Lord. A situation."

"We? *We* have a problem, do we? Don't tell Me: the singing fish and her friends again." God examined a speck on His robe.

"A twitchy sort, fishies. Great flippy-floppy things all full of themselves," said Bim, trying for a diversion.

"The fish is irrelevant; she now has her own problems, having to work for a living and all. Let her be an allegory of My wrath. And as horrendous as Lipchutz, McMuckle and company are, they, even *they*, would not aspire to become singer-songwriters. Level with Me, Bim."

"I am watering the schnapps, God," whimpered the golem.

"Adulterating the bar stock! How you do elevate my dudgeon," said the God of Hosts. "Damn!"

At the word "Damn," there was a mild earthquake. Bim scuttled into a corner. "A little foresight, Shlomo Bim. Think ahead before you run out. How many times must I tell you this? Let My people fear the singing fish. I shall send more schnapps."

McMuckle Makes a Minyan was first published in the December 2007 *Ranfurly Review*, Colin Galbraith, editor.

A Modest Proposal

If having the author murmur in your ear is your idea of the total reading experience, you are invited to browse onetinleg.com's Free Reads section. These MP3 downloads are released under a Creative Commons license. They're free.

```
http://www.onetinleg.com/onetinlegRSS.xml
http://www.onetinleg.com/orange_virgin_RSS.xml
```

To take advantage of onetinleg.com's automatic subscription links, you will need a piece of (usually) free software that can 'aggregate' or 'catch' the podcasts you subscribe to. To preview the latest tale before subscribing just click 'stream' on the Free Reads page. How do you subscribe to these podcasts? Copy a URL from the above box into your preferred podcasting software (e.g. FeedReader, iTunes, FeedDemon, Snarfer, etc.). You will automatically receive fresh onetinleg.com podcasts each time they're published.

Chimaera Constant

A woman, light of hair—once auburn, now gray
—is attacking a ball gown of many ruffles and flourishes. The gown is being dismembered for a quilt. "A delicate case, clearly, Doctor," she addresses a commanding presence on the label of bottle of patent elixir. Elizabeth Profitt Pease starts her mornings with strong sweet tea and Dr. Pomeroy's Herbal Draft, an alcoholic infusion. It is now afternoon. On his label, Doctor Pomeroy wears a black serge box-back tailcoat, a foulard bow tie beneath his stiff collar, and a haircut center-parted. The dress is a prom gown, hand-stitched by Libby's mother—crepe du chine dyed blue in a watered silk effect, tulle netting at the bodice with a pattern of blue cornflowers. "I have worn it once. Once was enough," says Libby Pease. Her mother's stitches are sure and small. As a quilter of surpassing skill, Libby is envious and reaches for her tea.

"Sweet Jesus!" Elizabeth Profitt Pease has—for just a moment, a split second—the queer idea that there is an eyeball in her cup. "Uh... hello, eye." The eye does not speak. She takes a swallow of Dr. Pomeroy's straight from the bottle and shakes her head to clear it. She squints; the eye in her teacup squints back—the eye is hazel and clear. It is her mother's eye.

"Peculiar," says Libby Pease and drops the cup. Her mother's eye winks at her and disappears as the teacup continues on alone to the floor where it concusses with a sharp, porcelain shudder before shattering into pieces. The teacup—one of a set—had been her mother's, painstakingly gathered-in at the Willipaq Cinema's Thursday matinées.

Libby tries to picture her mother, Eurydice Wyndham Pease. She instead remembers Profitt Pease, her father, a man of adamant opinions, a stiff-legged banty rooster of a man with an Old Testament inflorescence of a beard. "The Blue Willow," sighs Libby, despairing of the scattered fragments. She sits and stares at the broken pieces, the scattered tea leaves drying on the kitchen linoleum. No mother is in evidence. This had been an eye without a face.

She rummages through attics of lost memory and realizes her mother had never had a face. Surely she must have; people had faces. Libby's mother has a *name*, Eurydice—a name fraught with possibility. "There are deeper meanings in a name if one looks for them," Libby's mother says as she pins a gardenia to her daughter's prom dress fifty years earlier. Her father is not one for deeper meanings—the world presents itself to him, is considered, and put in a proper order. "Dicey..." her father calls his wife by her short form, "if you keep fussing with Libby's dress..." Fussing caused wear, and dissolution followed—this is a tenet of the Pease household. That the dress will wear out at the pinning of a corsage is unlikely; Eurydice Wyndham Pease made the dress herself.

"Ahem." There is a perfunctory throat-clearing and the smell of molasses and plug-cut tobacco. "Don't mind if I do. A cup of tea?" says Sun-ripples-pool, a dead Indian. He is a regular visitor. He wears a loincloth and is well-muscled, albeit stringy. Libby offers him a thick white diner mug of tea. It is waved away. "Only in one of those Blue Willow teacups," says the dead Indian, a spirit-priest, "if there are any left, that is." Sun-ripples-pool munches on a triangle of cinnamon toast. The Algonquian spirit-priest is 400 years old and values his occasional treat.

Libby reaches down a cup and saucer from the third shelf of a converted pie safe. She checks first against the likelihood of an eye inside and dumps the contents of the white diner mug into the teacup. "Here. Careful, there are only three left."

"Nonononono," says Sun-ripples-pool. "Brewed fresh in a matching teapot. And it should be Lapsang Souchong, by the way—loose, not in the bag."

"There is no teapot comes with the set of matching dishes. If there had been a teapot, the theater would surely have said so."

"The Willipaq Cinema shut down thirty years ago, Lib. Remember? As they are now a parking lot they can not be expected to offer any guarantee on their dimestore dishes. Besides, from your psychic aura, I would say there is a statistically significant probability that you have encountered an eyeball in your teacup," says the spirit-priest. "Your missing mother—this is about her?"

"No. I mean I don't think so. Is it?" In a reverie engendered by the Dr. Pomeroy's, Libby idly traces the quilting stitches of a white-on-white that she had made many years before. The quilting alone took her more than a year to complete. The white-on-white is a quilt that hangs on the wall—its quilting is an intricate design of filigree and feathery plumes, stitches all but invisible except in the long diagonal light of a late afternoon. People find both Libby and her quilts difficult. "Artistic," is what they say.

"Ah. Do I detect a slight slur?" says the spirit-priest. "It's that Doctor Pomeroy's. You should really cut back on the booze, Lib. Have you a Fortean wild talent lying dormant beneath that placid exterior? Nurture it. You'll have the eyeballs standing in line for a dip in your oolong. You should feel special."

"Then that is all you have to say. You, medicine-man, had me believing you are all-knowing, all-seeing, and not just a run-of-the-mill witch doctor." Libby adds another dollop of Doctor Pomeroy's to her tea.

"Well, if this is not about your vaporous mother, then it is about you. Spirit visitations are impromptus. You can't pin 'em down: one day an eyeball in a teacup, the next day Mom wears a fishnet body stocking and comes tap-dancing down Broadway. It all depends."

Eurydice Wyndham Pease, Libby's mother, would have been disgraced to be caught scantily dressed, even in New York City. In a teacup—well, here there was room to move.

❑

The Blue Willow is a "self-liquidating premium" at the local movie theater where Dicey Pease attends the afternoon matinée in season. The plates are transfer-printed, the pattern a glorified decal, baked on. Libby has heard this while watching *Antiques Road Show*. They might be worth something someday.

"Movie dishes," says Profitt Pease, her father, to his wife. "Those tear-jerkers of yours." The Willipaq Cinema offers the whole set—eight place-settings. "Service for Eight, plus Serving Pieces," says the marquee, meaning a vegetable dish, the gravy boat, a platter, sugar-creamer pair and a condiments carousel, no teapot.

In her thirties, her mother housebound, Libby attended the Thursday ladies' matinées until the Cinema closed, driven into bankruptcy by television and the added expense of a popcorn kiosk. By Libby's spinsterhood, as her friends said of women unmarried and past the age of thirty-five, the population of the Blue Willow stood at service for five and a quarter. Libby scoured the yard sales and discount outlet stores to honor the memory of her mother. Blue Willow was out of fashion, even the Ben Franklin Store in Lincoln—a half-day's drive—had stopped stocking the plates in 1973.

Libby once comes home with a gas-powered lawnmower. The Pease house teeters uneasily on a granite ledge near the fish pier; there is no lawn to speak of. This is Willipaq, Maine, the leeward limit of North America, and a lawn signifies gentility.

"There's a war on," says Profitt Pease, deep in dementia, "and you are scavenging scrap. There's my good baby girl." This, also, is in 1973. Profitt Pease prowls the house in his pajamas while Libby pushes the

Chimaera Constant

lawnmower through their starveling patch of green. He will die the next year.

"My father thought the Germans would come marching up Key Street to attack the arsenal. Right to the end."

"You are having the nostalgias," says the spirit-priest, "a popular female complaint. Hot flashes? "

"Not yet. Not today. Yet."

"The mother without a face? was she subject to moody spells? And if so, what did she do for them?"

"She went visiting."

"Ah-ha. Spreading the hormonal joy around." Sun-ripples-pool gestures expansively. "You allergic?"

"Penicillin once—not that I know."

"Good. The Gatekeeper sheds."

"Gatekeeper..."

"We are going to Hell," says the spirit-priest. "It is time to cross that line, Lib. The underworld."

"We are going to Hell..."

"Everybody goes to Hell. From time to time. Well... sometimes, some folks. The celestial movers and shakers: Orpheus, for example. His wife got stuck in Hell with an expired visa. He had to bail her out. Wanna know her name? Eurydice—same name as your evanescent mother."

Sun-ripples-pool reaches down a dinner plate from its shelf in the converted pie safe and spins it on the tip of a finger. Libby tenses; she has seen basketball players do this on television. "The Gatekeeper—he is a coyote. We shall expand your vistas, Elizabeth. We too shall go visiting. To see your mother-without-a-face." He stops the spinning and holds the plate before her face. There is no reflection; the glaze has been worn off with many washings. "Look at the plate—the bridge. The two lovers."

Libby shuts her eyes. "Medicine-man..."

In the inner darkness of her closed eyes Libby sees an Oriental garden. Lovers—why should they be lovers? The two could be an old married pair out for their evening's constitutional. Or two men—the Oriental dress makes it difficult to assign any sexual identity to the strollers. "There are no lovers on the plates." A pair of doves, perhaps.

On the Blue Willow plate the magnolias are in bloom. Libby peers closer. "These are not magnolias. Surely they are sweet oleander. Oleander," says Libby. "...vomiting, diarrhea, cardiac arrest, decreased body temperature, death." Oleander, bitter and nauseating. "My mother..."

A gentle plash plash from a freshet springing at the footings of the tiny bridge. The distant mountain coughs—the clearing of a seismic throat. Libby pauses midway on the bridge's soft high arch to place a hand on a polished rail. She leans forward on her elbows to look down.

An oleander petal floats by, a water strider clinging to its back. Libby's own face regards her from the water. Beside her is a bird with the face of a man. It is Sun-ripples-pool; he is changing. The spirit-priest reaches out to her. "Come with me. You are afraid of meeting your mother?"

"I am afraid that she will be me."

"Daughters become their mothers—the Chimaera constant. You *have* a face. If you are to buy peace in the valley you must confront your fears. Things will be hunky-dory again."

"What do you get out of this?"

"I get you. And we will require a covered dish bring-along. Coyote loves his casseroles. No accounting for taste—the canine divine and all." His eyes grow huge; his ears are tipped with tufts of speckled white feathers.

"You..."

"What you see is me as I am. But this is not about me. This is about you. We are here on business. The business of the mother without a face who collected dimestore dinnerware at the movies."

"My grandfather might have brought them home. He was on a voyage. The *Barbary Princess*."

"Poppycock, Libby. Your mother brought them home, collected piece by piece at the moving picture show. We will have to fortify ourselves for a chat with your mother. More tea, if you please."

"The river—it has a name?"

"Lethe. Greek, go figure. Slim pickin's is better than no pickin's hereafter-wise. And don't drink the water. Coyote pees in it."

❏

The day before she went to Hell, Libby smelled cloves and peppermint. With age had come a rearrangement of taste and smell, and she was curious to see what she might have stepped in. "Cloves and peppermint—unlikely." Sitting to remove her shoes, she was prepared for the worst: a night-wandering skunk upwind behind the shed where she carried her garbage bagged and wrapped to be filed against collection day, this now smelled like sawdust, fresh and pitchy from the mill. The scents of childhood eluded her; they were masked and made repellant. The masquerade of cinnamon and nutmeg as chlorine bleach annoyed Libby Pease the most of all. It was like hearing words in a foreign language—a language she studied once but had forgotten. An Easter ham, the cloves. It is not Easter, so surely no ham in the oven. Peppermint. No, eucalyptus—like the mentholated lozenges she takes with a cold. There was a granularity under her feet, felt through her thin-soled house slippers called China flats. Sweeping compound from the Red and White—that was it, the smell of peppermint and clove. She had brought it home on her shoes.

The Red and White closes forty years earlier under a relentless onslaught of vinyl-floored mega-stores—the Pick 'N' Pay with its soulless checkerboard aisles and wire racks of romance novels near the bagged salads.

"The concatenations of desire," said her dead Indian. He had smelled gingerbread in the oven and popped in for a taste. "Orange and oily—spicy. Like those bodice-rippers you are always bringing home." Libby was a devoted reader.

"Wha..? I beg your pardon, medicine-man. I was woolgathering. I was a million miles away."

"The sweeping compound. Orange and oily. I felt it, too. Figured you were off on a toot, Lib."

"I thought I smelled cloves and peppermint. I am seeing things; the wires are crossed somewhere—smell, taste, mind. Everything is getting smaller—constricting. I am not the woman I was."

"So, the universe is shrinking, not expanding. Live with it. And you've still got a nice, tight ass. Spread out, but tight."

"You are quite forward for an apparition." Libby blushed but was secretly pleased. "I am sixty-eight years old."

"And I am four hundred—so? You remember your father's blusterings..." It was a statement, not a question. The spirit-priest's voice was muffled; his mouth was full of gingerbread. "You have told me this."

"And his face," said Libby Pease. "There is the picture." She gestured to a framed photograph on the mantelpiece. "He was a handsome man when he still had his teeth."

"I hesitate to mention this, Lib, but the picture of your father contains one half of a baby and some wisps of a female hairdo. The happy couple has been rent asunder with a scissors. Was Profitt Pease trying to send a message to his one-and-only, the delirious, ah..."

"Dicey Pease. That was her name," says Libby.

"A precarious name, Dicey. Short for, for... short for something I do not doubt."

"Eurydice," says Libby.

"Eurydice. Marriage is only a piece of paper, and divorces may be cancelled out by marrying again—although I don't know why anyone who has once had resort to the law would repeat the same mistake. Your mother was a spendthrift?"

"My mother was quite frugal, medicine-man." Elizabeth Pease was mildly surprised to find herself about to defend her mother's tight-fistedness. "She made do in hard times."

❑

Libby gets her hair done on the last Wednesday of the month. This is to coincide with the arrivals of her Social Security disbursements. There are colorful bottles—dried flower arrangements, baskets of potpourri—clogging the windowsills. There is the comforting gossip of the salon, but nothing to assist in Libby's search for her faceless mother. She is offered blue hair, tight curls. "No thank you. I shall have my regular bobbed cut. I am going to see my mother."

Elizabeth Profitt Pease—Bitsy then—swallows a watermelon seed when she is seven. The other girls giggle: *Gonna get a baby, Bitsy.* They knew that babies came from a seed; the Bible was full of seedings—the seed of Abraham, the seed of Israel. Pastor Brooks Havermeyer thundered seeds from the pulpit any admonitory Sunday. *Pregnant*, they said in hushed whispers—seed-swallowing came with a word attached. The Bible on its lectern—carved walnut feet of a lion, wings of an eagle—lay huge and heavy, edges kissed by peeling gold leaf, the words of Jesus printed in red, spoke of a mustard seed.

"I don't buy the mustard seed," says Bitsy's mother—the faceless mother. Eurydice Wyndham Pease's choice is the yellower-than-yellow prepared mustard, a sauce that came in faceted glass jars with screw-on

Chimaera Constant

lids. Empty of mustard, the jars would be filled with the Christmas candies she boiled and rolled and dusted with confectioner's sugar for the mailman, the milkman, and a holiday disbursement for friends and family. Libby's mother uses cane sugar, refined into twenty-five pound bags and flavored with essential oils in tiny vials that come in the mail.

❑

Blue Willow. There is an arbor, a trellis perhaps, clouds of blue against a sky porcelain white. A snow-capped mountain dominates the distant horizon. "A volcano," says Sun-ripples-pool. "Extinct, the volcano. Not to worry."

Libby holds a plate up to the light—to refresh her mind, she says. The figures have moved.

"That's you and me on there," says Sun-ripples-pool. "Getting on with things. Did you notice, Lib, that on the matinée dinnerware it is always two-thirty in the afternoon? I mean, the sun, the shadows. Come, this is our time."

Hand in hand, Libby and Sun-ripples-pool cross into her neighbor's yard where there is a geodesic play dome. A wood fire smolders inside. The seasonal dwellers from next door had built it from a kit the previous year for their sprawling brood of preschoolers. It is winter; they are gone. Elizabeth Profitt Pease and the spirit-priest crouch together under the dome. Over their heads, layers of blankets and quilts provide insulation. "Snug as a bug in a rug. What'd I tell ya, Lib?"

"You're sure this will be all right? With the ancestors, I mean."

"Huh. Dunno—let me check," says Sun-ripples-pool. He holds his right hand up to his ear, thumb and pinky extended in the mime for cell phone. "If you will—the sweat lodge is a tool. The spirits visit. They desire no offering other than an open heart."

"Or mind?"

"Ah, yes. The mind is your toy. The soul is God's toy."

Sun-ripples-pool shakes a turtle shell rattle under her nose. "This is a vision, Lib. Go with the flow." From the knob end of the handle protrudes the turtle's mummified head. The turtle's neck has been wrapped with red duct tape. Sinews extend from the turtle's head for the length of the rattle handle, Libby supposes. The spirit-priest makes several passes—around, under, over, paying special attention to her armpits and groin—with a scallop shell in which smolders a shredded bark smudge. It has an aroma of a fire of fall yard rakings. He fans the smudge with a large eagle feather, stirs the embers to full glow with the tip of the quill.

The outdoor temperature had hovered at zero when Libby tapped the glass as she left the snug confines of her kitchen. The glass was a barometer/thermometer lodged in the belly of a ceramic shepherdess which her father had mounted on the inside frame of the mudroom door.

They are abruptly in a field of yellow dock and red clover. In the cold, brilliant sun Libby can see for miles, as far as the horizon. Far down a steep slope is a network of green bogs and glistening lakes connected by fast moving mountain freshets. Broken bits of sunlight dart back up the hill to her in shimmering pinpoints. The hillsides are mounded with fall foliage of red, brown and yellow. And nearby, up close, a huge boulder. "This is a native hereafter, my Elizabeth. No ferryman here to pluck the coins from your mother's dead eyes, no nasty medievalisms like eternal fire, no three-headed dogs." At this, a large crouching beast—like a wild dog, but not, with orange eyes—ambles out from behind the boulder. "Hail, Coyote." The spirit-priest shakes his rattle to the six winds.

The coyote's coat is not well kept. Libby notices bald spots where creeping mange had left open patches of skin worn raw with scratching. "Hail, Owl-husband," says the coyote, sitting down and whiffling at the base of its tail. "Who's the girlie?"

"I beg your pardon," Libby bristles.

"No offense intended," says Coyote. "Spirit-wife, then."

"These days I am called Sun-ripples-pool, Guardian. And she has come for her missing pieces."

"Ah, Owl-husband, so many do. The Blue Willow, then."

"Correctissimo, Guardian. It's a woman thing. Her mother..."

"...collected dishes. A common maladjustment. It is good that she left them behind. The dear departed are a clutter hereabouts—and with baggage, well..."

"There are a lot of dead folks, I imagine," Libby says.

"Yes." The Guardian's eyes glitter, a warm paw touches her elbow. Libby wants to jump away but feels that would be interpreted as bad manners. She strokes Coyote's paw. Orange irises close to slits as the creature smiles an array of sharp white fangs. "Sorry about that. Go ahead—jump. First-time visitors always jump; I won't be put off."

"First time."

Chimaera Constant

"Some come back."

Sun-ripples-pool gives Libby a gentle jab with his elbow. "And the lost lovers disappeared from the plates of your mother's hard-won dinnerware? Ask about them."

"They were here once—of this I am sure," says Coyote. They were of the intuited."

"The intuited."

"Rocks," says Coyote. "And the silver birch weighed down by last winter's ice storm just before it snaps. Rocks though, mostly. Rocks, stones, escarpments. They have huge souls, escarpments. And the not so huge—like the skipping stone, before it sinks. Its dream of flight. But their aspirations... you could paper over the Sistine ceiling with a lithographed lover's dreams of flight. You brought me my casserole?"

From an insulated carrier a scallop casserole, hot and moist with a breadcrumb crust, is produced. "Excellent. For you, Owl-husband, no problem. I'll send the missing place-settings. Watch the mails."

"You have postal service in the spirit-world? And you are shabby," Libby thinks despite the luxuriant sable ruff encircling its head, Coyote needs a comb-out.

"Shabby is as shabby does. I think of myself more as a facilitator," says Coyote. "Slipping and sliding over the line." He passes a ceremonial pipe. "Here, have a toke."

"Line."

"Line... yes. An imaginary boundary that keeps the spirit-world and the material world from tripping over one another. Dicey Pease?" Coyote calls over his shoulder—slowly, deliberately.

From out of a roil of vapors comes a hooded woman. Auburn curls frame a face forever young. It is the face of Elizabeth Profitt Pease.

"Uh... is there a message?" Libby has heard that the spirit-world often sends messages to the yet living.

"I am transfigured," says Libby's mother. "I am content."

Coyote sniffs at Dicey Pease's ankles. "That's it? Your message for the home folks? A mite self-involved if you ask me."

"No, Guardian, I have no message. Besides, whom would you tell it to, Elizabeth?"

"I believe we can spare her," says the Gatekeeper. "If you'd like to take her home with you..." The Guardian flops over on his haunches to scratch at a mange spot.

"No. I will stay. You have gone to Hell to complete my place-settings—a dutiful daughter. This is enough." Her mother throws back her hood; the face is Libby's. Coyote licks her hand.

Libby notices that they are no longer in the sweat lodge, but back in her kitchen. There is the smell of nutmeg and gingerbread fresh from the oven. "My mother—I am she and she is me... But can we be? I am me," says Libby.

The dead Indian is now seated cross-legged atop Libby's Hoosier—Dicey Pease's repository of flour, sugar, tea, coffee and salt, herbs and spices—her mother's kitchen helper. This has come down to Libby with the house. "The picture. Of your father when he had teeth? Well-posed. Hometown photographer?"

Libby is seated at the table, quilting the reassembled fragments of her one-time prom gown. "Drat!" There is a knot in Libby's thread.

"Language, Libby, language," says Sun-ripples-pool. The spirit priest gives the Hoosier a mighty thump with his heel. "No moving parts, built to last. Like you and me. I like that."

"Elias Schoop was the photographer. He sold insurance. State Farm, as I recall."

"Do I detect a pattern here, Elizabeth? No face for Mom, but you can cross the Ts and dot the Is as to the occupation of a rural camera enthusiast."

"He was also the principal at the high school."

"Aha! A father-figure. Now we are getting somewhere." The spirit-priest has seen more remarkable things in his 400 years. "The parental ectoplasm—it's all in the winds. How they are blowing in the spirit world, if you get my drift."

❑

Libby stands at the kitchen sink watching black-capped chickadees and nuthatches browse the bird feeder. Mouse-gray juncos prowl the sere grass of last summer's yard, pecking at their scattered millet seeds. She moves robotically, content with motions much practiced, smoothed and honored by use. Libby is washing her mother's dishes with the careless rhythms of routine. There is a potato ricer in the drain board, its metal handles protruding. With a swing of an arm there is glancing contact, and the tinkle of cracked porcelain. The plate in her hand now has a chip taken out of its edge. She turns to the converted pie safe where her mother's Blue Willow is on display. Libby looks, surveying her mother's hard-won hoard. There is a longish scar where the gravy boat had been glued back together. The gravy boat faces front, a prominent placing.

The dishes are not to be used everyday. Once she had brought them out for a meeting of the Quilter's Guild executive committee, hosted by her. When the quilters departed, Libby discovered that a cup was missing. She suspected Valerie Trott. Valerie's mother was a collector, as had been Libby's mother. There were no accusations; Libby swallowed the loss and never used the Blue Willow for company again. It was, however, dusted each month.

The figures are no longer on the plates. "Huh. Moved on, we have," says Sun-ripples-pool.

Libby coughs, a deep raling rattle from the bottom of her lungs.

"Pneumonia. From the sweat lodge. Life is cheap; love and death both are hard-won, dear Elizabeth."

"I beg your pardon, medicine-man. We seldom discuss the cost of things." They sit on the porch swing. It is dusk with the odor of oleander in bloom. *Peculiar for Maine—and in winter*, Libby thinks.

"We could have been those lovers, Lib. Despite the difference in our ages," says Sun-ripples-pool. "All hot and sweaty, rambunctious and full of the juices of youth. But the Blue Willow patterns are not anatomically correct. So we make do with the hand nature has dealt us."

"They are not? I had not noticed. Have you said you were *not* meant to be my beau?"

The spirit-priest hastily backtracks. "Learn to think big while writing small. All politics is local. The devil is in the details," says the spirit-priest.

"There should be a, a... What is the word they use these days, medicine-man? Closure. Yes, a closure. Some finality. I shall have completed my mother's place-settings, after all."

"Dunno. I'd have to look that one up. We don't get a lot of closure in the spirit world," says the spirit-priest. "Death is an elision, an ellipsis. The dead go away and are quiet, and they tend to stay where you put 'em. I don't mean to say that ol' folks are to be forgotten entire. There should be a marker where someone has breathed his last—coyote scat or a fallen willow branch. Lib... *Lib?*" There is no reply.

Tissue thin, the blue-veined translucency of Elizabeth Profitt Pease's skin catches the long shadows that highlight the fine stitching of her white-on-white, the quilt that hangs on the wall, the quilt that took her a year to finish.

"Happy landings, dear friend," says the spirit-priest as he gently kisses Elizabeth and wraps her in the treasured quilt.

Chimaera Constant was first published in *Farrago's Wainscot*, October 2008, Darin Bradley fiction editor.

Daphne Longhandle's Last Flight

It was late morning on Campobello Island

and Daphne Longhandle was wrapped around a wind-blown juniper that overhung the slate beach where I had parked for a snooze. Daphne had little black wings and yard after yard after yard of muscular, scaly tail. Her snout was crusted with a slithery substance that had to be mucus, dragon snot.

"You are a summer person," Daphne sighed. "I always know when it's summer—people with brown knees, backpacks and nowhere to go. They mill about and take pictures. I have never been anyplace, mostly."

Waiting for low tide, I had parked my car on the beach. Or what passed for a beach on Campobello—gray slate, shale and boulders. I had been dozing in the sun, my head hanging loosely out the window of my rental car. A steep drop to the ocean lined a narrow, curving road of many switchbacks with neat houses and wild gardens of hollyhocks and ditch roses, goldenrod, fireweed and purple loosestrife.

Oh yes, I am Harry Bronson, semi-retired editor of the *Sauk City Sentinel,* the newspaper of record in south-central Wisconsin. The *Sentinel* boasts a devoted albeit shrinking readership. As the paper doesn't like its supernumeraries shuffling about and getting under foot, sabbaticals were mine for the asking. I had taken two months off to see lighthouses in Maine and the Canadian Maritimes.

"What we're talking here is hopes and aspirations, Bronson," said Daphne Longhandle. "Eleanor Roosevelt, f'rinstance. She is one of those reserved public women whose depths of passion are only revealed on close examination. And again of course, there is her famous macaroni and cheese recipe..."

"Eleanor..."

"Eleanor—the same. I can see how Franklin fell for her. I think of her often. She, too, is a summer person; I'd be surprised if you didn't know each other," said the dragon. "Get out of your tin can and we'll talk. You don't have any oatmeal cookies in there, do you?" said the dragon.

❏

The story of Daphne Longhandle rightly begins ninety-plus years earlier with a tall, angular young woman standing on a dock.

"Franklin! Your favorite!" Eleanor Roosevelt called to her husband out on the water. She wielded a four-foot-long megaphone with the authority of a young mother who wishes to be heard. Her wide-footed stance said she meant business. Her husband was sailing, a favorite pastime.

Franklin, an assistant secretary of the Navy, tacked over to an anchor buoy, belayed his sloop and swam to the dock. Eleanor's macaroni and cheese was legend. She added nutmeg with onions and chives. Franklin loved it.

The previous evening they had stayed up late to watch the night sky together, a romantic moment. That, too, had been a macaroni and cheese night. By then, of course, it was too late. It was in the eyes, a secret knowledge. Some women do that, you know. You could ask them what they are keeping hidden and even they couldn't tell you. It is a gift.

"See that, Franklin?" said Eleanor.

The husband followed the direction of his wife's upraised finger.

"That's O'Brien," said Eleanor.

Franklin observed a line of stars on the eastern horizon. There were four. "That's Orion, dear, not O'Brien. And shouldn't there be only three stars? I must get my glasses changed."

"Oops, sorry." Eleanor nodded at the constellation, O'Brien, and the fourth star blinked out. "I have renamed it after Mister O'Brien—Adelbert?—that nice man who rows the groceries over from Eastport?"

"How did you do that?" asked Franklin, referring to the disappearing star.

"My secret," said Eleanor. "Smell the nutmeg?" Another secret of Eleanor's, that macaroni and cheese recipe. Franklin was a lost man. The questions were dropped. Nutmeg is a well-known aphrodisiac.

❏

"Ahem." Daphne was waiting for a reply.

Eyes closed, I stretched and scratched then lolled against the dashboard, my head cradled in my arms. "Wake me when it's over."

"Would you like to hear my joke?" Did I tell you Daphne had a keen sense of humor? "It's about a knight. Saint George. You look a little like him, you know? But it's been a while."

Daphne Longhandle's Last Flight

"And you have seen him, I suppose? Saint George?" I opened one eye for a peek. "Joke. Umph..." I closed the eye quickly.

"St. George's Cross," she said. She waited expectantly; then threw the punch line. "...and the dragon is *really* pissed off. How about that?" This was followed by gales of laughter. Whackhoop! Arrgh, arrgh, arrgh! The creature snorted a cloud of sulphur, brimstone and mephitic halitosis: the usual stuff if one is a familiar of dragons. I sneezed.

"Bless you," said the dragon.

"Thank you. Ouch." I had a welt at the base of my neck from the door handle.

"There you are," said the dragon.

"Where, exactly, am I?" I said. In the mud below the road's steep shoulders, the ribs of a barge eaten by shipworm looked like a beached whale.

"Sleeping away a glorious sunny day on your fat fanny in a tin can with no oatmeal cookies while I haven't had a good night's sleep since Franklin Roosevelt broke his promise."

"FDR? Roosevelt made you a promise? In person?"

"Of course in person. That he and Eleanor would visit some day. You think we get a lot of telephone calls here? Charley doesn't believe in me. But we talk."

"Charley?"

"Charley O'Brien. The lighthouse keeper. Macaroni and cheese is his best shot in the galley. Should be, I taught him the same recipe I taught Eleanor. Wipes the lens, fires up the generator when we get a nor'easter. You know—a lighthouse keeper. He gets a month off a year. The lighthouse goes on automatic then. This is Charley's vacation. Soon it will be automatic all the time. No Charley. Nobody at all. I shall go stark, screaming bonkers."

"We were talking about FDR and a promise he made you. *The* FDR?"

"Franklin Delano Roosevelt, the very same," she said. "Of course, that was when he used to come here, to the island." There was a wistful sigh. "We had some good times. That young Eleanor was some cookie. A definite babe. Franklin and Eleanor were summer people—light housekeepers, not lighthouse keepers..."

Arrgh, arrgh, arrgh! The dragon erupted in spasms. I supposed it was laughter. Her breath reeked of cigars. "Eleanor was a looker. You should have seen her when she was eighteen."

"Eleanor Roosevelt..." I recalled the photos of the First Lady I had seen in grade school—liverish complexion and a pouchy face like a cake fallen in the oven. "...you mentioned knowing Eleanor Roosevelt and St. George? Both?" There was a massive slithering as of construction machinery and the dragon unwrapped herself from the tree. The tiny wings were sort of pitiful against her bulk.

"I did. I just know I did," said the dragon. The creature's huge eyes flashed lime green highlights, verdigris and gold: a summer housefly buzzing at the window. "I distinctly heard myself say just that thing—Eleanor Roosevelt, she was hot stuff. Of course the nutmeg helped."

Until I met Daphne Longhandle, I figured dragons tended to eat whatever came along. The macaroni and cheese was a bewilderment. I decided it was time for the formalities, so I extended a hand.

"Bronson, Harry Bronson, emeritus editor of the *Sauk City Sentinel.*"

"I am Daphne Prydferthbwytawrganawyreni. PRYD-ferth, bwy-TAW gan, are-ANY. It's Welsh. Damned if I know how Mom got her talons on a Welsh dictionary. It's a dragon thing, I guess. I was abandoned early on. Mom went west with a crew of migrating geese.

"PRYD-ferth, bwy-TAW-gan, are-ANY," repeated the dragon. "I am told it means beautiful eater of airplanes. See, even fresh from the egg I had my future all mapped out for me. We don't even get to choose our own names. Dragons are a lot like you humans in that. Daphne is my favorite nymph, however," she added.

"Prydferthbit... That is a mighty long handle, gets my tongue all tangled up with my dental work. Suppose I call you Daphne Longhandle?"

"Panache, I like that. But just Daphne will do."

"How do you do, Daphne?"

"Pleased to meet you, Harry Bronson. Likewise, I am sure. I am the last of my kind—*après moi le déluge* and all. Unless Mom met up with Mr. Right amongst all those geese. Hardly seems likely. Does it to you?"

It didn't, and I had to say so. "I am only one of your summer people. Here to see the lighthouse," I said.

Daphne Longhandle's Last Flight

"Then surely you have heard about Saint George and the dragon. Well, I'm the dragon," said the dragon. "Only three—the Blessed George, Eleanor and you have been able to see me. Consider yourself pretty lucky," said the dragon. "Let's go somewhere comfy and chat," the creature said almost as an afterthought.

"Uhn, I don't think we can go to my place."

"Well? Weren't you coming to mine?" Her logic was irrefutable; we were up and moving. The pattern of the car's upholstery was embossed on my sunburned legs.

"Summer person," she said.

The dragon strolled along by my side. Along and along and along. Because of Daphne's size I had to abandon the car on the beach, above the tide line. We went to my place.

❏

"Come on, Bronson, push."

"I *am* pushing. You've got to help. Flap your wings or something."

Daphne breathed a sigh 45 yards long. "You will have to excuse me if I'm a bit gassy—all that macaroni and cheese." She shrugged and fluttered her tiny wings. Then lurched forward. "Ooh! I'm in!" From inside the room there was a crash as chintz, lamps and dried flower arrangements went flying. I fell off the borrowed stepladder and barely saved my nose from getting bashed by grabbing at a window box. A clump of petunias came loose and hung dejectedly. I dusted myself off, righted the ladder and climbed in after her. I listened at the door. Pinned to the inside was a placard: Rules for Innkeepers. No Pets. Installed in, around and under the cozy ruffled chintz four-poster in my room was a dragon, a myth.

"I hate to be a bother, but you wouldn't have that match would you, Bronson?" the dragon again asked hopefully. Between her bared fangs was installed the now-defunct butt of a thick, black cigar. "If you are a non-smoker, some dahlias or macaroni and cheese would be just dandy," said Daphne. "As I may have mentioned, I taught Charley Eleanor's macaroni and cheese recipe. The surefire one with nutmeg, guaranteed to turn men's knees to jelly? No effect on Charley. He's the great-grandson of Adelbert O'Brien, by the way."

"Adelbert O'Brien?"

"The same. Eleanor renamed a constellation after him. I showed her how to excise unwanted stars, too, a neat trick." The dragon scratched her ear with a foot. We sat together on or near the sofa while Daphne told me the tale of Eleanor and Franklin that you read at the beginning of this story.

"Level with me," said Daphne Prydferthbwytawrganawyreni. "I've got some dahlias waiting. You clearly come from an adventuresome stock. Why, then, do I put you off? Don't spare my feelings. Equanimity is my middle name. If I had a middle name."

"You really knew Eleanor and FDR?" was the best I could come up with.

"And the kids. If they saw me, they didn't give a never-mind. But Eleanor saw me. I was wrapped around the lighthouse, basking. She didn't faint away as was the practice then. She walked right up and struck up a conversation. A lot of spine, that girl." The dragon swiveled her head a full 180 degrees to admire her tail. "Now it's only Charley, macaroni and cheese and the occasional raid on Eleanor's dahlias," she said. "I do get to hankering after Eleanor's prize dahlias. Mighty tasty with jam."

"You have jam at the lighthouse?"

"No, only macaroni and cheese. I have to pretend."

❑

In bed that night, Franklin rolled over and nudged his wife. "Nell, how'd you do that?"

A muzzy "mmph," a waft of nutmeg-scented breath, then a long languorous stretch. "All women do it, dear," said Eleanor. "It is a mystery. As Assistant Secretary of the Navy you won't have the time or energy to experiment with each and every one of us. Therefore I shall have to do."

"Wha..?" said the Assistant Secretary of the Navy.

"I am a woman ahead of her time; don't worry about it," said Eleanor.

"I meant the star. You made it go out."

"Only a trick. A fiddle-faddle a friend showed me. Somebody I met on the island."

"A man?"

"Jealous? Mmm, yummy. No, a woman actually. Daphne is her name."

❑

Daphne Longhandle's Last Flight

Campobello Island is remote, only a blip on the radar of boring, boring history for most kids who have to study the Franklin Roosevelt years. Daphne had lived in the lighthouse since it was built.

"Franklin pretended he could see me, I think," said Daphne. "To keep Eleanor happy. Through Eleanor he offered me a war job. Plane spotter. I coiled myself around the lighthouse and watched."

"See many?"

"Nope. No planes. Ever. He forgot to tell me who were the bad guys and who were the good guys so it wouldn't have made much difference. Franklin couldn't really see me anyway. He was only humoring Eleanor. Did I tell you she was a babe?"

"You most certainly did." My eyes were watering and my sinuses screamed for relief. I was enveloped in a cloud of noxious blue smoke as Daphne sucked a last remaining spark into life. "Where do you get your cigars?"

"They're Cuban, a gift from Winston Churchill; and to tell you the truth, I'm about out. Franklin couldn't abide cigars and Winston sent him several cases aboard the cutest little Royal Navy cutter, a Lend Lease job with brand new paint, the *Crofter*. It had a little airplane with pontoon floats tethered on its rear deck. The jolly tars winched the airplane over the side and lowered the crates of cigars. Eleanor felt sorry for me, being invisible and all. I got the smokes. I know a good thing when I see it." The short stogie glowed dangerously close. I had a choking fit and ran for the bathroom.

"What you are coughing up is Winston's last cigar," called Daphne. "It's over sixty years old."

"So am I," I replied. "And I was hoping for sixty-two." The dragon opened the bathroom door with a flick of her tail and chucked the last inch of her cigar into the toilet.

❏

Franklin and Elliot were up on the summer porch putting the final touches on a model biplane.

"Franklin?" called Eleanor.

"Nell?" Her husband looked up from an adjustment he was performing on a miniature aileron cable.

"I have decided to ask Adelbert O'Brien to put in a flower garden."

"That's nice. Go right ahead."

"Dahlias, I think, the dinnerplate variety. Daphne is especially fond of dinnerplate dahlias."

"Ah, the mysterious Daphne. When will I get to see her?" asked Franklin Roosevelt.

"That eventuality must reside in the company of the imponderables," replied Eleanor, who as a girl had shone at declamatory presentation. She turned to where the children's play had become rowdy. "Annie! Don't push James; you are so much bigger than he is."

❑

"I did so look forward to having some company," said Daphne Prydferthbwytawrganawyreni. "All I ever wanted was a family, a little egg all my own. Being the last of my kind, the Roosevelts are as close as I'll likely get. When the lighthouse goes automatic there will be no Charley to cook macaroni and cheese. Set loose and alone in the world I would starve, not knowing how to open a can. And these oatmeal cookies Charley speaks of—they are in a can?"

I explained oatmeal cookies to Daphne Longhandle, Beautiful Eater of Airplanes. She allowed as the cookies sounded delicious but put away pining for them to a later date. For the moment her catalog of melancholy was full. "I haven't seen Eleanor much lately," said Daphne.

"And Winston Churchill?" I asked. The dragon did not reply.

"Let's go and visit her garden," I said.

Frolicking on the Roosevelt lawns, the dragon seemed more like her old self. "Eleanor told me Franklin, Churchill and Stalin were getting together to divide the world after the war. I was so excited. They would be coming to Campobello. I dreamed of nibbling dahlias and jam with Stalin, Roosevelt and Churchill. They went to Yalta instead."

"Eleanor Roosevelt is dead."

"I know that, silly." Daphne wiped away a tear from the corner of a giant eye. "But I have to hope. Life is a tradeoff: dahlias to nibble versus the hope of Eleanor Roosevelt and Winston Churchill coming for a visit. The odds are pretty slim, I know. Hopes and aspirations, Harry Bronson, remember?"

"I feel like a monster."

"This is how we learn, Harry. You are the monster this time. Deeds and not appearances define who we are."

Daphne Longhandle's Last Flight

I picked a huge yellow dahlia from the garden and offered it to her. The dragon's lips gently accepted the flower. She munched thoughtfully. I picked two more dahlias, one for her, one for me. We sat in the shade of an old tree to eat our flowers. I thought, this tree shaded Eleanor and her children as they played together generations ago. The tree, a surviving elm, reached out its branches to a set of con trails high above the fair weather clouds.

"G'zork!"

Daphne was gently snoring. I went back to Eleanor's garden for an armload of dahlias.

"G'zork!"

My arms were laden with flowers. I gave her an ungentlemanly poke with my elbow.

"Huh? What? I must have dozed off. We are inveterate nappers, you and I, Harry Bronson."

"Daphne Longhandle, you have a great heart and in that heart lies your great beauty. Please accept these dahlias, courtesy of the Campobello International Park Commission. May I come to your lighthouse and watch for airplanes with you?"

"Well... Charley is away, but I think it would be all right. There's some leftover macaroni and cheese in the fridge."

"About Winston Churchill..."

"I'd rather not hear any more. Thank you for the lovely afternoon."

She shrugged her rudimentary wings and turned to leave.

"If I could fly, maybe I could come and visit you, Harry Bronson."

I explained that the Midwest was over a thousand miles away.

"Do the geese fly there?"

"They do indeed, then turn south down the Mississippi."

And that was that. We ambled along side by side to the far end of the island where young Eleanor had sailed with Franklin.

Eighty-three feet high, the lighthouse was painted with St. George's Cross. Its shone as a fair weather beacon, bright against glaring titanium white. I huffed and puffed my way up the circular inside stairway; Daphne Longhandle simply coiled herself around the building. We met at the catwalk surrounding the great glass lens and then watched for airplanes together from high atop the Head Harbour Light.

We watched the sky until sunset. And said goodbye. "I would so love to get a piece of mail addressed to me—me personally," were Daphne Longhandle's last words as we made our farewells. "Those postal cards with the pictures. The summer people buy them. They are so beautiful, particularly the pictures of my lighthouse with the big, red cross and the shiny glass lens. I would save your letters in my scrapbook. Is it all right for me to keep a scrapbook? Not presumptuous, I mean. I have saved clippings from the newspapers—pictures of Eleanor and Franklin. And the children. I get a sense of time passing by watching the pages yellow and shrivel."

I pointed to a con trail miles above, a jetliner turning toward Newfoundland. "There is the farewell of an airplane, ice crystals they leave behind. They go very high and very fast."

"Not quite the same thing as feeling the wash of the propellers against your face, is it, Bronson?"

"No, not the same."

"Bronson?"

"Yes?"

"I had thought you might ask me along with you on your travels. But this is my lighthouse. I have to stay. Franklin may come back and I promised him. He promised and I promised. He might ask if I saw any airplanes."

❏

It was an election year in the Midwest and my dreams of far off lighthouses went on hold. By attrition I was an elder statesman. To keep my paltry honoraria along with health coverage, the paper insisted on an occasional assignment. I got to cover the state conventions of those fringe parties without a hope with which the *Sauk City Sentinel*'s management didn't deign to waste the time of its younger rising stars.

I took a break from the harangues of the Farmer-Labor Party and, instead of heading for the nearest watering hole, ended up at an outdoor flea market—antiques, collectibles, ephemera and junk, the usual stuff. Couples slumped behind their offerings.

"You will write to me?" the dragon had asked.

"Of course." Well, a promise was a promise.

An oldies station blasted from speakers mounted on light poles. The tune was Stealers Wheel's *Stuck in the Middle with You*. Behind a table of antique postcards, a woman with lacquered bangs and iridescent nail polish sang along with the radio. Her husband was passed out in a folding lawn chair, beer in hand.

"Well, if you've got to get stuck," she gripped the table and stared me straight in the eye, "...the middle is a pretty good place. When it comes down to push or shove, like." She dissolved in a puddle of giggles.

I took this as an invitation to browse.

Shoeboxes of old postcards were arranged by Travel and Events. I bought the first Ferris wheel from the Colombian Exposition in St. Louis, the Tilt-A-Whirl and the Cyclone from Coney Island. Some of the postcards with gold leaf curlicues of an ornamental border were still intact. Sepia-toned bathers with middy blouses and bloomers, I hoped this would evoke memories of the Roosevelts at the beach for her.

Whenever I stopped for the night, I mailed a postcard. Chicago, Racine, Minneapolis. I scrupulously included my home address on each card. Not that I expected a reply.

And I got none.

❏

"Dear, look, little Annie is working on a scrapbook."

"Hmmm," Franklin leaned over to where Eleanor and Anna were exercising a paste pot and brush over a thick album with gilded covers.

"Postcards. Very pretty."

Although he had reports to read, his golden-haired daughter was the apple of Franklin's eye. He put down his pipe, blew the smoke over his shoulder and scrunched crosslegged down on the floor between the two.

"Look, daddy. Here's one with our lighthouse," said his daughter. "It has a funny address."

"Sauk City, Wisconsin," read the president-to-be. "Someone named Daphne must have a sweetheart who is far away."

❏

The honking of migrating geese makes me look up when our Midwestern autumn comes. It twists young and burly round the chimney corners with the first maple leaves of another fall, and I am called out for one last time to rake the yard and bundle up my roses for winter. I keep a special stash of large, rank, delicious cigars for just this time.

On the off-chance that my Beautiful Eater of Airplanes has found her wings I mix up a double batch of oatmeal cookies and smoke on the porch. I have never figured out how the young Roosevelt girl got that last postcard of mine, the one with the Head Harbour Light, to paste in her memory album. But that happened almost 100 years ago and I was not yet born.

Daphne Longhandle's Last Flight was first published in *The Aputamkon Review II*, Fall 2008, Sarah Dalton Phillips, editor.

The Tirewoman Gabriel

Harry Hirshberg, my surgeon, swims into a fragile focus. Harry's face grows huge and menacing, then dissipates to scuttle and scamper in an array of miniature whirlpools. Harry picks up the phone and whirlpools are sucked down a hospital drain. A potted begonia nods knowingly from the bedside table.

Scree-click. Harry has the nasty habit of exercising the metal spring on his clipboard as he speaks. I am in a tubular white hospital bed cranked at 45 degrees. Harry still has his gloves on; his mask dangles by its strings. He tells me he is keeping me in for a couple of extra days for some tests. Scree-click. He goes on to speak of an enlarged prostate and bladder problems. He had taken a tissue sample while I was under the anesthetic and sent it off for a biopsy. "If it is cancerous, we can operate and save your life, as it is early." Scree-click.

"What are my chances, Harry?" I ask, watching my urine flow through a catheter.

A pause, then the verdict. Total loss of sexual function or a lifetime on the bag. "Maybe nothing and you go home Monday. But won't it be good to know?"

Pain and inconvenience. My future. Heavily sedated, I slide into a trough of lessening expectations.

❑

Twice a year and regular as clockwork, when Barbara's School of the Dance trots in the latest corps of majorettes and ballerinas, the classic backdrop—Mediterranean hillsides with Raphaelite shepherds and shepherdesses discreetly about their distant businesses—was always requested. In addition to shepherdesses on their backs in the grass under fluffy clouds, there is a backdrop of a convent garden at dusk. Giant bumblebees prowl thick wisteria, vines knot to frame a lovers' bower. Before the foreground, hogging the floor, lies a toppled faun, his lips curled in a sneer of passion. At his side is a sawed-off fluted plaster column with a shattered capital nearby suggesting old ruins. I could not bear to throw the stuff out. Some day someone would want to be immortalized with a leering, panting satyr.

Thirty-two pairs of eyes stare into my lens with a migraine intensity. The Gumdrops have come to pose for my camera. A woman stands naked at the kitchen sink, gently crying. I do not know her but she has a maimed beauty that makes me wish I did. That and, of course, her nakedness. A flush of acne scars blends with freckles on her high cheekbones and swoops to the bridge of the nose where eyebrows almost meet. A bizarre effect. Tears roll down her breasts and over her belly to shimmer on her freckled thighs.

I have hurt her, as always never quite sure of what I have done or said, if anything. Are her tears for me? In my anesthetic delirium I name her Gabriel. A name is who you say you are, the gift that, unasked for, forms you. To her ethereal, blemished beauty I have given her the gift of a name.

As I reach to comfort her, I see a pool of blood widening at my feet; it is my blood. The Gumdrops giggle: silly man, bleeding on the floor. They do not notice Gabriel's nakedness. The Gumdrops are a troupe of bandy-legged girls, skinny and pre-pubescent: the lineup for Barbara's School of the Dance yearly group portrait. They are early, the Gumdrops. I must check my appointments calendar.

Helen, my daughter, arrives barefoot and in her pajamas and we kneel and hold each other. Thirty-two pairs of eager eyes look on expectantly as the blood puddle widens. From the front hall a telephone is ringing. It will be Barbara, of course, asking after her Gumdrops.

The flowing faces of Gabriel, Helen, the Gumdrops, scuttle and scamper through a drug induced euphoria. Sin and Death will have to wait for future ripening Gumdrops ready to kneel for the reaper. This is a metaphor, for Sin and Death flourish far from the neat yards of cautious Richmond families with the extra income for dancing classes. There is a military ambience and the clatter of the Gumdrops' toe-taps. This is not a metaphor, as the girls' glossy headgear imitates dragoon guards' high silk tasseled helmets. I seem to have survived Harry's procedure and I struggle up and out of the ether. A palette of smiles from rictus to smirk ripples across the Gumdrops' doughy young faces.

The phone rings and I awake to discover I have lost an entire day to Harry's medicaments. It is Sunday and Helen has caught up with me in my white metal bed after months of silence.

Helen says she is going to die.

I tell her so am I. I sleep peacefully. The call is a release. As it turned out, Helen, my wife, did die.

Barbara Langerhans of Barbara's School of the Dance had struck a deal with a costumier for epaulets in bulk. Cellophane-wrapped lavender plaques with orange yarn dangles arrived to be mother-stitched to the shoulders of bolero jackets. Each child carried home a package and a note: "Please, *please* make sure that Jenny wears these for our Gumdrop Parade number in the Pageant." Barbara bustled about draping her nymphs into wooden poses before collapsing, glasses pushed back on the top of her head, into a canvas director's chair. The chair creaked as it accepted her 250 pounds.

"Roy," says Barbara, her tone suggesting that I had joined with the furniture in a lost battle for her attention, "You are the best. You have such patience with the girls."

I ignore her in return.

But Barbara is speaking.

"That one over there, the coy little minx in the spangles. What do you think of her, Roy?" The Gumdrops all wore spangled outfits, home sewn. "That's Melissa Bradley... one of the Bradley girls...?" I am hoping to get them all in the shot without squeezing them together.

"A piece of work, that one. But talent...? You better believe it." I nod agreement: she has succeeded; she has broken my train of thought. Barbara is in charge.

"People... *People!* We're on stage. This is the real thing. Attention!" The Gumdrops freeze into snappily dressed lines. Barbara runs a tight ship. We are approaching the terminal perimeter of when the kids still think this was great fun. Soon they will start to fidget. They will take their turns in the tiny lavatory and, having wasted half an hour, reassemble refreshed but looking arch, stiff, and posed. These fair-haired moppets posing for my camera and one another are oblivious that they may be an enticement. "Steady, old goat," I whisper to my fallen satyr. "Don't bite." He leers back at me.

There is an abrupt crash. We have lost a Gumdrop in the last row, knocked offstage.

Barbara addresses the missing Gumdrop. "Dorothy Mead? Dorothy!" Gumdrop Dorothy struggles back up.

"I dropped my baton, Miss Langerhans." Gumdrop Dorothy extracts a wedgie and squirms standing on one leg.

"Well, pick it up." Dorothy is left to fend for herself. Barbara keeps on talking.

I am the home town boy. I am safe and reliable.

❑

But ah, my two Helens. I shall tell you about my late wife as though she were a naughty, petulant child who, playing the piano or giving a recitation from memory, has done something precious, inadvertently achieved beyond her years. In life nobody would have patronized Helen. She was brilliant, attractive, and painted technically adept watercolors that, while sufficient to make her a glittering phenomenon in the artistic firmament of Richmond, Indiana, had the style and emotional depth of hotel wallpaper. Helen might shine, but not rise.

But now our daughter is performing for company.

Helen, my daughter, really plays quite well and has presented us with this week's lesson, a divertimento she had by heart in less than the allotted time. But one lacuna, a brilliant improvisation with hardly a hesitation, and she is through.

No one has noticed. Helen would like to leave but stays seated at the piano.

"Sooo..." They turn to me.

The guests have lost their places in the predictable flow of a Sunday visit. "Soooo... Roy, that's quite a kid you've got there."

The Sunday visitor swirls his empty drink. He is waiting.

George followed me out to the kitchen for refills while Sylvia and Helen talked about school. Helen missed an older woman in the house and the thought of the girl's missing mother, distant and near death, got George's wife dewy-eyed and deep into a discussion of my daughter's sixth grade social studies project.

While I wrestled with the handle on the ice cube tray, George let out a whoop from the back porch where he had strayed glass in hand to admire our Indiana Sunday afternoon. He had taken a skid on the wet, soft boards but caught himself and had his arms wrapped around a corner post at the head of the steps to the yard.

"Roy, that porch of your is as slick as a Rush Street hooker," said George, referring to one of Chicago's seedier districts, supposedly unknown to the citizens of Richmond, Indiana. He held out his glass which had survived the skid intact. I gave George four fingers of scotch over his ice and he studied the drink appreciatively against the light.

"Ahh, that's just the ticket. Shall we join the ladies?" He did a pantomime suggesting a carpenter driving a large plane down a board. George is a sketch.

We joined the ladies.

His wife's gaze is trailing absently after the departing Helen, diminishing over the patterned linoleum and through the kitchen door to where backyard baseball was forming up. Sylvia's eyes have the forgetful, misty glaze of a childless middle age. Helen goes out to raise hell with the neighborhood kids.

"Sooo..." Sylvia synthesizes. Thesis, hypothesis, synthesis: a flicker of genius has been indulged and left to gutter under the blanket of patronage. Her half-turn on the velvet sofa reveals very much of her very marvelous legs. Sitting all day on a high stool at the cash register is what does it.

George and Sylvia own the hardware store.

"Sooo... Simply marvelous, Sylvia. You must spread them for us more often." The words are not said. This was an absent-minded lapse for Sylvia. Conscious of her husband, her knees snap together, the tramway to the Promised Land temporarily out of order.

This, of course, is a conversation we did not have. The fiction is that my wife has gone to paint. To the Sandias, which is where the thin air seems to be in Santa Fe, the thin air so clear and pure you could spit and hit Albuquerque, sixty-five miles downhill. And for her lungs—her health, the shadow of tuberculosis. We are children of the 19th Century who in late middle age have not yet accepted Roosevelt or the germ theory although our reason tells us otherwise. For The Consumption, a trip to the mountains.

"But seriously George, I'd really love to screw your wife." Not said.

"She'll be back healthy as a horse and rosy as a pippin." Sylvia really says this. She means my wife. Horses and apples speak of health.

Sylvia's veiled promise and Helen's distant death are not to be spoken of.

"...and there are these injections I hear about..." She means antibiotics. Streptomycin and mountain air. If Helen were tubercular and gone for the cure, they would have had her back in six months.

Helen the child. Helen the child's mother.

❑

The call from Albuquerque has the ballooning effect of many miles and many connections to make the circuit.

"Hello, Roy. We had snow here overnight—two inches, it's so clear I can see Santa Fe. Imagine! Sixty-five miles straight up almost, in the mountains, and the air is so clear I can see all the way."

Helen is calling to say she will die. Not right now but someday, and she requires appropriate consolation, person-to-person collect. Helen Hilliard calling Roy Hilliard in Richmond, Indiana. How many operators had it required to complete this call from New Mexico to Indiana?

Helen found it hard breaking away from us. "I want you to know how difficult this is for me, Roy. Roy...?" Leaving behind a twelve-year-old daughter named for her makes her a regular caller, running up fabulous phone bills as one Sunday each month she rattles out irrelevancies.

Natural laws overcome even the momentum of the Bell Telephone Company. Order begets disorder and the resistance in the wire turns Helen's long silences into the spattering of distant stars. I have to shout into the phone.

"Helen, you have all that money out there and I have all these bills back here. Would you kindly ring back the operator and tell her you will be paying for the call? I can't afford collect calls from New Mexico."

We had only one such incident. After that, she picked up the tab for the calls.

"We are talking about our daughter..."

"Helen..."

"Roy...?"

"Helen, I will listen to you pre-paid, but I'm afraid I can no longer accept collect calls from you." A pause, then a bloom of dial tone and a disconnect drilled through the ear.

Her trip to New Mexico, like our marriage, was uneventful. Her painting, my photography. We were the artistic elite in Richmond, Indiana and we were expected to enjoy Debussy, cucumber sandwiches and discreet affairs. Twenty years in place and none of this had happened. Helen had been showing watercolors in Chicago when a wheelchair-bound tycoon fancied her and bought all her pictures. Helen had looked her delectable best in a floral print silk dress and high heels—her gallery uniform. She followed him to New Mexico. The difference in their ages she found a comfort and Jeffrey's lack of mobility was less pronounced where the houses were all on one level and his powerful seventy-year-old shoulders drove his wheels in passionate pursuit of Helen across the terra cotta tiles of his sprawling ranch bungalow. That the pursuit was passionate, I heard in graphic, panting detail when Helen was feeling particularly bitchy or particularly guilty about abandoning us. The whir of ball bearings and the flash of nickel plate from Jeffrey's discarded trolley as the legless tracker cornered her in some adobe niche and powerful biceps held her squirming on the tiles as they writhed their consummations western style. Particularly when she had been drinking, Helen laid out their trysts in the no-holds-barred, blow-by-blow style of Don Dunphy announcing the Friday Night Fights. At last she would become tearful. At those times her monthly call became a catalog of my inadequacies, Jeffrey's prowess. They were, however, apparently not tireless, for she always found the time to call.

Once a month, without fail, Helen would call. The knowledge that it was costing Helen and Jeffrey hundreds of dollars to call and turn my guts inside out, for what satisfaction it gave them, gave my small demon of spite room to grow and breathe in distant Indiana. I realized the telephone bills were small change to them, but since it appeared that small change was all I was destined to get out of this, I should be content to come away with anything at all. At the feast of the gods, one eats what is placed on his plate and is content.

Helen was a hometown girl and, aside from putting the screws to me one Sunday a month, she kept up her old associations in Richmond. Helen wished to be thought well of by these women, the homebodies, the flower-arrangers—the women who from their fortresses armored by a husband's daily drudgery in insurance, medicine or dentistry, pursued bohemian careers in literature or the arts and drove to Chicago for the symphony. But where were they in this scenario of hers, the stay-at-homes? This required a delicate positioning, for by implication, Helen was doing while they were still pretending. Clearly, she had it while they did not—the self-realization that comes from confronting Nature one-on-one armed with but a wet brush. A barrage of regular correspondence, weakly-but-bravely-facing-the-inevitable in tone, fortified her standing with the old coterie in Richmond. Helen had to tread softly for Helen basked in her perception of their esteem.

"Sorry for the shortness of his note, but..." Implying that she was saving her strength for painting sunrises on the mesas.

The notes were on Jeffrey's letterheads, paper handmade in Taos, and usually accompanied by a pencil sketch.

For the first year of Helen's calls I lost weight, saw my graying hair thin out, and rode a teeter-totter between diarrhea and constipation. The big blue bottle of Phillip's Milk of Magnesia on the nightstand, replenished weekly, had become an anchor for my sanity. My visits to the drug store gave a needed sense of continuity and purpose to my life. Ed Sanders, the pharmacist, took me aside one day like a Dutch uncle.

"Roy, that stuff's going to kill you," he was referring to Phillip's Milk of Magnesia. Ed spoke with the same depth of concern an AA sponsor might use on a postulant discovered with a quart of bourbon under his arm.

"Forget Helen, Roy, she's never coming back. Get a girl; get laid. Going on like this is doing no good for you or for your daughter."

I was long-suffering Roy Hilliard, abandoned by a woman who didn't know how good she had it, bravely raising a child on the cusp of puberty and facing life unbowed.

❑

Our old, comfortable back porch was springy with the wet of an Indiana summer all the year. A thin film of slippery green permanently colored the boards and made them impossible to paint. It was Helen's route to play with friends—skip rope, cowboys, dolls. A deeply worn shortcut like a game trail ran diagonally through the vacant lot behind the house to where lay the bigger world of a twelve year old—school and the Five and Dime. Since Helen's mother left us, the springiness had become more pronounced and I no longer trusted the porch with my weight. It was the property of Helen and the cats. No one passed our porch unannounced. In the winter the ever-wet porch modulated from the *sklitch sklitch* of summer to a *skree-chick* sound of deal pine turned stiff as freezer beef. This reminded me of Harry's, my surgeon's, practice of playing with the clip board springs of his patients' charts. I had to fix the porch.

Between the thought of porch fixing and the deed there was a winter of Sunday calls then silence on the long, long wires from New Mexico. That Helen might finally be ill enough to die far from home, I had viewed as a fond fiction by my friends and neighbors who were uncomfortable having daily dealings with an abandoned, impotent Roy Hilliard.

When Helen at last did stop calling was hard to tell. Her calls became sporadic and the gaps between them extended. The business of portraiture flourished. At least as often as Helen had once called, Richmond's merchant princes shepherded their wives and little ones through my doors to be defined for future generations.

It was a busy time. I went into the hospital for my prostate and parts of me were removed. In my anesthesia dreams I again saw the Gumdrops, my two Helens, and the naked woman who wept at the kitchen sink. I had given her a name once, but it eluded me. Names are given to baby chicks and kittens. Kittens are drowned; the chicks arrive yellow puffballs, are adored, pampered, thinned by cats and foxes, then eaten by Sunday visitors. Harry Hirshberg, my surgeon, slapped me on the back and fiddled with the spring on his clipboard. Scree-click.

One afternoon of the following summer as I was finally fixing the porch, Gabriel came home with Helen. I recognized her at once as the woman from my ether dream: a dislocated remembering of shadows within shadows. The two approached me across the deep path in the vacant lot, then our yard, a delineation marked by sweat and beer as each summer I pushed the mower ever farther into the no-man's-land of an uncontested boundary. They held hands. Helen was proprietary; her bearing said, "She's mine, but I will share." I sat on a sawhorse, smoking. Since her mother left there had been no one between my daughter and me. Now, it appeared, there was.

I felt that I must perform some act of welcome. "Name?" I held out my hand.

A name—the gift that, unasked for, forms you—was her only possession. Gabriel had been named Caroline Evangeline by a disappeared mother. She shed that name at the schoolyard, age thirteen: "Caroline Evangeline... will tell us the long thin country in South America that ends in Tierra del Fuego."

"It is Chile, Miss Prescott, and they give us olives and tin. And I am Nikki."

Everyone was pleased.

Helen stepped back. The girl stepped forward. She stood up straight and gracefully through her awkwardness, arms at her sides, a slight curve to the back. I was a middle-aged householder with his official paraphernalia—wide pencil, hammer, saw and two pounds of flooring nails, she, a knobbly-kneed, gangling girl, at first glance not much older than my daughter. Seventeen, eighteen, perhaps. "Nikki," she took my hand.

"An Alianora, that is what you are." Helen, my daughter, looked earnestly, first at the stray she had brought home, then at me. Our approval was important. "Alianora whom people called the Unattainable Princess..." This name was from the books Helen and I read together. We spent hours together lost in tales of chivalry and romance. And from the tales of knighthood, druidic spells, *Jurgen The Pawnbroker*, *The Silver Stallion*, *The Worm Orobouros*, the *Morte d'Arthur*, came a name for Nikki—she was the Tirewoman Gabriel.

"Alianora? That is hard to say. I like Gabriel," said Gabriel. "You are who you say you are; everybody knows that."

"Gabriel? Dad, is there a Gabriel anywhere in our books?"

"There is now," I said. We had given her a name.

Helen pouted but Gabriel put her arms around her for one of those energetic hugs that lifted Helen off the ground. "I am *so* a Gabriel. Say it."

"Gabriel," said Helen. We three agreed that it would be an excellent name. We shook hands gravely and it was done. *Mundus Vult Decipi*, I thought, the world wishes to be deceived. This was the motto of a princely hero of one our books. With the addition of Gabriel we became a family not again, for in the days of Helen, Helen's mother, we had not been. We carried a collapsible day bed down from the attic and Gabriel bunked in Helen's room. And so began our life together—Gabriel, Helen, my daughter, and myself. As long as could, should, or would be was what Gabriel said of our arrangement. Within two weeks she moved across the hall and slept with me. The first night, Gabriel and I made love in the dark.

I loved to watch her, lithe and limber, with the flexibility and curiosity and energy of her youth. "Why? Why me?" I asked. Her arrival in my life and the life of my daughter was a surprise, although not precisely unannounced. I considered her a blessing. Ed Sanders, my purveyor of Phillip's Milk of Magnesia, would have approved.

"If you have to ask why you'll ruin the surprise," she said with tears and a smile as she coiled herself around my body.

"Surprise? What surprise?"

"If I told you it would spoil it all."

"You don't know."

"No. And if I tell I'll never find out." She dug her face in against my chest and wept to shake off her paradox. She laughed as the tears flowed. "As long as could, should and would be," she said again. "I hate surprises."

"Me too," I said, accepting her gift.

❑

The telephone rang from its recessed niche in the front hallway. From the ring, a local call. But then with Helen dead, it would be a local call.

"Roy..." It was Barbara, her voice a theatrical tremolo not unlike a musical saw.

"Barbara?"

"That *thing!* There is a *thing* in there with my girls—the Gumdrops."

"A thing." She had seen the leering satyr.

Being the last to know was not a happy place for Barbara. And she suspected the satyr, tongue lolling, was a projection of myself. Roy Hilliard, goat-man. Huh! Now we all knew. Or, if she did not know for sure, Barbara had her suspicions—that I had been playing some dirty joke. I was a dangerous type. I held the potential for embarrassment.

None of my clientele—Richmond's merchant princes, their wives or daughters—had ever complained about the satyr. Somebody had snitched. Barbara had been called immediately. Our local calls come through clear and sharp with none of the atmospheric spattering of Helen's Albuquerque ravings. I heard Barbara set down the receiver and walk away from the telephone, answering a distant knocking at her front door.

Footsteps returning. Barbara. "Roy?"

"Yes."

"Roy, we have to talk." The receiver was firmly replaced, call over.

❑

"Is that me? Ohh... I am beautiful!"

She was beautiful and so was my daughter, who sometimes joined her. The tensions between the two, the child-woman and the woman-child, the fair and the dark, made them perfect objects. Their posing was so unforced, so natural, that this was a tacit fiction we all accepted—that when I held the camera, I disappeared.

There was the fear of a bad experience. A panic of blurry, unauthorized prints circulated in the boy's gym, the lurking suspicion of treachery at the drug store where the amateur photographer took his film. The thought of a drugstore clerk with suppurating acne and a hand in his pants thumbing my Gabriel, my Helen, all the while passing pills and poultices over the counter gave us some chuckles and no small titillation. I processed all my own film. The pursuit of fame beyond my Wednesday night bowling league and the plaudits of my clientele did not excite me.

Watching a print coalesce in my darkroom tray, I knew that Helen, my daughter, and I shared Gabriel. This seemed in the red of the safelight a natural continuation. It was not strange that these two women whom I loved should love each other. The surprise was that I had not seen it through the camera: the two young women, gently touching, the briefest of kisses.

❑

I awakened to Gabriel curled into a tight ball, her knees under her chin, sobbing uncontrollably beside me in our bed. I knew I could have beaten on her, hammered at her for attention, and gotten no reply. As the spasms passed, I fell back to sleep stroking her hair. I watched her relax into innocence, a ruined child, so vulnerable, drying to a sticky mess. The child with a child's fears so much more real than actual horrors.

In the morning Gabriel stood before the mirror combing at the tangles of her sweat-damp hair dabbing at a smear of little girl snot, red-eyed with a puffy face. "What? I did? It must have been a bad dream." These were secrets she meant to keep.

We were two again, Helen and I, with Gabriel growing between us. I often slept alone. When the loud and frantic scrambles of copulating mice grew too much—our room, our house, where I slept alone across the hall while the mice frolicked in the walls—I would reach out for Gabriel and find no one there. It was not an episode of madness I feared, but of an overwhelming unhappiness.

My daughter and I had become distant, formal. We communicated with silences. I finally just asked her about our Gabriel's nighttime horrors. My daughter was unconcerned.

"People are sad sometimes. Last night she was sad." That night Gabriel moved back in with me.

"I love you both but cannot have you both. I am driving you apart and will make you both hate me. Or me you. And sometimes I want just to run away."

"Why?"

"Because I am afraid of losing you, of hurting you and having you send me away or making me want to leave."

❑

I awakened in the middle of the night with the painful urgency of a middle-aged bladder. Moonlight and the well-worn habits of years guided me down the stairs. The engineers who designed the Richmond water supply had been content to get the privies out of the yards. They were railroaders, not city planners. When your knees gave out and your eyesight failed and a final illness left you confined to an upstairs bedroom, it was assumed there would be a dutiful wife or child to empty the chamber pot.

Gabriel stood naked at the kitchen sink, gently crying, her arms deep in the suds. She must have heard me directing my grateful stream in the bathroom, so I knew I would not frighten her.

"Gabriel?" I put my arms around her waist and, kissing her neck, felt the smoothness of her belly and moved my hands to cradle her breasts.

"As long as could, should, or would be. We said that, didn't we? About us—the three of us?"

"Gabriel..." I was going to lose her. Helen was going to lose her. Waking in the night, this one time her dreaming fears had not left her. She turned in my arms, so close, and kissed me, still sobbing. Her words were a torrent. About loving and about loving the both of us, Helen and me. And about the nights when, after lovemaking and full of me, she would cross the hall to Helen's room where they would make love as I slept. There were too many of us, it seemed. We had taken all she had to give. We had emptied her.

With a heartbroken cry, she plunged her arms into the steaming, soapy water and came up with our carving knife. I watched the knife in Gabriel's hands, the big, sharp chef's knife we kept for shaving thin, red slices from our Sunday roasts, glide into my body. We regarded the hilt protruding from me, just below the sternum; there was just the slightest trickle of blood. It was as though we had been summoned here and were now waiting for further instructions

"Why?" All I felt was a mild curiosity: so little blood for such a big knife. I was distantly aware that I was going to die. I was interested, but not very interested.

Gabriel tried to put her arms around me, but the knife was in the way. "Oh, Roy..." Her tears were dry.

My knees were loose and I followed them to the floor. There was a twinge of pain and I felt very tired. "Huh... Old Spaghetti-legs. Can't take me anywhere."

"Helen!" Gabriel screamed and knelt beside me on the kitchen floor. I reached out a hand to pat her shoulder.

❑

From the front hall, the telephone is ringing. It will be Barbara, most likely visited with a fresh complaint. How word got around; one good leer deserves another. Barbara will soon stand armed with but a clipboard and a whistle, her Gumdrops a kneeling phalanx before a charge of leering, prurient satyrs.

"Why?" I ask again. This is beside the point; it is all going to be my fault. Helen's telephone silences from New Mexico might have told me if I had bothered to listen between the spatterings of the stars.

"If I told you then it would ruin the surprise, wouldn't it?" That the Tirewoman Gabriel might be just another Gumdrop I can not just now accept.

"I hate surprises." A name is whoever you say you are. I am not so surprised, after all.

I shake my head to clear my eyes. Helen, my daughter, arrives barefoot and in her pajamas and we kneel and hold each other, we three. Our words are gone.

The phone is still ringing and there are no words for Barbara either. Barbara will have to improvise. True grenadier parade majorettes, Barbara's Gumdrops will have the determined look of a retail cadre standing firm for the January White Sales as they repel the satyr's charge. Will the Gumdrops miss me?

The Tirewoman Gabriel was first published in the February 2010
Necrology Shorts, John Ferguson, editor.

The Death of James A. Garfield

You probably picked up this tale expecting one of those conspiracy theory tell-alls. I mean from the title and all. Nope. In the middle of the Twentieth Century mysterious things were still reported in the Southern Highlands. There was this one item about an exploding deer that got buried in the back pages. However, in real life, hauntings, hexings and supernatural doings were as strange to the post-bellum South as pit barbecue, Winn-Dixie, Dr. Pepper and Royal Crown Cola were familiar.

The exploding deer thing happened when I was in the seventh grade. I was nowhere near the scene. It is important that you know I am not delusional about the death of James A. Garfield: He was shot by a disgruntled office seeker and his middle name was Abram, the A in James A. President Garfield figures in only minimally, delivering an occasional opinion from the Presidential hereafter.

My name is Harley Pigeon. I grew up in Mycenae, Wisconsin, just west of Elm Grove. And James A. Garfield, the Pride of the West, twentieth President of the United States, was shot and killed alright—the sort of abrupt ending that gives rise to ghosthood. There was an assassin, a guy passed over for a civil service appointment, but infection—blood poisoning—is what got James A. Garfield. Doctors didn't much bother to wash their hands in those days.

At the time this story starts, the late 1940s, the dust was still settling after those events which we who lived through them called World War Two—and harmless weirdness was a popular preoccupation. So Ed Seitz and I were not unprepared. Ed Seitz? He's my partner.

"Yeah, yeah, the tomatoes." That's Ed. "The Cherokee Purples—strange fruit, that's what. Harley, pull over; I gotta pee real bad."

Together Ed and I are Factory Findings—*not* incorporated. My specialty is brass grommets; Ed knows the industrial string and twine business inside out. The leaf springs of Ed's Buick sedan sag with sample cases and catalogs. He is a salesman to be respected. We pulled over to empty Ed's bladder; Ed pees a lot when we are on the road.

Short and overalled, a small figure stepped out of the roadside scrub and declaimed. "You are Lost. Lost Forever." Ed hastily zipped back up. We weren't looking for anything out of the ordinary. But not not expecting it, either. We were in one of those back-of-nowhere boondocks that abound in Appalachia.

The girl was freckled and red-headed. Her pale skin made her eyes look spooky—and wiser than her years. A large, black dog came gamboling up, wagging all over. It was a standard poodle, not your average Appalachian farm dog. The dog rolled joyously at the girl's feet. "Barney's not lost." She grabbed the dog by its ears and shook its head. The dog seemed to love this.

"Hello. Who are you?" I asked.

"I am Delilah," she said. "James A. Garfield has guided your feet. It's a sure thing. President Garfield never misses. After the tomatoes, of course," she said with wide-eyed innocence. This is a kid trick: getting inside your head so you trust them.

"Well, Delilah, I am Harley, how do you do? And we are never lost. We navigate by the sun. This is US Route 41. Or Route 40. We just don't know what town we're in."

"I told you you were lost." Her logic was irrefutable. "Follow me."

We followed her.

Ed and I stumbled over ravines, through gullies and, torn by brambles, stung by nettles, followed Delilah and Barney the poodle through an endless Appalachian outback.

"Here we are," said Delilah. She gestured proudly toward a tumbledown barn.

All the evidence suggested a massacre. Fresh blood was drying black and stippled in a neat three-foot pattern smack-dab in the middle of a windowless side wall. There was some dripping.

❑

Did I tell you I went to James A. Garfield Elementary? Probably not. We had cheerleaders and a losing basketball team for them to cheer for. School spirit saw to it that I was more or less informed about the late president. So for me at age eleven President James A. Garfield was a little anecdotal history and a losing sports team. Nothing more, nothing less. I missed out on World War Two because I was pigeon-toed. The pigeon-toed thing never fails to get a chuckle. It's my name—Pigeon, Harley Pigeon. And some suspicion that I might have been a war slacker.

Ask Ed Seitz. "Air conditioning and cheap labor, Harley. No unions," he told me, sharing a vision of the New South. This was in 1948. We were playing billiards at the Antlers Hotel in Milwaukee. We had never met before, just ankled up for a few beers and a friendly strangers game.

"Air conditioning, Harley. That is what will relocate Northern manufacturers to Dixie. These guys are going to pack their factories, run off and start all over again."

Ed did not laugh when I fessed up about the pigeon-toed deferment. "Hmm. Good for you. Four-F. You saw an opportunity and did your war work as a civilian." This, and the beers, made me feel I owed him something. Ed is not muscular on personality. But he knows what he knows.

Back to James A. Garfield again. Did you know that Alexander Graham Bell actually invented a metal detector to find the exact location of the assassin's bullet? Mr. Garfield had been placed on a bed with an innerspring mattress. Bell's device wouldn't work because of the metal in the springs. Mr. Garfield died.

Charles Guiteau, Garfield's assassin, wanted to be ambassador to France. He was a lawyer, go figure. And it was Garfield who got a song written about him, so much for Guiteau's fifteen minutes of fame. Everett Hoops, Delilah's grandfather, sang the song for me on the Carolina side of the Great Smokies right near where the deer exploded: "Oh, I'm feeling mighty lowdown low. I been shot down mighty lowdown low," said the song, meaning James A. Garfield. Mr. Garfield was not a happy guy. After all, he had been shot. And me? Ed Seitz and I were not looking for happiness per se, but business—which when you have enough of it is the same thing.

❏

In the hill country of South Carolina Route 41 disappears into that limbo of good intentions where highway projects languish. Dixie Duck and Process of Piedmont, South Carolina had landed a tarpaulin contract for mothballing every deck gun in the entire US fleet. They needed grommets, pronto. Through dumb luck and the grace of God, Ed and I were in their office the afternoon the order came through.

"You're sure your grommets will fit our dies?" asked Dixie Duck's production manager.

We were sure. "If they don't, we'll buy back the grommets and you're only out one day's down time. We'll eat the order." We promised overnight delivery, fools that we were. This took beaucoup driving with one of us always behind the wheel. In the 1940s tourists were few and far between and we drove pedal-to-the-metal. These coffee and Benzedrine runs left us bleary-eyed and reeking like a hamper of lapsed laundry. But our customers loved us.

When our rented rig with 6 tons of brass grommets pulled into the Dixie Duck and Process loading dock it was three in the morning and I was there to meet it. Ed had left Milwaukee the previous day. A very large black man named Wilton was at the wheel; he explained Ed was sleeping in the back of the cab. A steady diet of bennies and roadhouse coffee had given Ed double vision and for him night driving was out; he had needed a break. There, in the fog of a mountain switchback was Wilton Paine with a cardboard suitcase and his thumb in the air. Ed liked to pick up hitchhikers and let them drive. Wilton Paine obliged.

Ed clambered down off the sleeping shelf. "Wow, here already?" He knuckled his hair, then his eyes, and let go a phlegmy smoker's cough. He was wearing striped flannel pajamas. He crawled over Wilton and exited the cab. "Harley, meet Wilton."

"How do, Wilton."

"Hiya, Harley. Mind if I have a drink?" Wilton ratcheted the hand brake and pulled a pint from the recesses of a worn denim jacket. He beamed upon us, blowing clouds of smoke from his pipe, shaking his head in sad affirmation, "This is true, I can't deny it. I'm weak..." We passed the pint around. "But I'm a good man; I just get out of control sometimes is all."

"How much out of control?" The rig was a rental. We had a bond posted.

"Can't rightly tell. And 'cause I'm so big folks tend to write off any damage I cause." In the soft circumlocutions of South Carolina, Wilton Paine had a predilection for strong drink.

"He's been driving since Gary, Indiana," said Ed.

Good men were hard to find.

"You drink on the job?"

"Never."

That night Wilton Paine became Factory Findings' third partner. Clearly, he liked things the way they were; it was just that things could be better. And with a soft-spoken competence, he set about to make them better. I never saw Wilton out of control. I never saw him drunk and he never let us down.

Well, the dies didn't fit our grommets. I figured they wouldn't so, while Ed and Wilton were on the road from Milwaukee, I sunk our floating capital—200 dollars—into the local machine shop. There were three sets

The Death of James A. Garfield

of alternate dies ready for whatever might be on board when our truck showed up in Piedmont. I walked Dixie Duck's floor manager through the setup and told him to hang on to the dies courtesy of Factory Findings. We would be doing business here again.

Staying in the office Ed and I were losing money. On the road we made money. With Wilton spelling Ed and me at the wheel, we regularly beat contract haulers and Railway Express by days or weeks. At Valdosta, Georgia the sheriff's brother-in-law operated an axle-popping mudhole at the county line and he had the only tow truck in the county. The state police tended to look the other way. That mud hole got us once with Wilton driving and a load of 55-gallon drums of sodium bisulfite and ammonium salts on board for an alligator tannery in Ocala. Wilton told me to stay under cover in the sleeper and pulled an Oscar-winning "Yassuh, Boss" routine on the cops that had us laughing for months after the fact. They let Wilton through for free. Black folks knew how to work the system in Dixie. Milwaukee, Chicago, Vincennes, Evansville, then the Chattahoochee National Forest, Macon, Tifton, through Georgia to the Florida line. Our alternate route was to pick up US #1 at Waycross. The Route #1 swing took us into the beef and citrus belt of central Florida where we had only one account, the alligator tannery.

Like I said, word got around. We delivered and on time.

❏

Some months after Wilton Paine joined Factory Findings, Ed drove while I dozed. Through the industrial wastelands along the Gary, Elgin and South Shore interurban tracks, the route twists like the stitching on a major league baseball. Except for the red thread. Like Theseus and the Minotaur? Like I said, I grew up in Mycenae, Wisconsin where the Mycenae Boosters insisted that the doings of the ancient gods and heroes be taught in elementary school. I have been also known to read the occasional grommet and twine catalog.

In south Gary, somewhere between Inland Steel and the Falstaff brewery, the Buick swerved hard right, taking a one-hundred-eighty-degree turn at 40 miles an hour. Too fast. Tires squealed and I was thrown against the door; Ed's enthusiasm always picked up once we got past Chicago.

"Remember the bar with the stripper?" Ed had a frosty beer and a particular oasis in mind.

"The tassels." I remembered. We would detour.

Calumet City, Illinois is the fallen sister of Hammond, Indiana. That the Calumet River had once caught fire was legend among the guys at the

Antlers bar. The two towns straddled the state line. Calumet City was blue neon beer joints with electric country bands; all the bars had strippers. This particular bar was called the Calypso. The same woman as last time twitched above the bar, partaking of a private epiphany two feet from the end of her nose. At ten AM we were outnumbered only by the band and the girl. She was at the end of a long work day and moving just enough so that she might be dancing.

Now the stripper is important because every good story has to have a proper siren. The stripper with the tassels signified temptation of a sort. Her eyes stared noncommittally into space as she cranked out the mileage on her plywood stage. The tassels rotated lackadaisically, one clockwise, one counterclockwise.

"Just an hour, okay, Ed?"

"Just an hour, Harley."

Ed hung on in the Calypso for a twelve-beer hour. He left a fiver in the stripper's jar and waved to the band. The stripper nodded acceptance to the jar while ignoring Ed and me. Destiny was calling and I was driving.

Ed slept it off all the way to South Carolina. I jumped Route 41 and headed east to Asheville on US 40. Our coup at Dixie Duck had opened doors to purchasing agents at five other fiber processors.

The Burma-Shave signs were a touch of humor in the predictable procession of tarpaper shacks surrounded by junked cars, scrub pine, and leavened with the sporadic offering of flattened raccoon. You remember them? The Burma-Shaves grabbed me with their cornball versifying. Ed snored and I read.

> *Riot in drug store*
> *Calling all cars*
> *100 customers*
> *99 jars*
> *Burma-Shave*

The signs came in sets of five—the last sign a kicker for the sponsor, Burma-Shave.

Ed woke up on the Carolina line. "Harley, I gotta pee."

Ed had to pee. I cruised along, eyes peeled for an appropriate peeing grove. And passed another set of Burma-Shave signs. I only caught the last two lines and hit the brakes.

> *Little did I dream*
> *While in my youthful bloom*

The Death of James A. Garfield

For the murder of
James A. Garfield
I'd meet my fatal doom.

Not your usual Burma-Shave sign. I had a feeling of all-over creepiness that something was not right on this road.

"Ed, here's your pit stop. I gotta check those last signs."

"U-turn? You want a U-turn? Great, then I'll take a pee." Ed sprang out of the Buick and ran over to stand against a bridge abutment over one of those country creeks with which the South abounds. This is the part I told you about at the start of the story—where we first met Dilly.

"You are Lost. Lost Forever." The pale-skinned little girl, freckled and red-headed, appeared as if from thin air. Ed's look of distress said he was not through. Ed was dancing about and doing his best to hold it.

"Go on, pee. I'll wait," said the girl. Ed looked grateful and hustled off.

"Dilly? You there?" The call came from a scrub copse beyond the bridge abutment.

"Here, Grandpa," shouted Dilly.

"Don't you never let a chance pass you by," wailed an old man's voice.

"Don't you never let a chance pass you by," the child called back.

"Whatcha got, Dil?" There was a rustle from a stand of alders. A stoop-shouldered muscular man in bib overalls slid down the ditch on his rear end and approached us.

"Oh. People. Hello, there, I'm Everett Hoops. I see you've met Delilah. Lost?"

"No. We know where we are; we just missed a turn is all."

"They are looking for Route 40," said the little girl. "They don't know where that is."

"I recall someone from the state came through putting numbers on things. That was '06 or '07. You most likely want the Willardsville Pike," said the man in the overalls as he dusted off his fanny.

"My Grandpa is the Tooth Fairy," said Dilly.

Leathery crevasses etched themselves into the old man's walnut-tanned face as he displayed a warm, welcoming smile of many missing teeth. "I'll admit to being the Tooth Fairy. Excepts that I leave my teeth and take the money."

The girl gave me the once-over. "Not too likely material they've given us to work with." She puffed out her cheeks and let a suppressed laugh out through her nose. There was the smallest bubble of snot. The old man and the child struggled to contain themselves.

"Mr. Garfield has sent you. You have followed the call of the Cherokee Purples," said Everett Hoops. Then he threw back his head and burst into a song that was half singing, half talking. This was to be the first time I heard the song about Mr. Garfield, for whom my school was named:

"A preacher said to James A. Garfield, 'If you should die tonight where d'you think you'll spend eternity?'

Mr. Garfield looked up kinda sad-like and he give him somethin' like this:

'Oh, I'd make my home in heaven, Lord, Lord,

Oh, I'd make my home in heaven.'"

The old man sang through the gaps in his teeth. He was more authentic than an old country record; his tremulous high tenor sounded like he brought his own static and scratches with him. When he was finished, he hugged the child. They then faced each other and performed what appeared to be a familiar ritual.

"Don't you never let a chance pass you by," they chanted together.

"The Cherokee Purples told us you would come," said the girl. "Because you have been here before. In a dream the tomatoes had."

I was trying to hold eye contact with the girl in the bib overalls who was now looking serious as all hell. She broke a grin. Ah, I thought—they are having us on. Now we will all share the joke. Nope. They caught the giggles again, started laughing out loud and sat down together in the long grass of the verge.

"I know what you're thinking," said the old man. "But suppose I was to tell you tomatoes have a secret vegetable language? The Cherokee Purples, that is. That to those who can understand them they will foretell future events? Well, they don't; they foretell the past. What they will tell is what really happened. See, no one remembers what actually took place even a couple of hours ago. History is opinion."

"We're not lost," said Ed. "We just stopped to check out the Burma-Shave sign. My partner was curious about what it said."

"Well, that's a long story," said the man, "that I can tell you if you have some time to spare. Have you avoided temptation?"

The Death of James A. Garfield

I recalled the stripper in Calumet City. "Pretty much," I said.

"Then you get to come up to our place," said the child. She scrambled down the shallow bank, hopped the creek and struck out at a right angle to the road.

"Y'all're too late for the yachting cannon," Delilah called over her shoulder. "Grandpa was picking ticks all this morning. Off Barney. But I can show you the barn. Wanna come?"

I jumped the creek after her. "Barney is the dog?"

"Well, yes."

Ed was huffing and puffing as he waded over to join us, his cuffs wet from the creek. Everett followed. The old man and the girl shared another private glance. Ed and I were being set up.

"If we come along will you tell us about the Burma-Shave signs?" I asked.

"I might."

"If we come along, will you tell us what the hell you mean about tomatoes having a dream that we were coming?" Ed asked.

"Nope, you've got to believe," said the little girl.

By now the four of us were stumbling through a rolling pasture of daisy fleabane in full bloom. "Watch your step, gents. We only got three cows but they get around," said Everett. We came to a pair of small ravines, eroded at their bank sides by a recent gully wash. Undercut sod clung by tangles of roots dangling from upside-down bouquets of daisies.

"Jump good, now. Sharp stuff stickin' up down there." In ravine number two were the rusting remains of leftover agricultural implements—a dismembered horse-drawn mower and parts of a Cord truck. Four dome-shaped valve heads the size of young watermelons rusted red atop a cracked engine block that had oozed its oil onto the soil. The oil spill had hardened into a thick dark varnish.

"And there's the barn." Weathered and unpainted though not dilapidated, the small barn stood straight on unrotted sills. The barn was immaculate except for where an elephant or other large ruminant had strayed into a fusillade of automatic weapons fire. Snuffling and the delighted moans of a dog rolling in something good issued from under the wide planked floor.

"Barney?" A low hanging pall of black powder still lingered around the sodden shingles under the eaves.

"Yep. We named him for the barn. Groundhog," said Delilah. "He got the skunk last week." There was no dead elephant in evidence.

"Damn ticks," said Everett. "They drive Barney crazy."

"Grandpa and I pick off the ticks and drop 'em into the cannon. Then boom," said Dilly, patting the muzzle of what looked like a miniature deck gun from a pirate frigate. "I get to shoot it."

"Yachting cannon," offered Everett. I decided not to ask how a muzzle-loader used to signal ocean racing for the idle rich had made it into the hills of Carolina.

"We don't do deer bombs anymore," said Dilly.

"Just as loud as the cannon but too dangerous," said Everett.

This was information I didn't want to hear. I paused to reflect that I was in the company of a pair of folksy, down-home maniacs.

Ed was unsettled by the blood all over the barn's shiplap siding. These people were an unknown quantity and they had a gun, albeit a miniature cannon that would take considerable time to load and point.

"Not that I'm objecting. Knocking off ticks is a good thing. No, no, no, yes, yes," said Ed. "It's the splattering—isn't that extreme? That's just an observation, not a criticism."

Everett beamed on Ed. "You, sir, are a follower of thread. Like Theseus in the Labyrinth." Meanwhile, the girl had positioned herself between Ed and her grandfather, a defensive posture.

"There is a museum. Willimantic. That's in Connecticut..." said Ed, missing the classical reference. "...the shrine of twine." I never got excited about string, not like Ed. He was grasping for any plausible excuse to make a getaway. Right now we were behind schedule to meet with Wilton and share out deliveries among us. "When folks need thread or twine, that's where you'll find me. I travel with a line of twine and we are headed to the museum..." He pulled out his pocket watch. "They close at five; we should be going..."

"Connecticut is 500 miles away," said Delilah.

"...right now as a matter of fact." Ed looked imploringly to me for confirmation.

"Yep," I said.

The Death of James A. Garfield

"Like Theseus," said Everett. "The slayer of the Minotaur? You are a follower of thread. The thread was red—like the stitching on a major league baseball."

"Huh?" Ed.

"There you are. You have heard the call of the road and heeded the Name of Power. President James A. Garfield has brought you here to us. The stories get mixed up but they all make sense in the end. It was a red thread," said Everett.

"I am a traveler in industrial twine," said Ed Seitz.

"I thought so." The Tooth Fairy was satisfied. "Like to hear about the deer bombs?"

I said no. Ed said yes and sat down. He looked nervously at Dilly. She might misinterpret a refusal. Everett Hoops told us about deer bombs.

"The deer bomb. We did it all through the Depression. If you have a dead battery hanging around and everybody did; you dig a hole and bury the battery, leaving a pair of wires sticking out above ground. The battery has to ripen, build up a charge, in the hole for three to six months. Tape the exposed wires to a block of deer-lick salt. When the wires touch you will have one righteous explosion. A deer licking at the salt completes the circuit."

"And kaboom!" said Delilah with relish. "But we don't do them no more, the battery bombs," she pouted.

"When my father, Dilly's great-grandfather, died I became the caretaker of his tomatoes, the Cherokee Purples. From there on in they were to be my responsibility," said Everett Hoops. "No time for batteries."

"Oh, yes. Tomatoes," I said. If we had been inside I would have been edging toward the door.

"It's a good thing. Resourceful." Ed was not convincing. He was talking about the battery bomb, not the tomatoes. "A good thing, too. Yes, yes." Ed hadn't caught up with Everett Hoops' fast-flowing shifts of focus.

"And you're not objecting," said the girl to Ed.

"Not one bit. No criticism intended," Ed repeated.

"Well, you don't have to worry" Dilly was consoling. "We never really made a deer bomb. It's one of Grandpa's stories."

Ed looked relieved.

"But we could." I'd just bet she could.

"Why James A. Garfield?"

"Because nobody remembers him," said Everett. Ask a silly question, etc.

"And tomatoes're not rightly a fruit, you know." Everett Hoops didn't just retail his homilies on the simple life. He was ready for wholesale. "The tomato is rightly a berry."

"And your great-grandfather's tomatoes are why James A. Garfield appeared on a Burma-Shave sign?" I asked.

"It was to get your attention," said Dilly. "The signs. We put 'em up. The tomatoes only made the suggestion." They were enjoying this. We were probably the first entertainment they had had in a spell.

"My attention?" Here was a place I did not care to go. These two had been trolling for wise guys, traveling salesmen grinding their retracements over the choking dirt byways of the southern heartland. "Me? Me personally? My attention?"

"You. You are the chosen one. I shall be yours." Dilly. Her eyes said she was dead serious. I reminded myself that this red-headed, freckled kid would grow up to be a woman. Eventually. And a damned attractive woman, too. That is if one of the travelers she and Everett trolled for along US 40 didn't murder them and steal their three cows.

"You are seeking your fortunes armed with but guile, courage and a native wit like Odysseus in the old story," said Everett. We were smack dab in the middle of some traveling salesman joke. Except Everett, self-anointed Tooth Fairy, appeared sharp as a box of tacks and the comely daughter was only ten years old.

"President Garfield, James A. Garfield, has set your path to bring you to us. He has guided your feet as surely as Athena did for Odysseus. You have already passed through hell and escaped the siren call," said Everett.

The siren call. I thought of Calumet City and the ecological war zones south of Chicago. "We followed US 41," I said.

"You followed your instincts. You are a curious man; you despise a mystery," Everett said. "Dilly is the grapes of heaven and you must come back when she has ripened to an appropriate age."

"I only wondered who had been messing with the Burma-Shave signs."

"It was us," said Dilly, "We've been trolling for my prince for a coupla summers. You are the first. You are the one."

The Death of James A. Garfield

"Prince?"

"You are my chosen champion," said Dilly.

"Chosen by the late president, James A. Garfield," Everett said. Well, that explained everything. "You are what I leave to Delilah. With you, Harley, she shall wax fat and browse the pastures of plenty."

"You must read a whole lot."

"We have two books. Bullfinch's Mythology and the Bible. Dilly and I read aloud in the winter. The stories tend to get mixed up but Mr. Garfield straightens 'em out."

Without wishing to offend Everett and Delilah, I plunged right in. "Just how many years are we talking about here?"

"Seven," said Everett. "You will come back to claim your bride in seven years. She will be eighteen years old. Almost."

"I can hardly wait." This was meant to be sarcastic. If they caught on they gave not a clue. The grandfather played it straight.

"You must wait."

Okay, I had to wait. The girl was ten years old; I would be happy to wait. I looked over the pint-sized kid from whose pencil-thin shoulders faded overalls hung by suspenders. These people were weird. Weird and compelling.

"And all this is because of Burma-Shave?"

"Because you answered the call of President Garfield. Yes."

Of course. I sat down in the grass next to Ed.

"What if I don't come back for Delilah?"

"I am the Tooth Fairy." The old man was controlling a full-body laugh that started near his diaphragm. "If you find any teeth under your pillow, better check your wallet and your bank account. You'll be back. I'll see you don't forget."

❏

Ed and I finished that trip with our contacts outbidding each other for the privilege of buying from Factory Findings. We bought a semi-trailer on credit, with purchase orders for security. We had figured a way to cut transportation costs and therefore increase our share of the billing. This involved consolidating our bulk orders in one truck in Milwaukee then driving south. All we needed was a depot for offloading and breaking down our orders. Wilton fixed things up with the owner of a drive-in movie in Knoxville that was only open weekends. We would rendezvous with Wilton in the foothills of the Great Smoky Mountains. Sure enough, he met Ed and me with three panel trucks and two brothers-in-law. Wilton had married off a lot of sisters.

I waited seven years and went back to claim my bride.

Romantic? Well, frankly I had forgotten.

❑

It was Wilton who first spotted the huge and unauthorized checks drawn on the corporate accounts. Then he checked Factory Findings' certificates of deposit, those quick roll-over accounts where we shave a little off the system by parking our withholdings. Some had been cashed out. And not by us.

That same morning I found a tooth under my pillow.

That Ed Seitz and Everett Hoops might be in cahoots did cross my mind. Not that I didn't put Wilton and his brothers-in-law out of suspicion. They loved a good laugh. It was just a hop down the holler—five miles to the nearest phone and Alexander Graham Bell's singing wires—to put Delilah Hoops' grandfather in touch with Upsala 8478 where an ancient black daffodil telephone rang on the second floor of the Zabloski Bros. Bldg. Ed Seitz was sure to answer when I was away. That gave me more food for thought.

But then there was the mysterious tooth. Not a child's tooth. It was a molar, worn, yellowed and long in the shank. Human, I guessed, but I'm no expert.

As I drove south I nursed the unsettling image of Dilly and her grandpa out in the woods rummaging through a pile of deer bones scattered by a long-exploded battery bomb left over from Everett's father's predations in the Depression. Looking for a tooth. None of these explanations left me truly happy. I opted for the unseen hand of James A. Garfield uniting two lovers from the Presidential afterlife.

Everett Hoops met me by the same rural bridge abutment where Ed had stopped to pee seven years earlier.

"Don't you never let a chance pass you by, Lord, Lord," Everett sang into the alder copse.

"Don't you never let a chance pass you by," answered a full, strong contralto. My, my, how time had dealt kindly with Delilah. Beautiful and poised described her—to a point. There was still an endearing touch of

The Death of James A. Garfield

the bizarre about the young woman. And when she smiled, freckles danced across the bridge of her nose.

Thirty years later and those freckles still dance.

The New South bloomed, just like Ed Seitz foresaw 37 years earlier in the Antlers billiards room in Milwaukee. The Burma-Shave roadside signs were not maintained; they faded and fell in forgotten locations, no hands clapping.

Everett Hoops and Ed Seitz had by now gone on to raise tomatoes for the angelic swarm. I like to think Ed finally made it to the shrine of twine. Dilly and I tend her great-grandfather's tomato legacy: Cherokee Purples, Brandywines and Bonny Bests. We get back to the mountains to sort and save the seeds each year. Wilton Paine is the southern partner of Factory Findings with his home office in Gainesville from where he manages a fleet of seventeen company-owned trucks. I suspect Wilton spends most of his time over on the Gulf, sword-fishing. Wilton's reports reach us from time to time but, frankly, the man is making us so much money with his down-home managerial style that I feel guilty just reading the bottom line. Anyway, next year Wilton will be buying out Dilly and me to become El Honcho Grande for the whole operation. Dilly and I are on the road most of the time, pulling an Airstream trailer. The checks catch up with us with the same irregularity of Factory Findings quarterly reports.

❏

"Dil? Honey, where did we put the signs?" I figured it was time to visit Everett Hoops' Cherokee Purple tomato patch. I was rummaging in the garage loft. We were behind schedule on our youngest daughter, Addie. She had wanted to finish college first.

"What?" Delilah was shouting from the back porch but she ended up with a choking fit as she tried to hold in a belly laugh. Just like she and her grandfather had so long ago. I scuttled down the ladderway.

Dilly performed a pirouette on the porch, a presentation of herself. "Addie took them with her last week. She says we might forget where they were."

"The James A. Garfield Burma-Shave signs?" Since Everett died there had been no more omens or portents from President Garfield or the tomato patch. Dilly says it's not that the Cherokee Purples aren't talking, could be we just forgot how to listen.

"Fair child, fair children," she said, taking a bow. "Wanna go trolling?" The freckles danced.

We rendezvoused with Addie at her dorm and we are today headed south to find what is left of US Route 40. Then, if US 40 is still there, east on 40. We have the old James A. Garfield signs in the trailer. A father (or grandfather) never figures his daughter will ever find a man worthy of her.

A word about tomatoes. The Cherokee Purples have no opinion on the doings of humankind. They just pass on what they see, but you have to know how to ask. This is vegetable wisdom. The writers of history have their story; the tomatoes have theirs. Now, who are you going to trust? I'd trust the Cherokee Purples—they don't have a stake in the game. They just watch and wait. What exactly they are waiting for, I don't rightly want to know. Not yet.

The Death of James A. Garfield was first published in *A Fly in Amber* [http://www.aflyinamber.net/] July 2008

The Return of the Orange Virgin

Prologue

In the cellars of the Queen, the stones were holding converse. There was no sound, but the stones' deep resonances crept between their joins, leaping basaltic fissures with a lethargic iridescence. The Orange Virgin clutched at an ornamental drapery to steady herself. *How came I here?*

"Unbecoming and unrewarding, o queen," said the stones. "...your thought. You are here because we are here."

"Here is where we are, stones. It was ever thus. Have you any other pithy perorations or are we through?" The thick velvet of the wall hanging—shot with gold and silver threads and embroidered with emeralds and topazes, raddled to insubstantiality by time and rot—crumbled at her touch. A spider scuttled for safety in a fissure.

By their nature, the stones did not get around much, but they had compensated by evolving a great pride of place. Black basalt they were, striped with travertine, an outcropping of the world spirit—fashioned plumb, square, and true—and stacked perhaps at the pleasure of a backwoods warlord to keep the cows out of his celery and the neighboring feoffers out of his wives. The great blocks were meticulously quarried to a master plan that allowed but fine tolerances at their joins and little tolerance for intruders.

"You presume much for artifacts. Why am I here? You have some pronouncement or other, I can feel it. You yearn for company. I, too." The goddess aimed a kick at the wall. She had no leg. She had no body yet shared the affliction of all who travel fast and far: her bladder was overfull and shrieking for relief, a depressingly human state. But the bladder was elsewhere. In the stress of her need she reached for one of her long braids to chew, an idle habit, and found it likewise not there. "So! I would appear to have mislaid my parts. When my body catches up with me, then I will attend to its needs. For now it can hold it."

The goddess grasped her *whereness*, though why and to what purpose, malign or beneficent, she could not guess. Ignorance was unbecoming; she was, after all, a deity. "And a goddess is expected to know everything and at all times. Yes, yes, yes. I am familiar with the drill," she told the unremitting emptiness of the oozing walls.

"The child of clay—he will be one of them. A creature of flesh and the evanescent air." The stones.

There was a lengthy pause—a minute, an hour, a week perhaps. "And yet of us, do not forget." The stones added.

"He is mine," said the Orange Virgin. The stones ignored her. "Uh, hello?" Again, no answer. The stones had resumed their deliberations.

"They invent themselves, going backwards from the moment of their deaths, prey to violence, wistful longings and silly enthusiasms."

"These creatures have no sense of proportion but an immense capacity for forward motion. We will not become involved."

"But the child must be elsewhere—we would not be comfortable with the, hmmm... state of affairs. There is a duopoly, an overlapping here. Let the child be with those he resembles. Inform the Orange Virgin."

"Pompous pile!" The Orange Virgin kicked the wall. "Ouch!" Her body had caught up with her.

The stones were unperturbed. "Incompatibility—you are foreign to us, but we have tolerated you, Lady. It were best, hmmm... yes, best for all concerned—you and we—if you and he, this Cowboy Trueheart..."

"Bangtree. Biff Bangtree." The Orange Virgin stamped her foot.

"As you will. Trueheart, Bangtree, whatall... The golem must go, you too. Our comfort is in disarray. However, in his hour of final need he may return to us if he wills, for he has been manufactured from the dust of our world. In his terminal agony he shall find us waiting, as always. You, goddess, are with us, but not of us. You wrung the rain from the sky and quickened the wombs of the wild things and brought the wheat to sheaf. Blah, blah, blah. Ever you grind on with your tales of pathetic abandonment. Just who abandoned whom?"

"I was offered no choice, and this is not the present topic under discussion."

The Lady sniffled and, to hide a tear, told herself she smelled the fumes of belladonna that once wafted forth on the polished cobbles of the night.

Had it become her time to go yet again as before, those aeons past. "And here we are replaying eternity. Until we get it right?" The Orange Virgin hoped so. Smoky pine resin incense once rose heavenward to gladden the nostrils; her altars were empty, censers left swinging in their gimbals as horror-stricken votaries fled, sandals flapping, into the night to rouse the priestesses.

The Pig Killing

Harry took a pull from the screw-top pint of fortified wine. Empty. Blood and mud. Spring killing. This was the reverse order of things.

Harry Profitt Pease, white stubbled beard and nearing 60, walked in a dream of youth and beauty—firm, brown, country girls blushed by the sun. Their freckled breasts and legs pursued his waking hours; crisp floral prints tantalized with their formal exposition of girl flesh, close and aromatic, hors d'oeuvres of a promised feast to come. These were the girls of his youth: ever fresh with skirts that swirled as they took lazy, calculated pirouettes.

Harry came in bib overalls and with a two-weeks' beard, a tune from his mother's Victorola dancing through fumes of sugary wine. Rudy Vallee sang The Whiffenpoof Song. That Harry had been a basketball hero in high school should have brought some consolation to the pigs he killed—blown away by the star center on that championship team. Honor enough. Why, then, the fuss? The pig didn't know it was special, certainly not Harry, though it had a glimmering just before the end. Every pig was the same pig every time to Harry, an old, familiar face; he had no way of knowing this one was different. After he killed the first one thirty years earlier, introductions had been superfluous, "Hello, again. How are we this year?" as he swung a leg over the fence, a cabbage or stale bread under his arm. They followed him to the nearest dry, level place in the yard.

The firm brown girls in crisp print dresses, preserved from the rigors of late middle age, accompanied Harry and the pig to the killing ground.

Harry didn't trust his aim. Even at two feet, a yard or so, the alcohol sufficient to steady his hand blurred his vision. He leaned against the pig. The pig grunted amorously and nuzzled Harry's knee. He fastidiously replaced the cap and threw the empty bottle into the brown sere of last year's tall grass. It was spring—why were these pigs here and so big? Harry licked his lips for the sweet, sugary residue and polished his glasses on his shirttail.

Harry carried his cannon. Harry's Father, Profitt Pease, once calls the rifle that—his cannon. "Shit, I could hold off a regiment if they sent one man at a time every Sunday for brunch. And unarmed," says Profitt Pease. The cannon has a spilt stock held together with duct tape, Harry's father's gun. Harry's father's bullets, too: machine gun loads from the Second World War. About half were duds.

Harry fondled a cartridge of green patinated brass. "Duds..." Harry talked through his sweet, sweet wine, "...you're older than I am but half of you still work." The bullets are short for the chamber so he has to load them bolt-action style, one at a time.

Harry spoke to the pig, "I hope you don't mind waiting..."

Harry grew dreamy. Was this sacrifice really necessary? Harry was five again and waiting in a railroad depot with his mother during the war. Even miles were rationed. "Is This Trip Really Necessary?" The sign was over the ticket window.

Each year Marcus Hanrahan and his kids raised two pigs on kitchen scraps and garden leavings. By fall, they were haughty and indolent, ready for the transformation to unaccusing packages of freezer paper with masking tape labels. Each fall Marcus sent his pigs to glory. But not last fall. The young Hanrahans, now a quorum of five, had pleaded for the lives of their pet swine: "Oh, Dad, that's gross." The blood flowed somewhere else, not here, not out past the swing set, to fill the see-through polystyrene trays at the Red and White meat counter. Marcus relented; the pigs lived and stayed through the winter.

The pigs grew thin and anxious behind the house as their back yard wallow froze and was dusted with snow that, churned by their pacings as they studied their rectangle of sky for a sign, turned into black ooze. Their food kept coming—the garden waste and vegetable trims were replaced with dinner scraps, neglected toast and congealed mashed potatoes, ham fat and egg grease, muffin ends and cabbage husks from the dumpster out back at the WilCo Diner. But where they should have thrived, the pigs grew thin; they knew there was something wrong.

The kids fed them through the winter, and about February, feeling spring coming, they went back on their feed and they grew huge. The food kept coming, though the kids' attention wandered—trail bikes, hockey, and high school courtships replaced the pigs in the forefront of their sensibilities.

They would be chops and roasts. Harry was called.

Harry Pease, as a killer of pampered swine, favored close personal contact. Too shaky to stand back and take aim, he pressed it to them and blew them away. There was the inevitable spattering, but Harry never missed. He replaced his glasses and wiped his lips.

"To the tables down at Morey's, to the place where Louie dwells..." If Harry held onto the dream, someday the girls might return.

The Return of the Orange Virgin

Folks became attached to their pigs and the necessary step from the backyard pen and into the freezer called for intervention by an outsider. Harry Pease killed the neighbors' pigs every year; he had a regular round and welcomed the extra income from it. Harry's skills were honed by a vigorous consumption of alcohol, and if the old ammunition he used tended to misfire, the pigs were willing to wait. It was a leisurely process, a regular fall event. Harry was called and, in a week or so and right on time, his old truck with his poles, pot, and chain hoist rattling around in back struggled up the rutted hills of Willipaq, its suspension and shock absorbers flattened out by the frost heaves and gully washes of the county roads. The kids were bustled into the family sedan for a day at the Mall, four hours distant. Freezer paper and masking tape were set out on the back porch and beer was left in the fridge.

"We are poor little sheep who have gone astray, Baa, baa, baa... "

One special girl moved forward from the throng, Alma Nightingale. His hands on her waist, she had placed her graceful bare arms on his shoulders and stared into his eyes, a small, dreamy smile of possible surrender touching the corners of her mouth. They had danced close and he had kissed her—once—where her long, sculptured neck met her shoulders. Alma had a beautiful neck that paused elegantly at the edge of her cotton floral print before swooping beneath the taut fabric to become the hidden wonder of breasts, waist, armpits, and eventually, Harry supposed, thighs. A dream of galloping bosoms held in check by the mystery of cotton appliances dissipated and Harry picked up the song again.

"Gentlemen songsters off on a spree, doomed from here to Eternity... Baa, baa, baa..."

As the day wore on the song pulled itself together—Harry had all the lines by heart, but they slid around, dictating their own order.

Harry shot the pig. Eyes closed, head turned away, he held the barrel to its head and pulled the trigger.

Noise. After the shot the pig gave a long slow sigh and sank to its knees, then rolled over. Harry trembled, a long lethargic spasm. There was blood on the muzzle of his old rifle. Not looking at the pig, Harry wiped off the barrel where the plaid lining showed at the bottom of his pants leg, twisting it around in the rolled-up cuff.

Turning his back on the three-legged pyramid with its chain hoist where the pig still twitched, Harry stumbled around to the tailgate of his battered pickup. He chucked the rifle at the far end of the load box. It slid along a drain slat and disappeared under a mound of shredded nets from the herring weir he maintained with two partners. They were last year's and meant for eventual mending. The partners, like the herring, had gone away and left Harry with a pile of useless tack and memories of found money. Once canned, herring became sardines. But a pig became pork. Harry wrestled a 16-ounce can of Seadog beer from its plastic yoke and popped the tab. Drinking it empty, he threw up on the grass, spattering his other pants leg.

Harry felt cleansed of his deed of murder, and turned to his work. Get the pig in the air. Pyramid power. Upsy-daisy with the chain hoist, bleed and peel. He let the blood flow onto the ground.

The second pig nuzzled Harry's overalls, angling for the cabbage.

❑

An April morning. A woman reclined, naked and glorious, on a ledge of basaltic granite high above an eddying tidal pool. Pulling the pins from her coiled hair, she shook free the nine three-stranded braids to fall below her waist. Her red hair, curly and thick, extended to her knees; she stood and spun it about an extended arm, much as a haughty waiter standing by with a towel after the presentation of finger bowls. She stretched, luxurious in the sun, and thumbed a fresh wedge of chewing tobacco into her cheek. She held a book, Bullfinch's Mythology.

The Orange Virgin closed her book with a snap, flattening the dappled sprig of medicinal hellebore she had picked to hold her place. "Ten thousand years and this is the best I can do? And the tale has yet to begin," said the Orange Virgin. "If I am to return to the world of men I must read up on what they expect of me. Silly book, but then devotion is all about appearances. My sacred swine must again be murdered. By this account the gods are stretched back on a cloud with our socks off, reclining with a mulled ale and portioning out the conclusions of destiny. They have forgotten me—a lint in the navel of nowhere. 'Twere sweet to be remembered yet again. I am weary with doing for myself. Sometimes, I wish, sometimes..."

Harry Pease—eyes hazy with cheap red wine and the vision of a red-haired woman—licked his lips for the sweet, sugary residue and polished his glasses on his shirttail. Harry replaced his glasses. One shoulder strap on his Big Yank overalls flapped loose, its brass-plated snap hanger jingling when it hit a rivet.

The Electric Virgin

The Queen of Heaven, Orange Virgin, Fata Morgana, etc., etc. shuddered as the first pig died. On the Other Side, the strain of the sacred pig was breeding true again. And she had not known. How and when does a pig know it is holy and dressed in the raiment of joy? A new pig, a pig of the ancient line, not yet self-aware until the revelation of the final, fatal flash—the pig and its kil-ler knotted in their mutual innocence. "One gets out of touch... I am explain-ing myself. This is all wrong."

There was a grunt from the hole at her feet. The diggers' backs creaked as they chucked the dirt up and over. A sidelong glance, a pause in the rhythm of their digging again acknowledged her presence. Then another shovelful of dirt flew over the revetment, to spill and scatter at her feet. The two were hairy, sweaty; they labored shoulder-deep. They were not hairy all over and matted like woolly mountain sheep, just hairy and sweaty and honest come by both. The tufts that blocked their noses and ears like kapok escaping an unruly mattress challenged one to look away, thus demonstrating good man-ners. Morgana had come looking for them. They must want her in return. "A moment..."

In the hole a throat was cleared—gravely and raspish. The Orange Virgin wanted a favor of her elder dwellers, the earth-spirits of her world of ban-ishment, and she turned her attention to the task at hand. The goddess leaned precariously forward to look over the edge. "You are my tenants. Mine. You are immortal but keep busy. I like that." She was awkward; they had been here first after all. "Oh, dear, I had so hoped we could become good neighbors," said the Lady. "I have a friend—well, not quite a friend but my most newly-anointed priest, albeit he is not yet aware of this. He is much like you. I should have preferred a woman. Oh, dear—I hope I haven't offended you."

The two went at it with a steady pitch and roll, one swinging a mattock, the other nipping in with his shovel under the silver arc of the pickman's return stroke. They appeared to be digging a well while standing in it. If they were aware of her presence they gave no sign, and she pointedly ignored them. There was a protocol to meetings such as this that the parties were content to allow to play itself out. An indecipherable something, most likely a muttered insult, then "...well enough for a displaced divinity," from the hole. She was then ignored again.

She experienced a winging hope, tinged with almond and wintergreen and forgotten these millennia. The line of the White Sow of Naxos—orotund, fast and fierce, the old tub might come again with her spotted piglets to roam the dooryards of Paradise. "She was me and I was she, the White Sow. And a tough old party I was to be sure. A nice sacrifice would bring me up and out of this lethargy of exile." The

Orange Virgin did deep knee bends and jump-ing jacks to clear her head. No, she could not return—but a pig had been killed all the same. Pigs died daily, this was no wonder to be remarked upon. Their hecatombs and myriads privy to a reserved destiny, their bacon and their hams hung in the rafters with garlic strings and braided onions. Unre-markable. A man had killed a pig—that it was a man she was almost certain. Why not a priestess? This was a knotty conundrum. Wide-eyed, fat and trust-ing, a pig soul sent flying to pig heaven whosomever did the deed of murder. He will probably now eat it. Why do they never think to stop and ask?

As long waves of morning light penetrated the curve of the world, The Mor-gana ignored the elder-dwellers in turn and spoke to the ambient sunshine, as though careless of a casual listener. "Morning comes in on an angle, the new day slips up on us. Wagon-wains of business will wait for noon. See how the filtered light plays over fields of long-stalked daisy fleabane; shadows of dew-heavy flowers speak of early Spring or early Fall: an indicator of new-ness."

Or early morning. Something early anyway, an epoch, perhaps, thought the Fata Morgana, stretching, pleased with herself and the moment. The Queen of Heaven squinted against the rising sun, sure that in some compartment of her being she had ordained all this.

"Or if I did not, I should have. Or someone much like me who was here first. This is all such a comfort..."

There was a second grunt from the shovelers in the hole, a break in the rhythm of their digging. Here was a major irritation: they were not used to an accompaniment while they worked.

Pleased at eliciting a response, however small, the goddess continued her colloquy with the sky, the day. She stood on tiptoe, arching her back, and held the pose, relishing a delightful cracking at her joints; then, pivoting languorously at the waist, passed through all degrees of the perpendicular to let her arms dangle loosely to the ground.

"I have touched the empty heaven," she announced to her toes. Crisp blue skies and, upside down and backwards between her legs, an isolated flotilla of upwardly exploding cumulus clouds ambled by. The reversal of perspec-tive said the clouds were 'down,' the ground 'up.' The Queen of Heaven swung gently from side to side, limbering her hamstrings. "And, having col-lapsed like a dime store jackknife, blessed the ground where I stand. Morning devotions, matins to myself, all in the off chance I will be overtaken by a fit of exercise. There is an economy in this and I am pleased." She touched al-ternate toes and enjoyed a pleasant giddiness as blood rushed to her head.

The Return of the Orange Virgin

Swooping to the reed forest along the river bottom, a pair of mating insects stopped in the air, hovering. Morgana straightened to watch them, iridescent green with long striped abdomens and double wings—dragonflies? She let her eyes slide out of focus and followed the traces of their aerial maneuvers to see if they had left her an intuition. They had not. Smells of honeysuckle and jute blossom from the bottomland wafted up the hill. The now dazzling sunlight and the thin, cool air spiked with aromatics carried no other mes-sage. Soaring and dipping, tracing accidental figure eights, the dragonflies flew back up to her over a half mile of hilly pasture. They played out the complexity of their passion and parted to rest on separate twigs. A sunny day in the making with the buzz of coupled insects flying upside down and the growing irritability of a captive audience in the hole at her feet: this was truly life as it was meant to be.

The rising embankment made it appear they had dug deeper than they actu-ally had. She stood an hour and watched them slowly sink into the ground; they paid her no further mind. Eyes bulged and muscles corded with the height of the throw. Their mound was shutting the sun out of their hole and threatened collapse; soon they would be to the rope and pulley, one man down the hole, the other above.

She called down to them. "You are here from the old dispensation." This was an observation, a statement requiring no answer, something they all knew; but, ready for a break, the diggers stopped. There was low talk, unintelligible, then louder for her benefit.

"The Lady wants to talk then, nar?"

"Seems so. Time for a rest then."

"Hoy, Alf, give us a lift." One laced his fingers together to form a foothold and boosted his partner out of the hole. He scrambled up the side of the mound, dislodging a cascade of clods and loose gravel. There was an of-fended "Oof. Hey!" from the hole. Up top, knees were dusted, a cap re-moved.

His proportions were not quite human; under the rolling fabric of his clothes, muscles knotted and bunched in unfamiliar clusterings. A pleated white mus-lin shirt with a ruffled front was drenched with sweat and soiled beyond re-pair.

"Aye, Mum. We wuz here with the Dancing Lords who raised your castle. Meaning no disrespect." He slapped his thighs and raised clouds of dust from maroon corduroy breeches, sandy mauve with blushes of imperial purple where the nap had been worn down by sitting, kneeling, and bulging pockets.

"Your grandfathers' grandfathers' grandfathers were. In service to my prede-cessors, that is—and no offense taken, by the way."

"No, Mum. We were."

"You are immortal, then."

"Never thought much about it. Reckon so. That about right, Alf?" He called to the one left in the hole.

"What's right?" shouted back. "You deal with her, I can't hear for shit down here."

A bad beginning. This was not going to be easy.

"Can't she see we're busy?" The voice from the hole. "Tell her to come back later."

"If you are trying to be offensive, you are succeeding. I am afraid your atti-tude is adding an unpleasant edge to what had started out to be a beautiful day. I am struggling to hold together the shards of my tattered good feel-ings."

"Gobble my goo, but don't she just about talk, then." The voice from the hole held genuine wonder, as if confronted with a reversal of nature. A toad or a bird had acquired the gift of tongues and was declaiming the algorithm of a complex knitting instruction.

The Fata Morgana caught a petulant tone rising in her throat and choked it back, chancing the hiccoughs. She paused, breathed deeply, and began again. "Oh, things are starting off all wrong. I did so hope us to have a meaningful conversation."

"Eh?" from the hole.

The Fata Morgana strode to the edge, leaned over and shouted. "Friends. Let's be friends."

The shorter, sandy-haired one—Alf—looked up and past her, his eyes fo-cused on a point somewhere in the sky. "She wants something."

The Fata Morgana shouted again into the hole, "I am the goddess of Spring, Life, and Beauty, you redundant bumpkin!" She turned on her heels to face the digger who had joined her up top. She dropped her voice three registers and projected moist, insinuating charm. "You may adore me. Misters...?"

"Lamprey and Tawse, Mum—Jack and Alf, if you will. But begging your pardon, we're not into that sort of mumbo-jumbo."

The Return of the Orange Virgin

"I do so hate it when things start off like this. I indeed require some service from you. Sweet reasonableness dictates we should have spoken long before this, being neighbors and all. But... things came up."

"Twelve thousand years," came the voice from the hole, Alf. "Give or take."

The goddess allowed herself to be amused. "We have been aware of each other for millennia and just look: our first meeting and we are in disharmony already, all sixes and sevens. That is a handsome hole, Lamprey, skillfully wrought. But with your friend in the bottom of it and me up top conversation is difficult."

"What is she saying, Jack, she wants to come in our hole? She wants favors; she should be polite."

Lamprey scrambled up the oblique angle of piled earth, sending another fall of pebbles down upon his partner.

"Hoy! Easy there."

"She is suggesting both of us join her on the verge. What say—give it a rest?"

The Orange Virgin followed Jack to the edge and leaned over. "Hail, Tawse. Yes, please join us." Morgana noticed they had dropped their colorful dia-lect. Jack braced a foot against the side of the mound of tailings and pulled his partner up.

The hole had a dry bottom—good footing—and had gotten wider as they got deeper. How did they know where to dig? Thinking of affinities and ever-flowing water, Morgana looked into the ground at their feet. Through the strata she saw a cleft in the limestone shell of the aquifer twenty feet yet lower down—a chancy strike with considerable digging. "There is water closer to the surface, a new spring ready to break through just a hundred me-ters up the hill."

"We are diggers. If we don't dig, what are we then?" Alf paused deferen-tially, lowered his pickaxe and rubbed a handful of earth between his hands. "You mean well, but water that comes easy can go away again just as easy." He felt he had made his point. He looked to Jack for approval.

"You are of the earth and I bow to your superior opinion." Morgana smiled, trying not to patronize. "You are diviners, dowsers? I know there is water there, how do you know? You must be very sure to expend so much effort."

Lamprey—Jack—nodded assent. "Nah, I don't have the skill as a water-finder. The Old Ones—the Dancing Lords—they said here was where to dig should we ever be of a mind to open a pasturage hereabouts."

"Sheep. We have took a fancy to a hillside dotted with woollies."

"That is a handsome hole you have constructed. How'd you like to come and work for me?"

The sandy-haired one looked at her, shielding his eyes from the sun. "Gov-ernment work, then?"

The accusation of a public works project hung in the air. There was quiet. Alf delicately lifted a water strider from the surface of a bucket of water and la-dled out a drink, gulping with a throaty clacking and spilling down his shirt.

"I have decided to lay on electricity."

The clacking stopped and the ladle was passed to Jack. They stood around, uncomfortable with eye-to-eye contact. Lamprey and Tawse shuffled their feet. I am royalty, thought Morgana, feeling the awkwardness appropriate. But they wanted convincing.

"Dirty old wires."

"But in the wires the singing of the hearts of stars."

"The singing wires. Oh, and don't she have a way with words, then? Dirty old singing wires. Where's the magic, the wonder in that, then? Eh? For a little convenience."

"You'll piss away our birthright, then?"

"Pardon my inference, but if you were not born, how then can you have a birthright? Enlighten me, Dear Alf."

"The right to keep on going as we have been. Why this electricity? Progress I'll bet you call it. To run kitchen appliances? To light a filament? And read dirty old books? What's happened to tar and pitch? They give light aplenty; and smoke, too, so's you know where your torches are. Reading rots the brain—keep at it and soon you won't remember a thing."

The Fata Morgana etched a grandiloquent gesture encompassing the sky, the hill and trees. "Living with your heads in the dirt has made you grumpy and out of sorts. This is small recommendation for the conditions of this 'birth-right' of yours. All this is mine. Join me where the air is fresh and clean."

The Return of the Orange Virgin

"Wholesome and energetic, this one, all out-of-doors." Alf stood on tiptoe to stare her in the face. His breath smelled of recently extinguished cigars. "And this is yours, say you. And now ours, an open gift of your munificence. The sun and sky and, by implication the stars at night too, I suppose. Generous."

"You were here first. All I offer in return are open-handedness and civility, an area where you have been short sheeted. It is settled: you are immortals and hence have no birthrights. You are kobolds."

"That is what others call us, Lady. We have no hidden powers." The implica-tion was that she did and that they wanted no part of her. He turned his back.

"Surely, then, neither have I, dear Tawse. Come, let us be friends; you are from the old dispensation and have many secrets I would share. And for my-self—I, too, have no magic quackery."

"You have your beauty and the powers of religion, Lady. We are tenders of the earth. It was your place to speak first."

"I have spoken just this minute—right now. The present I remember quite clearly." Morgana hid a smile. "Can we now be friends?"

"And now this electricity." Lamprey shuffled, acting out a deference he did not feel. "Bear with us, Lady, for we have something to say. It is beneath you, this electrification. We were happy to live at a remove with you, our new suzeraine. Live and let live, eh? We each go our own way. We earth, you sky. Spare us your 'conveniences.'"

"I thought to brighten things up a bit, bring the blessings of technology to the Old Ones' torture pits."

"They was called 'The Dancing Lords.' Not to their faces, of course. They was great leggy beasts, they was," said Jack.

To far-away hearers of their legend, the name suggested grand court balls, courtiers and courtesans exquisite and graceful, intimate with closely whis-pered invitations, twirling as fiddlers skirled exotic threnodies from their tor-tured strings. Cytharae thrummed tempi of seduction and the great drums thumped out a meter concocted to please a drowsy libido—brocaded silks and perfumed beards, braided and pointed with oil of citron and patchouli to lure a lady's favor. Shaved heads with plaited topknots twined with ribbons, pointy-toed slippers glide over floors of polished finely veined adamantine.

No.

"Not hardly human at all, though that weren't necessarily a shortcoming. If you catch my drift." Jack Lamprey was not human and, if you had asked him, proud of it. Jack would volunteer this in the case you neglected to ask.

"They was a twitchy sort, the Dancing Lords," said Alf, Jack's partner. "And their speech was all lispy with strange words."

"Did you understand what the Dancing Lords were saying?" asked the inter-viewer.

"Nar. They wasn't about long enough to bother learning the language," of-fered Jack.

"But they built and they built. Canals, revetments, donjons, castle keeps..."

"They was a lazy lot. Used slaves. Wore 'em out at a pretty clip, too. The slaves of the Dancing Lords suffered. Oh, they suffered. Made me and Alf sad to watch it. But what could we do? They was mortals and none of our business. It was dizzying to watch them all flow by. The Lords wore out every morsel of life native to this planet big enough to swing a pick axe or haul timber baulks. Took 'em generations to wear 'em out. The local stock was sturdy stuff. And they hated the dying; it was hard. But they died."

"The Lords used up anything that could walk or talk. Nothing left when they were through with their building. Except for us."

"And the insects," said Alf. "Don't forget the bugs."

"And all the fliers and the stilt-walkers—the big blue herons that dip for pickerel in the narrows. They survived. Me and Alf was some heartsick to see it all. Can't abide waste. By the time they was through there was nothing left but the dragonflies, the stilt-walkers and us two."

"The great glaciers come down twice to the castle when the Lords was here." Alf.

"They had forgotten their wisdom by then, I figures—thirty, forty thousand years makes even a Dancing Lord forgetful."

The Orange Virgin felt she was losing her grip on the direction of the interview. "Nonononono. What I propose is simply stringing some wire. That is all."

"I have a thought she will have us tunneling in windows next," said Alf. "Fresh air to gladden the lungs of the tormented. Lightscapes and hanging baskets of ferns. Sanding the floors. Nasty, noisy business. Then varnish and paint."

"The dancing lords are gone, the tormented and their accusers forgotten his-tory. You are about building a museum of rent-flesh, then? You would outfit poor Lamprey and Tawse with shiny-billed patent leather caps and we will be collecting admissions. Bright, shadowless electric light to brighten corners where millennial screams yet echo. We will be stumbling over busloads of day trippers."

"Nar, Lady," said Alf, "...you tunnel in through the water table and the moat will fill up your cellars."

A silence surrounded her and reached out to include Lamprey and Tawse. The dragonflies returned and settled in her hair. The diggers wanted to be back at their well, but all three sat quietly, listening to the day about them. The sounds of the sun, the hill, passing clouds. "Oh, dear, I had so hoped we could become good neighbors," said the Lady.

Lamprey stood, dusting his trousers, and broke the silence. "Knowing of your beauty was enough. We are shy folk, enny?" A large jackknife was pro-duced and tossed to his partner. "Give the hooked blade a strop, eh, Alf?" Alf, who had been oiling the blade of his shovel, caught the knife at the end of its arc without looking up.

Morgana sat on the pile of earth and replaited a braid.

Lamprey hooked a fresh dipper of water from the bucket and studied it, stir-ring with a finger. "That you felt it necessary to bestow the reality of your radiant presence..." He drank, slowly, quietly this time, and finishing found the water strider in a patch of vetch and replaced it in the bucket. "... you hold us in low esteem. We are diminished by your being here and being beautiful."

Alf, making a display of having no part in their discussion, had put down the glistening shovel and was stropping Jack's knife, running the blade alter-nately on the haft of the shovel and the instep of his boot.

Jack held a cat's-eye marble to catch the sun. "Here is beauty."

Running a ridged thumbnail around the agate equator, he peeled a layer off the stone to reveal an identical marble within, smaller only by the tissue-thin shell he removed. "This is earth magic, Lady—that everything is exactly as it seems. There are no hidden meanings." The cats'-eye, a crystal flaw in the marble's agate heart, stared unflinchingly from the second layer. "You have come looking for us, him and me. You are the stranger. A name would be appropriate, goddess. You know who we are and want a favor."

"You are not human."

"Can't fault your reasoning, Lady. Then, neither are you. So human is now the standard of beauty?"

"I am finding out just who you are." Morgana focused her attention to the brass pivot in the center of his suspenders. He stooped deliberately to set the cat's-eye down on the ground, rose and began to scratch, keeping his eyes on the marble as though it was in immediate danger of theft. His brow wrinkled, indicating a mind at work. Then he leaned forward and covered the stone with a foot. His brow smoothed and, relieved of an apparent anxiety, he con-torted himself to get after the itch, always just out of reach.

"Ohh..." An awareness spread over his craggy face and a smile teased the corners of his mouth. He turned to look up at her. "Finesse. I like that. A simple itch—no tsunamis or volcanoes. Your credentials are accepted. True bona fides, Oh Sender of Aggravation. You are who you say you are. But I do not recall you having said who you are. If adoration were your due, we may not worship you, sorry about that." Moving his shoe, the digger re-trieved the cats'-eye and polished it on his shirt. He held it to his eye, screw-ing it into the socket like a jeweler adjusting his loupe. After a minute, he turned to her and winked. The pebble popped out to be caught in an open palm held at waist level. He pocketed it.

"We have our own priorities, and they do not include you. Our rhythms are not yours. You are not of this world: an Earth Mother of another earth. And what does an earth need with a mother anyway?" He stamped the ground with his heel. "Poor old duffer, got no Mum then, eh?"

Morgana observed abdominal convulsions held bravely in control: the two of them found this all immensely amusing. "You may address me as Queen of Heaven if you wish." Their faces remained immobile, but their contained spasms continued in silence for some minutes.

"Challenge—change. She is trying to buy our loyalty by offering us excite-ment, an escape from our humdrum, everyday routine." Lamprey gave a snort and his eyes bulged as tufts of hair shot forth from his nostrils accom-panied by twin pillars of dust. He stroked his nostril hair, rolled it into little conical twirls then stuffed it back in.

"Sounds bogus to me," said Tawse. "A come-on."

"You call yourself the Queen of Heaven." His eyes intent on the cat's-eye, Jack Lamprey indicated the blue sky over his hole with a casual wave. "But not this heaven. You must mean another heaven, then. Good.

Then if this other heaven is such a great place why are you not there instead of messing about with us and with our well?"

"I can see you are a rocky garden in which to plant the seeds of the new technology." Morgana, too, songs from the hearts of the stars notwithstand-ing, felt wires were beneath her. The benefits of electrification were to be a gift for her star chamber. "My history is laid out for you in the design on a pebble? You are insightful and prescient."

"And you are yanking our insightful, prescient chains, Oh Queen. Here the stones rule and things move at a slower pace than you are accustomed to. But they do move. We are not so isolated as one might think here away from the glamour at the fast-paced center of the universe."

"Which is, of course, where you come from." Sandy-haired Alf thrust his cigar breath between them. "It is always where they come from, the basis by which all other things are compared. If things there were so great, what are you doing here? It was the same way with the Old Ones. And where are they now I ask you? Extirpation was their mete; and we are but humble antip-odean well diggers scrabbling away in the dirt here in the bunghole of crea-tion."

Fishing the marble from his pocket, Jack spoke to its last peeling, his words low and conspicuously private. He then held it to his ear. Apparently satis-fied with its imperceptible reply, he threw the marble away and spoke. "She is talking fairies. Moonlight dances with tiny toads under mushroom fairy rings. She would have us flit about in our underwear, hovering on little wings, quaint, non-threatening relics of times long dead for the edification of her tourist hordes."

"Pouring wine for her guests. Busloads of blue-haired daytrippers on holiday come after a peep at the past of their imaginings."

"Charon, a suited-up salaried employee, come paddling them through by the barge load: fallen warriors from Knossos, a theme park for the mutilated shades who gladly died, her name claiming their last breaths. See, we know your history, you and your Greeko lads and lasses."

"Then play military waltzes on the pipe organ for the layings-out."

"I am bringing in an electrical generator. Powered by steam, bitumen."

"Bitumen—ugly smelly stuff."

"Dirty old wires."

"Fetch and carry, mop and polish. You are after charnel house janitors. You flatter us with a spurious interest in our well, but you are recruiting pimps and procurers. You would have us flit about on gauzy wings while we plant ferns and sand the floors."

"Hoy, Alf—don't leave out the butt-fucking."

"Aye and then we drop our drawers, tiny diaphanous Greek things though they be, for your gentlemen callers. And where will you be when all this is going on—lapping away at your parlormaids? Not too bloody likely. Thank you for the blessings of your imported civilization, but no thanks."

"You have posited a bizarre scenario of the way things are. Isolation has ad-dled your brains. You are caverniculous fools."

"But fit to serve you."

"Fit enough."

Meet Biff

The Fata Morgana was not expected to kill her lover. Still, the idea was not unattractive. It was just one of those ideas that came to one. Like checking under the bed to see if life had coalesced from the dust balls, or "when my nose itches someone is thinking of me."

She stopped to scratch her nose. "In days past and forever lost, my frenzied women would have lapped up the spillage along with the blood and torn pieces of the bridegroom, tidying. Consummation, then the meal—the wedding feast.

"I had done it because it was expected and now someone is thinking of me and I want to do it again. Damn old White Sow of Naxos. Bloody, savage old thing!" She had hoped to lead her worshipers to an appreciation of the finer things. "But no—blood and guts, blood and guts. Nothing else would satisfy them. I tried." The White Sow was one of her attributes and the cause of the Levitical prohibition against eating pork. "My blood communion and they were jealous. Those camel jockeys couldn't deal with a little competition."

She postulated a conversation with the hypothetical pig-killer. It was only an everyday pig, probably an accident, one of those confluences of malevolent serendipity where everything lined up for no particular reason, and here she saw it as a summonsing to slaughter her love-slave, "...gigolo, dancing boy, whatever. The pig is incidental," said the Queen of Heaven.

The Return of the Orange Virgin

"So are we all. Tell that to the pig," the alleged slayer would say.

"You killed it."

"I was an instrument of forces beyond my control."

"A hairy and time-worn excuse. I used to use it all the time."

"Nonetheless, you postulate that your pig is dead. What are you going to do?"

"Do? Do? What is all this rush to do something? There has been time and enough for these twelve thousand years."

"And you did nothing. Perhaps that is why you are called."

No comfort there. She cut off the invented inquisition and kicked a pebble from her path. Her deposition of the hypothetical accused was over, but the voices continued.

"Blood must answer blood. Kill your automaton then we'll talk."

"He has no blood. You are dismissed. Go away."

Her isolation had made the trivial immense and the immense itself was trivialized by the fleeing eons. It had been a nice touch, the blood communion, and a wakeup call. Whose touch? Whose call? Once a corps of eager priestesses would have done the deed for her. Here she would have to do it herself. Where was the fun in that?

She scratched her nose again.

Things here were not as they had been, yet ever so often she hankered after the thudding hooves, horn tips dipped crimson in the blood of a careless bull-dancer.

"They took such delight in the killing and forgot me at the end. I would really rather have my own snowplow or a little red truck."

❑

Meanwhile, the object of Morgana's brown study responded to a rumbling in his stomach. Tummy, actually. He was tall, lean and broad shouldered—a hero. If he called his stomach a tummy, who was to argue?

Biff Bangtree backed out of the buttery, his pockets full of doughnuts. Biff Bangtree was not yet his name, since Morgana had neglected to call him anything. That he have a name was not a vital component of their lovemaking. "Oops, I beg your pardon," he said as the kitchen door's double swing hinges caught up with his momentum and gently nudged him through. He paused some moments, then quietly slipped back in. Just a few feet, just making sure. Biff had troubles with leaving a room. He felt compelled to check if he was really 'here' or if he had left himself behind. He studied the door's gentle back and forth as it described an ever-shrinking arc. A wide Cheshire smile exposed polished rows of teeth too white, too straight for even expensive orthodontia. No one there. This, then, is me. Giving the swinging doors a hefty push, he dived through just in time.

Passing a mirror, Biff stopped to check if he might be in there and, noticing his cheeks all puffed out, remembered the doughnuts and swallowed. A long brisk walk through the honeycomb of corridors would help him outdistance his uncertainties. When he saw himself, he liked what he saw but felt unworthy. Each mirror was a fresh adventure. Would the handsome stranger in the glass have been recalled, metamorphosed into something less palatable? Biff's anxieties peered out from what he suspected was a disguise to see if it had slipped, parading his good looks in front of an endless succession of reflective surfaces. Putting on an innocent, carefree air, he swung whistling down the hallway.

He was pretty and knew it; his self-admiration could be considered a normal, healthy manifestation. Biff liked what he saw. He ran a moistened fingertip, addressing the composition of an eyebrow. What woman would not be proud to love such a creature?

"Desire is an honest emotion. Never be ashamed of it," Morgana had told him. "Furthermore, it is right that you look to me for nurturing, for you are my chick that I have hatched from the egg of the world we both stand on." Another puzzling metaphor. Biff felt warm, reassured and comforted when she said the words, nonetheless. She had pulled a set of knee-length checkered knickers from a creel she carried slung over a shoulder. "These are pants of the kind called plus-fours. I want you to wear them when you are out and about where the parlor maids may see you."

Swinging around an ormolu panel screening the service stairs, Biff sat on a step and let out a deep, deep sigh that started at the soles of his feet. He had this feeling. A feeling that somewhere deep, deep down in his makeup, something had gone wrong.

Slumped on the stair, his knees supporting his elbows, which in turn held his chin, Biff felt a depression hovering nearby. He had told Morgana about these episodes, but all she said was, "Growing pains, that's all. They will pass. Take an aspirin."

The Return of the Orange Virgin

One of his hands strayed to an ear, toyed idly with it and then, feeling an itch, vigorously went after relief, his little finger diving deep into the auditory channel.

The ear came off.

Biff sat there looking at the ear in his hand and the depression settled lower upon his shoulders.

"Oh shit! Just simply shit!" He threw the errant ear across the hall and reached up to the side of his head where he felt the swelling nubbin of its replacement starting to grow. There was a twinge in his belly. Dinner time. All this fighting the blues and growing new parts took energy. Biff decided another raid on the buttery was in order and stood. The thought of doughnuts and cookies startled the depression and it flew away.

The Raspberry Dream

The dawn chorus of larks and thrushes spinkeled, spattered and trilled. From far off there was a regular, steady thwack as a small boy all alone and bored idly hit a tree with a stick. His continuo offset outraged cawing as a flight of crows worried a homeward-heading owl to roost.

A curlew dived past a swath of sunlight—across, through, and out of sight beneath the riverbank. Last night's frost boiled away from the brown sedge and seregrass, leaving last year's winterkill flattened and wet. The sun, its energy at this hour dampened by its distance from the solstice, was building an illusion of nightfall, not sunrise—twilight on the moors—turning ground frost to steam and the steam to a clinging mist that hovered shoulder high. The Fata Morgana leaned far out to watch vapor traces boiling off a dilapidated hoarding that clung over a vertiginous plummet into the bailey, one hundred feet farther down. An array of scrofulous spikes cold hammered out of bog iron peeled their layers, showering walkers beneath with red rust flakes when the great ospreys shook its timbers with their landings. This year even the birds had given up on the hoarding. Soon it would fall.

Vertiginous, indeed. She allowed herself a shivery thrill at the heights. A momentary self-indulgence. There was no danger for her here. Not here and now. A wry smile. Falling into a moat was at this juncture not what occupied her. It was a long way to the ground just the same—130 old feet. The king's foot. Old feet, old king. That she had not met the raisers of the castle was a regrettable oversight, too late now for a remedy. "Time—a silliness." She shook her head to clear away the moisture from her eyes. "Childish. But I am not a child." In her peripheral vision a pale, red-haired girl flickered and disappeared, leaving a slight tang of horse sweat and daisies. *Who is this child?* thought the goddess.

The Fata Morgana wrinkled her nose and shook her head again. The pretty girl, naked and with high piled coiled red hair returned; she was astride a great chestnut horse. "Well!" said the Orange Virgin, "...if you are who I believe you are, I am certainly glad I felt the psychic wind of your passage and roused myself to give you a proper welcome."

"If I am who you think I am, might you not have prevented ourselves from getting into this stuff all together and saved us both some inconvenience?"

"And who do you think I am, anyway, and while we're moving right along my pretty, just who the hell might YOU be?"

The girl stood—straight, supple, young and beautiful. Her hair unbound falling to the horse's withers. She crossed her arms at the wrists, holding them before her tiny breasts, a mythopoeic gesture the significance of which was not lost on the goddess. "I am the Fata Morgana." The child giggled; her horse snorted.

"That's nice. So am I. Glad to meet you. You are a phantasmagoria fashioned by the norns to plague my thinking. You are an aspect of myself. Go away." The child faded; the horse was left browsing a patch of watercresses, then it too disappeared with an apologetic cough. The Fata Morgana breathed a saffron-scented sigh. *Time and to spare, but for today I shall act my age.*

At the tip of an eyelash a tear formed, glistened, and fell to the empty channel far below. The tear caught Morgana quite by surprise. Tears have their own reasons. She observed its downward spinning through the mist, the tear's coiling descent a path that circled in against itself. The mechanics of its fall changed it from a tear to a sphere, turning the crystal pearl over and over in its flight, examining it as if for flaws. No flaws found, perfection prevailed and the last ten feet it dropped like a rock, inspected and approved, impact assured. The empty moat accepted her tear with a small splat. There is a photographic compression that cheats time with a single motion picture frame exposed at regular intervals that holds to scrutiny the mechanics of flight of a hovering bee, falling water, or the unfolding blossom hidden in a bud. This, of course, is not the real thing but a cinematic trick for the delectation of a posterity that should properly have better things to do during the leisure hours that follow good works. However, posterity doesn't care.

The Return of the Orange Virgin

Turning her gaze back to where the bird had disappeared under the bank, she followed the long rays of the rising sun where they made a trail in slate and muddy gold tones across the river. The ripples generated by the cobbled bottom of the spillway gave the reflection a look of ball-peened pewter with peeling appliqué gold leaf. The sun was higher now, the sky cloudless, all the makings of a fine spring day. The hour of deceptive shadows was done. The only indicators of the season were the white silhouettes where the trees of morning had left an imprint on the grass of their long sunrise shadows. The mist below thickened, ground fog becoming sea smoke, gradually rolling by its own weight to fill the river and overflow its banks, gathering in coves and hollows. The fog settled, waiting for the sun to burn it away. She stretched deliciously, feeling the sun. It was warming up nicely.

The curlew reappeared about its business.

"Welcome to the cosmic capitol, Master Bird," she called, "You will be happy here."

She was the Fata Morgana, Queen Mother of the World, and had built herself a love slave to assuage the lonely days. A handsome piece of work if she did say so herself—wide of shoulder, slim of waist, courteous, considerate, quick to restoke and deferential even when spent, a comely dream of passion fit to set mortal pulses pounding no less than hers. Not human and yet not of the gods, his discretion was guaranteed for at night she simply turned him off. But it was too easy—a household appliance, one would have hoped for more in a lover.

"I have been too indulgent. Why do I have these concerns at being caught out with a gigolo? I make the rules. Such amorous thrashings-about as we have had, it were a pity to tie my enthusiastic stud in a sack and drown him in the moat. But no, the moat is dry and word would get about, and how could I face them then, eh? To put my darling in a sack, which it seems is what I am about, would appear mean-spirited. There has got to be a better way."

She spoke to no one, to clear her mind. Her pretty had to go but she could not bear to part with him. At her feet a vortex of light snow developed. Flurries swirled around her as she set her feet up the rocky path. "The snow will kill my raspberries. Enough, I have done enough for today."

Morgana walked until twilight, an aimless meander. As her mood softened, the snow no longer followed her. The grasses and flowering plants straightened and bloomed as she passed but she perceived this only at the margins of her mind. When a twisted linden tree appeared for a third time, she realized she was retracing a circular route. The path wound up a ridge ascending to the base of one of the castle's great supporting plinths. A clustering of peat and thatch cottages nestled on the far side of a gully. Morgana paused to eavesdrop as a mother and child studied the darkening sky. The young one was working hard at staying up later than usual.

Morgana gently touched the child's mind. It was past her bedtime. She was watching the sky for a sign, hoping to stay up for another hour.

"Ohh, mommy, look." A bright blossoming flared and faded past her finger's end.

"A star exploding." The woman had been a mother many times over many years. The night sky held no new wonders for her. "They do it all the time. Come to bed."

The child had to think quickly. "A minute more, please. I am looking for the V of the eidolons."

The Fata Morgana touched the mind of the mother. Everyday weariness and a gentle concern. She calmed the mother with pride at her wise child.

The mother peered into the afterglow left by an expired galaxy. "Silly girl." A pause. "What is an eidolon?" Eidolon. A new word from school. The little ones were ever bringing home new things; it was hard keeping up.

"They are the wild flying pigs of time, unwinding the stars." The two sat together in the deepening dark, watching the sky for flying pigs.

A wiser child than mine—chalk one up for inventiveness, thought the Queen of Heaven. *I like that child, though her imagination hardly beggars reality*. The Queen of Heaven leaped the little ravine. The sound of her landing startled the two and they jumped to their feet, then bowed deeply.

"Just getting some air. There is wisdom in the stars. Study them well."

"Yes my Lady."

Turning her back, Morgana hunted for the cobbled footpath she knew was somewhere about. She followed it through twisting switchbacks to the castle's foundations where a sally port door was left unlatched. She slammed it behind her and stalked to her suite of rooms.

"I must exact retribution for the death of my sacred swine." The statement sounded harsh and bloody left ringing in her ears. She had been out of practice with summary doomsaying these millennia past.

The Return of the Orange Virgin

"Ah, there, my dear, do you mean exact in the sense of precise or are we back to a mass distribution of wrath and let the undertakers sort out the guilty parties. Let us take stock. To date this day, I have lost a pig I had never met. I stood and wheedled two graceless tinkers to do my bidding—'your rigmarole, my Lady; we trust you find it impressive, we would rather play in the dirt.' Waiting for me at home is an empty-eyed son and lover, my toy who makes me feel foolish and I must destroy. My yearnings for him are a riddle wrapped in a conundrum. He is so easily swept away: 'Destroy the toy,' I snap my fingers and he is dead and I am not satisfied. I shuffle my feet and he is alive again, but I am still not gladdened as are the giggling little parlormaids—'A handsome man stands dancing in the mansion, Ma'am.' They become snippy, delighting in their pretty turns of phrase as they do in their pretty ankles. Home again, home again, jiggedy-jig. Morgana the Queen and her magical pig. Huh! What would they make of that? What do I make of that? Things are becoming more complicated than at any time in the past twelve thousand years. Life has been too simple for me. Cabbages, red kale, onions and the laundry have been my preoccupations. I ask and yet I get no answers. It used to be so easy.

"I must ask myself—self, has someone back where I come from reinstituted my worship on her own hook and without a by-your-leave? I must find her to thank her or destroy her. Or him, though that would be a disappointment. More destruction. Hmm—makes sense today, but then it always does. Aren't we getting all bloody-minded?"

The Queen of Heaven grumped about the castle, content to let matters slide. In a week, Lamprey and Tawse showed up at the quartermaster's, requisitioned spools of wire and headed to the cellars.

❑

The next day, the Queen of Heaven tended her garden, metaphorically, for her preoccupation was indeed with beauty. She spoke to a man, tall and slender, with all the lineaments of male beauty, childishly eager to please though with an absent look about the eyes.

"To have you stalking the halls, my pet, will surely improve the lubricity hereabouts, but nothing would get done. I'm sure you understand." She suppressed a feeling of irritability as she caught herself explaining herself.

"Indubitably, my Queen," came a mellifluous baritone, "Your reasoning, as your beauty, is beyond dispute." Handsome and vacuous, he stood naked at her side. Fair, thin, translucent skin showed off a lean, corded musculature that invited the touch. Morgana ran a moistened fingertip from his chest to where a fresh tumescence was already beginning.

"No," She caught herself. "Enough is enough. I'm sorry, but you've got to go." She traced again her finger's path from a nipple to his groin, pausing to fondle perfectly molded buttocks. All the inviting hollows and protuberances, recycled back to atomic numbers. It did seem a waste.

"Wanna fuck?" her child of clay asked hopefully.

"No, not now darling. Hush, mother is thinking." Conversation was not his métier, but with such an endowment words were superfluous. She had had a bad time with consorts blessed with a quickness of wit and quip. They demonstrated an annoying proclivity to want to move in and take over. Morgana was prepared to return her lover's constituent parts to their respective places in the periodic table of the elements when a passing regret stayed her hand.

"Barefoot and poignant, thus was it ever," sighed the Orange Virgin. "I have discovered feelings for you, and shall not run you through the dispose-all after all."

"Thank you my Lady."

"Oh think nothing of it. As a matter of fact, think nothing at all. Forget me, forget everything. You are embarrassing to have around. Go stand in the corner till I figure what to do with you. Come here first."

"I am here, my Lady." The deference might have contained a spark of wit.

"Your skin."

"My Lady?"

"Your skin, my pet, that integument that your beauty is only as deep as. I would touch it once more ere I turn you off. If only I had made you lobulose and jowly, I could do away with you in a moment. But then you are not lobulose and jowly, for in my inscrutability I have made you more than I intended. I have developed an attachment for you and must look inside myself to discover why. I am deep indeed, for how may I question my own ways?"

A caress followed by a lightly sketched gesture of dismissal, and the golem strode to a corner, to become furniture.

"Did the mechanisms of sacrifice appear in a dream? How did the pig announce itself to my priestess? 'Pardon me, here is my pedigree, I am dedicated to the Lady of the Wild Things, please kill me now.' Highly doubtful. Anyway, I have done no dream-sendings. This was a part of the covenant when I went away.

"Enough of conjecturing," she announced to the naked backside of her silent lover, "the time has come for thinking." She poked up the coals in an incense brazier, added charcoal, and put a kettle on to boil. She crumbled dried leaves of raspberry in the fire and dropped a handful into the pot. When the water had boiled, she threw herself into a chair and put her feet up on the table, breathing in fumes of the raspberry tea.

"Whoever this priest or priestess is who is calling me, one assumes he has a reason. Aha! It is a he... getting my feet up with a cup of tea was always an efficacious maneuver. Let us let my hair down."

She straightened, pulled the pins from her hair and let it fall free, then settled back, her feet again on the table.

"We are also divining your future, too, old stud. You might show some interest." Her lover stared impassively at the wall. "But, of course, you are silent. This is proper."

She sipped at the steaming cup and fell into the half-sleep of raspberry dreams.

Some minutes passed. When she looked up, the puzzle had deepened.

"Almost certainly my priest is a man, gray-haired and wise beyond his great age." There was something wrong with this picture. She again sipped the tea. "Oh, not wise, then. But an athlete, a hero, and fallen on hard times. I am disappointed my priest is a man. It must be women have lost the knack since I departed. This will require some looking into. Gray-haired and wise then, a canny conjuror. But a fool. These are confusing signals. And why is he calling me? There must be a reason."

Harry Does the Lawn

Harry Profitt Pease finished the mowing of the library's lawns, the carefully rationed movements of his afternoon a masterpiece of ergonomics. The last swallow from the final can of the sixteen-ounce Seadog six pack went down simultaneously with the final spin of the riding mower.

Harry was a part-time permanent fixture at the Valiant Memorial Library. In intervals of sobriety he had even been seen washing the windows and swinging a mop in the entry hall. In all his years as the Valiant's quondam sexton Harry had come to look upon the trustees' monthly check as his personal entitlement program. The Valiant's endowment was being eaten up by inflation with each passing year, but of small change there was sufficient to cover the day-to-day expenses: rough-and-ready gardening, storms and screens in season and the occasional heavy lifting.

As the blades of the ganged reel mower heads bounced over a final tussock, Harry pulled his machine to a halt behind the frilly Victorian bandstand and carefully positioned the last empty can behind him on the saddle. "Rest, oh my chariot." A turn of the key, then total, dead quiet. The following cloud of white and blue exhaust hovered and dissipated; there was a few seconds' pause as his hearing returned, then the world welled up around him, filling the ringing silence. Too late to go and shoot baskets. He hitched up his suspenders and looked back on the perfect pattern the mower had laid out with its last 180 degree turn. A neat semicircle, satisfying. Where there had been engine noise was now birdsong, distant children's voices and the slam of a car door from the Red and White parking lot. The good life.

The beer left a pleasant haze and a mild residual buzz, and Harry Pease sat and pondered, watching the lights on his multi-band scanner. Long shadows in the afternoon, the time of rest with the smell of gas, grass, sweat and Seadog wafting heavenward. "Lord, I have labored and now I seek my ease." Harry's pronouncement of the work ethic. Work, now play. But before play, rest.

A Velcro strip on the dash plate held the scanner on the riding mower. There was a Velcro strip on the dash of Harry's truck, too, because you never knew when something might happen. Nothing was happening now, no activity on the bands, just the march of red LEDs on the sequencer, and it was good, good to sit at rest in the afternoon and watch the lights in their chase from left to right. Harry sat on the mower listening to the police and fire bands until dusk.

Alma Nightingale's flower print sashaying down the hill called Harry from his reverie. If pressed, he would have admitted to dozing off. The determined swing of Alma's hips brought her through a budding bower of sycamore and maple gapped with the stumps of great elms. Her progression reminded Harry of youth and joy. He switched off the scanner, dusted the drying debris of scattered clippings off the knees and out of the rolled-up cuffs of his coveralls, and moved down the hill.

Their paths crossed at the after-hours book return box—a regulation government mailbox painted blue and welded shut. Vandals had regularly dumped snow into the box in the winter, and in the summer, the library's hours being so inconvenient, the few pensioners in the neighborhood who did check out books returned them at the desk. It was a monument to well-intentioned futility. The trustees eventually had given up on the box, and during a meeting later written up in the newspaper, in which they hotly debated the proposed sale of the heirloom grandfather's clock from the library's foyer had, with no objections, no abstentions, voted to call in Harry with his acetylene torch to close it forever. The meeting broke up in acrimony over the clock. A faction that favored selling it to buy books for a children's reading program adjourned to the WilCo Diner for coffee. The clock, the children's books were never spoken of again. However, the after-hours book drop got welded shut, removing forever a relatively innocent outlet from future generations of vandals who, deprived of this middle ground criminality, would move directly to larceny, grand and robbery, armed.

"Oh, hello, Harry." That was all. They had gone out a couple of times in high school when Harry was a basketball star. Alma had married Vern Nightingale, a reliable man. Harry's star had fallen on bad times.

Harry recalled that Alma had asked him to fix a broken washing machine once. Was that last year or last week? Anyway, he should by now have a replacement machine for her in his sights. Maybe he did; things got confused. "Hiya, Alma. Still keeping my eyes peeled for that washing machine you're after."

As a child young Alma Nightingale had daydreamed a life beyond hanging the laundry, beyond the Red and White, a life worth writing down. At sixteen she bought an empty book—padded pink satin covers with a clasp—and had faithfully kept a tally of everyday doings all through her sophomore year. Her life, the lives of her friends and all she knew, were dull, common, ordinary, boiled ham and buttermilk uneventful, their yearnings without substance except for those things she would never write in a book for fear of an unauthorized reader prowling through her possessions. Alma wished she had the spunk to make things up. Instead she put it by.

She had picked up the diary project again when in her thirties, feeling quite the young matron with the kids out of the house and the strangeness of free time in the middle of the day that was hers and hers alone to fill as she pleased.

Reading the entries from twenty years earlier, a year's worth of round exercise book script riding the blue lines, Alma remembered wondering as she wrote, Will I ever read this? What sort of person will I be when I read this?

She had had an image, a spiritual template of the woman she would become in maturity, a woman like the summer people she saw each year—sophisticated, a busy wife and mother, a woman at home in the world wearing jeans, casually unconcerned with the appearance she presented to the world—a kerchief about the hair driving a station wagon on her many errands. These women and their children came in early June, their arrival heralding the start of the summer season. They opened houses, spoke authoritatively with electricians, nurserymen, carpenters, plumbers, the deliverers of bottled gas; they and their money were in command. Slim and stylish with a dab of potting soil on the cheek, a stray lock of hair springing from under their bandannas, they drank in the afternoons and bought gin and scotch at the state agency liquor store. These women kept diaries, wrote, some painted all through the summer—seascapes and landscapes that to Alma were startlingly good, well executed. These were women who did things well, who were beautiful, worshippers at the shrines of their own inner fires.

In August the husbands arrived by train from Connecticut, New York City and Philadelphia, pale and overweight wearing khaki pants that had been ironed just like dress pants with creases, sweaters that had been dry cleaned, not blocked and dried on towels on the floor over the cold air return. The men got off the trains smoking king-size cigarettes to be met by the station wagons. The couples kissed. The men wore belts, not suspenders. The husbands put on floppy hats and pottered about their yards, drank in the afternoon and played tennis—mixed doubles with other couples from away—on the asphalt courts behind the high school.

At sixteen the blank pages had been a duty, a responsibility to her future self. She had seen herself years hence, a stylish matron weary of ceaseless involvements and obligations, seeking sound advice from her younger self, slipping back into the silent past and rediscovering how things really were before they got complicated.

Things had never become complicated. Alma's husband died punctually and in good taste after thirty years of boring fidelity. There was a modest annuity.

Alma found herself thinking of Harry often—more often now that Vern was gone—as the years piled into decades separating them from their high school romance. Was it a romance, really, or had they only gone out together a few times?

The smells of fresh cut grass and oily exhaust with the roar of a two stroke engine two blocks away had said Harry was doing the library lawn. He had been at it for hours and that meant he was drinking. Riding circles and massaging the turf till the beer or the gas gave out.

They met at the useless blue book box, both feeling a vaguely remembered call of the glands. Alma had put on a flowered print silk dress, a summer frock, and wore her hair up. Too early for silk, but down parkas and thermal underwear cramped her style; she had a lovely throat and shoulders.

"A... washing machine. That's nice." Mild surprise although it was he she had come to see.

"Gotta go, Alma." Harry, embarrassed at being drunk, did not meet her eyes and dived into the open bulkhead doors that led to the library's cellar.

❑

The wonder of the approaching 21st Century was not totally lost on the Valiant Memorial Trust Free Library of Willipaq, Maine, U.S.A. A hundred-year-old brick building and a superannuated librarian, thirteen volumes of the Oxford English Dictionary, a Britannica, a World Book and the complete works of Louis L'Amour in paper and hard back, and yet Mrs. Gladstone, the librarian, wanted more. She dreamed of a computer lounge where patrons might log on to the state catalog and browse electronic books with the click of a mouse. "Buck Rogers and Willipaq, Maine," she confided to Alma Nightingale as they despaired the future over sherry and cookies one evening, "Are ships that bump in the night." It was Mrs. Gladstone's second sherry and she was tiddly. The library was open afternoons Tuesday through Thursday, noon to eight on Friday when slides were shown in season. Against possible future need, an opaque projector was kept at ready in the attic. "The overhead projector brings such life to a flannel board presentation," Mrs. Gladstone remarked, the seminars and meetings that big city libraries hosted never far from her mind.

The trustees felt their responsibilities keenly but not actively, for the local library was a popular legatee. With every will probated yet another bequest filled out the shelves with more mysteries, westerns, romances in paperback, and the timely passing of a quirky science fiction collector had filled one bay from floor to ceiling with book club editions. The trustees were solid men, steady and with a sense of history. They felt the Valiant Memorial could afford to wait and let attrition pack its stacks with poundage.

Joyce Gladstone, at an age when the obituaries were the first item turned to in the paper, avoided that page, apprehensive lest her interest precipitate another vanload of books. Sometimes the thought of Harry Pease and his collection of Popular Mechanics and Playboy magazines stalked her nights, interrupting her blameless sleep. She dreaded finding Harry's name listed among the newly dead.

Morgana and the Eidolon

There was a summoning and, distracted, Morgana lost her raspberry dream. She was wrenched through a curtain of red ruin to a place where a universe waited to be born. There was nothingness. But not quite. Spinning. Forgetfulness and no sense of self. Spinning and an awareness of something gone wrong. Everything was gone but a throbbing that would have been pain. Now that was silly, either it was nothing or it was something. A wanderer in the void, she caught at it, held it, cherished it, and felt the pain, drowning in a firmament of agony.

The throbbing now came in waves, and in the interstices, grateful for the relief, a sliver of self-awareness glimmered and made itself known.

This, then, must be death. I am dead. But I am something. The nothing is not me. Whoever I was before whatever happened must have possessed a fine sense of irony; that at least, has survived. And unless I am mistaken, more than an irony has come through whatever catastrophe precipitated this nothingness, for I appear to be an "I" and the "I" I appear to be is consciously cogitating.

The accretion of smugness that was these thoughts winced, cowered and forgot as the pain struck.

The agony rolled in waves, surrounding her. There was only the pain, obscuring tantalizing wisps of memory at the edge of consciousness. Yes—a loss! She had lost something precious! If she could only hold back the pain long enough to remember. The paralyzing pain rolled in another wave, mocking her, leaving her numb and empty. The pain! And with the pain a sense of futility and mockery that obscured tantalizing recollections.

Yes, she had forgotten a precious thing; if only she could get a handle on it. She was a hiccup in the cosmic process and she was bewildered. There had been a familiar, comforting presence, and it was missing. Power! That was it; she had none. Power defined by its absence gave small comfort. She had had it—now she didn't. The Fata Morgana felt a melancholic longing for her departed power. Not power to do anything in particular—threaten, coerce, destroy: illuminate a city, tighten the skeins of a siege engine, or wind up the bowels of a child's clockwork toy—just power to have around. Just in case. There was this feeling—what had been hers, was now not, and that troubled her. There was that in the emptiness that defied a firm grip. Just the familiar, reassuring bulge of potential, there to quiet her unease was not much to ask. But who to ask?

In the permeating emptiness, a bland, featureless wall announced it would be pain again if she would but allow it. In measureless time awareness returned, and with it discovery that the pain had lessened to a throbbing which, in turn, as stars were born and galaxies defined, diminished to an annoying tintinnation. Born anew, the universe boiled, simmered, and went off to cool—just past the edges of her perception, to wait. She awoke.

Now that was strange, I distinctly remember nothingness. All this would appear to be a somethingness. But where is it? I recall Chaos through the fumes of sleep, and Chaos, at least, is something. "Where am I? Who am I?"

"Very appropriate," said a voice close by. "Your utterances, that is, for you remember nothing and you want some answers. At the moment you are a point, a very big, very heavy point—a point with a past—but still a point, and an awareness, not much more. But at least you are someplace, and that is considerably more than what you have left behind can say for itself. Being someplace is what a point is all about," the voice added gratuitously. "Even Eternity's gotta start someplace, right? Don't worry, be happy."

She looked about and saw a shimmering curtain, an aurora borealis of dancing pinks and fuchsias backlit in blue. A bird poked its head through a rift in the curtain. "Poetic, isn't it? A beaded curtain in a house of pleasure, seen through the haze of passion, a forest fire just over the horizon and always out of reach." It was the voice. "You will never see the real thing. You may only infer its existence from secondary manifestations."

The bird, a duck, motioned her over, and to her surprise, the goddess discovered she possessed a volition. The wanderer stretched and felt her strength, small but there. She approached the bird.

The bird flipped a coin, a considerable feat for a duck.

"What happened? I remember nothing, but there was something: pain, a great noise..."

"You have an admirable facility for understatement. What you have just witnessed and cannot remember is the end of everything and a new beginning—the Big Bang. Yearnings, struggles, joys: all the paradigms, apotheoses, covetousness, sloth, envy, etc., along with dandelions, cabbages, butterflies—the hotel reservations and weekend painting projects of a googolplex of individuals are over, caput, finis—sucked through the eye of Eternity's needle, pushed out backwards on the other end, and here you are. Simple, really."

The goddess was spinning and dizzy, and the ringing in her ears encompassed the cosmos.

"No excess energy," said the duck, "but sufficient to your needs. We remember what went before, but when the Big Bangs come, all else is lost. You have made it through a Big Bang. You are the only recorded case of a redundancy. There is nothing done without a reason, except ever so often to keep us on our toes, and there is a reason for this, too. You are an anomaly, my friend, so keep a low profile." The bird snuffled about under a wing as it groomed its feathers; it flipped its coin.

The coin spiraled into the air, an upward silver waterfall. "This is money. Look and remember it. This bit of money will be ever buried in the flow of commerce, known only by the transient, nugatory phenomena that follow it—a stuck abacus ball, a well-formed formula that won't factor out. A bump, a blip, a nit, a nubbin, a trifle—the snake that can swallow a goat has gulped down a cherry pit. Few will possess the coercive intent to lure it out into the open, for seeming to have value, it has none: it is a symbol, a marker, a pretty bauble that I picked up and for which I have discovered an affinity. A token of sentimental value exclusive of its intrinsic worth—detect its contrariness against the passive background of commerce. The money is an allegory, all money is an allegory, do not be deceived by what it seems to mean."

The duck carelessly flipped its coin and looked meditative. The coin accelerated up and away. The Orange Virgin, Fata Morgana, etc. and the duck waited for its return. It did not return.

"They, the raisers of temples, the populations who sought to forestall your rages and propitiate your insouciance—a bother and a needless drain of public monies considering where we stand today—they have happened to you no less than you have happened to them." The duck produced a large, thin sheet of a crinkly stuff and spread it flat between them. "This is a newspaper picture, a representation of something else—not it, but it. Get it?"

The Return of the Orange Virgin

"I forget. Refresh my memory." The goddess had seen pictures before, but where eluded her; the gate to yesterday was locked.

On the page a giant railroad engine billowed steam and cinders, tall sticks with looping wires that lined a traction system of parallel rails were a blur as it sped past. "Look closely, for this is an allegory; if you are going to be of any use, I must explain you to yourself and allegories are easy and fun."

The picture was in shades of gray except for a blazoning of orange letters on the barrel of the steam train's plated boiler—'Santa Fe.' The great machine was going at a pace to somewhere off the page. The land it traveled was a desert, but distant green mountains gave a promise of verdant rainfall and hospitable conditions. Orange letters proclaimed 'New Mexico—Land of Enchantment.'

"Don't worry about the content of the picture, the representation is meaningless. Look close." The page filled more of the available cosmos, nudging accretions of stellar gas out of the way.

"It is made up of dots," said the goddess dutifully.

"Those are the people," said the eidolon. The paper once more lay manageably between them and spiraling clouds of incandescent gas rushed back to fill the place it had been. The dots were no longer observable as when 'New Mexico—Land of Enchantment' filled the void.

"Follow the dots. Hmm. Dots are an algorithmic convention for chance. Fate, my exemplary Fata Morgana, is a straight black line, unbroken. The dotted line represents some small hope for a future. For you, at least. And the pathetic groundlings with which you populate your creation. They worship you, old puissance. *The morons do love to have their heroes.* That's an H. L. Mencken quote."

"Who?"

"The Doctor or the pronoun? Picky, picky, picky. I could quote Mark Twain, if you like. Shakespeare should have something appropriate to a disenfranchised goddess. Let's see…"

The eidolon pretended to fuss with the New Mexico poster.

"We were talking about connecting the dots."

"The dots make the picture," the duck thrummed. "People are the dots. You are the picture. That is a metaphor. Get it?" The duck studied nothing in particular.

A yearning to be once more alone subsumed her fears and gnawed her being. There was a thought that at another time she would have wiped the duck to Limbo with a wink. No. Its voice was annoying, but it was all she had and she clung to it for fear of being left alone in Chaos with the yearning.

"Who am I? Who are you?"

"You are dead, old puissance. But for my intervention, as dead as planked mackerel. It's all over for you and you are as blotto as the most tenuous ephemeron. But don't let this get you down. Keep busy. When you're dead you tend to let things slide and that is a regrettable sloppiness. Stop keeping up with things and they go all to hell. I am an eidolon, an image on the edge of things, and you are one very fortunate prime mover who has been granted a second beginning. Don't ask me why, I just work here. And there." The voice indicated a place beyond the present absence of anything.

"A prime mover?"

"And spectacularly lacking in wisdom and restraint. For one all-wise and all-powerful, that is. Your intransigence precipitated the inevitable. The end came early because of you, but don't be glum. Inevitable, right? Just early. The reality plateau just blown away might have bumbled along unconcernedly for just-about-ever, but all that has been precluded by you. You just don't remember it because it's all gone. I am here; you are here. All because you dived snoot first into that raspberry compote you love so well. Got it?"

The voice signaled a shrug and the goddess sensed a preparation to depart. "No I don't 'Got it'. Please stay and explain." There was a pause, largely for effect, and the eidolon continued grudgingly.

"You are here today and alive because a pig has died; a human has shot the Morgana's prize pig. 'I'll bet the Morgana didn't even know she had a pig, but she is sure to do something impulsive, running madly in all directions and that.' That's what they're saying, you know. The pig didn't know it was yours either, my dear, but ignorance is what makes bacon. Nor did the man who pulled the trigger know what he was about. He was drunk at the time, no excuse." The voice became businesslike. "'A pig has died and she will be fair puggled,' that is what they are saying."

A pig. The goddess felt the inner passages of her nose tingle at a full aromatic assault: piquant overtones of sizzling bacon—spicy fat with wood smoke seasoning. And salt. Salt—she squirmed with pleasure at the evocation of taste. There were fleeting images of sausage curled into ropes. A curly tail. Four legs and pink.

"You have wrapped yourself in an institution and, seeking the safety adoration brings—incense, offerings and prayers, find instead your radiance eclipsed, obscured by a body of commentary. The giver of light and law, you are now defined by the faithful, and your obsequies expropriated by them; you are lessened, codified and trivialized, and eventually absorbed into the body of the faithful who made you and whom you made. The dots have called the picture back for an accounting. They have co-opted your coercion. You, oh Great One, have failed them, and they turn upon their creator. Dots and goddesses—money talks and nobody walks. They are the parts but you are the power and will not be diminished. In one final blaze of glory you extirpate your constituency. Silly girl, there has got to be a better way. It would be pusillanimous to say that you and the humanity that worships you are beneath our notice. We just hadn't bothered with you or them till now. Unfortunately, we have inadvertently waited for the last minute, and it is nearly too late for a fix. *Now*, of course, is a moderately subjective concept; and since you are here in a robust good health lingering on at my pleasure, we shall use my definition of what, where, when and why *now* is. This is no small thing, I hope you appreciate this."

The smugness was becoming much to bear. Hoping to get close enough to throttle the creature, the goddess nodded her appreciation.

"Good," the bird went on, "It is not our agency to become involved. You will be our agent."

"Agent? A hireling, an employee?"

"Of a certainty, for there has been a collision of interests and we must all swallow our pride. The Orange Virgin will be returning to the Earth of her exile to look after her pigs and her passions. She will be a royal pain in the ass—this is what they say. This much I will reveal to you," said the duck. The creature made to depart.

"Wait! You raise more questions than you answer. Who is this Orange Virgin?"

"Somebody. Oh, yes, definitely somebody. An old friend—you perhaps. Meanwhile, you wait. Sit back and enjoy the view. But don't be taken in by externals, things are not always what they seem. F'rinstance, here I am a duck. Think about it."

The goddess pondered that.

"You are not a duck."

"And you are a crafty, incisive schemer and have seen right through my little artifices. We understand each other. Keep the lid on things for me and you will live. 'The Morgana is returning,' they will say, '...all wrought up over her stupid pig. She will want to change things.' I like things the way they were. Baseball has been very good to me..."

"Baseball?"

"The local idiom, you'll get used to it. Things have changed since your departure; I am all you have, remember that. You were once called by a plenitude of names in as many tongues. Men held you in their hearts and prayed to you in their despair. But all that has changed. They are gone who worshiped you, their fountain of mercy and well of grief, and all the books and movies too, that glorified your name glorify Mine. Ah, yes, *your* Name."

And the Orange Virgin remembered who she was.

"You! El, you double-dealing, patronizing, duplicitous conniver. You are no eidolon; you are flimflamming me."

"Tush, tush. Morgana, please... Remember where we are."

"I remember very well where we are. Nowhere. This is neutral ground. We speak as equals here."

"I need you in place, in the world of men."

"You are contaminated by your constituency. You are even talking like them."

"Darling girl, it's your pig. Do you want to live on through eternity and never know what went wrong?"

Silence, then a sigh. "You've got a point there. What has happened?"

"Very well, then—plain talk. I haven't the slightest idea what happened but I am prepared to cut you a deal."

"You want me back. To pull your chestnuts from the fire. I remind you, I did not seek to be reinstituted. On the world of the Dancing Lords I am no threat to you, sky demon."

"Nor I to you. We are both playing our parts. Well, just see what we have here." The flipped coin returned, spiraling down from an extended absence. The eidolon reached out and caught it.

"Parlor tricks. I would have expected something more elaborate. I had not finished speaking. I have demands upon my time."

The Return of the Orange Virgin

"Which is unlimited. Spare me that, Morgana. You were romping with your honeypot. The golem is symptom, and not the malaise. Seduced by comfort you have risen to the bait. You have lost the game and you didn't even realize. The penalty is to play out the events of someone else's choosing."

"And you are that someone. Don't make me laugh. Ha-ha."

"If you inflected your laughter it would sound more sincere."

"Ha-ha. There again. You want me to wander in a shadow play of linear existence among the poor bozos who walk *your* Earth? This is indeed a chuckle. What do I get out of all this? It is to be a comfort to me in my sunset years to know that you have so graciously conceded to me a part, however small, in your master plan. Who am I, after all, but the mother-creator of the object in question?"

"Please, we are discussing a situation, not an object."

"Any situation must be an outgrowth of your incredibly convoluted machinations. El, you were always such a schemer."

"You belittle the universe with your spurious profundities, my chickadee. I defer to you because you were here first, so figure it out for yourself. If you had been paying attention you would have known this and saved yourself the bother of a call. Have a nice day." There was a boreal trembling indicating imminent departure.

"Wait! You called me."

"So I did. The eons must be catching up with Me. I will allow you in to straighten things out. With your looks you could be anything; how's about a little collie dog?"

"Beg pardon?"

"A dog. The acoustics are a mite shabby here at the birth of creation, I concede, but you heard me clearly."

"I hear you well enough, my old and rare. A dog will be fine—a spirit-beast as my aspect. I can relate to this. It is the race and flavor of said canine to which I object. A little collie dog is so redolent of Lassie and Timmy. Something big and yellow, I should think. To go with that snowplow or the red truck which I was promised but never received."

"Fine. A big yellow dog, then. *De gustibus non disputandum*, as they say. You are invited over—no strings. Only a few conditions—the dog thing among them. It won't do, after all, to have you charging back all naked and glorious and grabbing up everything that isn't nailed down for yourself. Someone would be sure to recognize you. I need to know if this is an accident or if there are other hands at work. If we make this a mutual effort—yours and Mine—there can be no question of hanky-panky if the Great Author calls us to account."

"Aha! I get it. You think you are being audited. Have things gone that poorly then for humanity in your patch?"

"*Comme ci, comme ça.* Iffy as always. They meddle with the building blocks of creation, but they are ever the same. They think they have discovered the principle that drives the cosmos. What do they do with it? They play electric guitars and boil tea. Now, I ask you... They are such monumental bunglers as to present no immediate threat. To Me."

"But to me. Ah, I see. You have a problem. And you want me to negotiate an elucidation."

"Yes, Lilith Mine. You are still accomplished at your dream-sendings? I have just the companion for you. A noble chap. I have a name for you. A name and a location. Harry Pease. Harry Profitt Pease. Your priest. Prepare the way, then."

Sarabande

"Harry Profitt Pease, eh?" The Queen of Heaven opened her eyes. She was home. She drained the cup of raspberry tea. "Smooth, El. Simply smooth."

She rose and swatted her golem on his backside. "Whether to destroy this Harry or let him play some deeper game; you shall help me to decide. I shall delegate, and solve two problems at once. You have received a reprieve, my embarrassment, my love. Thank you for the tea and sympathy, my silent lout. We shall prepare an education for you and bond you to this priest all unawares, weird and tanist as in the old days, for I fear he has not the slightest idea what he is about. But you must be born again, an inconvenience for both of us, I am sure." She touched his toes and the top of his head. "Spin, please."

She held a spindle of transparent material that stretched and clung to itself in successive layers. She wrapped his body as the silent golem rotated lazily about the pivot points she had established. "You must gestate by yourself, for I have business elsewhere. Inside your cocoon you should be free of all interference by eidolons, demiurges or whichever displaced deities. My old adversary is on the prowl. He would send you back as a paraclete. 'Are they not waiting for a comforter, after all?' says he. I shall send you first, on my own hook, as it were. We shall

---

The Return of the Orange Virgin

peel back the layers of your personality as the jolly tinker with his 'earth magic' peeled back the layers of his marble. And when you emerge—viola!—a butterfly. A malleable personage more easily slipped past the guardian spirits of this world who, in your present form, find you indigestible."

She turned to leave the room. "I think we will find you a tutor, build you a nursery, and get you an education. You shall be a fine, upstanding, uh... golem."

❑

A transplanted humanity had flourished in the soil of Morgana's new world. She seldom troubled with them and they in their turn regarded her with proper awe and gave a wide berth when she walked among them. They signaled their deference and respect at a safe remove and went about their lives. It was like having pets. That she should feel envy of them was not a question. Going one-on-one with these hothouse flowers was a melancholy necessity. Their time was so short.

"And I am theirs as much as they are mine. They bloom and fade, then die. And I do not die and they do not find this strange. Why do I? They invent themselves, going backwards from the moment of their deaths, prey to violence, wistful longings and silly enthusiasms. These creatures have no sense of proportion but an immense capacity for forward motion." By the time one had finished a sentence there was a new one, a son or daughter or granddaughter or great-great-grandchild standing in the place where the young Pettifoile or the pretty Sarabande had stood just a blink and whisper before, now shriveled, dead and gone to dust. "They have no room for doubt—I am the faith that gives them meaning. Could I not have seen it in her eyes, little what's-her-name from the other day?"

That look of guilty surprise when I come upon them unawares. "And how little what's-her-name had jumped when I caught her stroking my golem's naked belly. She was absolutely bug-eyed at his erection." *Doesn't she know he is always that way?* "Why the child was positively gibbering—drooling lust become terror in an instant of discovering me there. Am I not the Mother of the World? Could not I have foreseen this?" *A little more prescience, please.*

Exiting into the hallway, the Queen of Heaven latched the door behind her, a thing she could not remember ever having done before. She jammed one of her hairpins behind in the channel with the latch shuttle, an announcement to her fragile mayflies that it should remain unopened. *They are secure in the knowledge that if I do this sort of thing, their husbands are safe. But yet they are tempted. So I go to the cellar to talk to stone heads*

She marched along a vaulted arcade and into a cloistered patio open to the sky. Geometrical plantings of household herbs, rosemary, borage and thyme, displayed early flowers. She found their precision calming, and trod gently among the early budding herbs.

The goddess, spying a familiar face with a hail, accepted the reverence due her, graciously acknowledged her postulant, and picked up their conversation from its last stopping point. There might have been a lapse of centuries as humankind counted the years so scrupulously, having so few of them.

"Oh, Sarabande, as we were saying the last time we so fortuitously met..."

And the hauntingly familiar features, delicately, diaphanously Sarabande—petite, lovely and attentive—wrinkled in surprise that the goddess had singled her out for a chance converse. "Oh, my Lady..." Kneeling in the fresh spring mud of the greensward, she ruined her gown.

"Sarabande, look at me."

The averted eyes rose to those of the Fata Morgana. Adoration, some trepidation, worshipfulness. No fear there—faith, adoration, trust. How to ask the question?

"Sarabande?"

"Lady?"

"Sarabande, I know this is becoming tedious for all of us, but you are not the Sarabande to whom I last spoke, are you? I mean you are truly beautiful and there is that in the curve of your mouth and the shape of your ear, the very turn of your hair—the way it exposes the notch, that tiny irregularity at your widow's peak when you tie it back like that. You *are* Sarabande, the Superintendent of plantings and the Herbarium?"

"Assuredly, Lady. But the one to whom you spoke was my great-great-great-grandmother. The time you appeared to her has been treasured by our family, and I and the mothers and daughters before me have your request picked out in the embroidery of all our chemises, lest we forget and by so doing inadvertently dishonor you."

Morgana felt inexplicably weary. Their lives were so short. "And the reply?" She asked the lovely mayfly.

The Return of the Orange Virgin

"Yes."

"That is all—yes? What was the question, I mean what is it you have accomplished or I have caused to be performed that you and the line of Sarabandes before you have deemed of such moment so as to incorporate your reply into the embroidery of your petticoats?"

"The arbors of honeysuckle and wisteria, Lady." Had the Goddess forgotten? Sarabande pulled out her shirttails and proudly displayed an intricate stitching of whorls and flowering trellises, evidently the rest of the message. "We have moved them to the far side of the bailey, as you asked, and installed a planting of bellwort and lattice flowers in the shape of a Mycenaean spiral hedge. The labyrinth is completed since the time of my grandmother. We hope it finds favor in your eyes, Lady."

The weight of her fine blonde hair—but for the triple-stranded braid that held it back from her eyes—falling free to her waist, crowned with a wreath of plaited daisies, her eyes respectfully downcast, chin a-tremble at being in the presence of godhead, Sarabande was one of those tragic crumbs of life's picnic the wind blew about. She looked so like her great-great-great-grandmother. The Sarabande who had received her orders had spoken through the lips of this fair child, trembling with love, not fear, here this afternoon.

"It does, my child. You have done most excellently. When you perform your solstice obligations, tell your grandmother's spirit she has wrought well and I am pleased."

Sarabande made a curtsy and backed off a few paces. As she departed, a saucy swing articulated her slim waist and wide, shapely hips. In her mind the audience had gone well.

And in my mind, too, thought Morgana. *Though we have arrived at differing conclusions. The golem—my child and lover—he is closer to them than to me.* "So the child has eyes for the golem. How well she hides it." There was a thump and a backfire from out behind the postern gate. An oily billow of black smoke rose to the sky.

"Ah, my electricity. The jolly tinkers have prevailed."

The thump again, then a steady throbbing, and an acrid wind with the smell of smoldering bitumen. Morgana sneezed.

"I see progress has its price," said the Lady as she wiped her nose on an embroidered sleeve. "The price is advice. I shall follow the jolly tinkers' wire to my star chamber and have some converse to cleanse my mind."

Electricity Comes to the Star Chamber

The house that was a city grew and, as is the way with cities, buried its past beneath an ever advancing present. In the cellars of the Queen, where three corridors met to form a Y, three stone heads graced the capital of a buried pendentive. They were figments, and existed nowhere in nature. They were the past and they were buried. They had been surrounded, enveloped and eventually forgotten in a subcellar of the great masonry sprawl as addition after addition was piled over them. The settled dust of thousands of years had raised the level of the floor and grown hardened by the footfalls of passing errands. Lime leached from all the stories above had marbled the black granite walls and joined with the dust of the floor to form a polished cement. The heads were malign at first glance, a dead craftsman's nightsweats and horrors: vaguely a cow, a goat, and a manticore. Each had some resemblance to the beast it portrayed—and not without an idiot twinkle—but seen through a glass cast with a ripple in it, reflected in a mirror with peeling silver. From the clustered heads a tongue thrust well into the corridor at ankle height, a peril to trip the unwary.

Mineral deposits had whitened the Goat's tongue and striped his head so that his tongue appeared to have paused in the fastidious licking of an ice cream cone. The Goat's dead eyes were rolled back, hollow stone pupils positioned to stare up the kilt of any passing visitor. This was a nice effect, although by accident of positioning rather than of prurience, for the level of the floor had risen. In former times he had been out-of-doors and his gaze had been heavenward, away from the temptations of the earth and the flesh, an allegorical figure. Some sincere soul had in ages past painted a green trim line at shoulder height perhaps as a guide suggesting direction though there were only two available, thither and yon. It was a nice touch, imparting an institutional hominess. But all it evoked was a thought that perpetual wanderers in these depths might be in need of cheering up.

It had been a long time between entertainments. The Cow, the Goat and the Manticore entered into silent transports as Lamprey and Tawse one day appeared. Or night, the difference here was moot.

The well diggers were sweating and cursing, trailing wire behind from a spool they carried threaded through with a pikestaff. The requisite paperwork had been completed and the quartermaster had sent them into the dark. Today the generator was down and Lamprey and Tawse were denied the consolation of even the rudimentary dimness of a work light. They stumbled ahead, the carbide headlamps on their miner's harness

The Return of the Orange Virgin

etching shadow pantograms on the walls. Tawse foresaw an interminable future as a supplementary and semi-permanent work detail for the Lady. He turned to his partner. "This place is not natural, not rightly of our world: reeks of the Dancing Lords. It gives me the creepy-crawlies."

"It seems to be three chaps with their heads stuck in the wall," said Jack Lamprey.

Tawse winked at the three heads. "Gladdening the hearts of the tormented then, eh?"

"Who's this fella?" said Lamprey. "Ain't he but a mean-looking cuss?" Even a holy scholar inured to deciphering the identities of obscure saints in isolated shrines where all the images looked alike but for their associated implements of martyrdom would have been hard pressed to peg the Manticore right off.

Tawse tumbled right away. It was the Manticore. "This one, f'rinstance, is a man-dragon. If he was real there'd be a scorpion's tail tucked away on the other side of the wall. But he ain't real, not now. He's a figment." Tawse patted the comforting immobility of the solid rock. Striking a light for his cigar on the Goat's tongue, he held high the guttering stump of a wax match and, puffing blue mephitic clouds, studied the Manticore.

"One wonders what presumptions they were guilty of to offend the Queen of Heaven. Poor old duffers."

"Nah, they're not even human. They never lived at all. These are decorations from the time of the Dancing Lords." Tawse was proud of his memory.

Lamprey stared, pondering the faces in the wall, then stooped to pick up a hand maul. "According to Herself, modernity indicates auxiliary lighting against an unspecified emergency. Love it or hate it, we've bought ourselves a task and the sooner we're through, the sooner we're home. Shake a leg, we've got five more of these things to get up. Then we can be back up top with our well and our woolies."

Lamprey leaned into it with a will, swinging the maul while Tawse held the drill. They punched two mounting holes into the blank stone, pressed in lead slugs and bolted a battery and lamps in place. They then picked up the spool of wire and prepared to disappear further down into the dark.

"Hoy, hold up a bit." Tawse set down his end of the pikestaff. As a final gesture to the fears that grow best alone and in the dark, he returned to install the now defunct butt of his stogie between the Manticore's bared fangs. "Ain't he quite the dude."

They laughed uneasily and departed, trailing their wire behind. They had been here long enough. There was a numbing air in the labyrinth down the stairs, and most who went once avoided a second visit.

Prince and Morgana

Pen Harrington jerked awake as the red liquid fire of a charleyhorse shot up his leg. The muscles of his lower back and upper thighs joined in a cantata of agony; they had shrunk to conform to his scissored slump over the kitchen table. He tried to stand but he was wedged in. He had been fighting his demons of despair for the past six hours and forty-two minutes, head in his hands, moving only ever so slightly to refill his cup. He had passed out in a chair and now he was trapped, stuck in this ridiculous position, his circulation gone, his limbs no longer his to command. Elegantly, exquisitely, the pain flowed up his legs to his back. His knees levitated, hitting the kitchen table and setting a half full bottle of cut-rate bourbon to doing uncertain circles on its base.

"Dumb table." The bottle settled down, but a small pool spread out from his coffee cup, soaking into the bare wood. He put his hand in the spill and wiped it on his shirt. He would spend the remainder of his days at the center of an ever-contracting puddle of agony as his whole body joined in the spasm.

"Damn dumb table." He interpreted the spilled bourbon as a betrayal. That his own kitchen table would let him down thrust his agony into the background. Half rising, Pen grasped the table's edges and began fine-tuning it, trying to reconcile its wobbly legs with the irregularities of the floor.

"Damned floor." Getting the thing level became a study in concentration, lining up the tumblers in an unfamiliar combination lock. The whole place was off plumb and out of true, but there was a magic spot where everything was steady and reliable. He had found it before; he could find it again. Shoulders wide and arms spread, like a bus driver taking a wide turn, Pen manhandled the table. As its four legs found their usual depressions in the linoleum the table corrected itself and the charleyhorse relaxed. The pain subsided.

"Good work, team." A celebratory draining of the coffee cup and he passed out again. From a far corner of the kitchen Pen's yellow Labrador retriever looked up curiously, scratched, stretched and rolled over hoping to have his belly rubbed. No luck, Pen had nodded off—nothing out of

---

The Return of the Orange Virgin

the ordinary, but a dog could hope. Prince scrabbled back into his favorite spot, wedged between the refrigerator and a steam radiator.

❏

Once Pen Harrington had been young and eager and had prospered. As a lad, Pen Harrington reveled in pastures watered by tourist dollars. A young goat, supple of knee and quick of breath, he had been content to nibble the flowers of the season. He had a job, as a full-time counterman, selling auto parts. Once Pen owned a house. He still owned the house and thought of it from time to time. The winter winds, summer gales, the wet salt air, freezing fogs and Fundy southeasters had prized up the nails from its clapboards and rotted its sills, but the house still stood. Empty and without him, it teetered on the Willipaq ledge, high above the tides, secure enough. He had bought it at a tax auction but he did not live there.

He visited the house in flights of sporadic fancy, toting a toolbox, with a baseball cap set back on his head, radiating steely determination and with a line of credit at the lumberyard. His good intentions accumulated non-negotiable credit in the Methodist afterlife his mother and aunts had promised him when he finished his vegetables and went quietly up to bed. His mother and aunts had then played cards. Pen Harrington grew up and drank. Not all the time, but the house went to hell anyway. This was all before he held forth with snappy yarns and a sympathetic ear as a part-time bartender at The Willipaq Casino—no gambling, only a pretentious restaurant with a cocktail lounge and an attached marina. There was no local trade; loose change was spent at the laundromat or the liquor store. The bartender job saved Pen from becoming one of the shirtless dropouts who haunted the breakwater in summer, draped over the benches placed by a Rotary bake sale. They compared muscles and tattoos, got nice tans, drank beer and hustled tourist girls.

The last time he visited it the house had been standing empty for fifteen years. The weather had come in through a broken window and heaved the floor but the joists and sills were serviceable though shaky and would hold, Pen estimated, till he got around to jacking up the house and sliding a new set in. How long ago had that been now? Ten, eleven years. That the house—his house—still stood he was sure, for the tax bills came regularly and on clear days he could make out its cranky roofline as it huddled on the ledge across Willipaq Bay. It was a thirty-mile drive.

Prince had settled between Pen's feet where he twitched with the private anomie of a dog dream. And his ear itched. That exquisite itch that could never totally satisfied—his favorite kind. Still asleep, Prince flopped over onto his hindquarters and scratched at his ear. From his collar a jingling of interlocking links rang a percussive counterpoint.

"No superpowers today? I would have thought one such as you would not be troubled by an everyday affliction of the flesh." Prince looked up. Interesting dream—he was somewhere underground and the walls were speaking to him. The walls were striped green and white with mineral accretions. The head of a large animal, a cow, looked down and nodded wisely. It had a secret. "I know who you are," said the Cow.

"So do I," said Prince. "May I have a sniff?" He ranged about seeking the Cow's hindquarters but they were hidden in the stone of the wall. Prince raised a leg.

"I wouldn't do that if I were you," said the stone head. "I am a sphinx. Cleopatra loved me."

Prince put down the leg. "Silly, you are a cow. Champion Guernsey milker by the look of you," said the great yellow Lab. Prince had seen cows on the cartons of milk Pen Harrington struggled home with. "Cleopatra is a name for a cat. You are not a cat, you are a Cow." He was surprised that he had made words but this seemed nothing out of the ordinary, so he let it pass.

"I am an allegorical figure to confound all who come my way," said the Cow. "I am the guardian of the castle of the Dancing lords."

"You are a silly cow and you are deep underground."

"As are you, silly dog. I was once high atop the postern gate. Fierce I was. But the parts you refer to—those that would produce milk and tell me if I were a common cow or, indeed, like the ancient guardians of the Hittites and Sumerians, a great, giant horrific charging bull, full with the blood of kings—are alas embedded in the stones. You will have to take me on trust."

"Believe, me, you are a cow. Milk smells bad." The cows and their cartons were torn open to take the bite out of too-strong coffee, then forgotten and left to spoil.

"And you are a silly dog and no olfactory beauty yourself. If I am a sphinx and confidante of Cleopatra, then I am reputed to have information. All the stories say this. There are no stories about silly dogs."

"I have heard stories." Prince had heard stories of trouble and women, basketball and the weather, smelled the heady thick perfume of beer and crispy cheese snacks. Pen and Harry Pease told stories for hours as he curled close to the wood stove under the crackling glare of Harry's television.

"You have heard but you have not listened. Any reliable tale would have reported that you are an uneducated dog. You have listened but not heard, the wind blowing through a hollow tree. You sleep on the floor and drink of the natterings of foolish old men. Your head is empty if you do not crave knowledge and wisdom that it brings. This is about to change."

"I, I..." The ideas—wisdom and knowledge—were strong and bigger than he was. Prince had no words to reply.

In his mind, a dream within a dream, a chestnut horse lay at rest in the meadow, knees tucked in under its glistening body. A child, a young girl with a length of red hair tumbling over her shoulders, lay at full length atop the horse, stroking its long nose, whispering reassurances—an exchange of confidences. The child was naked. The horse kept his head turned away, pretending indifference as he nibbled watercress, but his eyes rolled backwards in their sockets, riveted on Prince. Clutching at the horse's mane with her hand, the child leaned over to caress his head. "Speak, dog," said the Wise Child.

Prince's lips parted. He licked the tip of his nose for reassurance, and spoke. "Wisdom is conferred. And a riddle is what you are said to have for me before I may pass this point." He spoke the words even as he realized he did not understand what they meant. Words, he had words.

"Had you wanted to pass this point?" asked the Cow, getting along with things.

"Not really," said Prince. "I am happy just where I am. Here there are smells and kibble."

"Here," said the Cow. "Well, since you are somewhere, you obviously know part of the answer to my riddle already. There are three ways to get anywhere—the way you know, the way someone has told you and the way that is intuited for you."

"I am already here, so that leaves two."

The Wise Child swung down from her horse's back and threw her arms around his neck. "Very clever, Holy Dog, but you are in the way of outsmarting yourself. Careful, lad. Don't set yourself up with a lifetime of misery just to show off. And show off to whom? A Cow stuck in a wall? Oh, really, silly hound." The Cow pretended to chew its cud.

❑

"Gotta have a smoke." Pen's eyelids fluttered as false dawn was gloaming, its long rays competing with the fluorescent ring in the kitchen ceiling. His hand made exploring circles and found nothing. Pen Harrington was desperately hung over and trying to regain control of his body. One flailing leg struck his dog in the ribs. Prince's dream—the Cow, the Wise Child, the great chestnut horse—was gone, blown off like early morning sea smoke. Pen slapped his chest pocket for a pack of smokes and, finding none, levered his hams high enough off the chair to give his pants pockets a squeeze. Definitely out of butts. Prince stationed himself in front of the door, wagging his tail. Time for a walk. Pen stood shakily, the action setting off a flurry of thumps as the great dog's tail hammered against the door.

Pen Harrington, the provider. Man the hunter. Prince loved Pen and Pen loved Prince. They sometimes shared macaroni and cheese dinners when there was no kibble left in the bag. Prince remembered where the kibble came from—C&E Feeds on North Street. Twice a month his food came down the alley with Pen stooping under the weight of the fifty-pound bag balanced on his shoulder, Prince trotting importantly at his side. Trips were special. Even though the dog and the man went almost everywhere together, the anticipation that, yes, we might be doing it again, made Prince's blood race. There would be a rustling of preparatory activity, lacing sneakers, unpegging a windbreaker from the coat tree in the hall.

"I am totally, miserably hung over. And out of cigarettes." His options were two: quit smoking cold turkey or stand up and get moving. Pen braced himself for action. Pen rolled his head around on his shoulders, massaging his sleep swollen jaw; time to face the elements. Look at that—five o'clock in the morning and still dark. It seemed it was always dark here at the leading edge of North America, a hazard of infelicitous positioning.

"Feet do yo' stuff." Cigarettes meant a trip, ready or not; there were aspirins in the bathroom.

Testing his equilibrium, Pen caught hold of the ironing board left up from the last time he had used it. Three weeks—four? The ironing board collapsed, its scissored legs splayed in a position suggesting bicycles in love. "Uhn, sorry about that," he apologized. Testing his equilibrium, he decided he was in no shape to drive. He would walk over the bridge to Canada where there was a 24-hour convenience store. From past experience he knew Customs Canada would stick a tail on him if they smelled liquor driving through. License hassles from the Mounties Pen did not need. He reached his jacket down from its peg. The thumping became a rapid-fire staccato as Prince's tail threatened to splinter the panels of the door. Pen clipped a leash to the dog's collar. "Just for show, fella. We're going over the river." Pen dropped the leash and returned to the table where he examined the level in the bottle. Half full, enough to maintain his deepening depression at an acceptable emotional plateau till the stores opened up. Booze he could get cheaper in the States. Prince followed expectantly.

To those up top in the sunshine who still thought about him the consensus was that the best thing about Pen Harrington was Prince—big, loving, gentle and not too bright. Where Pen went, Prince went, and preferably by car. Prince sat in the passenger's seat giant and yellow. The ebullient, effusive Pen of the days of summer girls, summer boats and summer money had gone away. When he thought about his house on the ledge at all, it was as a haven with an address where he would receive the government entitlement checks that would start in twelve years if he lived, a roosting place to await the inevitable while inflation nibbled at his monthly stipend.

"Twelve fucking years till Social Security," Pen grumbled. Years of uniform sameness: companionship at the diner, crony talk at the hardware store, winter afternoons watching basketball videos with Harry Pease. Pen was a lover of women past their bloom, the night waitresses and night duty nurses about town: lonely women he met while he was at work.

With his blue warm-up jacket half on, one sleeve dangling, Pen Harrington executed a quick and perfunctory circuit of Things To Be Looked Into Before A Trip To The Store. That was the giveaway. Prince plomped all of his 102 golden pounds immediately in front of the door and, thumping his tail on the kitchen linoleum, blocked all exit.

The pantry doors were warped from decades of winter overheating and the penetrating damp of all other seasons. Pen inspected their larder.

Squeak.

"Hmmm."

Slam-chunk.

"Needs toilet paper and macaroni and cheese dinners." Prince thumped harder, the metronome of his tail picking up speed as Pen turned to the refrigerator. A putrid presence forced him back. "Phew!... something in there doesn't like us, eh, fella?" He hadn't been this deep in since he cleaned out the beer last weekend. "Maybe we do some defrosting today."

Prince wagged faster and changed his tail's direction. Its angle of moment now struck the crossbucking of the door's bottom panel, making the screen door on the other side bounce at each hit, its rusted spring giving little squeaks.

"Well, that's just what we'll do." Pen bent to unplug the refrigerator and, leaving it open, fished the trash barrel from under the sink. "Today we begin anew, facing unafraid the challenges of a fresh start, the promises of a new dawn." He tied up the barrel's contents and skidded the leaking bag across the linoleum toward Prince at the door. Prince scrabbled out of the way to take refuge under the sink with his food dish. Pen installed a new plastic liner, scooped in everything he could pry loose from the congealed ice of the freezer compartment, took a deep breath, held it, and knelt before the vegetable keeper. He pondered over how shapes and colors changed over months in storage as he dumped liquefying greenstuffs from the hydrator drawers into the barrel. He liked to have salad stuff ready at home, just in case—a concession to healthy living.

Pen felt himself turning blue from lack of air. He slammed the lid on the plastic barrel and boosted the empty drawers to the sink where he turned the hot water on full force. The smell got worse. He turned his back on the open refrigerator, consigning the problem to the healing powers of time and nature.

"Let the damn thing drip. We'll put these things out in the sun and hose 'em off later, huh?" Prince agreed. His stomach was not now empty and rumbling with reminders that some kibble would be nice, so Prince forgot what he was doing under the sink at his dish. He took a lap at the water bowl, then shouldered his way through the door to the yard. Pen had preceded him. When Prince pushed open the door Pen rose from the steps where he was lighting up a cigarette to clear his sinuses and chocked the door with a bag of garbage. "Air the place out, OK?"

In the old days, when Pen was freshly broke, newly arrived and with a residual spring of youth in his knees, he and his new puppy had done a lot of walking. That was before the car and before the women. They had just moved into two rooms and a bath and there was no spare change for transportation extras. A technological level higher than foot power would have to wait. At the supermarket Pen would wave to Prince, waiting uncomplaining and eager in the street, as he rounded each aisle. They had gone to the store together several times a week. Walking home there were two full big brown bags, usually cans. Lots of canned goods and macaroni and cheese dinners, canned tomatoes, canned spaghetti, peppers and onions in polypropylene bags from the produce section, coffee and always some loose packs of cigarettes. Even though cigarettes cost dearly by the pack, Pen bought these daily, relishing the human contact. His strong arms full, he and Prince continued their progression to the bar where Prince snuggled into the sawdust while Pen got drunk and forgot about the groceries. The bags were safe at the bar and eventually—after some hours, sometimes a whole day—he would notice they were missing and man and dog would pick up the thread of their original errand and spool home again with their groceries to the security of the kitchen.

Prince picked up his leash's loose end and marched on to the next new attraction—outside. The smells! No less pungent here, but different, always different. This was sometimes puzzling. Pen Harrington did not change. Pen was Prince's pole star. Everything was right because that's the way things were: Pen was here and all was well. Prince padded off to decorate the tires on the line of parked cars. Often they would not be where he had left them. The night before he had marked them all with a badge of reference, and now some were gone, some had moved. This implied a malleable, mutable existence as changelings. This was puzzling and disturbing. Time was when lifting a leg had been the happiest exercise of his heritage; Prince felt never more fulfilled than when he was letting fly from his bottomless bladder. Recently that had started to change. A nagging doubt that troubled the canine mind returned: the slightest suggestion that there could be more to life than kibble and bits and curling up on the linoleum.

It was the girl-child woman-person he saw in his sleep, he was sure. It was a recurring dream but he had never before remembered it in the daytime. Prince paused, leg in air, against a '78 Volvo. He had been in a lush pasture where a young girl leaned against a great chestnut horse. There was a Cow stuck in a wall. Strange.

"Hello there, old fella, I am the Fata Morgana. Remember me," was all the girl had said as the dream faded. "Be seeing you, old pup, when I come through. But first I will send a woman to be my priestess. To wrest my rites from this usurper—this Harry Pease." Prince snuffled puppy-happy at her feet.

Video Poker

Arsenault's was a blaze of light, the only human habitation in Loupe du Jour, New Brunswick with lights on. High yellow sodium lights on sixty-foot pylons ringed the gas pumps, casting few and deceptive shadows. Arsenault's One-Stop and Family Sundries was also the bus stop. To this it owed no small portion of its success. In an age of specialization, Theo Arsenault was a generalist, with gas pumps, a soda fountain, over-the-counter drugs and notions, and a wall of coin-operated gaming machines. Plus lottery tickets, tobacco and magazines. Canadian taxes added over five dollars to the price of one pack of cigarettes as soon as you crossed the bridge. The tobacco trade was stay-at-home: Canadians proud to do their share for National Health by shelling out the excise, and tourists who had money enough not to care. Pen and Prince were regulars four times a month without fail, during the weekend benders when Pen reviewed his career mobility and analyzed the slights and indignities of the week just past. The unsteady man and the huge yellow dog received only a cursory glance from two teenage toughs plying the video poker machine, full packs of Pall Malls rolled up in their T-shirt sleeves. Pen noticed the slick black leather jackets tossed over the pinball beside them and was comforted that the great mandala had rolled around one more time.

An attractive, bewildered-looking woman was pressing a sheaf of bus receipts on the night clerk.

"Lady, I'm sorry, but it just hasn't gotten here yet. Freight isn't like check-on baggage. They send it on when they have the room to spare." He was gesturing to the empty shelves behind him emblazoned with the Atlantic BusWays logo.

"But there was lots of room. I was the only passenger on that bus."

"That bus, miss. There are others and they are full. Your bag will probably come along tomorrow." Seeing Pen, he reached down a pack of Players from the overhead cigarette stacks. "S'cuse me, got a customer." He favored the woman with a smile, a wall of friendly, attentive indifference.

The woman turned and gave Pen the once-over, sizing up this latest manifestation of the predominant local life form. Pen's hands and feet felt oversized and his neck started throbbing. He was very conscious of his condition and appearance and wished he had met this woman sober and by daylight. She was magnetically beautiful and he spun a fantasy scenario of the two of them walking barefoot on the beach. Compelling, that was the word. He found her compelling. She radiated a spirituality usually lacking in bus passengers, something ennobling. Prince sensed this too, and made a small whimper of recognition.

They made eye contact and Pen quickly diverted his attention elsewhere, very aware of how he must look—human refuse, it might be catching. Mothers hastily draw their little ones to them, clearing a path, holding their breaths as he passes, protecting their children from the fumes of failure and neglect. He was a spreading stain of social wreckage at a spiritual and magnetic moment.

Pen tried to look busy. There was the urge to check in a mirror: "Sorry, forgot my tie; it's at home with the good suit." He cast about for a plausible object to hold in his hands. Snatching a copy of Modern Fly Fishing from the magazine rack, he furiously leafed through it. Resentment flared against himself, the world at large—everybody and everything that was not him, could not understand. Prince also felt the call, but had none of his master's inhibitions. Trailing his leash, he walked up to the woman and stuck his nose between her legs.

"Well hello there, big fella. You're not in the least bit shy are you?" Not intimidated by a dog almost her size, the woman knelt down, and putting her nose to Prince's, shook his head by the ears.

Pen hurried over, muttering apologies. "Sorry about that. He just likes people is all."

"Well, I like him, too. He's just a big love." She formed her words well, an educated, big city girl. She rose and extended a hand. "Hi, I'm, I'm..." There was no name. She scanned the shelves for an inspiration. "Granola. Uh... Margaret Granola. Call me Maggie."

The simple, everyday gesture caught Pen off balance. He was prepared for a quick getaway, but in that instant it was all over. Pen was awash on the shoals of beauty, his compass demagnetized, his ready anger put to flight by her directness. He heard himself mouthing formulas of apology for his dog. Modern Fly Fishing was twisted into a paper party favor.

Her hand hung between them. She pressed it forward, coming closer; there would be no easy retreat for Pen Harrington. "Are you a fisherman?" She had noticed the crumpled magazine in his hands.

"Oh, me? No." There was a pause. Prince thumped the floor, approving. Her eyes were dark and clear, friendly without a trace of amusement at catching him out. His rage flushed and faded. "Lose your baggage?"

"No, my baggage is fine, or so the man here assures me. It's just not here yet. I'm the one who's lost."

The hand was still extended. Pen dropped Modern Fly Fishing and took it. "Welcome to Loupe du Jour, New Brunswick, Canada. Pen Harrington."

"Well, Mister Harrington, it's simply grand to make your acquaintance. And besides, my arm was getting tired. I'm... actually, I don't seem to know who I am. Maggie is probably not my real name. I hope that doesn't bother you. It should bother me, but it doesn't. My ticket says I got on in New York City, but I don't remember a thing."

Pen chilled. "Amnesia, huh?" She was too good to be true. "There's a lot of that going around."

Immediately, he regretted the wisecrack, but she seemed not to have taken offense. Such openness, such sincerity. This had the all hallmarks of a setup for an unnecessarily elaborate con game and Pen Harrington didn't care. His eyes must have given him away; she picked right up on it.

"It does sound awfully bogus. I mean... doesn't it? It's all so involved," Maggie said. "Don't worry, your life savings are safe. I mean... wouldn't it be simpler for me to just ask for spare change?"

"You can't remember anything? I mean who you are, where you came from?"

"I know came from New York, it's right here on my ticket, and I was hoping I'd find some clues in my suitcase, only it's not here yet."

Pen allowed that if she were an adventuress out on a big money scam and posing as an amnesia victim, a cruise ship or international air terminal were more likely locations to stalk her prey. "You know your name, that's a start."

"Oh, Maggie? That just popped into my head when I saw you and, and...?"

"Prince."

"Prince..." More thumping and the nose was back in place—a low, happy glottal rumble as ears were scratched by the exciting, wonderful woman, "...I knew introductions would be in order. Prince and I are going to be close. Very close."

Pen Harrington was in love but did not trust the feeling. He examined it with the pitiless precision he usually expended on the level of the bottle waiting on the table at home. Love, too, was perhaps important. She was beautiful, wonderful, pure and fine, and all Pen could think of was getting her in the sack. He despised himself. "You could stay at my place."

For Prince, big and yellow, the arrival of Margaret Granola known as Maggie was another fresh event in a life already crowded with newnesses. The great yellow Lab rolled over at her feet and fell asleep, snoring loudly. By comparison, the moment of recognition for Pen Harrington was pretty tame stuff.

The Return of the Orange Virgin

"I know I should be more concerned, but I'm not. I am on a mission—that I remember. That and a voice." Maggie regarded Pen archly. This was a test.

And Pen passed the test with flying colors: she heard voices; she was a whacko and it didn't matter.

"And I suppose I am a jogger," said Maggie. "Because of the shoes?" She lifted one foot, showing off an expensive, high-tech sneaker.

Pen Harrington was feeling the wandering, unpredictable itches that were never where they said they were when you went to scratch them. His body wanted a drink. At the same time he wanted this woman more than he had wanted anything in his life. His attention strayed; he had lost her for a minute. She was talking to him.

"Are you all right? I asked if you were a jogger."

"Not lately." He had done no exercise of any description in over eighteen years. "Track in high school," he added weakly. In the operating manual we are given at birth there is a hidden command. It tells the bearer, This is it. Put down your pencil, wrench or screwdriver, land the airplane, bring this ship safely to berth and cease all superfluous activity. You are in love; go for it. This is the big one.

Maggie took him by both hands and looked deeply, closely into his eyes. "That's all right, we'll get you back into shape."

A decision had been made to which Pen did not recall being a party. All his life had been quick flings and easy liaisons. He looked at himself from space, a satellite photograph. Its taut surface mimicked depth while being shallow and immensely, incalculably wide—a great sullen puddle after an unexpected passing shower, calm in the repose of easy commitments soon forgotten.

"I am on a mission. You don't think I'm crazy, do you? It doesn't matter if you do. You know what they say: 'A pretty girl can always find some nice man to look after her.' You are a nice man. I trust you."

Pen Harrington fell like the last of the forest giants before the chain saw of wide-eyed disingenuousness. Prince snored and dreamed of a child astride a great chestnut horse.

The three left together and Maggie moved in. "Some soap and hot water and a little elbow grease and we'll make this place sparkle."

At times like this one is expected to overlook little flaws in one's intended. You make small talk and the phrases ring down the ages.

□

Meanwhile back at Arsenault's One-Stop and Family Sundries, the night clerk, Gerald Bronson MacKechnie, had replaced the toughs at the video poker machine. He slammed it with the heel of his hand. Gerry was a solid citizen who saw himself as a free spirit.

Thwack!

He found this satisfying and did it again with the same minimal results.

Thwack!

Inside the gaudily painted cabinet the tiny fields of a memory chip collapsed, sending its stored contents winging away to chip heaven. On a video display framed by irreverently stenciled plywood, a Jack, deuce, nine and a pair of red tens blanked out leaving a field of low-resolution scan lines. Gerry MacKechnie had been plugging the quarters he had boosted from Arsenault's till hoping for a twenty-dollar payoff against all good sense and with no encouragement. He was the lone dweller left remaining in Arsenault's, the woman and man with the big yellow dog having sorted out some misunderstanding over luggage and left thirty minutes earlier.

No one had seen and he could hope for a quiet getaway. He had put off going home until he had broken even and now he had broken the machine. Three AM. Sheila would give him a frosting—no nookie, cold feet in bed and up with the kids at six. And Arsenault was sure to notice the missing money. He would blame the teenage toughs. Drinking beer, driving the back roads with the radio loud, then hanging out and playing video games again was heady medicine.

After a moment of furtive embarrassment, he thought what the hell, and knelt to see if the plug had come loose from the wall. It had not. "Shit." Gerry hit it again. Nothing. Not even the satisfying jingles and rattle of springs and linkages you got in the good old pinball machines. "I thought there was a special Providence that looked out after these things," said Gerry, meaning the Provincial Lottery Corporation.

"There is," replied the machine, "and it doesn't like muscleheads abusing Church property."

A cascade of coins fell into the trough. "But for you this night there will be a plenary indulgence. Take a cab."

Gerry looked around. Theo was fussing with a clipboard out at the gas pumps, getting totals. This must be some new program from the Lottery Corporation. He scooped up the money and reached for his jacket.

The Return of the Orange Virgin

"Be fruitful and multiply," said the machine.

Struggling into his jacket, Gerry hurriedly backed from the store.

"Quack, quack, quack," said the video poker machine as a duck appeared on the screen, stalking back and forth with a big cigar and a painted mustache. Doing a Groucho.

The picture flickered and was restored. The screen filled with the Corporation's usual come-on—Youth, Beauty and an annuity somewhere in an ill-defined future all for a dollar investment. El was pleased with himself. The parceling out of human fortune was going well...

Biff is born

It wasn't easy being born.

The golem of the Fata Morgana struggled naked and alone, knees tucked to his chin, lying on a polished stone floor.

Wet.

He was wet, that was it. A pink starfish of blue-veined fingers covered with moist translucent skin filled his field of vision. The fingers glistened. He wiggled them.

Mine. My fingers.

Closer.

He tried to lick the wet from his fingers. My tongue. My taste, then, but a barrier. There is something between me and me. This is my hand and I am wet. He licked himself again, this time a knee. He sucked at it. The pliant membrane pulled away, leaving a blister filled with colorless fluid.

Some sort of covering is covering me and I am in it.

The observation pleased him.

I am in a placental sac and the sac is filled with fluid.

And with me, of course; I am in here.

How did I know that?

This is ME; I am thinking.

The blister he had raised wrinkled, shrank, and reformed itself to tight flawlessness over the pink, perfect knee. He caught at the membrane covering his hand and pulled at it with his teeth. Its further reaches gave and stretched, conforming. There was a feeling of tightness all over his body.

Body. My body. All of this is me.

Discovery and pride.

The pleasure at his body fled before panic at confinement, at being trapped in the sac. He pulled again and it stretched again but did not separate or tear. The tightness was tighter.

I've got to get out of this.

Frantic, he shook his head from side to side, a negation. This loosened the membrane covering his face, giving a little freedom. A regular pounding in his chest became deeper, rapid. Bite after bite he bobbed and tugged, his mouth and throat filled by tasteless, endless, accommodating film. As it stretched he felt his toes curl. As one end loosened the other became tight. Thup, thup, thup, thup—bubbles of film were being sucked in and expelled at his nostrils and mouth, springy and resilient.

He stopped his struggling and watched, fascinated.

Breathing. I am breathing. Was I doing this before?

Before. There was a before.

His breaths became ragged. There was no more air in the sac.

I am suffocating. Desperate, he clenched again with his teeth and gave the sac a furious shaking from side to side.

The covering stretched and pulled his heels up tight against his buttocks. He paused, exhausted. Thus far he had moved only his fingers and his head.

He watched exhausted and watched the bubbles—thup, thup, thup. I can breathe; there is air. If I do not struggle it will let me breathe.

The membrane relaxed, reformed, and he lost the few centimeters of play all his efforts had bought him. Flaccid membrane filled his mouth, stretched and striated, used up, no longer a part of the game.

A game! It is playing with me.

First curiosity, now fear.

I must think. These are new feelings.

All feelings were new feelings.

Discarded membrane lay about his head. What remained still covered him, but there was less of it. Thanks to me. I did this.

The Return of the Orange Virgin

The membrane tightened. His nose flattened out against his face and despair overwhelmed him. As he watched, the membrane pulled itself together, recovered its resiliency, and flowed back over his body. His toes uncurled and his nose unflattened as the pressure was relieved.

He slept.

❏

The newborn dreamed.

"We have a window," the female voice rang with quiet urgency, "We have a window opening. Form a line and have your papers ready." Amplified hollowly, standing waves of words slapped back early reflections from tile walls. "The doors to healthier, greener lawns and celebrity tennis are open. Lawns to the left, please."

A male voice, not at all urgent, kept pace with him.

"Except for you. Don't waste your young self hanging about on line. Nothing here for you. No second chance." There was no one in sight. "You're dead meat, stuck in the garage. Leave it in park. You'll never make it."

The invisible speaker hurried off, bustling down an empty corridor.

The voices spoke nonsense.

"All form and no content, that's it. You are catching on. Welcome to the world."

The newborn woke.

There was something in the air that made his head hurt. Light.

He discovered his eyes and closed them, his teeth again tugging at the membrane.

It popped and shriveled. He was free.

❏

"You'll get used to it." The Fata Morgana approached the golem where he stood fearful and confused, dazzled by the light. "I know it's bright but your eyes have been closed."

She handed him a towel. "Here, dry yourself off, then we'll have a talk." His hand reached out for the towel but could not hold it. She draped it over his arm and kissed him lingeringly on the mouth.

"I am afraid I have again made you too beautiful, my pet, my peccadillo. We but work with what we have." She took his face in her hands and kissed him again. He did not respond. Unflinching and impassive, he stood silently as she traced gentle whorls on his cheeks, lips and forehead with her long middle fingers.

"You have forgotten all that was between us. That is good. Frankly, you had become an embarrassment. Although you are still too good-looking by far, much has happened since we were last together and you have much to learn. We shall have to look to your education in areas other than knotting sweaty sheets."

He sat down amidst a jumble of alphabet blocks, his eyes wide and adoring. His head ached from the urgencies of flailing thoughts trying to draw meaning from each other.

"You retain no memory of our past unions; you are beginning life all over again. The funny feelings in your head will pass. Trust me." Morgana recovered the towel from where it hung, unused, over his arm and tousled his hair with it, giving a vigorous rubdown. "You know your letters?" she asked.

He rummaged through the spill of blocks and came up with two. He held them up with proud accomplishment.

"Alpha and Zed. Very good, my darling. You are coming along swimmingly."

Basking in the sunlight of her praise, he rummaged again through the scattered blocks and came up with B I F F. The Orange Virgin knelt next to him and gave him a big hug. "Biff! Yes, you know your name and can find all your letters." She thrust her tongue in his ear and gave it a loving nip. Biff laughed and squirmed.

"I have slipped up somewhere and will probably regret it later. By rights you should not yet know your name, but I am under the gun and we have got to get cracking; these impromptus are ever fraught with peril. But... Mama's got to get a hustle on and you will be on your own for a while. Sex will have to wait. We shall start you out with Ovaltine and Space Ace."

Morgana clicked on a mahogany radio receiver, its cabinet peaked like a cathedral window. "We are tapping into a world where ghost whispers bloom through a sub-etheric sleet into comfortable suburban parlors." She spun a large central knob and a white pointer chased through rows of glowing numbers on an indicator panel. "Think of it—the clacking needlework of a Mom accompanies the warblings of the unseen guest as a cloud of blue, pungent smoke rises from a pipe set by in a floor-standing ashtray. Time is slippery but this is probably the youth of my pig killer. A family at ease—a Mom at rest after her busy day as a Dad puzzles over birdhouse plans in the latest Popular Mechanics. It is their way; this is a time they have set aside. This is the Family Hour and they are listening to the radio. Later, Mom will go to the kitchen and bake a quiche. A quiche is perfect balance—an imitation of life. We must teach you about quiches. Ask me later."

"Raydeeoh..." There was a scramble for the appropriate alphabet blocks. And a shimmering as a miniature aurora borealis assembled itself near the ceiling and dropped down to surround Biff and the radio. He reached out to touch the dancing strands of blue; a spark leaped from the tip of his finger.

"Biff, Biff, are you there?" It was Morgana. She was now talking through the radio.

"Uh, yes. I'm here.

"Put your finger in your mouth, there's a good boy. You have just got yourself a nasty burn."

"Ouch!" His finger was glowing and his flesh bubbled.

"Ouch! That's right, darling. Please be more careful. You were built for pleasure, not for pain. You have no safety margins. Finger in?'

"Mmmmph."

"Excellent. Now listen to me very carefully."

"What are you doing in the radio?"

"I'm not in the radio. Forget the radio. I have a very important grown-up job for you to do and I am only going to tell you this one time, so listen up."

Biff placed an elbow on his knee and, chin in hand, leaned toward the radio. He cocked his head to one side, a posture indicating rapt attention. He had a feeling he was not alone. Morgana's voice was in the radio, but the radio always had voices in it, so that wasn't it. He swiveled his head around. Just on the other side of the shimmering curtain of pink and blue spangles, silent and larger than he remembered her, was Morgana herself. This was not right. Morgana was motionless; her golden eyes stared fixedly ahead. She was performing a ritual gesture, her right hand elevated, supported at the elbow by the heel of the left. Her right hand had the thumb, middle and index finger raised, the ring and little fingers folded into the palm. Her left hand accomplished a ritual gesture of aversion, index and little fingers extended.

The radio crackled and gave forth with a reassuring squeal. "Oh, her. She's there, then, the Destroyer. One of my aspects, I'm afraid. Good. She's me but it is not me; it's all very complicated. I will be going away for a little while, and I thought to leave behind a likeness for you to remember me by, to give you a sense of direction. She is my essence, as I was at the beginning: the basic me. She is perfect and will be content contemplating her inner being unless you do something absolutely wrong-headed like trying to draw her out in conversation. I—me, that is—have been tempered by wisdom and folly, compassion and mercy. She has none of these shortcomings. Don't get her worked up; she is righteous and implacable. She is the Destroyer; she doesn't do quiches. Don't mess with her, got it?"

Slicing through a thunderstorm of interference, Morgana's voice was tense and rushed. "If she gets on your nerves, have housekeeping put a screen around her. You, my child, are to have nothing to do with her, at your peril."

Biff managed to choke out, "Yes, I understand," though he truly did not. Biff distractedly reached out to tune the radio and Morgana disappeared in a bloom of static. He had lost her! He panicked and, falling backward, just missed colliding with the motionless Destroyer. He noticed she wore a necklace of tiny human skulls.

A heterodyning squeal and Biff looked to the receiver. An urgent baritone filled the room. "And now... Dolby Jenks, Space Ace, brought to you by Chocolate-flavored Ovaltine."

"This is today's lesson, study it well. You will do daring things." The voice of the Fata Morgana filled his head. The radio had never done this before.

Stone Heads and Mayflies

A phosphorescence heralded matter in transition. The corridors were narrow and inclined down although frequent short ascending flights of chiseled steps and the gentle grade of the courses between made the constant descent less apparent. The pitch of the steady slope was such that the Fata Morgana thought 'down' no matter whether the way she trod rose or fell. Darker stains on the walls and increasing damp underfoot told of the nearness of ground water; faint highlights flowed and danced over mineral accretions that clung like dripping wax to the roof and walls. At every twist and turn, she felt the weight of scrutiny, that the very stones were reaching, yearning from where they had been lifted and placed by hands long departed.

The emanations of the stones said none who descended ever returned, but were sucked into the bowels of the world to become one with the lithosphere. On the stones' part, it was curiosity and boredom that drove them to strain and reach out to the traveler, stop him for a while and hear tales of other places. Hyperbole notwithstanding, the stones did not speak: "Pause... tarry with us..." The breath of eternity that filled their sails of sentience was not sufficient to form the words. They were deep but slow, their utterances longer than the living memory of a single human. By the time the words were shaped, considered, formulated and ready to go generations had loved, fought, lain and begat, leaving ever new crops of scrappy, ragtag toddlers to drag dead cats by the tail in the dust that was their progenitors.

Ever so often a straggler from the litters that bestowed immortality on the local genotype, its child mind as yet uncluttered by the everyday usages of speech, would hear the stones and stop to stare, twin rivers of snot separated to dribble down and around a thumb plugged into a tiny mouth, big eyes fixed at a spot on the wall. There was an affinity between the very young and the very old, but there was little communication and the demands of the body would come crowding in upon the moment. The child would be distracted and move along to eat, to pee, to grow and beget. Hence, the stones got little satisfaction from the flickering, fluttering lives dwelling in the spaces they defined. Nor were they particularly quick-witted even by their own lights, and their thoughts, when they thought at all, were particularly tedious, for not many decisions were required of them and they took the long view.

For the stones, the threat of adsorption of passersby was an exercise in deceit, for any census of the messengers who plied these warrens—shuffling geezers or light-footed equerries bustling about their imperatives—would have shown that most returned.

❑

The Fata Morgana, Orange Virgin, Lady of the Wild Things, etc., etc. hurried along, her feet raising a two-foot high dust cloud that hung motionless in her wake. Her long strawberry-red hair she wore braided into a beehive that extended her already statuesque beauty to an aerial climax, and she swung her hips with the steady determination of someone who knows what they are about. Her breasts were bare, as were her feet, and she wore a pleated kilt. She bounced down flight after flight of narrow stone steps, her bare feet slapping shivery echoes to announce her coming.

She stopped abruptly, her footfalls fading ahead of her, and put an ear to the wall. There was a gurgling of the river, faint and distant, and the scuttling of small creatures that thrived in the crevices where mortar had crumbled and fallen out. She took comfort from the bounty of life that scrambled in to fill all available vacancies. The tiny things flourishing behind the stones were a reassuring sign of continuity. Voles, shrews and water rats were welcome.

"If the moat were going to collapse our foundations you would not be raising your families here, would you little brothers and sisters?" The Queen of Heaven smiled a sunny, broad smile and sat on a step, listening to the scuffling behind the masonry.

L-shaped staples the size of pitons had been driven in near to the ceiling. They supported an electric wire that looped from staple to staple and disappeared into the feeble gloaming ahead and down. Dimly glowing bulbs were set at intervals close enough to offer the barest minimum of light to guide the passing pilgrim.

Her hairdo would have forced her to walk crouched over. "Below the moat, tradition is an encumbrance..." She pulled strategic pins and her hair fell free. In the corridors beneath the water table the lintels were low and the head-room scant. "...but we must preserve the decencies." From the waistband of her skirt Morgana pulled a toque and placed it on her head.

The silence was utter, but she knew she was being monitored. In all their deliberations and with all their tedious wisdom the stones yet kept watch for changes in the millennial weather here underground.

She continued on and down for perhaps twenty minutes, stopping at a branching of the way where the three heads waited.

❑

Thousands of years—the life span of the great ice sheets which made their sporadic incursions down the mountain valleys to claim the rich river bottoms for a few shimmering millennia—Morgana had had the castle to herself. For a while it was good to be alone with the majestic dance of the glaciers and the prairie. Forward, dip and back, the foot of the ice advanced to touch the donjon tower with a brief, respectful hundred-year's kiss.

When the ice was in the yard, blue and green dazzled the eye from the miles-high cliffs of frozen torrent stretching away to the mountains. Time to think and heal.

Ever young, she appeared lost in a dream through the glaciation. Her preoccupation was with another time, another place, not with the thousand-year ephemeron at her feet. Then the sun would reverse itself, coming closer while the chickens crowed earlier each passing morning, melting the ice and filling the moat. In the hours past early midnight, Morgana watched the skies. The old familiar groupings had not changed, some comfort there. There was the Harper, the Cat, the Whale. And when the morning star brushed the crescent moon in the first watch before false dawn and an orange and violet curtain descended, the Queen of Heaven lay on her back under the midnight sky, its solitary beholder. She breathed in the oxygen-rich air from the wandering polar massif and delighted in a concert by the aurora borealis performed for her alone. The sky was closer in the times when the ice wrapped the world.

Other concerns had diverted her attention for what must have been several whiles. When next she looked, the ice was gone. "Huh!" remarked the Queen of Heaven, "...must be summer already. Pity, I had not done with the ice and the lights, but they will return."

❑

In one early time of ice and sun Morgana lay on the parapet, counting bubbles as the moat trout rose to careless mayflies: one perfect day with the feel of the stones warm on her naked belly. She lay at ease, dangling her arms over the edge. Thumbing a freshly cut wedge of tobacco into her cheek, she looked down to regard the decorations whereon she lay.

Three heads formed a triptych at the far corner of what then was the farthest projection of the stonework. She thought to animate the architectural horrors—two grotesques and one gargoyle, to be precise: a cow, a goat, and a manticore. How fine, how perfect, to have confidantes—a star chamber not continually jockeying for preferment, who would speak fearless of her displeasure, how refreshing that they should keep her company. Morgana arched her sun-dappled back to feel the breeze rustling the spidery leaves of a gigantic honey locust that had taken root on the parapet.

She spat a stream of brown juice into the air and waited, hearkening to hear its splat in the moat. A localized network of copper and lead spillways joined at the three where storm drainage would pour through the open mouth of the central head, the Goat.

"Gargle, gargoyle. Speak, grotesques, and amuse me this afternoon when the sun is warm on my back and the katydids are thrumming."

The Goat blinked its eyes and tried to say something. The sound was as of a rattle of pebbles cascading down a hollow pipe.

"Oh, how dry your uvula, Goat!" said Morgana. A local but intense thunderstorm assembled itself fifty yards behind them over a garden of skylights and ventilation horns that grew from the slates. A cannonading rain came pouring down the drainage grade to clear the throat of the Goat.

"That should moisten your dangling grapelet, Goat. Give us some words, and keep us company."

"Slow day, Queen of Heaven, that you bring your humble plumbing to life?" The Goat was her immediate favorite. "It is not enough for us to strike stark terror into the bosoms of the enemies who somehow seem never to come, plus drain the roof; we are now to entertain you, too. Well, what shall it be, anagrams, twenty questions?"

Morgana doubled up with laughter, almost rolling off. She grabbed at the Goat's tongue and pulled herself back. "Say it, Goat. Declaim the last prayer of the Dancing Lords—do it for my love."

The Goat cleared his throat and declaimed:

"Besash bilaigan pertanith gedun
Epillia graben, spilaga perphunt
Dilyaga, dilyaga, dilyaga
Bilaiganit belunkt
Epigal fridath, per fridath, onagonagnon punt.
Filladith, jagasch, per dalda spilaga.

"And, if I may, Lady, I have prepared a transliteration for the local tongue...

Approaching cerise, tender blossoms of the goddess-flower bow.
Shade-dwelling trefoil seeks bright umber.
'Boring, boring, boring,'
Says Her Worship;
And each of us, every last one, is cast down.
Tansy and hellebore cry our outrage."

❑

That was then, this was now, and she was not joyful. It had been some many centuries since she last visited.

The Cow's lip had a curl to it she did not remember, a slight inflection that made him look haughty and supercilious, like a banker about to break wind. She squinted and wrinkled her nose, making an arch of the freckles across its bridge. The Cow's name was Sid, a masculine form, to

---

The Return of the Orange Virgin

be sure, but with his hind quarters embedded in a good eighteen feet of masonry, his putative gender was irrelevant.

He had had no name before the Fata Morgana quickened him, and was content with the monicker. Sid it was, and short for Sidon, a town on the Punic coast where she had seen those eyes before. The folk there had once thought it wise to institute her worship. The Sidonian longshoremen, sailors, and the tight-fisted dealers in dyestuffs, a normally irreverent lot, had shelved their differences long enough to raise a shrine; times were good and there was money aplenty for religion. But when it came time to contract for a statue to fill the temple's empty sanctum, they had a falling-out over what attributes should be celebrated. The rollicking dock whallopers opted for the likeness of a thin-lipped Irish virgin to fill the empty niche, for they had traveled far. The sellers of Tyrrhenian purple had held out for something more traditional. They pored over the lore and settled on an idol for the sanctuary: a concession to the commerce that made them fat, for their dyes were extracted from the hinge of a mollusk. A compromise was struck and the factions were happy: the municipal sculptors supplied a Bronze Age Aphrodite rising from the sea on a scallop shell, half cow, half fish, whose eyes had held this same look of honeyed innocence.

Morgana had been favorably impressed, "This is truly the Land of Milk and Caviar," she said of Sidon, and blessed their efforts. She sat on her heels in the dust and studied the Cow's face, enjoying a flood of pleasant melancholy for the irretrievable past. Morgana's brisk departure from their last séance had left him with the look of an honored partaker at someone else's retirement banquet. The unflattering, unprepared pose showed surprise at having been cut off in mid-thought.

"Look how I have left you, old friend. We must remedy this the sooner."

The Queen of Heaven peered closer, nose-to-nose with the Cow. His lip trembled with an imminent profundity. Or an imminent flatulence? Amused at the thought, Morgana stood back and studied Sid's face. Yes, gas most likely. "Of the choices offered, the imparting of wisdom or the passing of gas, I'd guess the latter, old ungulate. Such a look of wisdom were wasted on after-dinner speeches. Yes, gas it is. Feather the edges is my advice, unhealthy to hold it in—higher exit velocity per foot-pound of backpressure, and quieter, too. They will mistake you for a distant flight of friendly zeppelins."

She stood. "Speak," she commanded.

Stone flowed into flesh and the words tumbled out. "Simply won't do, y'know. Bad form, this Biff business. Bury him, bag him, cut loose his constituent parts and set him adrift at sea. The stones are not pleased that you have made life from the clay of their world."

She was not yet ready to hear this and turned away.

"Speak, speak! Fine, that's easy for you to say," piped up Goat with his vanilla tongue and bulging eyes. "And we sit here in the dark waiting on your pleasure. Please understand that lately our experience is limited. 'Speak' indeed."

The beautiful Morgana sat cross-legged on the floor so as to look the Goat in the eye. "Well frankly, Lester, on the face of it that is a ridiculous statement. Stone is your nature; your character is inherently cold, hard rock and, barring a dispensation to which I am not privy, aside from our soirees, this is as good as it gets for you three."

The Cow leaned over as far as he could and spoke with a detectable edge of sarcasm. "Begging Your Wonderfulness' pardon, and stop me if I am getting out of line, but all the indications are that Your Wonderfulness has come here for advice and I remember hearing me give the very advice you seek just moments ago. Am I not correct?" He looked around for a second.

The far head chimed in. It was the Manticore. "Why let acrimony spoil what could be a perfectly delightful entrenous? It is wonderful to see you again, Morgana, though it seems like simply ages since you have graced our humble pit with your radiance. Lovely as ever I see, and by the illumination of your gracious presence, I am moved to poesy; for truly, the Dancing Lords were possessed of a classic tin ear. They ignored me—irony was not their strong suit:

> Ditch roses, red
> Mock hellebore, orange,
> The Goddess tired of us
> And put us in storange.
> She should go eat tansy and borage.

"I have achieved a hudibrastic rhyme scheme, I believe." He broke off in peals of laughter.

The Cow spoke. "There was a time, before your time, when we were the locus of all available spells and conjurations, and look at us now—obsolete technology. Just look at us."

"Look at us," the Goat, Lester, added with a note of wistful introspection.

"Times and places change, oh dolorous caryatids, not faces, and you are here, awaiting my call to need. And right now it happens that I need some conversation. Remember that you live at my pleasure and are animate subject to revocation. You are stone, after all, and eternity is a long enough time to learn some proper behavior." She was, however, pleased with them; fifty years was a while to hold a pose. That long? Fifty, forty, thirty, hundreds—no matter. It had surely been centuries since she called them from their chthonic catalepsis.

"Oh Queen of Surpassing Beauty, and meaning no disrespect, when one—much as we—is up against eternity, talk is really small potatoes, if you know what I mean." The Manticore paused, sure he had made a seminal observation.

Goat rolled his tongue out and made a noise like a New Year's party favor. The Manticore succumbed to another laughing fit.

"It is not sufficient that my aspect has shined upon you three? Oh, my playthings, this is not respect... Remember who you are and where you are and, as the Serpent of the World comes to bite his own tail yet again as all things roll round to their inevitable resolution, if you three ever hope to again see the sky, keep a civil tongue in your heads." She regarded the Goat. "And off the floor as best you may."

It was hard for a cow, even a cow hatched in the imaginings of a fury of demons, to be assertive, but Sid gave it his best effort. He rolled his eyes, cleared his throat and, bringing up a few pebbles and a frightened family of wall shrews, began. "Why do we talk the way we do? The delvers and hewers who gave us form are no more," the Cow declaimed, "for them we never spoke, but you have given us life. You tell us you are the Earth, our Mother, and we are but projections of that in you to which you dare not give voice lest doubt shatter faith and then where were we all? But this is not the Earth. We are in the earth, buried alive or almost alive—a thin margin if you ask me. This is logic chopping, a wobbly peg on which to hang our self-esteem. Even in the isolation which our unfortunate condition makes unavoidable we have heard that Morgana makes a golem to be her love-slave. Why should a mud man have all the fun? What are we?"

The Manticore was beside himself. "Well, fuck me sideways if our Sid isn't in a snit. Fierce, bad bossy, he's about a moover!" The Manticore threw his head back—as far back, that is, as the ruff of porcupine quills that ringed his head allowed. It was a face carved with subtlety—bared his fangs and racketed gales of laughter.

Squatting on her heels in front of the Manticore, Morgana flicked the remnant of cigar butt away with a disgusted swipe of her perfect fingers.

"Filthy habit. When did you take up smoking?" Thus saying, she pulled a pouch from her waistband and started rolling herself a cigarette.

"But, but... you smoke."

"Yes, I do. And I find it a thoroughly relaxing and enjoyable habit. But I make the rules, and you don't." She lit up, inhaled deeply, and exhaled toward the ceiling so as not to tempt the stone head beyond endurance.

Morgana felt a misting in her eyes. Was this a tear? There had been entirely too many of these lately. And, if a tear, what was the cause? Did she weep for her lover, beautiful for all his limited behavioral repertoire? Hardly. *A tear has its reasons and if I but wait on its own good time, it shall tell me why it is there.*

She stood quickly, catching herself in a stumble. Turning to face the wall, she examined the traceries of a cobweb at eye level, pretending an interest.

"Don't cry. Tell us about it." The Manticore.

If I am crying for myself, let my tears be for me alone. She willed herself to be lost in the wonder of the spider as it shuttled back and forth weaving its snare. Gossamer and glistening, the net maker coaxed her strand from a distended abdomen, wet and fresh, and in a pattern only she would make. Only once—this spider, this time—then never again.

"Bought yourself some trouble, Lady? Need some diversion? Advice or consent? The word has gotten down even understairs here that the Queen of Heaven, the Orange Virgin, is getting her love-tunnel greased by a golem."

"Correct as always. And, as always, only partly so. There is no hiding from the stones, nor do I wish to, since you appear to be finely primed on what is rightly my business." She paced a tight oval before the three of them, twirling a loose strand of hair about her finger. "I would be educated as well as flattered: tell me of your makers, the Old Ones who left you high and dry," said Morgana, changing the subject.

"Queen Rhea who coupled with a serpent to produce the Egg of the World would query us about the wisdom of the ancients? This is indeed a hoot. Ask on, then, Beautiful One, but by the bells that jingle at your anklet, question warily, slipping up on the subject roundabout. We will never lie to you, but talk is cheap and answers come easily as a mountain stream when all we desire is to be alive and to see the sky again."

"Answer me well and so you shall. Diversion, company, advice, please; but, as you say, let us talk around the topic of our séance, and thus approaching it unawares, perhaps weasel out some hidden meanings. It has been lonely here, even with the bustling human seed I have surreptitiously plucked from across the veil..."

❑

She had arrived in haste though not in disarray. At the start there had been only Morgana and the castle, empty and alone. The long-gone raisers of the masonry pile had passed her notice, and now that she was interested they were gone past recall, having striven, flourished, thrived, fallen and perished utterly, from blink to blink, their eternity the duration of a cosmic giggle. What cataclysm had left the property vacant concerned her not. But the people, what lives had they led here? Conjectural fantasies populated the world again with a warrior elite who hammered one another into extinction. But for all that, they were not the mindless savages such an ending would suggest. Ghost whisperings of silk and the snick of a scabbarded sword hastily drawn in defense of a tryst lingered in the far corners when the wind awakened echoes of the distant dead—not all brutes, they. They had loved and fought. And laughed. And from a store of cunning set by for a joke that needed no reason but itself, they constructed the three comic horrors to drain their slates. Terrible as they were, any attacker with murder in his heart seeing the Goat, the Cow and the Manticore rising from the predawn mists would have fouled his linen more with laughter than with fear.

"You were my first companions in exile and I hold a fondness for you..."

"You asked of the Dancing Lords. Whither have they gone who raised the castle and carved the Goat, the Cow and the Manticore? Alas, we were formed facing outward, and their recessional escaped our notice. Things just got quieter." The golden-eyed Cow tried to look sad. "All organic life that metabolized at a high enough rate to achieve thought was gone—blooey, just like that..."

The Goat punctuated the 'blooey' with his tongue. "If everything went 'blooey,' how come we didn't notice?"

The Cow tried a shrug but failed. "Neutron star, cosmic storm, a bad bowl of porridge shared planet-wide. Who knows? Anyway, they were gone: took the veil and withdrew, existence-wise. But while they were here they were about movers, as my long-tongued friend, Lester here, is wont to say. One fine day when everybody was out on the lawn for an energetic, uplifting session at bowls, they were fried by a passing celestial engine and disappeared lock, stock and caboodle." Eyes of honeyed innocence angled upward. "'Caboodle' is one of the words they used to use."

The Lady's eyes itched from her drying tears. She ground at them with her knuckles. "Have I been crying? No wonder you are looking at me strangely." As her knuckles were removed, her eyes widened and she sat in the dirt of the floor with a thud. "And here am I all tears and sitting in the dirt like a little girl with a scuffed knee. Well, it is my privilege to be a little girl at times. I have been so thick in the afterglow of the sky demon's bamboozlement that I did not see what was before my face. Yon spider," she gestured with her head, "is disassembling her web. This is not in the natural order of things. The pig killer is a summonsing. By whom and for what I will not even guess. But I am returning." She spoke to her perfect toes and wiggled them. "Am I not beautiful, capricious and inscrutable?"

"And insurmountable, too, for all I know." The Manticore chanced a quip under his breath. The goddess was naked to the waist, although from midriff to floor accoutered in a many-pleated bell skirt that thrust her billowing hips into immediate attention.

Morgana hiked up her kilt and directed a kick at the nearest head. "Time!... It is Time that is changing, and here I thought it was I."

"What time did you have in mind? Since you request an honest opinion, one must state that one has answered one," said the Goat. It was not his head Morgana had kicked, but threatened revocation was on his mind and a judicious reply seemed called for. "Endless time we are more than conversant with. Good times it has come to our ears you have been having with your, uh... friend. What time does that leave?"

"Just time and enough if I act quickly, my friends, for I have an intuition from my own tears and a spider's web." She threw her arms round the Cow's neck and gave him a kiss.

The Manticore felt moved to say something, though discretely sotto voce.

"Shut up, you ninny," whispered Sid. "Do you want to spend what's left of eternity stuck in a wall? Talk about the weather if you must talk."

"But we don't have any weather..." The Manticore trailed off, then pretended to be asleep.

"The spider, the people—they are all riders on the now." Morgana's enthusiasm was only slightly damped. "They define themselves by their passage from task to task through their brief, fleeting days. They fool themselves that they are going someplace simply because they have a name for it. The sky demon would not have pulled me to a tussle in Limbo if he were sure of the outcome."

The Return of the Orange Virgin

"They don't know where they are going. Does it matter? Look at us: we know where we've been. Big deal. Do you know where you are going?"

"Not really. I have forgotten. But I know where to start. My forgetfulness, my friends, is a symptom. The engines of creation are slipping and only I can save it. I think."

Sid was not reassured. "Shouldn't there be some planning? I mean, things must have changed. You can't just go charging in dressed only in your knickers and ask for your old place back. Perhaps they have forgotten you just as you have forgotten."

The Orange Virgin arranged her pleated skirt, crossed her knees and settled to the floor, this time gracefully. She stretched, hands together above her head, lifting her strawberry hair and twirling it into a loose bun, a theatrical gesture that lifted her breasts in the faces of the Cow, the Goat, and the Manticore. Pulling a set of nine ivory hairpins from her kirtle, she put them in her mouth and started replaiting her loosened hair. This was a lengthy process. The beehive confection rose, braid by braid, to the ceiling. When there were but two pins remaining, she spoke around them. "I have been so caught up in the flow of things so well ordered that I did not even notice. Time is changing. Fool, that I did not notice ere now. When eternity ends it will end all over: in the carbon blue molalities past the farthest star, in the wilderness of creation as well as at the corner grocery. And eternity will end here in my venue, on my watch—the worlds and times granted me by the Great Author in some ineluctable whimsy."

"Ahem!" There was a rattle of pebbles as the Cow cleared his throat.

"Yes?"

"Oh, Queen, you have come to us for whatever residual wisdom our makers may have left us when they went."

"Correct, friend. If you can arrange the nuts and bolts of whatever plan that in my own inscrutability I have obscured from myself, please do so."

"At the risk of overstepping our franchise, let me posit a question that may lead you through the fogs which cloud your vision. Ask yourself, O Queen, are you real—yes, you, yourself—or have you made a myth that you are living out? Meaning no disrespect, you have stagnated here away from the Earth of which you are the eponym. You have lost the rhythm of meaningful seasons. Sure, go back and wrestle with this godling who has supplanted you. Some healthy competition would be just the thing to get you back in trim. But they believe in him, not in you. Do not expect joyous welcoming throngs. Look on the bright side—perhaps the pig is not a sign. Enjoy yourself, lighten up. And in a worst case scenario, the end of everything is not necessarily a bad thing. What would be tragic is that it should be meaningless."

"The pig is incidental." The Goat.

"Tell that to the pig." Morgana. "He killed it, the man Harry."

"Then it would appear the aforementioned swine is not available for cross-examination."

"I want him, I demand him. One of El's for recompense—vengeance."

"Your isolation has made the trivial immense and the immense itself had been trivialized by the fleeing eons. Who better to know than us? Tussle for eternity if you must, but the little people—this accidental priest you tell us of—why not let them get on with their knitting unmolested?" The Cow.

"Revenge?" the Manticore held back a chortle. "Wet and messy for the goddess of life and Spring, wouldn't you say? Well, you do those things, don't you? Getting even is the portion of divinity. One word of caution, though. You are splashing about in the pool where the Kraken slumbers. Tit-for-tat. The sky-god will be forced to retaliate and once started, these things have a life of their own. Think first, my Lady."

The tear returned to tremble hesitantly on an eyelash.

"I have a feeling," said the Manticore, "That if I had a foot free—if I have feet, for I have truly never seen—I might scratch my ear and that would help me to think, for these are weighty matters."

The Goat ignored him. "And being lonely, it was appropriate that the Queen of Heaven create for herself a companion who, while more than human and thus closer to her, be less than a god, and thus too close for comfort. We are talking comfort versus discomfort then. You are not happy with the tireless thumper. This Biff Bangtree of yours is a household appliance—junk him. Next question, please."

"No matter how cozy we become, remember always that we are playing out our allotted roles in a grander scheme. Yes, even I have to play my role, just as you, my humble hippoglyphs—pardon the pun, for your makers have writ you large, though not entire. And though you surely scheme, your parts are less grand. Much less. But I am merciful and compassionate, and shall not only let you live on to fulfill your destinies, but shall grant you the boon you seem to crave despite that you tread dangerously close to lèse-majesté. I have an errand: some further conversation with the custodian of the world I left to come here is indicated. For the golem I have developed a sentimental attachment. There will be no more talk of killing him. You will watch him—one of you—and be his cicerone. Look after the tad and keep a lid on things. I will want to find everything as I left it when I return."

"A baby sitter?" The Manticore.

"Yes, a baby sitter—you, since you have just volunteered. Keep him out of trouble, and yourself, if you are able. I go to recruit a priestess to celebrate my Mysteries."

Pork-A-Dillos

"Linda?" Will Lambert from Human Resources stuck his head into Linda Winkelman's cubicle. Linda minimized her word processor and jumped to her feet as the latest chapter of her book—a work in progress—slipped away to the bottom of the computer screen. "I'm on those proposals, Will. Due tomorrow."

"It's not about that. There's someone I'd like you to meet." A stunning, statuesque woman in her early 50's elbowed Will out of the way and strode up to Linda, hand outstretched. "Me. And we are going to be the closest of friends, I'm sure." She was dressed like a woodsy Venus and braided her strawberry gray hair into a single heavy pigtail.

"Uh, yes. Hello, ahh..." Linda took the hand.

"leFaye. Norma Jean leFaye." Norma Jean plopped herself into a Le Corbusier swivel chair that had set Linda back two weeks' pay. Her feet went up on Linda's desk, wrinkling a stack of printouts. Linda grumped but kept any misgivings to herself—in the corporate world getting a roommate was tantamount to a demotion. Linda Winkelman had over the years, by skill and attrition, crept ever closer to residence in that coveted corner office on the forty-third floor. She made a show of moving her things closer to what was now her end of the cubicle. Will Lambert backed out.

The Woodsy Venus was pleased to tell anybody who would listen that, a survivor of the 90's organic exodus, she wintered in her summer cottage and heated with wood. "Keeping warm is a fulltime job—you are stacking wood, splitting wood, hauling ashes. And I spent a lot of time screwing a nice man who had a chain saw and a pickup truck. We counted Canada geese and listened to the loons together. I dropped out. Now I have dropped back in again."

Linda struggled with a sprawling ficus plant that occupied the space just inside the doorway. Norma Jean didn't raise a hand to help, just lounged languidly in the Le Corbusier chair and rolled a cigarette. "No, let the tall timber stand," she said. "And don't worry about your job. I'm a temp. They don't know that yet, of course." She held a finger to the side of her nose. "That's a secret, just between us girls. You may yet get a corner office with a window."

When Linda had excavated enough open space, the Woodsy Venus carried in a brace of L.L. Bean totes. "My book," she explained. "It took ten years, Linda dear. In the winter you're so busy chucking wood into the stove you hardly have time to do anything else. I do most of my writing in the summer." Linda now shared a cubicle, a secretary and a word processor with a woman who got herself up in L.L. Bean dressy tweeds with hiking boots for work, a fellow writer whose novel—historical?—was of an unspecified length and theme.

That the WV might be older than she appeared she felt to be an important bit of information to share with her cubicle neighbor. She was beautifully maintained and was studiedly aware that her appearance and anecdotal lifestyle did not reflect the norm for an advertising copywriter at Glasgow/Finn and Westcott. The Woodsy Venus made her connections, put on her persona, and flowed through the workday.

Linda was envious. "Uh, I hope you don't mind me asking, but—how old are you? I mean you look like a goddess. Is it your moisturizer?"

"You doubt me? Linda, you are a pretty girl, I like you. You will forget much of what I am going to tell you, it is for your own good. I am an old friend from work, am I not?" The goddess got a far away look in her eyes. She searched the middle distance, a shepherdess seeking lost innocence. Wrist to brow, she felt for a fainting couch with her spare hand. The pose reminded Linda of a Sarah Bernhardt poster she had had over her bed in the dorm for all four of her undergraduate years. The goddess leaned backwards, then fell down. "Shit! There should have been a velvet couch." She rolled a fresh cigarette.

Linda pointedly coughed and waved her fingers under her nose. A klutzy goddess, thought Linda.

"How perceptive of you, my dear," said the Orange Virgin. "And you must give yourself completely and of your own volition to my service. As my powers fade, which I am afraid will continue irretrievably, I am going to have to depend on you to look after yourself and our own shared best interests. I want you to have positive feelings for me and a predictable, calm, constructive and circumspect attitude as regards your own personal safety. We are going to change your mind in just the littlest way imaginable to make you amenable to reason. I seek a safe place for you. Go to sleep." Linda's chin fell forward to her clavicle. "All events that will or would ever occur in each and every universe or imaginable universe from the innards of the dust mote to the googolplex of stars have already happened. All and at once at the moment of creation."

"Wake up."

"Uh. Oh, sorry about that, I must have dozed off." The woman was a head case. In advertising, some eccentricity was de rigueur. She seemed nice and Linda realized if word of her delusions spread beyond the walls of her cubicle, there would be a rustling of termination papers. *Things must be lean in the woods to come back to the city and work as an office temp,* thought Linda. But the WV had made her break for freedom; what had she, Linda Winkelman, done for herself lately? All she had to do was to do it, make the break from the rat race. Linda wanted "more." More of just what she was not quite sure, but she was sure there had been a short-changing somewhere along the line. "A goddess. One of us said that. I think so, anyway. Aren't you, uhn, voluptuous for, for…"

"You are confusing me with the Virgin Mary. It happens all the time—all pale and white they keep her out in the yard winter and summer. They place a pot of flowers—in season and usually dead—at her feet. You have focused on the nub, Linda dear. They have robbed me of my attributes. The Little Flower they have demoted to a spirit guide for their afterlife. She is the Mother. I am a triple goddess—the Mother, the Lover and the Destroyer."

The answer was about what Linda expected—right in character for a sprouts and granola back-to-the-woods nutcase. "Uhn, sure... a statue. You are—were—a goddess. In another life?"

"And what a life it was, Lindy-me-love. But don't get me wrong; I'm still hot stuff."

"You are a neglected goddess, then."

"The neglected goddess."

Linda reached for her phone. "Maybe some of the guys in marketing, Creative, could get a handle on goddessness, uh... you know: religion?"

"…from the Latin," said the goddess, "religio, religionis—a moral obligation."

"A shrink, then. Professional help? Even the Pentecostals or the Catholics most likely will get a better handle on this than I can. I mean, um—religion is a fulltime job." "I have always found it thus. You are dithering. Forget everything that has passed between us. "Huh?"

Linda was thereupon suffused with a runner's aerobic high as endorphins flooded her body. The line separating dream and reality blurred and a cobwebby glaze covered her eyes. Her knees and elbows felt weak and warm as dream filaments twined about her feet and she swooned onto an enveloping pile of eiderdown coverlets where she gently bounced in slow motion, again, and again, and again. She had found a new religion, and it would not be denied—a faith of joy and, well... faith. Faith that kindled a small, desperate flame of hope in the Winkelman bosom.

"Faith. Joy. Warm elbows," promised a voice. "Bounce and forget, bounce and forget." Linda watched placidly as a flip card flow of her life was changed with a nudge here, a suggestion there.

❏

A chips and nachos conglomerate was introducing Pork-A-Dillos, a low cholesterol fried pork rind product, the latest scientific breakthrough. Linda had been named project manager for the new product's test marketing; if it flew she would be in line to direct the national campaign. At the brainstorming session with relevant personnel from Creative, the brand manager reached into a carton plumped onto the table piled with mechanical art, tore open one of the cellophane bags, 69 cents retail, and dumped the contents all over a billboard proposal.

"Here's a little something extra the guys in R&D thought you could get a handle on, Linda." The little Pork-A-Dillos were uniform tiny curls like the tops of Dairy Queen soft ice cream cones. "Little piggy tails... cute, eh?"

"Curvature of the swine. Very evocative, Sid," Linda said. "This is bullshit. I quit." And who the hell was Norma Jean leFaye anyway? There was no such person at the agency.

"Oops sorry, my dear. You are becoming agitated; I've been letting you drift. The corner office with the window—remember?"

A whispering in her head, must be the stress. Linda brushed at cobwebs in her eyes. "Like I said, bullshit." She had blown it all away. If she handled the account right—and the product was a shoo-in, she couldn't lose—the next stop was a vice-presidency, then a full partnership. Pork-A-Dillos was the step up she needed. Linda stomped out of the brainstorming and back to her cubicle. Grasping at the partition wall, she felt dizzy, disoriented. As if there were two of her. There was a rubbing against her leg. Affectionate. She looked down to see a black and white spotted pig untying her shoelaces. "Wha..." The dizziness returned in wave after coruscating wave. Linda sunk to the floor. The pig licked her face. "Relax," said the pig, "there is another of you—safely distant and with no memories of you or me. Or of this day, for that matter. She is in love. Isn't that nice? This is my mercy." The pig faded away and Linda stood.

Giving in to all the spleen she had saved up, she dragged a 30-gallon Rubbermaid waste container in from the copier bay down the hall. She emptied her drawers one by one into the garbage and stuffed her attaché case in on top when she was finished. She held a cup of pencils and paper clips poised over the attaché case as she stared out the window at the cityscape unfolding beneath her. No job, no money—that figured. And no office with a view. This was the last goodbye. She set the cup on her desk; this was no time to be sorting paper clips. Now she had nothing but time. And who the hell am I not to go to the woods and write my little heart out, too?

She should have been elated. Wait a minute! I am elated.

She had lost her job, she and her husband were growing farther apart with each passing day, and life was grand. The habit of work was ingrained, the rhythm of her life—security, the paycheck, rent—food, even.

But Tom! How to tell Tom?

"Why tell him anything? Tell him goodbye. He is a sponger—a good lay, a pleasant dinner companion, but a parasite." The voice was that of the pig.

"Hello?" There was no reply. "Huh." The pig was right; dinner and sex were Tom's survival skills, not hers. "Get on with my life. Make the break. Human Resources has my number."

Linda was staring out her window, her desk clear and empty but for the cup of pencils and paper clips. The cold, heavy rain had started about 3 o'clock. It must be just about freezing out, Linda figured. Wet enough to make a mess and cold enough to be snow around the rush hour. She dumped the cup's contents into the trash and put it in her gym bag with her sweats and sneakers. She squared her shoulders and shook her head. Must have been daydreaming. Time to get a move on, there were things to do. There was another fluttering of the pages of the day. She steadied herself with a grip on the edge of the desk. The dizziness would pass.

"I am so proud of you, my dear. Things are coming along swimmingly." It was Norma Jean, the Woodsy Venus; she sounded like the pig. "And forget Tom. He will be happy."

There was a crunch, accompanied by shouts from the street. A taxi, avoiding a delivery truck turning right from the left-hand lane, had climbed the sidewalk, scattering pedestrians and coming to rest against a light pole. The world was fraught with hazards for the unwary; there was a potential for sudden, unforeseen and lethal happenings here in the city.

❑

It was still raining, becoming what would be a wet, heavy snow as Linda Winkelman cast one final look at the polished brass revolving doors, shrugged and headed for the trains. The thought of reclining in a hot tub with a Kahlua and brandy close to hand gave her the strength to carry on.

"Oh, shit, my book. It's on my hard drive." She caught the brass revolving door while it was still spinning and rode the elevator back to Glasgow/Finn and Westcott.

The Woodsy Venus must have gone home. The L. L. Bean totes. Ahh, there they were, behind her door. Linda emptied the totes and neatly squared the loose pages into three piles on her co-logger-on's desk. She left a note—Emergency, I owe you dinner. I took the totes. Linda.

She undid the cabling from the computer case and stuffed it into a tote. The desktop computer went into the other bag. She picked up a well-thumbed Webster's Collegiate Dictionary from the mess scattered where she had missed the trash barrel and chucked it in, too. She latched the door and it snicked shut behind her. Linda put some effort into acting casual with the security guard. It was the company's computer. Linda was writing a tell-all exposé on women in advertising in the hours she freed up daily by being better organized than anybody else.

"G'night again, Ed. Forgot my homework." They shared a chuckle.

The cold blast of wet air in the street came as a relief. She could feel waves of body heat rising up to her face from her open collar. Linda felt the sweat trickling down from her armpits. Her face felt pink and moist and her sweater was starting to itch through her cotton sleeves. Her rolled umbrella, trendy with a shoulder strap, was slipping. She plumped the totes on the street and adjusted the umbrella, thrusting it under her arm.

Wrestling herself down the stairwell where Gimbel's basement had been in the years of her childhood, she decided on the IRT Brooklyn local.

"Any change?" She had almost reached the turnstiles when she was intercepted by the outstretched palm of one of the city's homeless.

Silence, a barrier of practiced denial; the offending party is not there, a non-person—blonde, with shoulder-length hair that he tried to keep looking clean. He had bushy eyebrows and a floppy handlebar moustache. He was homeless and slept in the subway tunnels under Grand Central Station. He had a key to the dispatcher's signal tower lavatory at an abandoned station. Linda knew him by sight. She brushed away the alms-seeker.

"Hey, be that way. Get cancer. Have a nice day," said the panhandler.

Linda threw him a smile. He smiled back; they belonged. She was drenched with sweat. Godammit, it must be eighty degrees down here. Linda put her token in the slot and slapped it through a residue of chewing gum with the flat of her palm. She advanced, sliding her stuffed totes over the slipway that covered the turret with its three metal bars. A comforting clunk as she hit the pipe with her hip. The next bar popped into place, pushing her through. The machine had found her offering acceptable. There was no going back.

She was trapped. The Woodsy Venus spoke reassuringly in her mind. "Animals are part of their environment. Remove, damage their dwelling places and they are extinct."

"Pithy. You think that up all by yourself?"

"No. You heard it on a nature show—TV. What is your environment? Maybe we could get you back where you belong."

"Huh?"

"The collective human mind. The collective unconscious. I am an archetype. You made me, I created you. Get it? And so we go on, hand in hand, for all eternity."

The rumble of her arriving train summoned a burst of speed. Crying, "Hold the doors! Hold the doors!" Linda looked around defiantly, claiming her space.

"You are pushing." A large bearded individual stared accusingly at her over a pair of thick, half-frame spectacles.

"So?" Linda turned to look. Her accuser appeared to be an Orthodox some-thing-or-other. A rabbi, clergy at least. "Uh, sorry."

"You were pushing. Admit it. Not to criticize, just a statement of fact." The large, bearded individual gave a classic shrug as he clapped a handkerchief over her nose. A heavy perfume filled her head. Linda recalled the smell from a childhood operation.

"Ether. But I already had my tonsils out." Linda said, aware how inane that must sound. Here I am being assaulted by a large, smelly person on the subway and that is the best I can come up with.

"Nope, chloroform," said the large bearded person. "Happy dreams."

Nowhere Again

In a dusty underground of sentient stones, at a branching of the way where three heads waited, the Orange Virgin squatted on her heels and stared ahead in the dimly illuminated underground dark, her eyes rolled back so that only the whites showed. After a pause that consumed the transit of one of her world's tiny moons, she snapped to. "Done. I have recruited my priestess." Her pupils dropped back into focus. "Now where was I? Yes, our young Biff. You will watch him—one of you—and be his cicerone."

"A baby sitter?" The Manticore.

"Yes, a baby sitter—you, since you have just volunteered."

"But..."

The Orange Virgin dismissed the Manticore. "And would you mind leaving through the kitchen? They're draining the moat today." The Manticore stepped forward out of the masonry wall. There was a creak as of never-used muscles being called into play as he attempted to swivel his head; he shook his back feet wonderingly. "Make it snappy." The audience was declared over and the Manticore shuffled off.

"What about us?" There were now two heads left at the pendentive where the arches met deep below the castle.

"Yes. What about you. I will take your status under consideration. Silence, please. I need to think. I have just had a wearying day in the world of advertising and public relations." The Cow and the Goat were stone once more. A day passed, perhaps two with their connecting night, and the Fata Morgana, Lady of the Wild Things, Orange Virgin, etc., etc. was quiet for several whiles, whiles that perhaps stretched to fill geologic times. A spider, adventurous, crept across her nose.

❑

It was a rainy, drippy day. It had been overcast for weeks with a vagrant glimpse of the sun only in the late afternoons. Moss and lichens were thriving on the shingling of the out buildings, strange fungi clogged the drains. In the kitchens of the Dancing Lords, the fires were kept burning night and day in the great ovens. Three families of woodcutters were kept busy manufacturing fuel. The castle keep was busy all the year even in the dry season. The castle was old. So old that some speculated that it had never even been built, but had always been there by the river.

The river was the reason for the fires. The river and its constant damp, the morning miasmas that clogged the lungs and fooled the vision, playing tricks with perspective, making near things far and far things near. The climate was free of cruel winters and blistering summer heats. The river was why the castle of the Dancing Lords was someday likely to fall down, why the constant fires in the great ovens burned whatever the season. Centuries of unrelenting damp had leached the lime from the mortar. What remained of the cement the original builders had slathered between the rows of basaltic blocks leveling their courses had turned to sand.

His passage mirrored in a hanging dangle of polished copper bottoms, the Manticore threaded through aisles of glistening enamel. The Manticore's jiggling image passed from pan to pan where they hung at their iron reticules, depended by chains from a ceiling beam thirty feet above. A breath of air would set them moving, a runaway cacophony of colliding utensils—a tinker's wagon careening downhill. But today there was not a breath of air sufficient to stir them. A cloud of vapor hung trapped three feet from the ceiling, a viscous caulk squeezed from the pastry tube of kitchen weather: cloudy today, and continued humid. A spectacle of glittering implements—steel, iron, tin and aluminum, quarts, gallons, missionary cauldrons, runcible spoons, shirers, boilers, broilers and basters, colanders, ewers, forcemeat forms, pâté molds, sieves, lids and ladles. Fluted tin forms braided like the innards of a mollusk's abandoned husk awaited gelatin confections, larding needles languished for a loin of pork. A shelf of ceramic rabbits awaited their pâté masquerade.

The Manticore blended well in the kitchens; the toilers and the peelers, boilers and slicers deferred to him. He made his way through the culinary clutter, passing easy banter with the workers, who saw him as one of themselves. Nothing out of the ordinary.

That the scullions, sous-chefs, peelers and broilers, the stokers of the ovens might have seen in him a figment from tales told by legions of cautionary grandmothers, a terror of nighttime fevers, did not occur to the Manticore, for he had seldom visited abroad in the days of the Dancing Lords. What the kitcheners, deep with sweat, wood smoke and the spatterings of hot oil, saw was a man, tall, black and elegant: a quartermaster minor, come to count onions or lash the recalcitrant stoker to greater effort. A not unusual sight in the days of the Dancing Lords.

"Better get a move on." The Manticore picked up speed, scuttling on all fours, claws rattling the tiles, quills extended from the ruff at his neck. Where he had passed the work continued unconcernedly. The Manticore was indifferent to the guises of chopped liver and salmon with herbs.

"Pâté-cake, pâté-cake," hummed the Manticore tunelessly under his breath. He wished he had a smoke with him. The Manticore thought of the Cow and the Goat, but kept his peace. There was no need at this juncture to muddy the murky waters of their uncomplicated minds. Where had they ever been, after all? They were stiff as salt cod and still stuck in the cellar wall, after all. And here he was, experiencing life, out in the world. The Manticore was sensitive about returning to the status of an architectural ornament.

"Oops!" The Manticore had spun around a corner and ran into a great oak refectory table. His forward momentum wedged him under the table and, when he tried to back out, his quills were caught. He wrenched his head from side to side and felt a quick agony as quills tore free and hung quivering in the underside of the table.

The Manticore lashed his spiked tail and splinters flew from the nearest table leg, a plinth as thick as the trunk of a 200-year-old tree, which indeed it was, carved and fluted, black with age and grimed with oil and soot from the kitchen furnaces. Now the tail was stuck, driven deep into the buttressing column.

He was trapped. Further struggles only drove his venomous tail and ruff of quills deeper into thick quarter-sawn planking.

❏

In an infant universe busily defining itself, much time had passed. The duck had left and then returned, a measure of these things. The Fata Morgana floated in a well of his intent, probing.

"You're back."

"I'm back."

"Haven't been hitting the raspberry again, have you, my love?"

"I am fact finding. I seek knowledge, not wisdom."

"This is good; I am not up to a raspberry interview. Linda Winkelman."

"What. Who?"

"Do not be coy, my Old-and-Rare. Coyness does not become Queen Rhea who hatched herself from the Egg of the World. Linda Winkelman. The name of your priestess. You have found her, split her, and hidden her duplicate at the edges of the human universe. I have loved you, my dear, but never trusted you. So, you were determined to come over, eh? *Mi casa su casa*, but I shall have counted the towels and put my initials on the silver before you are welcome here."

"You would never allow me back without some handicap."

"I would demand some concession on your part. About your appearance."

"I'm prettier than you. You're jealous. This is a ground we covered millennia past. What is it this time? You want me to have three heads and snakes for hair? Spare me the Bullfinch, my Leviathan."

"I feel a certain responsibility, a dedication to the mental health of my, uh... constituents. It wouldn't do to have you frightening them out of their wits with an evocation from their race memory. Can't have it, y'know: Mama Molasses popping up and making a stimmis. Simply wouldn't do, not at all. So these are my conditions: you may come over to troubleshoot, but no proselytizing. The status quo has been good to me. The status quo ante... well, it speaks for itself. Disorganized, what? All blood, ignorance and mumbo-jumbo. Gotta keep a lid on things."

"I will be able to speak."

"You shall, my cupcake. And to demonstrate that my heart is in the right place, I have allowed some randomness to enter the mix. In the tracking down of this self-anointed provocateur who is murdering your prize porkers, you are doing holy work, of benefit to us both. You will be yourself, intermittently, and at times unexpected and of limited duration. Just to keep you on your toes."

The goddess stared at a speck somewhere in the middle distance and, keeping her anger under control, calculated Pi to eight thousand places. "Pi," said the serenely beautiful one. El looked startled. "Irrational and transcendent, the number. Much as you and I, it just goes on. And now it is expected I should demonstrate humility at your generous open-handedness?"

"That I would expect from a robot or dancing chicken. You, Morgana-mine, are cut from a finer thread. We have a certain elegance, you and I.

Otherwise, what were we? Just dried peas rattling about in their pods. If this were something important I would perhaps give it my personal attention. But..."

"If I may reframe what you just said, you don't know what to do, correct?"

"Obviously. If I knew I wouldn't be talking to you, now would I? Silly girl. Run along and perform great works. We expect great things from you."

"But you don't know just what."

"Precisely. You are catching on. Come on over by all means, my dear. It has been simply eons. I notice that you have kept your figure. Attention to the little things—discipline, I admire that. But you are not enthusiastic. Have you ever asked yourself why you can perform more of what your human charges call 'miraculous' in your venue than I can in mine? Because they have defined you less. I am hobbled by ritual and usage."

"Poor demiurge. What would you have—the two of us charging in like the cavalry? Science does not smile on simultaneity; denying basic physics is lethal to gods and men alike."

"Nononono, my pet. Connivance and manipulation instead of intimidation. It's the wave of the future; believe me, you'll learn to love it. Admittedly, working through human agency is a tricky business. They are a pettifogging lot. I shall willingly withdraw. For a time. There are things that need to get done and you need a change, and I've got just the place for you. Here you are always welcome. Why let our irreconcilable hostilities drive a wedge between us?"

❏

Seated in the dust of her cellar, the Fata Morgana blinked her eyes. A spider had woven a web connecting the tip of her nose to the horns of the Cow. Satisfied, she rose and transferred a kiss from her fingertips to the nose of the Cow, then the nose of the Goat.

"Fare-thee-well, friends. Keep my secrets. We go to perform great works."

The Goat's lugubrious striped vanilla tongue lay across the floor; the Cow's blind eyes stared at nothing.

The Cicerone

A ragged red-haired girl, nine or ten years of age, hugged her chin to her knobbly knees as she sat scrunched up on the edge of a great carved oak refectory table. The child eyed the golem of the Fata Morgana appraisingly. "You are a remarkably good job," she said.

"Huh? Oh, yes. You are a little girl. Do I know you?" Biff's attention had been elsewhere.

"You will get to know me," said the little girl. "I am an aspect of the Orange Virgin."

"Then, how do you do," said Biff as he stared into the mirror. He saw the jagged peeling of strips of shiny painted-on mercury emulsion hanging from the reverse of the glass. Ah, there he was! He was balancing a cup of tea on one razor-creased knee, intent on saving his tennis flannels as he contended with a raspberry tart. There was an emphasis on form when one was invited to tea. Petit fours and cucumber sandwiches and a balancing act every time. Demitasse and tiny spoons, napkins on the knee. One liked to observe the niceties.

"Do you come here often. I mean..." Biff had trouble forming the words. He had never before had to speak with anyone other than the Orange Virgin. "I... I have never. This is my first time. Has this always been here?" He reached for another raspberry tart. It might be a long time between dinners. "Ow!" He bruised a knuckle on the glass. The tarts, the tea, the tennis flannels existed only in the mirror. Biff looked down; he was naked.

"The raspberry tarts. They're not real," said the child. Biff ignored her as he savored the taste of raspberries. "I am real. You have potential."

"I have been told this," said Biff. "I am to have an interview with my cicerone—a glorified babysitter from the way the Fata Morgana says it—one of those Morgana words that fills the mouth and bedazzles the brain." Biff Bangtree wished he could perspire. Biff studied his reflection.

"You are beautiful," said the Wise Child.

"Have you noticed? I don't sweat," said Biff.

Perspiration would be a healthy thing, agreed the Wise Child, as perspiration helped to cleanse one's pores. "My goodness gracious, but you are infectious," said the child. She had caught herself studying her own reflection in a polished steel omelet pan.

Tall, wide shouldered, narrow of hip, Biff leaned over the child, checking himself in the omelet pan, knees bent, bringing his face even with the girl's in the field of reflection.

"Checking to see if you're still there?" asked the child.

Biff was pleased his reflection existed in two places. But the child was beginning to annoy him. "All right, so I'm vain about my looks."

"You are naked, Biff, you dummy. You really should consider getting out more. So few men have the profile to strut naked. But you know what they say: too many trips to the mirror and you are an environmental hazard. Killing the fish, abrading the genetic structure of generations yet unborn. Don't suck at the mercury, there's a good boy. There's no one behind the glass. Just you in front of it."

Biff gave one last primp, indulging a final denial of what he saw. Whether sucking the silver off a mirror or licking the shiny bottom off an omelet pan, Biff liked to look nice.

The Wise Child sat on the table, admiring. The great refectory table filled the center aisle of the kitchen. "You will drive the women mad with desire, Biff," offered the Wise Child.

"Hi Guy," said Biff to his reflection, feeling silly, yet in the grip of a checking compulsion, he gave his high chef's hat an adjustment. With liquid joints and the easy grace of one born to admiration, Biff had the strut.

"And to think you make up all this nonsense by yourself," said the Wise Child.

"Shouldn't my teacher be here by now?"

There was a crunch and muted cursing from beneath the great refectory table. "Make things up?" said a voice from under the table. "Sounds very creative to me. We might begin your lessons with the study of creativity."

"Oh, that must be your babysitter," said the Wise Child. "He must be under the table."

"I say, are you stuck?" asked Biff. He crouched to behold a creature made up of many other creatures. Porcupine, man, lizard, eagle, scorpion. The creature seemed as surprised as he was.

"Ours not to wonder why, ours but to do or die. *Morituri te salutem. Ave atque vale*. Hail Caesar. Hardly a cheery reflection," said The Manticore. "Yes, I am stuck in the furniture. Here I am, sent out on a fool's errand therefore I must be the fool. So glad to meet up with you. The Queen of Heaven is tight-mouthed with her allusions, even for a goddess. She always makes things so damned complicated..." The creature seemed to be continuing a conversation with someone behind it. Biff looked up; peculiar, there was no door in that direction.

Biff got passing notice. "Hiya, Your Worshipfulness. The lad and I are going to have jolly times together." The apparition was speaking to the Destroyer, Biff realized. The statue with the necklace of skulls had followed him. Receiving no response, the Manticore spoke to Biff—a blue sizzle and a whiff of ozone, radio smells: "Well, I seem to be on the job already. Look at this—pants but no pockets." The Manticore had been stuffed into a set of plaid golfing knickers. "The Fata Morgana must have been distracted. Neat bonnet though." The Manticore tried to turn around and view its hindquarters. A horned Viking helmet was perched on a ruff of quills that encircled its face; its legs and feet were vaguely a lion's though covered with scales.

"What happened to your skin? It's all black."

A smile displayed rows of fangs. "Odd you should notice that. Damned if I know. This is a first time for both of us; I've never seen all of me before either. I seem to be in disguise, but you picked up on the pigment right away." Holding the helmet at arm's length, the Manticore tested the point of one of the horns with a fingertip. "Got to hand it to you—you're real observant." Any intended sarcasm was lost on Biff. The finger was quickly pulled back. A drop of greenish fluid welled up at a puncture. "Best to play it safe; you never know where these things have been." The Manticore put the finger in its mouth. Biff approved of this.

"I guess the horns are to keep us thinking." He sucked his finger for a while and looked at the Destroyer, then at Biff. The Manticore decided Biff was his best bet for conversation. The finger was removed. "Behold, my lad: the Hat from Hell. Far be it for the Fata Morgana, Orange Virgin, etc., etc. to send her humble operative into hostile territory defenseless." Holding the horned hat before him and at the height of his head, he advanced on Biff. "An investiture. You desire this chapeau?"

Feeling his way around some incidental furniture, Biff backed away. "No, no. No." Biff shook his head from side to side.

"So be it, then—no takers—another idea whose time has went."

The stranger allowed the helmet to pivot on the axis of his middle fingers until the horns pointed down. "Ave atque vale. Sic semper offensive headgear." He dropped the hat and it struck trembling, each horn embedded a full inch in the floor. "That I should be here at all and uttering such things is, in itself, a patent absurdity. My mistress seems to have packed me with a com-pendium of phrases for all occasions, and inflected in an argot to compliment my aspect. You have met my hat. I am the Manticore. Call me Manny."

The stranger walked forward, hand extended. Biff hesitantly took it and asked, "Are you a private eye?" The radio had told him of the adventures of Sam Spade; Nick Carter, Master Detective; The Thin Man; The Fat Man; Johnny Dollar, The Man with the Action-Packed Expense Account; and Mister Keene, Tracer of Lost Persons. They were 'operatives.' They did things, went places. Biff Bangtree knew he would look neat in an ice cream suit and a snap-brim fedora or summer-weight Panama hat.

"Could be, kid, could be." The Manticore held Biff's hand longer than was customary with handshakes; but Biff could not know this, for this was his first. The grip grew tighter and tighter as The Manticore's steely gaze held Biff's eyes. "You're not human, are you?" With that, The Manticore wrenched off Biff's hand.

Biff was dumbfounded, shocked and struggling; people were not supposed to behave this way. The Manticore's hand—a stiff arm with five powerful splayed black fingers and a flattened palm the size and weight of a manhole cover—in the middle of Biff's chest kept him immobilized while the sundered part was examined at length, turned over and over.

"Good work. She do it?" A tilt of the head indicated The Destroyer. "Furniture you can't sit on. Must be art. Can't say that she adds much in the way of comfort to the old place."

Comfort. The word brought memories of steaming bowls of oatmeal with cinnamon and sugar mornings, baked apple with brandy and a dollop of whipped cream evenings. Biff nodded eagerly, trying to get past the fence of fingers and back together with his property. The stranger spoke in conciliatory tones. "Yes, yes, of course it's yours. Just having a little look-see." The Manticore dropped his guard and, as Biff fell forward, seized his forearm with a paralyzing strength and slapped the hand back in place, locking it on with a quick quarter-turn and reverse.

Biff wiggled his fingers. The Manticore had wrenched him apart, then reassembled him. In spite of this abrupt behavior, Biff was encouraged. "I am experiencing Life. It has begun and I am on my way."

"I expect that is so. You are certainly naive, but right on the money." Wings behind his back, the Manticore was having a stroll around the room. "Glad you think so. Not the most auspicious start, but a start.

Definitely that." The Destroyer looked on implacably. "This your old Mum, eh?"

The stranger let his eyes roam over the distant ceiling where painted fluffy cloudscapes interspersed with gilded beams. Feigning unconcern, he then quickly swung around trying to catch the statue's eyes following him. She stood unmoving. "Her intent must be decorative." The Manticore poked the Destroyer's belly with a finger and jumped back.

This strange creature must be the teacher Biff had been told to expect.

"In the absence of any firm direction, your apprenticeship begins here."

"Uh, I am learning to make a quiche."

"A quiche baker, eh? She didn't tell me that. Seems a lot of bother, but if that is the destiny the Queen of Heaven has mapped out for you." The Manticore turned his back, absorbed with the immobile goddess. "You are what you are, my boy. But this..."

Biff was dismissed; he hurried to catch up with the conversation. There had been a question—his old Mum. "Uh, yes. She is, but not all of her. The rest of her is in a radio."

"'Sir.' You may call me 'Sir,' and I know what a radio is, you boob. At this moment the Queen of Heaven is on a Piranesi staircase through a wall with no backside and on a spinning orb a ninety-degree turn from nowhere. She is stranded all the way from Tuesday, much as I was. This one here is stiff as a cigar store Indian. Or would be if I knew what a cigar store Indian was. It is the place of the Fata Morgana to be constantly refashioned by the eye of the beholder. It is her place to be everywhere at once and at all times, whereas we stand on an endless linear now surrounded by the wreckage of the past. You and I are dots on a line. She is the line, and she will return. You didn't know that, did you, young laddie-buck?"

Biff hadn't the slightest idea what the stranger was talking about. What was this that he was supposed to know? He found the stranger's way with words confusing, but he seemed to be implying that whatever he was doing here had to do with Biff's future, his career. Biff gave it a test.

"Uh, were you in the radio? You mean Morgana won't be coming back? What is a cigar store Indian? Can you make a quiche?"

"No. Yes. This. And perhaps."

"What?"

"What, 'Sir,' please. As a golem you are a fine job of work, but a bit of a rattlebrain. Pay attention when I talk, boy. I can whip up the damndest most glorious quiche you ever laid tooth to and will show you how, but you must first ransom your credibility by giving me your undivided attention and cooperation. It's you and I, young laddie-buck that, in the absence of her puissant loveliness here, are left to carry on all manner of good works."

The Manticore grasped the Destroyer by the nose and started her spinning. The creature got down on all fours and, as the Destroyer spun faster and faster, picking up momentum, slid one hand under her whirling feet to gauge clearance. "You'll excuse me, but I found her presence disquieting." He dusted off his hands as the Destroyer spun faster, her increasing velocity creating a fearsome roar. But there was no wind, not even a perceptible breeze. The Manticore produced a cigar from within his ruff of quills and patted his golfing pants in search of a pocket with matches. He was pleased. "Your basic gyroscopic effect."

Slowly, gracefully, the Destroyer began to sink into the floor, leaving a neat, polished borehole.

"Wow! Where did you learn to do that?"

"True, boy, true. Impressive it is—neater than a quiche and no cleanup after. And were her apotheosis to return without warning, she could do me much mischief. Believe me, Biff-me-boyo, she doesn't feel a thing and with her out of harm's way, I can devote all my energies to the matter at hand. To wit: your education."

"Uh, I'm afraid you're going too fast for me. Could you slow things down a bit? That was a neat trick, though."

"Slickness, my boy, is a learned response. It's all in the presentation. I don't do tricks; you do tricks. What you see happening, what you apprehend to be marvelous goings-on, are a mere window dressing. The dazzled beholder must look behind the flash to find the form, the substance. It's all in the interpretation. I do what I have to do and you will follow along as far as your limited perceptions allow."

The stranger was implying he was a conjuror, or a god.

"Right on both counts. And your thoughts are as transparent as your vacuous, sculpted, aristocratic face. Close but no cigar." He flourished his stogie. "I am conjuror sufficient to our needs and the messenger of a goddess. De minimis—a little hocus-pocus goes a long way. This has been your first lesson."

The Return of the Orange Virgin

He waved at the borehole where the Destroyer had all but disappeared. "Right now I am happier with that old trout down the hole. You and I must have some time alone. Look at me."

Biff looked at the Manticore.

"I inspire trust, do I not? Come; be honest. If I am to be your tutor there must be no barriers of doubt between us."

"You don't look like I had imagined."

"You were expecting me?"

"Not exactly. You said you were an 'operative'. I know about private eyes."

"I'll just bet you do. Ah-ha!" Scooping a packet of wax matches from a tabouret near a bronze brazier, the Manticore tried to light up his cigar. He squinted with concentration; the little wax matches burned quickly. A second guttering match end fell to the floor. "Ahhh..." The Manticore coughed, exhaling a rich blue cloud of banded Havana.

"Are you sure you should suck it in that deep?" Biff was delighted: this was a tough guy, although not quite as he had imagined Dolby Jenks, Space Ace would look.

"A habit long deprived, me laddie-buck, though even with cement lungs caution is indicated." A series of ecstatic puffs, and his eyes rolled back beneath the forest of quills. "The universe is about getting boiled with its socks on and here I am speaking, living, breathing. And puffing on this admirable stogie. Whoa! Hey, there, I do believe I just felt my tail. Let me give it a check. Yes, definitely, I feel something there." He turned his head around, body following, but came up short against his quills, knocking the ember from the tip of his cigar. There was a smell of burning. "I don't suppose you have another match?"

Biff shook his head.

The Manticore sighed and stuck the cold cigar behind one ear. "Later, then. We are going to play a game together, you and I. You, because you seem real but are not, and I, who am not but seem real. A paradox and a conundrum, what a pair of private eyes we shall make, eh? Close your jaw; its hanging there betrays your astonishment. A gentleman is never astonished. And I shall make of you a gentleman, or at least an intimate bore, close and confiding. Ah, how you shall charm the ladies, but don't forget the breath mints."

Placing an index finger at the top of Biff's head as a pivot point, the Manticore took Biff's right hand in his left and, their arms extended together, began shuffling his feet.

"This is dancing, a social grace. The sinister and the dexter, left and right, working together to their mutual betterment. The spirit of cooperation, much as you and I will help each other. Now—just how much of what I have said do you remember? Don't strain yourself; just offhand, what do you immediately recall?"

"Uh, that we are dancing, charming ladies and boiling socks, sir. Why are we cooking the socks? What are ladies?"

"A dismal start. But at least a start, this in itself is promising. You and I are castaways here in Morganaland till we can work effectively as a team: the old school try, give 'em what for, and appended bullshit. I shall play cicerone to your Caliban. Know what that means?"

"Uh, no, sir."

"You will by the time you stop spinning."

The Manticore whipped him like a toy top and executed a handoff, leaving Biff spinning on his heels. As he picked up speed, bright stationary objects in the room became continuous ribbons of color.

The Manticore stood back and admired his handiwork. "Man of clay, you are back again on the potter's wheel, Caliban's centrifugal womb. This time, however, only for a few adjustments."

Biff hugged his arms to himself for fear of their flying off. The spinning was hauntingly familiar; he felt the pangs of birth again as the contents of his head pressed out against his ears. "Is this really necessary?"

"Not in the least. It simply keeps you from asking stupid questions till we're all through and tidy. See? Already that was a perceptive question."

Biff felt his ear on the move again. He was picking up speed and the roar of his cyclonic tunnel made the Manticore shout to be heard.

"You are a boob! We shall un-boob you, then! Oh, stop that damned spinning, it gets on my nerves."

"But, but..." There was a sudden stop and the traveling ear flew off.

"But, but..." The Manticore mocked. "You sound like a farting ungulate. Now, what is a cicerone?"

Biff didn't feel any smarter, just dizzy. "I still don't know."

The Manticore retrieved the ear and handed it back. "Yours, I believe. The Fata Morgana has eons to play around with as do I and, it would appear, you. But I am easily bored, nothing personal. I find freedom exhilarating and, frankly, want to step out." The Manticore turned and walked away. "Come, let us have a converse. If memory serves, there will be a game park outside. The Dancing Lords were proud of their manicured lawns and arboriculture. Quite conducive to creative reflection."

Set deep in a recessed arch was a small oaken door with heavy iron nails studding its crossbucks. The door's arched top was no higher than Biff's chin. The Manticore undogged the latch and stepped through. "Hold your head low, boy. Whoa-oo!" He clutched wildly at a rickety scaffolding that creaked as he scrambled to recover his balance. He had walked out into thin air high above an empty moat. "A demonstration of the ever-present unforeseen which surround us. A cicerone is a guide, a teacher helping you find a thread of meaning in the commonplace. This, for instance, was a surprise." He regained a desperate composure. "Don't look down. The last time I looked down from high on a parapet, there was dry land out this door. Dry and level. I see things have changed and not for the better."

Trying to appear unruffled, the cicerone—scorpion, eagle, serpent, porcupine, and lion with the face of a man—walked out onto a plank no wider than a single footfall, grinning broadly. The plank bowed precariously under his weight. "Truly limber lumber. But dry and cured. It should hold." He balanced in the middle of the plank and jumped up and down a few times. There were creaks as the timber butt advanced and retreated almost to the edge of the doorsill. "Close enough, but only one at a time. Follow me." The Manticore sauntered forward through the air. The trelliswork swayed and bounced. As he reached the other side he called back, "Well, what're you waiting for?"

Biff gulped, closed his eyes, and charged across.

Safely over, Biff looked down. It was a good sixty feet to a hard landing. The caked and cratered mud of the exposed moat bed was littered with construction debris and decaying kitchen leavings, some recent and green, some older and gray. Fumes arose; the accumulation was distressingly high; a rat scuttled away. Biff caught at his ear and hurried to catch up with the Manticore who was gesturing expansively as he strolled ahead over a well kept greensward.

"I have plans, me laddie-buck. Freedom is a new feeling to me. We are destined to strut, you and I, but there are some problems. For the time being I am looking after the interests of a considerable and, ahem, distant employer. But I am about doing great things, and you shall be my assistant."

Biff's heart—and he had a heart, for he was anatomically correct—leaped within his bosom. "Is that like a job?" He remembered the radio. "Like a Dolby Jenks, Space Ace, in the real world?"

❏

They strolled until dusk. The Manticore expounded while Biff grew reassured listening.

"Art—music, poetry, the fletching of arrows, well wedged clay thrown on the flying wheel into perfect proportions—is all inside of itself. As we practice art we pretend we are reinterpreting the world around us, getting outside of ourselves. Words talk to words, nothing grander. Art practices us even as the hoary general, shaking with delirium, his boots full of piss, calls for the charge. The soldiers shoot each other; they do not cook quiches. A sloppy expedient—the imitation of life. The Old Ones, the Dancing Lords, did it all the time; I know all about it. It is safe within a discipline, think you? Dreams are about dreams but they can lure you in, even as music explains nothing even as it makes you a part of it, a slippery pole to nowhere."

The Manticore knew everything. There was trouble and they were going to fix it. They were partners, like the private eyes on the radio. When they arrived again at the weathered bridge of planks, Biff walked right across, eyes open, scattering a flight of carrion crows who wrestled tidbits from the garbage below.

❏

All was not as they left it.

"Up, bup, bup..."

"There you go, the farting ungulate noises again. I would have hoped our times together would have imparted some self-assurance. Talk in sentences, lad."

"Buh, bup, bup..." If the cicerone had had sleeves, Biff would have been tugging at them.

"S'matter boy? Uh-oh." The Manticore executed a slow pirouette in time to observe a whiskered pink muzzle rise over the side of the Destroyer's hole. It was speaking.

"You are here to welcome me to your sunny shores. Yes, that's it, how foolish of little me."

The Return of the Orange Virgin

From out of the hole rose a small spotted pig with the easy grace of an absolute monarch treading gently through a crowd of deserving poor. "No, don't move; I want to remember you always with your jaws hanging out like that. Sorry to ruin whatever surprises you had planned but your gloomy lazaret was, well... dark, so I thought I'd come on up and join the fun."

"Well, I am almost impressed." The Manticore, who was frightened, decided not to show it in front of Biff.

"I would prefer to believe you two perpetrators didn't chuck me down that hole out of spite, but someone has to accept responsibility for this high-handed treatment and you're it." The pig floated to the center of the old oak refectory table and touched down on point, balancing on the tips of all four trotters. "Explain yourselves, please, and don't be tedious. Thus far your definition of fun has been sadly lacking." The pig—a spotted china with a tight brushy tip to her tail—stretched, sat, and raised a desultory hind leg to scratch an ear.

"You have the advantage," offered the Manticore. "You know us but we do not know you. I do not recall chucking you in the lazaret, if this is what has you exercised."

The pig hopped down from the table, made a circuit of the borehole, then sat down and licked her crotch. "I thought it was an excellent likeness, too. Everybody is a critic." Looking up from her grooming, she addressed Biff. "You, mud man—switch my wickets if you aren't the sanest of the lot. Miss your old Mum, eh?" Biff looked nervously to the Destroyer's hole. "Your protégé, Manticore, is made of finer clay than most people, and you would be advised to use him gently."

"You have a name for me, madame swine, but I as yet have none for you," said the Manticore. "I should be impressed, I know, but I fear I find you little more than a preposterous ball of porcine adorableness."

"You do not realize who I am? On a scale of one to ten, I find you likewise deficient." The pig curled back her lip, showing rows of white teeth, long and sharp, then twisted around to worry a something at the base of her tail. "You will be receiving no references. I am not a happy camper. However, a beneficent, charitable nature allows me to overlook the accommodations in my pit of durance vile." The pig finished her grooming. "You really don't know, do you?"

The Manticore tried to recline on a couch, but gave it up, his scorpion tail kept getting in the way. Instead, he perched on a stool. "Well, you are not a tourist. Your hostility would indicate that you have been bushwhacked and abducted. Not by us. This is all very sad, but we did not throw you into the hole. You are pretentious and irrelevant. Your continued presence will contribute little to the progress of our great work."

"'Great work' is it now! And it is I who am deemed pretentious. For all you know, I am a messenger of the gods, an unrecognized blessing on these, your frowsty shores. Oops, sorry! You moved and here I'm all out of film. Your time is up and you are presumed guilty."

"I, too, am sorry, but you will have to go. No hard feelings, nothing personal." The Manticore hopped off the stool and lumbered forward as the pig executed a flanking maneuver around the far end of the table.

"We have had a battle of wits which you, Sir Manticore, have lost, not even knowing we were engaged." She turned to where the horned Viking helmet was embedded in the planking of the floor. "Come."

Her eyes crossed slightly as she concentrated. The helmet trembled and strained and, with a squeal of a rusty spike exiting old oak, it popped free and settled on her head. She charged the Manticore, neatly stapling his ankle to the wall. "Oh, yes, I was listening as you dithered about. And I consider it poor-spirited for you to have dumped my likeness down a hole. And who am I? I am the Fata Morgana. I have been wrestling in Limbo with the god-king of otherwhere. And now with you. A full day. By the way, I love your pants"

The Manticore tested the strength of his bond, tugging gently at the helmet. The horns were stuck fast. "Will you always be a piglet? Or do you get a rematch? Of course, then you might end up as a sofa or an end table."

The pig paced a tight semicircle in front of the Manticore, whose seat on the stool Biff had commandeered. "Snappy cracks, and my, my, just look at you." The pig executed a four shouldered shrug. "You will have to do better. As a teacher you were unique and available. I make use of what is at hand. I admire that in myself—I am resourceful. Imagine my surprise when you two decided that I was in the way and popped me down that hole."

Biff spoke. "Uh, why are you a pig?"

"I thought you'd never ask. His Wonderfulness has been having His little chuckle." There was a 'pop' and the pig disappeared. The Fata Morgana, Orange Virgin, etc., etc. was leaning back in a chair, feet on the table. Biff stared at the place on the floor where the pig had been. He crawled about feeling the tiles. They were warm. "Perhaps I should have stayed a quadruped," said the Orange Virgin. "You're really quite cute bent over on all fours like that."

The Return of the Orange Virgin

"Would you mind awfully, while the lad is down there, having him help me with this staple?" asked the Manticore.

Morgana nodded and Biff pulled the helmet out of the wall. "I can't leave you two together alone for a few hours and you are hatching a revolution. Wonderful! This is just the spirit I hoped you would show." Biff and the Manticore relaxed as relief washed over them.

"YOU!" The Manticore felt flattened against the wall by the force of the goddess' invective. "You are a pompous, overblown mucker-about in the closets of deceit. Fomenting discord, are we? I am proud. Yes, proud of you both. You are so inept as to make able shock troops should I call you to my aid in the isles of unwisdom."

"I-i-i-isles..."

"Of unwisdom. Just a figure of speech. The Other Side, you know. I was getting comfortable as a pig." Morgana shrugged. "I found having four shoulders so expressive. Well, soon enough again."

The censer pot of a bronze tripod that had been sedately glowing in a corner shot forth a shower of sparks, the thurible swinging on its chains. "Yoo-hoo, anybody home?" The voice came from the glowing coals; a funnel of sparks rose and scattered against the ceiling tiles. "Having a family gathering, I see. I thought since we had broken the ice, so to speak, I could just pop over for some fraternal interaction."

"Who is that?" Biff walked to the brazier and held his hand over the coals.

"My putative adversary, and unbearably chummy. Hot, darling, no. Don't do that, you'll smell up the house. Yes, El, of course. Why stand on ceremony. Do you have something to say or are you just passing through?"

"Tush, Morgana, there you go again, painting me with too black a brush. I just stopped by to impart a bit of friendly advice, some intelligence that will save us both a lot of needless bother further down the road."

"Don't be facile, El; I am sure there are a plenitude of demands upon your busy schedule. Speak your peace and go."

"Someday you will thank me for this, Morgana, believe me. Your priestess is careening around over here and with a supreme lack of direction. I know she is yours: she is wearing the moonsign of the Fata Morgana but hasn't the slightest what she is about. Hardly your style, my dear."

"She's there already? This Linda, Linda..." The Orange Virgin blocked her mind from an attack by the sky-demon. He would discover the existence of the duplicate Linda. This would not do.

"Winkelman, Linda Winkelman. My dear, I do these things for you and you can't just go and forget. She is yours. No wonder she has forgotten her name when you've forgotten it too. Or so it seems. Did you feel my touch?"

"Forgotten. She's there? Touch?"

"And decidedly not ready. You see, my dumpling, I know everything. She has attached herself to one of the less distinguished of my flock, A crony of this Harry Pease of ours. She is flopping about like beached squid. I sense a gap between action and intent here. Have you been into the raspberry again, Morgana? I have been so looking forward to this, having you over—exacting blood for blood, wreaking havoc: the Eumenides charging about, flailing at whole populations, extirpating them all for the sins of their king. I love it. Just like old times."

"Keep talking. Your enthusiasm persuades me to stay home and forget the whole thing."

"Ever the ingénue. Pish-posh, Morgana, you are as curious as I am."

"Wait a minute. If she is there and I didn't send her, then she must be one of yours. She and the pig-killer, too."

"A nasty innuendo, the way you phrase that."

The Manticore shuffled anxiously; his cigar had gone out. He approached the charcoal brazier for a light. There was a shower of sparks and he jumped back.

"Butt out, fuzzy. Your mistress and I are talking. Go stick your head in the stove."

"She shouldn't be there yet, "said the Fata Morgana. "I had only prepared her way. There was a dream-sending..."

"To her boyfriend's dog. You sent a dog on a god's errand. What'd you expect him to do? I don't know where you found this woman, and I don't want to know, although something tells me I will be intimately involved with her before we are through. Anyhow, she is there, on the ground, and you had better go recruit her, albeit after the fact. She is here to do your bidding—go bid her. Hustle your buns, Oh Princess of Light and Love."

"El... *you* told me about the dog, Prince. I only introduced myself."

The brazier assumed a disinterested tone. "Get to your knitting—dragoon the wench and get her straightened out. Read her whatever articles of initiation your witches need to know. She is here right now, all sneakers and granola. Exact your vengeance. Get the job done and get out. Let Me get on with My life."

"I shall have to catch her before she leaves. Oh, how I hate this. Life was simple and beautiful and because you let things slide it is becoming all a mess."

"She's waiting for her baggage. Send it." The brazier flared. "It was your pig started this, Morgana."

The brazier sputtered and went out.

Linda in Wonderland

Linda Winkelman opened her eyes the slightest possible and found the light painful. An effusion of cinnamon and yeast that hung in the saturated air made her nauseous; there could be less steam, please. What she saw through a latticework of lashes was a large, echoing cavern—spotless. A center aisle stretched toward a hearth whence issued the smells of baking. This had to be a kitchen—it was hot and steamy; but not the sort of kitchen where you imagined a wizened granny happily concocting dinners for hungry threshermen. Walls and shelves glittered and bloomed with implements but a forlorn smell of buns gone wrong pervaded the ancient air. She was experiencing the kaleidoscope vertigo and ringing ears of a mild hangover. Walk it off, that was it. That must have been one hell of a party.

Her last memories were of the 7th Avenue local. That skanky man, the one with the smelly overcoat! Linda gagged and found that her mouth was taped shut. An unpleasant odor of unwashed citizen and a large hand reached from behind to remove the tape. "*Ouch!*"

"Sorry, my dear—that should help you breathe easier," said someone from out of her sight.

"Who are you? Where am I?" No answer. *Oh, Jesus, I'm not dreaming, there was no party. Register terror, please.* A fresh smell of burning mixed with the stale cooking odors of many yesteryears.

Her brain was receiving messages from far away places of her body that now was not the best time to make any sudden moves. "Oh well, it's now or never." She tried to stand and was pulled up short. "What?" Her wrists and ankles were bound with white surgical tape. That brought her eyes wide open. Yes, she was tied up, definitely tied, and seated on a wooden bench at a long polished table. An empty spool and a pair of shears lay on the floor at her feet. Whoever had tied her up had taken a few turns around the bench, leaving a short tether, then apparently run out of tape.

Sweet reasonableness said she should now be in a blind, paralytic panic. Nope—no goosebumps, no horripilation or trembling, just wobbly was all. Here I am cool as a cucumber and mightily pissed-off. She held onto the anger and cherished it. She was tied hand and foot, a prisoner of person or persons unknown, most likely drugged and unconscious minutes before, and she was making plans. Linda started to laugh, the laugh became a sneeze, she reached to scratch her nose and was brought up short by the tape. The unrelieved itch was more demanding than uncertain prospects at the hands of her captors. She stood and the adhesive tape tore. With both hands still tied together she joyously scratched her nose. No longer attached to the bench, she could turn, and if need be, hop about. She tried unwrapping her hands with her teeth, but with minimal results. "Huh." People did it in the movies all the time. Well then, feet first, hands later. Before bending to undo her ankles, she took a deep breath and looked around. Close by were tangy overtones of burnt eggs and cheese and haphazardly tended bread whose yeast had worked too long. A blocky, bearded, well-muscled man she recognized from the subway was occupied at the stovetop burners of an enamel, iron and nickel plate range. He wore a high starched chef's hat and an apron knotted on his chest. He was stabbing at an omelette pan with a spatula.

Linda paused to monitor her heart rate. Good. Regular, not racing with terror, just like in aerobics class. Goes to show you never know how you will react in a crisis until the crisis occurs. "I assume that I have been kidnapped." Her voice did not sound as confident as she felt.

The man looked up at her, still digging at the omelette pan. "You are conscious. Excellent. Sorry about the tape, but We like to observe the forms. Isn't that what kidnappers are supposed to do—the tape, I mean? I'm new to this hands-on stuff. You were becoming restless and I had to inject you. I had feared I got the dosage wrong."

"You chloroformed me, *and* shot me full of dope? I want you to untie me. NOW."

"Damn!" The burly man started, jumped and dropped the pan. At the expletive, a moth dropped like a rock from where it had been fluttering at the ceiling in a mating frenzy with a light bulb. "No need to shout," said the man. "Softly, please."

"I am not up on the etiquettes of abduction. Untie me. *Now*."

The Return of the Orange Virgin

The man ignored Linda. He was on his hands and knees under the stove, muttering. The pan retrieved, he set it on the table and started unwinding the bandages. "Sorry about the chloroform, my dear, but My powers are limited these days and I have had to fall back on chemistry My wonders to perform. Deity become a footnote—a sad turn of events. But the she-witch, the succubus, who throttles your mind has been likewise affected; I am comforted. You hear voices?"

Faith. Joy. Warm elbows, said the voice in Linda's head, a woman's voice. *Bounce and forget, bounce and forget.* "Norma Jean leFay from work," said Linda. "Just something I have already heard. It'll go away. And if you are saying I am nuts, I should point out I am the kidnapped one. You are the nutcase."

"So, the Orange Virgin is with us, My own lovely adversary, the same. Thank you for the gratuitous tidbit. I would have uncovered your, ah... penetration on My own, of course, but..."

"Your 'powers' are limited? You have no powers. You are a sociopath. A rapist even. People are 'conspiring' against *you* and *I* hear voices? Paranoid schizophrenia. You need professional help." Linda pulled back as her abductor leaned close to whisper in her face.

"Do you ever dream about the slaughter of pigs? No need to answer, we are not assigning guilt here. Or uniform tiny curls like the tops of Dairy Queen soft ice cream cones? Low cholesterol, the latest scientific breakthrough? Just wondering."

This guy is certifiable, thought Linda. A slaughter of pigs. Linda harkened back to that morning's brainstorming with Creative. "Pork-A-Dillos, yes."

"Crackly salty tidbits of fried pork rind? My, but aren't we just breaking all the rules. Read your Bible, darling—Leviticus Eleven, verses 7 and 11." The man unwrapped another winding of tape and knelt to massage Linda's ankles. "There, give it a bit till the circulation comes back, eh? Hope We haven't made you too uncomfortable, but We had to get you out of the picture for a while. The Pork-A-Dillos led Us right to you. Funny."

"Funny? I don't think this is one bit funny." There was an icy note of calm in her voice.

The Tevye guy babbled on. "We homed in on you like pigeon in a dovecote. We did it, Herself and I. The Fata Morgana, I mean. Much as I, she can make holes in time and start new solar systems spinning, upend the pyramids and unwind the skein of probability in a dozen different realities, but she can't come back home till I let her." He suddenly stopped, as though having said too much. He waved the omelet pan under Linda's nose. "Just look at that—a quiche of welcome. I forgot all about it in the excitement."

"The Fata Morgana. That is your partner? The voice in my head? You don't have to be anxious about giving anything away; I most likely wouldn't understand it anyway. Everything you have said so far is gibberish to me."

"Sorry about that. And this, too. I was only trying to be helpful." Her kidnapper batted his eyes at her and flashed a leer of many yellow teeth. "It was chloral hydrate, Mickey Finn, you know—that was what We injected you with."

Linda rubbed her ankles. "That may be the name of the dope you used, but who are you? *All* of you. And where are we and why are we here?"

"I have been called The Rider on the Storm—a prime mover, if you will. For now you may call me, ahh... call me..." El patted his vest. There were usually papers if one had the sense to look for them. He consulted an inside breast pocket full of pens and mechanical pencils. There was a nametag. "Gershon Meyrowitz, since you ask. And this is a sub-cellar of the Hotel Taft. They walled it in when the hotel closed. And I do hope that you are asking a simple question of names, backgrounds and map coordinates. There could be a..."

"Problem? I'll give you problems, buddy. For starters, I would be pleased to hear about just what the hell is going on."

"My dear, charming and very, if I may say so, acerbic Linda, you shall have all the answers your heart desires. All in good time. A lot could be read into what you have only just now disingenuously spilled from your cupid's-bow lips; nonetheless, I am prepared to reveal all to you, viz: what the countryside looks like beyond these walls, for your freedom while you are here will be unrestricted. You already have our names and our histories shall be forthcoming. As to the why-ness, I am prepared to discuss why my colleague and I are about what we are, though if you wish to explore the metaphysical aspects of why-ness, of Linda-ness, or the whatness of if... I shall have to refer to my notes." He opened a loose leaf binder the size of the Chicago Yellow Pages. "Observe." He riffled the pages under Linda's nose. The pages made an appreciable breeze. They were blank. "While I am prepared, my notes are not." He levered a pot lid open on a huge iron range, exposing glowing coals on the grates. "Metaphysics and the comforts of philosophy I fear, will not be ours today." He dropped the notebook into the firebox and replaced the lid.

The Return of the Orange Virgin

"So much for instructions. Well now, like a spot of tea?" Without waiting for an answer, he started fussing with a kettle and cups.

"This is bullshit. You're talking like some character out of Alice In Wonderland. I just asked a question; you didn't have to answer. Thanks for the street theater but 'shut up and sit down' would have been more to the point."

The man, Gershon Meyrowitz, looked crushed. "Oh dear, and I had so hoped to make a good impression. This being My first time and all..."

"You have certainly made an impression, you and that chum of yours. Forcible detention, abduction, shooting me full of dope and tying me up. And that getup! If I'd had my glasses on I'd have been laughing too hard to move. And now you give me some broken-down routine from the Kiwanis revue. Oh, I'm impressed all right." Shoulders slumped, gaze averted, her captor continued about his tea business. She had hurt his feelings.

"Chum? Oh, you think I have a little helper. That female voice in your head, then? Delightful." The kidnapper rifled through a bay of cabinets. "I believe we have some Oolong about somewhere..."

❑

Some hours earlier, and on the other side of a shimmering picture wall, Morgana had watched windings of white surgical tape form up into a decorative macramé requiring a level of skill to which the average desperado would not aspire. "It's El, sure as shit and twice as ugly. White Sow of Naxos, the old letch is putting on a show for her. What a lizard! He knows I am watching."

Biff and the Manticore looked on bewildered.

"This Linda Winkelman is not an extraordinary person, but sharp-witted enough to give me the slip. Nothing in her life will have prepared her to be the priestess of the Fata Morgana, Queen of Heaven, Orange Virgin, Lady of The Wild Things, etc., etc. My priestess has selected herself, by exemplary deeds or conduct most likely. All I have got to do is catch up with her. We are going to join her in her past. Hopefully recent."

The Manticore, not yet translated into the Cicerone of Biff, golem and quondam paramour of the Queen of Heaven, pulled enthusiastically at a newly-given rank, black cigar. "Hopefully? You exhibit a lack of precision I have come to expect from the goddess of life and joy."

"Could you blow your smoke in another direction, there's a good fellow. Realize those stogies are a plenary indulgence. Remember where they come from. Your continued supply is contingent on a devotion to my efforts." Morgana unwrapped gold foil from around a sticky chocolate nougat. Biff looked on interestedly. "Sorry, this is the last one. Really, I can't be spending all my time supplying treats for the personnel. Such a stew of life. Just look at that."

"Where? I don't see *anyanyanyany...!*" Biff clutched at Morgana as the facing wall fell away—no prefatory clearing of the throat brick-and-mortarwise, it was just gone. The room had become an open-ended box and, for all Biff could tell, they were flying and swooping at gut-wrenching acceleration through wispy swirling cloud cover toward what, at the rate it came charging up at them, could only be solid ground. Biff was going to be sick. They were going to be dead, and no chance to clean up after, crushed against the onrushing whatsis down there materializing through the clouds. He buried his face between Morgana's breasts.

"Silly boy, how nice of you, but if you're going to be sick, please do it in a bucket." She grasped Biff firmly by the ears and extracted him. This all transpired in a misty might-have-been—for with godhead many things are possible—a place outside of common reality albeit Pi was yet infinite and four-and-twenty an even number of blackbirds. "This is grownup business. Pay attention, there may be questions later. We are going to crash the barrier separating us, our world, from another just like ours but not as nice. We are poaching on the sky demon's preserve today." The Queen of Heaven was peering closely into the mists where the wall had been.

"Uh... where are we?" said Biff brightly.

"We are here, where we have always been." Morgana ruffled his hair and gestured at the swirl and swoop before them. "All this is but a simulacrum for your education: not real, but real enough." Biff peered at the speeding maelstrom of colors and shapes. "And where they are is midtown Manhattan." The Queen of Heaven performed a high-velocity inverted U to avoid a thicket of television transmitter antennas masted atop the highest of many tall buildings. Biff's knees buckled as they dodged a tower. He would be sick a lot, and not in a bucket. Then with a child's kaleidoscopic mood shift, his resolve weakened as something far below caught his eye.

The ground was covered with little specs hurrying to and fro. "Oooo... there are people down there. Just like us." It looked cold and wet down there. And dirty. Very inhospitable.

The Return of the Orange Virgin

"People, yes. Just like us, no. If they were just like us we wouldn't have to be at all this jiggery-pokery, we could just walk right in and talk sensibly. Let's move in for a closer look."

The people became bigger; Biff could pick out individuals. The image blurred as Morgana swung back and forth looking for one particular individual.

"I don't understand."

"Of course you don't. You'll have to trust me." Sensing a presence more vital than the surrounding low-energy ambience of people at their daily grind, she slipped into the consciousness of a Broadway denizen. He leaned casually against a mock masonry store front with its chicken wire lathing oozing out in places where the neighborhood idlers, moochers and art critics had been picking at the appliqué bricks. He pressed himself into the wall, lit up a joint and eyed a tangle of boy prostitutes coming on across the street to the tunnel traffic from New Jersey.

"The local color, Biff, my dear. Perhaps when you're older."

There was more swirling and swooping. "There. Biff Bangtree, meet your long-lost sister, my priestess. She doesn't know about you yet, but I think you'll get along famously."

"Why do I want a sister?"

"A genuine question, genuinely put, but the truth is too complex for a genuine answer. You want a sister because I say you do, that's why."

What they saw was the face of a pretty, auburn-haired woman, agitated and becoming more so. She was negotiating a revolving door with two large totes and an umbrella, her face screwed up in a lubricious clown grimace complete with protruding tongue, indicating intense thought on a tricky problem. Her struggles to get herself and her cargo into the rotating cubicle thence to the street had raised her skirt, exposing a quantity of calf and thigh. The show got appreciative looks, but no help from bystanders.

It was Christmas in New York, a time of tinseled windows, slush coming over the tops of transparent plastic rain boots. A wide-bodied Checker cab spun into the taxi stand at the corner, trying to use the parking lane for an illegal turn to catch the light at 33rd Street. A spray of brown slush stippled Linda's panty hose all the way to her knee on that side. "What the fuck!" She flipped a bird at the departing cab and forlornly watched the mixture of oil and ice crystals trickle down her left leg. From the passengers' compartment, five beefy, red-faced men packing camel's hair coats and attaché cases registered conflicted emotions. One on the jump seat facing backwards gave a sheepish grin and a small shrug of excuse—sorry, the human condition, etc. A twenty-five-dollar tip for the driver if they made the 5:03 to Dobbs Ferry. "Plus my stockings," Linda Winkelman addressed no one in particular. People hurried by blank-eyed and self absorbed, wrapped up in their own concerns. The only witnesses to the drama were its participants. Only hip waders would have saved her from a drenching. "Just look at that!—low heels, two inches of slush on the sidewalk and I'm soaked." Linda was a eyewitness to the immutability of natural law. She had wet feet.

"Cute cupcake," the Manticore thrust his head between Morgana and Biff, "and she wears an expression of extreme distress. An easy conquest."

"Too easy" The colors on the wall swirled and the woman faded in and out. Biff craned forward and caught himself as he went off balance, clutching at the back of the Fata Morgana's chair lest by leaning too far he fall into the picture.

Morgana stared fixedly into the mists as the woman returned. "I do so hope she likes pigs. I've got a lot riding on this."

Biff stared, too. The woman was blank and immobile. Had something gone wrong? Linda was standing stock still with her neck contorted as though she was trying to scratch her shoulder with her chin. Her ankles were crossed and she appeared to be looking backward while walking forward. She was balanced on one foot and her weight must surely drag her in an inexorable spiral to the ground.

"She's the one, no doubt about it. But we want to enter this transaction a mite earlier. Some adjustments are indicated."

Morgana stopped short; she felt confused emanations: hers was not the only power here. There was an interloper.

"I am the Queen of Heaven. I do not get confused."

"You are not Queen here," a voice spoke in her ear. A syrupy voice, moist and urgent. "Over the millennia you have been relegated to the shadow world of false legend and prophecies unfulfilled. I know, I wrote the Book. Oh, and welcome back."

"And you get your book in all the motels. Yaddita-yaddita, smug as ever. A thing of small consequence, so does the telephone company. And without your blood-thirsty medievalisms."

The Return of the Orange Virgin

The picture wall shimmered. "What a pair we were, you and I, Morgana. And, I sometimes dream, again?"

Chocolate for the Queen

Twinkling star showers dazzled Linda Winkelman's eyes from the inside. She wished they'd go away; they made it hard to focus; and maintaining her focus was the only grip on reality she had at the moment. Linda doubled over, retching again and again, but bringing nothing up. The Tevye guy had returned and was standing at her side. He smelled of lavender sachet, barnyard and goat. From her posture of abject misery, she could see his feet and the hem of a moth-eaten robe. From under the robe protruded two large and spectacularly untended feet. Cracked black toenails and a nacreous shine on his skin proclaimed this pilgrim had been a long time between water holes. He was wearing sandals! Sandals were strange footgear for winter in New York, but Linda was not prepared to debate fashions in the wholesale district. She hugged herself and rocked gently, trying to keep from passing out. So his feet haven't been washed for a while and he has scabby black toenails. So what? Was that a velvet robe he was wearing? Linda tried not to look up.

"Yes dear lady, I have slipped into a little something more in keeping with the gravity of the occasion, and if it were not for your discomfort, which will pass, you would have noticed that I have also donned the Horns of Power. Very Mosaic, nu? I got all dressed up for the Visitation. You are the instrument, the vehicle, if you catch my meaning, of a meeting of vast teleological implications. At this very moment, even as we speak, so to speak, the emanations of the demon-queen of Sumer and Babylon are invading your persona."

Leaning forward, her abductor patted Linda's cheek and let out a mighty sigh. "Ahh, but you are concerned with your current distress, not to chat about cosmology. Let me assure you that what is happening is non-invasive, in the physical sense—except for memories that you will treasure for years to come and that will make you the envy of every other human creature. But they'll wash right off if you so elect, leaving you none the worse for wear. You are to be the vessel for the return of the goddess-mother of the world. Care for a mint?" He peeled back the foil from a 2-pack of peppermint patties, took one and offered her the other. Linda groaned and turned away.

"Look!" He waved a magisterial hand down the stained front of his robe, "For this occasion we have rolled out the regalia so as to be in tiptop form—to be any less were to be a failure of magnificence." He took a bite and held his peppermint patty six inches from her nose. His body heat was melting its chocolate coating and the odor of peppermint was powerful and sickening. Another wave of nausea wrenched her forward. Not noticing, the man who called himself Gershon Meyrowitz prattled on.

"Our darling Rahab, our loving Rachelle, our Tiamat..." Her abductor flourished what looked like a credit card. No, it was a crescent shaped gold coin... with tooth marks. It was the peppermint patty somehow turned into a golden coin with a bite taken out of it. He noticed her eyes widen.

"Yes, a bite is out, and it has a picture of a birdie, see?" He held the coin down to where Linda could see it. There was a representation of a loon at rest on a wilderness lake. "We will put it where it is all warm and cozy and the heat from your body will melt the coin like the mint that it was. It will seep in your soul and disappear. No cleaning bills, no chocolate mess—just like M and Ms." He folded the mint wrapper's silver foil around the coin, making a tight triangular package, and reached into Linda's blouse to tuck it down her cleavage. This hairy, smelly individual was actually intending to lay hands on her! This was the New York you didn't read about in the guidebooks. He leaned forward, mimicking a favorite relative pressing coins on a prize niece. "See how it is shaped like the gibbous moon. Auspicious. It is not every day we have a Visitation, in fact, this will be the very first—an occasion that should be dressed up to, *gans gleich?* I am God, how do you do." She tried to move away, straining to raise an arm to ward off his fumblings.

"There," he said, buttoning her back up, "That should keep it snug and warm." He gave her left breast a pat. "I have marked you for the Orange Virgin. For exactly what, even I do not know. But remember that it was I who marked you. You are Mine if I will and I shall derive comfort from knowing I can catch up with you later."

Linda's vision had the fisheye distortion of a fever dream and the someone—yes, there definitely was someone else in her head—was playing with her focus; the store, everything, was zooming. The Tevye type shuttled and pumped in time with her magnified pulse beat. Her head felt stuffed, too full. It took all the will she could marshal to try to fend off the man's attentions, but her body wouldn't respond.

Just relax, my dear. I won't let him harm you. It was the woman's voice in her head, which at that moment was more crowded than Linda could recall it having been in the preceding thirty-six years.

The Return of the Orange Virgin

Trust me, insisted the woman. In spite of her better judgment, Linda Winkelman trusted. The voice inspired trust and, whatever was happening, she needed a friend, and fast.

"Whoever you are, get me out of this." Linda surrendered. A wave of euphoria rolled through her body and Linda was distracted from the full and undivided attention she felt she owed her impending unconsciousness. Air, she needed air. Ahh... the Storm Rider was opening her coat. That should help. *This guy has the balls of a bandit,* thought Linda as she passed into unconsciousness. *Damn, it's hot in here!* Salmonella poisoning, that was it. It was that takeout sushi they had called in for lunch.

Bunching up a fold of flesh from her cheek, the demiurge who was Gershon Meyrowitz held it between his thumb and forefinger, toggling her head back and forth. "Hotsy-totsy, Morgana. You in there? We've been expecting you."

What had been Linda Winkelman rose from a curled-up position, muscles stiff and cramped. She stretched to stand on tiptoe, arms extended. "Whew, what this poor girl has been through!" Golden eyes glowed around green pupils as freckles danced across the bridge of a nose that had not been tilted seconds earlier. Long red-gold braids cascaded to the floor. "There's got to be a better way. By-the-bye, beyond reading off a name tag, do you know who it is that you're wearing?"

"I am no hedge wizard. I am in control here. None but the ever-present lunatic fringe question my actions. Besides, as you and I know full well, 'possession' of a subject not sufficiently flexible, intelligent or mentally adaptable can kill them or drive them mad and that's no fun. Besides, does not Gershon look the part?" Heels together, the Gershon body made a wide, florid bow. "And a lifelong immersion in the articles of faith makes him a most amenable host. He's been waiting for me, right? Besides, it has a serendipitous location, this place of his. Convenient to subways, buses, the Pennsylvania Railroad, not to mention the young lady so suddenly and charmingly tenanted by you."

"Thank you, El. Always the cavalier. In ancient days you came to me with perfumed beard and romance on your mind. Look at you now."

"Yes, look at me." The pride of ownership. El flexed Gershon Meyrowitz' burly shoulders, and like a heavyweight contender warming up, feinted a few jabs and hooks, shadow boxing.

"I'll bet the poor man hasn't had a bath since you moved in. Certes, my lord, this model might better have been left in the showroom. For his own good."

"And My good? The greater good, as I sincerely believe?"

"You might at least keep him presentable. Those feet are a disgrace. How long since he's been home? I'll bet he hasn't seen his family in weeks."

"No, months actually." El cracked a grin, "They think he has run away with his bookkeeper." An all-encompassing gesture became a two handed shrug, index fingers indicating that somewhere within a plump worsted vest or its contents dwelt home, hearth and little ones with a weeping wife languishing in distant New Jersey.

"Such concern for the little people; you've mellowed. Integrity never was your strong point, El," said the Fata Morgana. Linda Winkelman resumed her pose of thoracic agony.

The Valiant Buffet

Harry Profitt Pease looked sideways into the mirror, hunting for a place to part his hair; clippings from a do-it-yourself haircut clung to the sink's porcelain sides. He doused himself with Lilac Vegetal, then wrinkled his nose and tried not to breathe. That evening was an illustrated lecture—a slide show—at the Valiant Trust Memorial Institute Free Library. Alma Nightingale was a known regular. "What the hell. Why not. I've got her washer for her, haven't I?"

The slide presentation on the Holy Land was a grand old standby of the Valiant's biweekly offerings, usually wildlife and nature oriented. Often some-one from the Audubon Society would give a talk on bird watching, a park ranger from the wildlife preserve an illustrated nature walk. The spectacle of green foliage up there on the beaded screen in the reference room on an icy winter's evening with the Nor'easters howling past in the Bay of Fundy made Alma Nightingale dream of donning her silk with the tropical flower print.

Reverend Murtry from the Methodist parsonage had actually been to the Holy Land but had run out of film. He had filled out his slide show with stock shots available at the tourist kiosks: grainy cliffs of Masada in rotogravure orange alternated with Kodacolor transparencies of the Via Dolorosa, Bethlehem, and tract housing in the Golan Heights. Rev. Murtry had typed out his commentary. The lights were dimmed and by the light of a lamp on the lectern he started a cassette player. He had prepared a tape with music and automatic pulses to advance the slide carousels while he gave his full attention to the narrative. The Reverend rattled his script and checked the audience. There was no audience. The convivial knot of Friday night regulars had clustered at the refreshments table—coffee, fruit punch and cookies, the Valiant Friday buffet. Abandoning his slides to continue without him, Rev. Murtry joined the throng. Perhaps Mrs. Gladstone had spiked the punch.

A bright young couple from away was tied up in an intense conversation with Alma. More circumspect and less outspoken when sober, Harry caught a snippet of conversation while cruising the refreshments table. "...full of charming, picturesque, bearded people whom I want never to work on any major appliance again..." Jaws snapped shut as they caught sight of him. Aware of Alma's earlier acquaintance with Harry, they were inquiring as to any other jack-of-all-trades available locally. They were looking for a fixer learned in the ways of automatic household washers and dryers. Harry vaguely remembered doing some work for them the previous summer. Even after forty years, he was proprietary about Alma and moved right in.

Harry's approach to the huddle of small talk generated a ripple effect. This was a problem of ventilation. The Valiant Trust committee had argued quire reasonably that taking down the storm windows in the spring was only inviting trouble—a building after all, was sort of like a bottle of wine. Unbuttoning one's edifice to let it breathe with the advent of the warm months, taking down the storm windows for other than routine maintenance, say every five years or so, was borrowing trouble. The summer gales caused weather damage to exposed interior casements, in the knockabout trip down the bulkhead hatch to the Valiant Memorial Trust's basement snuggery some panes were inevitably broken, requiring replacement. The exterior double glazing thus stored acquired a layer of dust and needed washed before being put back in place for the winter when it would be discovered they had shrunken in the dry of the cellar and had to be painted and caulked about the seams when re-hung.

Despairing of fresh air, early each spring Mrs. Gladstone herself popped the storms from the clerestory windows at the opposing sides of her office space that welcomed borrowers and book returners as they climbed the three steps from the entry foyer.

Enough fresh air for one librarian and the occasional browser, this was not enough for the Friday enlightenments plus Harry. Harry's body heat was cooking the emollient of his afternoon as he trod manfully toward the cookies and fruit punch in a vapor haze of Seadog beer, grass and sweat. The pallid figures clustered about the paper covered library table stopped their talk, held gestures uncompleted.

Lo! Conan the Barbarian has come to wassail at the gates, thought Joyce Gladstone (Mrs.), librarian, suppressing a titter.

Harry noticed the quiet of the usually chatty Friday night crowd and guessed it might be him. Were these, his friends and neighbors, sending him a not-so-subtle declaration that he did not belong here? They looked like the little figures architects put into their models. Tiny elongated people interspersed with shrubberies and trees made from sponge, dyed green with painted shadows to suggest a sunny afternoon.

Was he out of place?

Harry was not a regular communicant at the Valiant Trust's Sabbath-eve menu of uplift; he was getting the transparent treatment. Admittedly bad timing for a raid on the goodies but he was nursing a hangover and wanted to go home. He didn't feel like staying for the show, besides after the lectures the buffet was so picked over it was hard to do it any heavy damage.

Joyce Gladstone caught the whiff of Harry bearing down on her and charged right on with a cheerful determinedness, hoping to cut him out of possible intrusion by keeping the conversation bright, up, happy and busy. She turned her back on the circle and it tightened defensively, as if wolves prowled outside their campfire.

"Doesn't Alma look pretty," said Joyce. "You always had good chemistry, you and Alma, Harry. Don't put her off. She's going to ask you to fix her washing machine. Do it Harry... for me? It's such a little thing to ask. I'm not comfortable with this stuff yet." She nodded at the tableau of the Valiant's Friday-nighters. The familiar faces had a snapshot quality. Reverend Murtry tinkering with his slide projector, Bobby Farrell waving his finger—they had been having a sports conversation Harry recalled—pressing home some fine point about basketball statistics with the Rev. while sneaking a peek down the front of Harriet Hopwood's dress. Mrs. Gladstone blinked and stared blankly from vacant, puzzled eyes. "Was I speaking?" she asked Harry. "Distinctly thought I heard myself talking. Strange." She turned back to the circle; the stockaded wagons parted to welcome her.

There was a splash as a ladle fell into the punch bowl. "Land's sakes, can't take me anywhere." Alma's voice. Harry turned; she was dabbing at a stain on her silk print dress. There were small movements and the sounds of lungs being filled as respiration resumed. A tentative guffaw, most likely Bobby Farrell, and then conversation broke out as the party restarted itself. A continuo of manly resonances, hesitant hushed chirpings, percussive shufflings and rustlings and the staccato cough of a smoker coming in from a quick toke joined the counterpoint of Alma Nightingale's crystal glockenspiel as with a susurrus of silk she stirred the ice cubes in her tureen of pink citrus soup. The group was realigning itself with small talk. Their unconcerned random chatter broke through Harry's haze. Harry tried concentrating but the ebb and flow of people in their huddles and clusters made him dizzy.

He cut Alma Nightingale out from the herd and focused on her. Just how much had he had to drink today? Hmmm... figure it tomorrow, count the empties. He made an effort to bring his eyes into focus. He tried walking and found he needed to maneuver by shifting his center of gravity, letting his feet follow, stiff-legged. The room was swimming and to keep from falling over he had to balance on a very fluid pivot dead center in the middle of his hips. Damn! He wasn't that drunk. Funny how the beer catches up with you all at once. Harry had reached that plateau where the accumulation of alcohol gets the body drunk but leaves the brain alone to try to sink buckets from the free throw line of social ruin. He'd feel his balance start to go and his lower body would shuffle forward, trying to keep centered under the wobbly load.

"Still dreaming about a girl from high school, Harry?" Harry turned to see a pig hopping up on the window seat next to Alma, claiming a warm depression vacated by Mrs. Gladstone. Harry stared. The pig was a spotted china with a tight brushy tip to her tail that hinted at purebred bloodlines. "You wouldn't have a cabbage left in your truck, would you?" the pig added.

"Huh?" said Harry. "Oh, yeah. Sure." He shook his head to clear it and the pig was no longer there.

❏

The Orange Virgin was scheming. The Fata Morgana, Orange Virgin, etc, etc., had discovered a minor petulance. She fought it off but it persisted. "We live on the bow wave of perceived time. Time is a comforting figment, a subjective place humans have dreamed up to give superficial meaning to their paltry lives. Everything is all there and a glorious moment it was. We can never live it at once. We are merely writing its catalog as it unfolds. Merrily we roll along." She spoke to a cat that lolled in the sun at her feet. The two were high atop a turreted tower to observe the progress of an excavation far below. One of the gardener's boys had gotten a bad bite transporting the swans to a corral on the river as they readied to drain the moat. The Orange Virgin entertained hopes that the swans might also attack the diggers, Lamprey and Tawse, at their pick and shovel work.

"The shovel, a useful instrument," remarked the Orange Virgin. "It asks little in the way of affection, has no moving parts and runs on dried out crusts, cheese rinds and yesterday's ale." Some time had passed since her interview with El the sky demon in the cellars of the Hotel Taft and, after the manner of time passed beyond recall, there remained an air of melancholy tempered with a vague unease. "And speaking of useful instruments, I shall require much pocket change, eh sweet puss?"

The Orange Virgin wore a checked flannel shirt and a culotte with hiking boots. "Aha! Money—that is the answer." Morgana's big gray tomcat gave a burraow, bleep, bleep, rubbed affectionately against her ankles then, seeing a gloriously fat horsefly buzzing, forgot the moment and was after it in a pell-mell dash up Morgana's tresses and off the top of her head. Suspended over nothingness high above a hard ending on the sun-caked mud floor of the moat 30 meters down, he gave with a miaow as if in farewell to a foolish, pampered life. "Not yet an end for you, my pretty, a panoply of voles, moths and milk filled saucers lies yet ahead, sweet puss," said the Fata Morgana. She snatched the cat from the air. "Follow the money. Remember this."

A Roundelay of Rust and Rot

A month later Maggie's baggage arrived. Theo Arsenault called Pen Harrington, "There's ten cartons here, strapped with filament tape. They're addressed to you."

"Me."

"You. And a pet carrier. The stuff came spread out over three different Atlantic BusWays out of Quebec. The baggage claims match. Your lady friend's... you know."

"Be right over." Pen set the phone down.

Maggie was all smiles. "Oh, wonderful, now we'll know." She performed a series of dance steps, wrapping a dishtowel around her hips.

"Arsenault says it's your stuff. Here. Addressed to me and sent before you left. But we never met until you arrived."

"Pen Harrington, don't be an old sourpuss. Trust me; these are the imponderables."

"Yeah. Well, but..."

"Ten boxes, wow. I must have been moving in for the long haul. I must have known you'd be here."

To Pen this sounded weak, but Maggie's eyes held a look of trust and innocence. There was no room for deviousness there. "I'll call Harry. He has a truck. He'd be happy to do us a favor."

"Harry Pease. What a wonderful idea; he's got all that room."

"Your stuff... take it to Harry's?"

"All of it. In case there are questions later."

"I thought this was all about finding out who you were."

"Silly, don't you get it yet? I don't want to know. Not now. I am just happy here with you. I don't want it to stop."

"Arsenault said there was a pet carrier. You have a pet cat?"

"Pig. Harry lives alone, he'd just love a little piggie for company."

"Pig? No one said it was a pig."

Pen dialed Arsenault back.

"Yeah, it's a pig all right. A real survivor if you believe the dates on the waybills. Cute little critter. She's made a regular conquest of Gerry MacKechnie."

❑

Even though it was his day off, Gerald Bronson MacKechnie was back at Arsenault's for an afternoon of video poker. Sheila had chased him out of the house and he was feeling low. He leaned on the baggage counter waiting for a roll of change. This was a losing day.

"Hiya, buddy. Want to do a girl a favor?" Gerry looked around. The voice was coming from a pet carrier up front and at eye level on the baggage shelves. He didn't recall it being up there the night before. "I've been holding it since Montreal."

"Beg pardon?"

"Unlatch the door of the pet carrier, there's a good fellow." Out of the fiberglass and nickel plated latticework of the pet carrier, a black and white spotted snout poked itself in his direction.

Gerry started backing away.

"No, no, no," said the voice. "None of that, no apoplexy, no seizures. Just do as I say. Pretend I'm Sheila. Right now I've got to pee something fierce."

"You're a pig."

"Pigs don't pee? Come on, make it snappy. There's a pile of newspapers under the desk. Spread them on the floor. And turn your back."

Gerry thumbed the spring latch and a black spotted pig jumped down. She stretched then vigorously shook her head. "Well?"

"Well, what?"

"Turn your back."

"Uh, okay."

Behind him the muted trickling went on for a considerable time.

"Gerry."

"Uh, yes." The pig knew his name. Well, why not, it knew his wife's name.

"I'm through. Pick up the papers and put them in the trash, then we'll have breakfast. Wash your hands first. And be sure to come back, I don't like being stood up."

Gerry stood for a long time, holding his hands under the blow-drycr, turning them over and over. What the hell, he had nothing else on today. He went back to the pig.

"Took you long enough. I'm famished." The pig nodded toward the luncheonette. "No pork fat and a side of cole slaw, please. Cheeseburgers will be just fine."

Gerry pulled a quarter-folded ten-dollar bill from an inside jacket pocket. He unfolded it with an apologetic expression.

"I get it. You're broke," said the pig. "No problem, just take a cruise by the video poker on your way."

Gerry did as he was told. The pig was here, too, superimposed on a flashing screen of rampant royal flushes. The machine spoke. "Here's the funds." It whirred and a winning chit for two hundred dollars was ejected. "For your trouble. Here's for the food." Twenty shiny gold loonies slid into the tray. "Make that double cheeseburgers and hold the pickles," said the machine.

❏

Harry Profitt Pease pulled into the bus stop in Loupe du Jour vaguely wondering why he had come. The phone call from Pen Harrington had been quick and cryptic. What the hell, he owed Pen a favor.

He left with the pig riding next to him in the front seat.

After drinking all day, every day, for twenty-five years, that Pen's girlfriend's baggage might contain a talking pig made sound sense to Harry. "Stop here," said the pig.

Harry hit the brakes.

"I like that about you, Harry. You are ready for anything."

"Uh, yeah. But why are we stopping?"

"Because I say so. You have money?"

Harry took a swallow from the wine bottle under his seat and pulled a scrunched-up wad from his overall pocket. "Fifty dollars."

"Fine. Rent some videos."

"Huh?"

"Some videos. Anything. Love, war, you know. I have a lot of catching-up to do. And Harry..."

"Yes."

"I forgive you."

Harry stared at the pig. He was trying to think and drive at the same time, a bad accommodation. "Forgive me? Forgive me what?" He pulled into Customs on the U.S. side.

"I forgive you for being a murderous, self-centered, unthinking son of a bitch."

"Huh?" Harry's foot confused the brake and accelerator pedals and he slid into a crosswise stop across both lanes. The truck stalled, blocking access to the customs shed. With an airy gesture of a trotter, the pig indicated herself. "And you may call me Lady."

"Lady..."

"Lady of the Wild Things. I have now introduced myself. If things go further between us I shall have other names. For now, plain Lady will do."

"You are a pig."

"And you are a dirty old man. Don't belabor the obvious." The pig rummaged in the truck's glove box and, coming up with an archival Mars bar, settled herself comfortably in the passenger's seat.

The immigration agent waited, radiating forbearance for as yet unspecified crimes, as Harry jerked up even with him using the starter and battery power. The government man slid his window half open. The truck kept going right on through and stopped six feet past the shed.

"Oh, great." Harry fired it up again, flooring the accelerator. He fiddled with the gearshift, trying to get into reverse. The motor flooded and died. Fortunately, there was no line and a familiar face was on duty.

The man walked over to the truck and leaned on Harry's window. "Hiya Harry. Bringing anything back?"

"Yeah. Personal baggage. Mercy run for Pen Harrington. Customs declarations already on 'em."

"The pig is yours, right? A pet?"

"A pet. Yes."

Immigration shrugged him through and walked back to his shed; the window slid shut. The motor caught and Harry eased his cargo into America. He turned to the pig with a harsh, raspy aside. "What have I ever done to you that you should have to forgive me?"

The pig curled over in the passenger's seat and licked her crotch. "Oh, Harry, dear, you sound so eager and raring to go. Passion is for later, first the movies."

❑

Harry's place.

The trip had taken a little over an hour with stops for video rentals at two crossroads groceries. A low tide smell grew ever thicker as they mounted a series of hills and dips announcing the ascent of a precipice; the haphazard grading of the town road ended just before it ran out of dry land. There was a maneuver with downshifting, brake and accelerator as Harry aimed for a pile of gravel. He jerked the wheel hard right and killed the engine as the truck nosed over into a precarious thirty-degree drop. A practiced yank on the emergency brake brought a squeal of rusted brake cable, and the pickup lurched to a stop against a raised hummock. The stop left them listed over on the passenger's side. Harry wobbled the shift lever a few times, making sure he had it securely in second where it was less likely to pop out.

The Return of the Orange Virgin

The pig propped her trotters against the dash. "Nice ocean view—straight down. Next stop, Nova Scotia. You do this all the time?"

"Every time." Harry jumped down and chocked the back wheels with a pair of bricks. "So far."

The stack of movies that filled the seat between them had scattered over the floor. Harry reached in and gathered them up. He headed to the house with a double armload. "Pit stop. I'll be right back."

"Yes, you will." The pig curled up on the seat

❏

When Harry Pease had been drinking, which was all the time, he saw the world differently from the accepted norms. Harry Pease was a gentle eccentric whose only affront to the social code as defined by Elizabeth Profitt Pease, his sister, was that his toilet gurgled over the edge of the ledge on which his house rested, and the law offered Elizabeth, known as Libby, no relief. Harry's solids went through a pipe straight into the ocean. That Harry Profitt Pease's wastewater, the gray and the effluent, fed the fish was an embarrassment to her. As she stood on line at the Red and White supermarket she was asked, "How's Harry—still going over the edge?" That this might be a double-entendre escaped Elizabeth Pease. Harry's straight pipe was protected by law as long as Harry lived uninterruptedly at his present address and performed no major repairs. This was likely. The town's sewers would eventually catch up with him, but until then... A shrug at the Dept. of Public Works. Floating a bond issue so some geezer on the ledge could join the Twenty-first Century was not in the cards. Harry's house had the best ocean view in Willipaq. "So goddamned beautiful you could just shit," Harry had said, popping a Seadog one fine fall morning.

Harry returned, hitching up his suspenders. "Where's the boxes to?"

"Beg pardon?"

"The boxes: where do I put them? Your pet carrier got left in Canada."

"Assuming I am in charge, aren't we, Harry? Well... correcto, I am. But this is your house, after all."

"Just asking."

"Well put. Count them first. Tell me what we've got."

Harry unchained the tailgate and skidded out the first two. "What looks like a computer—new, still has the factory tape."

"And?"

"And eight others."

"The computer is yours. We will learn to play games together. The others are mine. Unload them, please." The pig sauntered toward the house where she inspected the washing machine he had promised Alma Nightingale. It stood where he had left it—on the porch, connected by lengths of green garden hose and an orange drop cord to the necessary utilities. "Ah—the epiphany of a major appliance." She circled it, inspecting. "Unprepossessing. Like you, Harry. Who could have guessed?"

The remaining boxes were identical in size and weight, about twenty pounds, give or take. Harry slid them off the tailgate and lined them up in two rows, four deep. The pig returned and circled the rows, a tour of inspection. "Frankly, Harry, your house is a mess; it needs a woman's touch. I arrived in the nick of time to save you from prodigal disorder."

"As you said, this is my house." Harry Pease prided himself on his rough-and-ready housekeeping, and he felt he needed to defend himself.

"The boxes. Cut one open and dump it on the ground."

Harry unsnapped his belt sheath and brought out a folding knife. The plastic strapping gave with a pop, curling back around the box. "Dirt. It's full of dirt."

"Ballast. Just when I thought El was committed to a slipshod performance, he surprises me. He has made up the difference of Tom Winkelman."

"Tom Winkelman?"

"Just a name. You may forget it; he no longer exists here. Pour away." Harry poured. All eight boxes held finely sifted gravel. From the next to last box an agate sphere separated itself from the gravel and rolled under a wild rose bush.

"Ah! Jack's marble has made it through. An oversight by my quondam consort, but Lamprey would be pleased." The pig circled the mound of dirt approvingly, then picked her way up the little gravel hill and sat, studying Harry. He was tall and spare, with a full facial inflorescence of lordly beard giving him the mien of an Old Testament patriarch. "Your full name?" she asked.

"Thought you knew. You seem to know everything."

"Mmmm. Maybe. I want you to know."

"Pease. Harry Profitt Pease. Pease the patronymic, Profitt my lady-gift, from my mother's people."

"Prophet, profit. You live up to your name in looks, not in business. I'd say most of your life between binges is scavenging junk from house to house and picking over the dumps."

"Now, that's not entirely fair." Harry did a brisk trade in pipe frames and springs for the bed-and-breakfasts.

"And you kill pigs."

"That I do. Uh, used to do." Harry looked away and ground a toe into the dirt.

"I have forgiven you, but I am curious. What has driven you to murder is clearly bad influences in the home. This..." she gestured expansively, "roundelay of rust and rot has driven you to savage deeds. Why did you kill the pigs?"

"Thirty-five dollars, I'm good at it. And no one else will." Harry thought of his gun, leaning in the corner by his bed, next to a metal softball bat. The household armory—if this pig was here for revenge. He quickly put the thoughts away. "A boat. I have a boat." He pointed to a thirty-foot lobster tender on blocks in the yard.

"You have a boat. Good. This will take us places we have not been before. Like straight to the bottom. The seams are open, showing daylight. Might this boat be another instrument for my assassination?"

"No, no." Harry felt a trickle of sweat down the back of his neck. "I mean we could fix her up. One-lung engines like this haven't been made regular since World War II." The engine had a plaintive, evocative sound. Chunk, chunk, chunk. To go from forward to reverse you stopped the engine, then restarted it, spinning the flywheel in the opposite direction. Harry did this sometimes, there in the yard, when the Seadogs had caught up with him.

"An antique, it might someday be valuable. Like you, Harry. You are valuable. And thank you for putting by your musings of violence... and voluntarily, too."

The pig had been reading his mind.

The pig smiled, lips curled back to show capable tusk-like canine teeth. She nodded. "Yes, I have—your thoughts, that is—but not all of them. That would be prying. Let's get this straight. You have, with your boat, taken the pigs to the Mother Sea to bathe them prior to sacrifice. This is proper; I approve. Pig! That is so generic. Sit still, you little bastard! Not you, Harry, the flea." She doubled back on her haunches, nibbling fiercely at the base of her tail. "You were trying to distract me, I believe. Please continue. You kill lobsters, too?"

"No, I don't catch lobsters. The boat has been parked, high and dry, for fifteen years."

"You have, then, in the past, taken pigs for their last rides in this boat, like your gangsters. You drown them, too, with cement on their feet?"

"This is a lobster boat."

"The lobster, as the pig, is sacred to me, likewise the colors white, green, blue and scarlet, the periwinkle and the scallop, and the spotted fish that sing like thrushes in my honor, for I am a horny old trout. You have eaten them, these lobsters?"

"Well, yes." The question held an implication of cannibalism. "Everybody does—when they can get them."

"Harry, Harry, what am I going to do with you? You are freed of the sin of lobster boiling. We shall bring the pot to judgment, and not the cooker. We shall be lovers, but later. Bring the videos."

"You are a pig."

"For now and here, yes. Come along."

The Mouse

Meanwhile, in the sub-cellars of the Hotel Taft, Linda's face was turning blue. Quite becoming, actually. El was prepared to be entertained, but took inventory of his better impulses. From the Winkelman body, twitters and whistles were being choked back and becoming a gargling. A musical interlude, then? Definitely not Morgana. His intent must have gone forth, summoning a traverser of the realms—what the more imaginative and impressionable of his parishioners once called demons.

The twitters and whistles became words: "Identify yourself, please. I mean, really!" Definitely testy, with a note of perplexity.

"I will not be patronized!" A voice not Linda's and yet not the Fata Morgana's issued from the Winkelman lips. "Explain yourselves if you can. I have been co-opted by your tampering with forces you in all likelihood do not fully understand. I must warn you, whoever you are, that such actions are strictly prohibited by the Comprehensive Code of..." Here more twitters and whistles. An affronted dignity entered the voice.

"Oh, Great Filladith, there's a sentience in here, too! You've invaded another being's persona and suppressed her volition. Release me before I am forced to deal harshly with you."

"Whomsoever you are, you are not enthusiastic about My exchange program," declared El, the demiurge. The Orange Virgin, no: a known quantity, she was definitely hostile, but would call him by name. This was not the Fata Morgana. Here was a new force to be reckoned with.

"I am from..." here a series of chirpings and whistlings, "...and the being's name, this being you have co-opted. What was that again, dear?" More twitterings. "Linda is the closest I can come."

"Linda. And you are sure she is helpless? This is what My intentions were."

"She is not happy with your arrangements."

"Tell her to pack it in for the duration. We require her body, no more. Her opinions are beside the point. Give her something to keep her busy—anagrams, Scrabble, long division, logarithms."

The twitterings and chirpings slowed to an approximation of articulated speech. "I assure you as a prebendary of the Church of Temporal Affliction, we don't hold with such goings-on..."

"And I am the Master of Creation; call me El. How do you do?"

"How do I *do*? Young demiurge, I'll tell you what I *will* do..." more twitterings. "But my doings are beside the point here. It is your doings which concern the Consortium."

"So. You are an eidolon. Ah, yes... The eidolons, busybodies of eternity—unfeelingly meddling with things properly beneath their interest—are putting us all to a great deal of trouble. Time is yet a cenotaph marking a kingless tomb and we have to fix the angle of the gnomen, reset the clock."

El took Gershon for a stroll about the basement of the Hotel Taft. Behind him the dialogue continued, but now two voices shared one larynx. This new voice sounded not unlike the redoubtable Fata Morgana, Queen of Heaven, Lady of the Wild Things, etc., etc.

The Queen of Heaven's tones were calming and conciliatory: "On behalf of myself and the snarky individual pretending to meditate in front of an air duct, welcome to the Hotel Taft. We will of course, give all considered assistance to speed you back to where you came from."

Linda's face was no longer contorted though sweat glistened on her forehead and stained her collar. Her normal color was returning. She sat stock still, body rigid, her eyes rolled up with pupilless whites staring vacantly while her hands carried on an animated conversation with one another. A medium-sized spotted pig materialized at her feet, curled in a ball.

"Excellent, Lord Eidolon, only too good," said the pig. "My old adversary in our perpetual tussle—he, the Sky, and I, the Earth." The pig indicated Gershon Meyrowitz.

El/Gershon prodded the pig with a sandaled toe. "That is you, Morgana, is it not? Well, my stars and garters, we have done it." He turned to study a carton of rigatoni on a pantry shelf. "Everybody's got to be somewhere, right? You should feel honored. Even I cannot just manufacture something out of nothing, Lord Eidolon. One loose piggy more or less will mean nothing to a casual observer, but the biota here is teetering at critical mass. I mulch, recycle, try to set a good example..."

"So you snatch a citizen from a probability vector where neither of you have any business, no authority..."

"...thus hatching a whole new supply of extraterrestrial mother-ships sightings in their universe? Fiddle-dee-dee." El/Gershon shrugged as if to indicate irrelevance. "So we are becoming the space aliens of another universe: legends in the otherwhen, someone else's time? Big deal. When we're done, we just give her back her body and send her on her way."

Linda's body turned to face the Rider on the Storm. "That's a lot of information," said the eidolon. "I think I will rest now; I trust I have expressed the Consortium's concerns. Please call me when it's all over. Nice meeting you, I'm sure."

"Lord Eidolon, wait," said El. "This woman had a husband, it seems. This would be an encumbrance. There could have been uncertainties if he were left to his own devices. I have dealt with him. I am always thinking of you, my responsibilities... the Consortium." El's mention of the Consortium was added on after a pause. The air was heavy with rebuke. The sky demon again pursued the evasive piece of lint. "And Myself. I like to feel I am backing a sure thing."

"You have killed him, Linda's husband! Oh, El, how could you," declared the pig.

"Easily enough. Calm yourself; he is well. I slid him through on the back draft of your crossing-over, Morgana. You produce an admirable shock wave at your passage, my dear. He is for now a wandering minstrel in your asylum, an assistant to a poet. He will love it there. Look after him for me. My constituents are finicky about their marriage vows; these, after all, I have ordained. If word were to get about..."

"Afraid. You are afraid of them."

"Well... yes. They could interpret any lack of action on My part as tribute to the 'pagan demon-queen.'"

"Which would be me, I suppose. Although I can't say as I am overjoyed with the characterization. But that, it appears, is that. We can sort him out later, if need be." The Fata Morgana spoke from the pig on the floor, who stretched—trotters forward, tail in the air—and yawned widely. "For now we have to get busy. Try out your sea legs, my dear."

Looking perplexed, Linda Winkelman stood and stretched. Then fell to her knees. There was a bone-jarring thump as the world seemed to drop three feet. Linda clutched at walls that were not there, her only reference being a runaway elevator. A flash resonated around Manhattan. A blown fuse. The fluorescents? Nuclear attack?

El probed Linda's mind for a possible source of mischief. The eidolon had thrown up a static field and gone to sleep.

In the streets outside a welter of voices called alarm. The closely-packed anxieties of a myriad of humanity broke upon the Orange Virgin like a tidal surge, then retreated as the world realized it was all in one piece and with hardly a hair out of place. A small presentation for a portentous phenomenon.

"Holy shit, what was that, the end of the world?" Linda stood and rubbed her eyes. She stared as a shimmering figure materialized beside her. The speaker had become a tall, red-haired beauty, naked. Her kidnapper had regained his feet and was dusting himself off.

"I compliment your self-possession, my dear. Your figure of speech is truer than you dream." Morgana reached out to comfort her. Something had gone dreadfully wrong. "El, you are despicable, contemptible!" She kicked the demiurge in a rage, hammered on him with her fists. "Marooned! I am stuck here with you in your smarmy world."

Gershon Meyrowitz ducked his head to avoid her blows. "A bissel earthquake, perhaps. They have them here all the time."

"Plate tectonics don't explain this." She made a sweeping gesture that included herself—a show stopper even in midtown Manhattan. And no longer a black and white spotted pig.

"I said you would be yourself at times unpredictable. This, this, ah... dislocation is one of those times."

"And you didn't predict it." "That is what unpredictable means, my lovey-dove. Anyhow, My word is incontrovertible. Whatever has just occurred, I have remarked upon it, said its name, and now it is so. Learn to live with it, we've got troubles in the here and now."

Linda decided it was time to speak. "Let me get this straight. You are God, right?" El nodded. "How do you do. There's this guy who lives in a cardboard box under the 79th Street transverse who says he's Jesus and I always wanted to meet his family. And you are," She gestured histrionically toward Morgana, "No, don't coach me, let me guess: Mary Magdalene, Madonna, Britney Spears. Hey, you really look great naked, you know? But of course you do, otherwise why go around with no clothes. Do you do this a lot? I mean seeing that you both are walking around and not in an institution someplace..." Linda's voice broke. Morgana made a move to comfort her.

"Linda, you have been through a lot. Give it a rest, relax. You are on the verge of hysteria, and we have enough on our minds at the moment. Trust me. Recognize my voice. Sit down please."

It was the voice from her head. Linda struggled, then sat as calm suffused her body. From habit she reached behind to straighten her skirt. In a panic, she reached into her brassiere. The coin was gone. There was a tingling there, but no chocolate mess. The clerk—God, or whoever-the-hell the madman was—had spoken the truth. She clung to that as an anchor for her sanity and sat once more on her string wrapped carton. The two—the goddess and the god?—were talking; they had completely dismissed her.

"Well, El, nothing up your sleeve, not even a teeny tiny plenary indulgence? The child is right, you are God here and you are helpless. Perhaps we should adjourn to Central Park and check under the 79th Street transverse."

"For the moment, no. And your sarcasm is not lost on me, I assure you. When Tevye here..." he again checked the name in the clerk's jacket, "...when Gershon is back to glorifying My name and on the bus to Teaneck remembering nothing of this day, then I'll believe everything is hunky-dory and not before. You see, I'm as stuck as you are right now. Untangle My holy innocents, Morgana. You are in this continuum for weal or woe since in a fit of melancholy yearning I bonded the body of this young woman with your old moon sign. Will I or nil I, a goodly part of you is here on My side for the duration."

The Return of the Orange Virgin

Morgana eyed him coldly, "Duration of what?"

"Damned if I know," said Gershon/El.

"I claim seniority. I am older than you by geological ages. Well, hello, there." A cat had carried in a still-twitching mouse and laid it at her feet. "Someone remembers who I am. Give me some credit, El, to have at least the brains of Gershon's cat. The Old Ones are yanking our chains."

El executed a small deferential bow while blanching. "You show an admirable proficiency with the local idiom, my dear, but even between ourselves, there are some names better left unsaid." Not to be mistaken in his intent, the cat again picked up the mouse, this time dropping it on Morgana's foot.

"Me again." It was the eidolon. "It is but a small token, and a promise, for the eidolons have found your constant self-indulgence worthy of recognition. Narcissism has its place and, after all, you are supreme beings. But there has been a slipup. Oh, it had to happen eventually, but 'why now and why to me,' I'm sure you are asking. In a like manner, I might ask, why me, and why on my watch? Because it has always been my watch." The cat looked on, approvingly.

"Lord Eidolon, you are an alarmist. Pardon me, I must share this well-intentioned offering." Morgana sat cross-legged, facing the cat with the mouse between them.

"The mouse will wait," said the eidolon. Linda stared empty-eyed as her lips made the words.

"To me it is religion, to the cat it is lunch, and lunch won't wait." The Queen of Heaven bit the head off the mouse and handed the remainder to the cat.

"Ah, Morgana, you always were the clever one, and I would rather see you disporting with shepherds in some bosky dell than blown to smithereens. But our destinies are intertwined in this, so hear me out. Assessing blame after the cat is out of the bag will not clean the shit from the fan. That is a metaphor."

"That is two metaphors, Lord Eidolon, and you become a dreary bore," said Morgana regaining her feet and slapping the dust from her behind.

A trace of irritation entered the eidolon's voice. "Bear with me, this gets interesting. When you first began your romp as blushing hegemonists you were rare and beautiful godlings with a promising patch to improve. This you have not done. And although limitless continuity does give one a sense of perspective, not-being we do not yet seek. What the doers have done, the doers must undo. The Old Ones have determined that, by the start of the next Great Year, all this will be no more. That is a promise."

"All for one little pig? That, the schism, it was but a bump, like jumping off a kitchen table."

"My dear Lady, at the risk of patronizing you, what does the earth weigh?"

"About six-and-a-half billion trillion tons, I believe. That's long tons. I believe my figures are accurate."

"Well, just you drop that off your kitchen table. If there were a place for this reality to impact upon we would have a dandy mess, wouldn't we? As it is you shall have landed upon yourselves, which is an anomaly, a paradox, and nature doesn't allow paradoxes. A Great Year, remember, is 25,800 earth years—a full precession of the equinoxes—so better get a hustle on. You have till Thursday."

The cat burraowed and rubbed along Morgana's leg.

Card Tricks and Cheap Tricks

At a comfortable remove from the failing cosmos, snug in a sub-basement of the former Hotel Taft on New York City's Seventh Avenue, the Fata Morgana blinked and said, "Thursday... But, but..."

"Thursday as defined as an ordinary day in the equinoctial precession—a wink and a whistle, actually. That's a give or take," said the eidolon. "Nature doesn't allow paradoxes. I repeat: What the doers have done, the doers must undo. I am but a messenger, and that's the message." The eidolon turned to stare at El who was fiddling with a watch fob in a pocket of his host body's vest. "Isn't there something you should be doing? I mean somewhere else."

"They say New Jersey is lovely at this time of the year," said the Orange Virgin with an un-goddess-like smirk. There was an icy note of calm in her voice.

"Nonsense. I am everywhere," said El. "I can make holes in time and start new solar systems spinning, upend the pyramids and unwind the skein of probability in a dozen different realities, but he can't go home till I let him." El specified the burly bearded frame of Gershon Meyrowitz with a two-handed gesture. Gershon bowed. The cat hissed. He hissed back, chagrined at perhaps having said too much. He looked mildly frantic and waved the omelette pan in the cat's face. "*Not Teaneck...*" El/Gershon flapped his arms and brandished the scorched omelette pan in a futile gesture of menace.

"You have burned your quiche, godling. An insignificant farrago," said the eidolon. "Compared with..."

"Funny." Linda Winkelman giggled.

"Funny? I don't think any of this is one bit funny," said the Fata Morgana, Orange Virgin, Queen of Heaven, etc., etc. "Forget this, Linda. Forget everything. I'll get back to you as soon as I can." Linda's head fell forward to her chest; she made gentle snoring sounds.

"...Teaneck, New Jersey," continued the eidolon. "There is no option. You may interpret this as a direct pronouncement from the Old Ones. You are underfoot and together the two of you are creating an incredible hash of things. One of you should be elsewhere. You. And get that poor man a bath," said the eidolon. Squaring his shoulders, the demiurge shambled to the service elevator.

"And now for you, Miss Piggy." The eidolon and the cat turned as one to stare at the Fata Morgana. She sat down.

"Ouch." She had hurt herself. She stood to check her rear end. There was a curly pink tail—the tail of a piglet—protruding at the base of her spine. "A cheap trick," she bellowed at the sky. "El. I know this is his doing—not yours nor yet the Old Ones, this on-again off-again piglet business. I thought it was a convenience for befuddling this pig-killer of mine, this Harry Pease. While I realize I am at your mercy, Lord Eidolon, and here under your sufferance, there is no requirement in our dispensation to thus be constantly hectored. Return my own regal fundament to its proper condition. Please?"

"Please and Thank you—the magic words. No. Not immediately, O Beautiful One. There is an issue." The dislocation traveled on, taking her with it as the eidolon flapped leisurely alongside.

❑

In the cellars of the Hotel Taft, Linda was left alone with the cat. There was an insistent scratching at the door. She tried to rise and found her knees stuck under the table. She was wedged in tight. "It's open." She must have ordered out for Chinese.

The scratching was louder now, more insistent. "I said come in, godammit," Linda shouted as she fumbled around for loose cash. She was broke. Where was the checkbook..

The door splintered and fell open. The cat gave out with a yowl of abject terror and departed vertically, up the side of a stand of stainless steel shelving that reached to the ceiling.

"You wouldn't have a match on you would you, girlie?" the visitor asked hopefully. The creature was a distillation of the fears that grow best alone and in the dark: a Manticore, a myth. Between its bared fangs was installed the now-defunct butt of a thick, short black cigar. The Manticore exuded the odor of rainy childhood afternoons, pious old people and the chemical composition of the afterlife. The creature's eyes flashed lime-green highlights, verdigris and gold: a summer housefly buzzing at the window.

Linda Winkelman breathed in the odor of her great-grandmother's kitchen curtains: wood smoke and cinnamon, a smell of fly-speckled pictures, peeling kitchen paint and the slops bucket under the sink. With the smells came a recollection of Sundays and hellfire from a pounded pulpit, a reluctant child dragged along to hear the litany. The apparition was a visitor from her great-grandmother's blameless grave.

"Do you believe in Hell?" Linda asked. "Sorry, that was a dumb question."

The Manticore sighed, a draft of wet paper matches sputtering. "No question is dumb. This is how we learn, honey." He was diffident. "This Hell, though—no, can't say that I have." He scratched his ear with a foot. "Heard of it, that is. Believing is something else. My turn. What is Hell and why do you ask? I mean, I have suggested this to you, right?"

"The red-haired woman with no clothes on, that skanky guy who needs a bath. They are your partners, ancient gods and goddesses, whatever? You don't have to worry about giving anything away. Everything they said was gibberish to me."

"Sorry about that. And this, too. I am only trying to be helpful." He batted his eyes at her and flashed a grin. Weird and strange, the creature reminded Linda of the big, dumb, loving collie dog she had as a child. And, like the dog, its smile showed many rows of sharp teeth. She cast about for something—anything—to defend herself with. Ah, the frying pan. The Manticore regarded the charred remains that clung to the pan. "A kidnapper's quiche. Mighty tasty, I hear. I am the Manticore. It was chloral hydrate, Mickey Finn, you know—that was what they injected you with."

Linda rubbed her ankles. "That may be your name, but who are you? All of you; there seems to be a porcupine in there with you. I know where we are but why are we here? More to the point why are *you* here? And what are you?"

The Manticore again scratched at an ear. "Actually, the story is much more interesting than the mere facts. The stones," he said.

"The stones..."

"Bedrock, the castle keep. I mean tens of thousands of years—more or less—and a fellow buried up to his neck in cement there's a lot of time for reflection. My companions were not much for serious conversation. The Goat—a joker, I couldn't get a word in edgeways. The Cow—all wrapped up in his own affairs. A silent fellow, Cow."

"He..." Linda rubbed at her chafed wrists. The Supreme Being's cords had left a bruise. "A cow is a she. You are confused whatever you are."

"A Manticore, as I have told you. A long and illustrious line. Now set to tending after tumescent toddlers by the Queen of Heaven. Or one toddler. He looks full grown, our Biff. You haven't seen a male personage about—stark naked with the lineaments of an ancient Greek god by any chance?"

"I am sure I would remember..."

"In the usual course of things, I agree. Remembering is what separates us sentient beings from the lesser creatures."

"I remember that I haven't seen a naked man hereabouts. This is the basement of the Hotel Taft; all sorts of things are possible on Seventh Avenue," said Linda. "Have you checked Times Square?"

"You will have to pay attention if we are to be getting on with things, young woman. We were speaking about cows and sex. A popular topic in the dungeons of the Lady of the Wild Things, let me tell you. Cow insisted that he was a bullock. Goat ragged on him mercilessly, thus raising the spiritual temperature of our fetid underground. Dudgeons were raised. We bickered and quarreled but to no avail. The tell-tale parts of Cow's anatomy were firmly fixed in the stones. There was no possible way to ascertain the truth or falsehood of Cow's assertions."

"I'm afraid that you are only a figment. You are nothing but a bad dream and I shall presently wake up and get about my business."

"How distressing. That you do not believe in me. I do hope that you are asking a simple question of names, backgrounds and map coordinates. There could be a..."

"For starters, I would be pleased to hear anything about just what the hell is going on."

The creature looked crushed. Linda had a flash of recollection from that life before now, when she had been somebody else. When? A neighborhood boy had shown her his collection of matchbook covers and wild birds' eggs. She had laughed, then afterwards felt bad.

Linda paced. Though an infrequent smoker, she craved a cigarette. "You are not answering any question I ask. You are making a big show of making a big show. You are making every effort in fact, to avoid answering my questions while all the time trying to appear helpful and cooperative, and I simply don't believe you for one minute. You are a kidnapper plain and simple. I have been abducted and I want to know why. And right now, please."

The Manticore performed a stagy bit of sleight-of-hand and pulled a package of cigarettes from behind her ear. "The tobacco's okay, pre-war. The good stuff. I get them out of the radio." He thumbed one up and offered her the pack. "Here."

Linda accepted gratefully. *He gets them from the radio.* She decided not to ask. The creature touched off a broom straw at the stove and offered a light. The kettle El the demiurge had set on to boil whistled a summons and the apparition busied himself with tea things. Filling a porcelain pot with leaves and water, he wiped off two cups and straddled the bench. Leaning an elbow on the table he stared at Linda. "You haven't asked me if I can read your mind."

"Can you?"

"No. Can you read mine?"

"I don't have to, and if you think coming on to me is going to get you off the hook, think again. I want some answers."

"Irony and venom both, pity. That you can't read my mind, that is. Because I find you quite fascinating and that is the simple unvarnished truth." It stood up. "One of our people can read minds but she's occupied on the Other Side right now. Uh, where you come from, that is. She can put on a real crackerjack of a show. Actually you have met her already. But here, our tea is done and I'm getting ahead of myself. The truth of why you are here is sort of complicated and doesn't lend itself to easy answers. Let us have a nice walkabout and you shall learn everything."

Linda stood, stamped her foot and smashed her teacup against the iron range. "I do not want to be diverted, I do not want to be talked down to like a child and I don't want your goddamned tea and unctuousness. I want to know what the hell is happening and I want to go home. Now."

"A violent punctuation. Your words would have been sufficient." The Manticore waved a taloned hand majestically in the air. "Get a load of this," he announced. A flickering blue and pink neon sign appeared. Its pink parts fluttered and sparked irregularly, something was arcing. There was a smell of ozone. Strong steady blue lettering proclaimed Say Goodbye To Unwanted Hair With The Amazing Remov-A-Tron.

"And you do tricks. How charming." The visitor with the tail of a lion and the quills of a porcupine definitely had her attention. Linda feigned indifference. "That's very nice, but I don't see..."

"Well, of course if you don't like that we can always try again. You will have to pardon me; I am a little peckish today. I'm not used to spur-of-the-moment performances, but I think I can come up with something stirring." Linda was making him sweat. "Ta-Dah!" This time the sign was orange, the letters large and even. There was no smell of ozone. WELCOME TO THE NEW JERSEY TURNPIKE. REDUCE SPEED APPROACHING TOLL PLAZA.

"That's very nice. A regular touch of home." Linda walked around the letters expecting backwards writing, a mirror image. No matter which way she looked at the turnpike warning it read forwards. The letters had no back. "Neat. Does it do anything?" The sign vanished with a small 'pop.'

"Being is what it does. Or did," sighed the Manticore. He had tried, really tried. Next she would be asking for card tricks. "It's Art. It is its own reason for being—it doesn't have to do anything."

"You don't do any card tricks, do you?" Linda asked.

The Ministry of Responsibility

Elizabeth Profitt Pease thrived on challenge. Although but two years younger than Harry, Libby the kid sister cast a proprietary shadow over her brother since she was able to walk, form the necessary words and claim her place under an admonitory sun. Her brother was hard to control, a scapegrace, a challenge. Sixty years later and she still battled the forces of darkness for Harry's soul. Harry grew wild and big in the shade of sister Libby's intent. The arrival of Maggie, an amnesiac with a clean slate for Libby to write on, proved a welcome distraction for her brother. Libby found Maggie's Upper West Side Manhattan accent exotic and therefore suspect. She took it upon herself to instruct Maggie in the niceties of social intercourse—when is a doily an antimacassar, which fork to use for salad and why lime jello with diced chicken parts and green grapes with an aerosol whipped cream topping is favored at covered dish suppers—things a savage islander would need to know to survive.

Over the passing months Libby's suspicions that the young woman might be a Papist faded. "Everyday people," as Libby said, giving Maggie her stamp of approval. "Down-to-earth," "Amnesia," said Libby's compeers in The Daughters of Milo as they went about their good works. Libby's affections were natural and unforced: here was a fresh challenge. Brother Harry rejoiced. That Libby Pease would open her heart to a voyager from parts possibly beholden to Rome—certainly foreign, the pink places on the map and therefore suspect—was less celebrated by Pen Harrington than it was by Harry.

The women planned things together and Pen, while grateful, felt left out. Not that there was jealousy as such, but a distancing: You go to your church, I'll go to mine; but we'll walk along together. Elizabeth Profitt Pease and Maggie Granola flourished rosy-cheeked in the starshine that was the younger woman's reflected love—not quite young, certainly middle-aged, but nonetheless passionate.

"Well, now that Libby has after all these years found a new project," David Morrissey had offered one afternoon at EAT, "It would appear that the heat is off for Harry."

❑

EAT. Cousteau McClonaghy thought that said it very nicely, a lure to gear-jammers, evocative of golden fries and truck stop mamas. We Serve Salada Tea was flocked into the screen door; the screen stayed up all winter, all summer, twelve months a year. The Salada Tea Company bought him the door 30 years before—a usufruct of cooperative advertising, he'd be damned if he'd take it down. Maybe some paint. Its highway department green was flaked down to the bare wood. Next year for sure. Cousteau was more poet than cook; his mom had named him after The Undersea World of Jacques Cousteau, a daily event on the only television available during her confinement. It had been a long labor.

"Welcome back to the land of paper towels and howling bowels, David," said Harriet Hopwood, playing the flirtatious waitress as she cruised their booth. "What'll it be—coffee, tea or me?"

The Return of the Orange Virgin

"I sense some tension here, but we are resigned to our mates and real people don't do things like that except on TV. Besides, my wife's father would have my guts on toast."

Pen studied the daily specials. They really changed daily, but what Cousteau served up in the realm of desserts and entrees demonstrated no relation to what the public might want. The specials changed with no discernable pattern but the flow of the zodiac: Cousteau makes it, you eat it. You don't eat it, Cousteau chucks it in the big green dumpster out back and is grumpy all next day. An organic farmer paid him twenty-five dollars to haul away the dumpster twice a week for composting. The specials were Dutch Apple, Cheese Cake, Date Squares, Grapenut Pudding, Bread Pudding. Pies: Coconut, Toll House. Lobster Roll $9.85. The lobster roll was mayonnaise salad with lobster meat on a toasted hot dog bun. The sign hung over a collection of the extra large styrofoam takeout cups with the waitresses' names magic-markered on where they dumped their tips.

"Harriet, level with me, has anyone ever, ever in all your years of slinging hash in this excellent establishment, has anyone ever ordered the Grapenut Pudding?" Pen ordered coffee and a toasted English, Morrissey covered his half empty cup with his hand and waved Harriet off with the other. "Yes, indeed, the heat is off Harry. Probably for good and all; and there's a story, probably apocryphal, making the rounds..." Harriet leaned close as Dim Lights went on with a conspiratorial stage whisper, "...that when Libby surprised the kids screwing on her parlor sofa, she was so enthralled by the spectacle of young love triumphant, she just slipped a doily under them to save her upholstery and made away to the kitchen to busy herself shucking peas until they were finished."

"Be that as it may, she has let the papers lapse on Harry's competency hearing and Harry's shooting baskets and swilling beer as in time past, unmolested. A happy man."

❑

"Pennn... Hey!" Maggie splashed along the sidewalk, driving her overshoes with the balance of a cross-country skier. "Golly, Pen, wait up; I'm all out of breath." She grabbed at Pen's ears and, drawing down his face, kissed him roundly on the mouth. She exuded the crisp, tangy glow of health children have after playing out of doors. "Phew! Oh wow. Golly, Pen, nice spring day, eh?"

It was the next day and Pen was recovering from a night of bachelorhood; Libby being busy working out the kinks in Maggie's bowling technique. Pen was in love with a woman who had no past, except for a little history inferred from a bus ticket issued in New York City—mocking laughter from a broad, answerless void. He checked on what little information they had and was stonewalled by the bus company. The ticket had been bought over the counter at the Port Authority, not from a travel agent. "We sell upward of sixty-thousand a day. You see what I'm saying?" Pen saw. The welter of indifferent humanity whose interlocking lives held the secret of her past had flowed together behind her, filling in her footprints. The threads of Maggie vanished into a transcontinental anonymity. It seemed too easy; the world had forgotten her. Did that mean she was his to keep? With so many places to look, why look anywhere?

Lost in the marvel of their couplings, his head pillowed between her breasts, he wondered at an odor of chocolate and mint.

"When I met you..."

"Yes."

"You said something about a mission. And a Voice."

"Did I."

There had been a fishing-about for her new glasses. Swearing she had never worn glasses, Maggie had held out for less than a week, crashing into, down, and over obstructions till Pen packed her off to an optometrist. He figured her old glasses were languishing unclaimed somewhere in the visceral convolutions of the Atlantic BusWays Company. With some fussing she got them settled on her nose, stood on tiptoe and stared him in the eye.

"I guess I did. I remember that. I wish I knew what I meant by it, but don't worry."

Pen thought of Maggie as a gift tagged for some deserving soul, and here, gratifying his own worthless flesh. Intercepted, gone astray, a gift of the gods, perhaps unintended, her being here with him was a karmic miscarriage; too many questions might be apt to call this to the attention of donor or donors unknown who would surely want her back. A dark ferment of doubt struggled to make itself known, but Pen suppressed it. She smelled great right out of the shower.

"I was afraid I'd miss you." They hadn't seen each other for four hours. She had left him sleeping to go to work: new life, new job, the first week. "How've you been?"

"Holding back the ravages of middle age, which I choose to regard as an aphorism rather than a fact. Fifty years and holding." Pen held his arms out and did a turn. "The demographic spike is right behind me, the doctors, dentists and accountants comforting in their numbers. But they are closing fast." He kissed her again. "I'm headed to the gym." On the days he was uninterruptedly sober, every day since the advent of Maggie, Pen was at the gym pushing the weights around.

A carload of cruising adolescents approached, sending up a tsunami of slush. They slowed and whistled. Maggie turned, smiled and waved back. The kids, partly paralyzed by six-pack beer and unused to receiving a response, slowed further to avoid splashing Maggie and Pen. They smiled, waved gaily back, and tooled off around the courthouse corner, sending up a shower on Bob Sawyer, the Happy Time Bread man.

Another kiss. "Can't do lunch today, Pen. Dr. Morrissey is typing a report. Maybe I can slip away later." David Lewis Morrissey, a.k.a. Dim Lights Morrissey, wasn't doing the typing, Maggie was. And it was not a report; it was David's Ph.D. thesis disguised as grant proposals. He was two years late getting it in. David used the 'Doctor' as a courtesy while he produced his overdue homework on company time with company employees doing the grunt work. Maggie worked at a word processor at the university extension. She had fallen right into the job and made herself at home, a natural.

"David Lewis Morrissey, almost Ph.D. Right-O, sweetheart. See you tonight." A peck on the lips, and Maggie crossed the street.

Pen watched her retreat to the office with dreamy delight. Pen liked to look at Maggie. In an age of one-size-fits-all panty hose and shrug-in brassieres, Maggie favored silk stockings and a garter belt, usually with knit sheaths. On her they looked good: straps and harnesses in bas-relief, a grand and reassuring sight. In a seamless world it was a solace to catch glimpses of female foundations.

Pen slopped across Main Street through the salt, gravel, and loose brown ice mix and hiked the two blocks toward Canada on the sunny side of the street. Maybe some coffee. Sure. Hold the Danish.

Slop, slop—galoshes on a sidewalk wet with spring ice melt. Willipaq, Maine: a sleepy border town, population four thousand souls. The big excitement in Willipaq aside from the arrivals of the new rental videos on alternate Wednesdays was an infrequent hot pursuit by the Mounties. Canada and the United States maintained a tentative mutual presence at three bridges and two ferry landings. Drug sniffing dogs and excise officers alike grew fat on takeout food.

Penfield Harrington slopped along, collar up, chin hunkered down into his mackinaw, with the isolation of his thoughts and his own galoshes' noise. Pen stopped at the curb and reconnoitered, listening to see if there was anything catching up with him. He ducked behind a light pole and avoided a shower of slush as the bakery truck passed. He checked the other side of the pole where, shoulder high, slush trickled dispiritedly back to the gutter. The Mounties got their man no more often, nor less, than the Happy Time Bread man, and they, too, were courteous and friendly.

The Happy Time Bread man warped his tonnage into a hubcap-deep berth in front of the Cousteau Diner. The driver was Bob Sawyer, part-time deputy, a county mountie. "Hiya, Pen. Sorry about that. I saw you duck behind that pole. Did I get you?"

"Hiya, Bob. Missed me this time; I am developing a sixth sense. How's the basketball?"

"Just great. Game Tuesday night. Come on out." He swung down from the high cab.

"We'll see." Bob always asked; Pen always deferred—the worn convivialities of winter with the earth not yet warm but the smell of spring in the air. Bob undogged the back latch, rolled up the gate, and slid out a stack of wire racks. Pen balanced on the running board and leaned into the cab; Bob's badge was pinned to the truck's sun visor, his gun belt rolled up under the high seat. "Just checking to see if you're armed. Glad to know you're on duty."

"I'm always on duty." Thirty years and he had never drawn his gun outside of pistol practice. He delivered babies and talked drunks out of trees, the kind of cop that made folks comfortable just knowing he was around. Violent crime seemed to resolve itself before anybody thought of calling the sheriff. Either that or the State Police showed up; they had the radio cars and the base station. And a good pension plan. Deputies had been known to lust after the dispatcher's job.

Bob shouldered his load and turned toward a flashing blue neon sign. EAT. "Going to Cousteau's?"

"Yep." Pen hopped down.

Bob Sawyer weaseled his toe under the Salada Tea screen door and pulled it open with his foot. Pen caught it and held it for him. Bob and his bread passed through.

Pen stuck his head around the door hoping for a clear shot at the geezer's table. Cousteau and his cronies held forth there from 7:30 to 9:00 every morning but Sunday, spilling coffee and shoveling eggs, deciding on how the world would go. Cousteau McClonaghy had a table radio always on by the cash register, an old five tube AM set that had heard Roosevelt declare war. He had had it rewired so the jukebox piped through the speaker. The geezers listened and pondered. Public opinion never slept. Cousteau was sensitive to the pulse of the street and he and his pals programmed the jukebox by what their old moms liked to hear, country tunes, Lawrence Welk, and light classical. The geezers had adjourned and the field was Pen's by default.

In gumboots and tweeds Dim Lights Morrissey straddled a stool at the counter. Morrissey was a very married man—a walking advertisement for stir-fry veggies, watching the cholesterol and regular exercise on the bicycle to nowhere, doing situps and leglifts. With his hawk-like features and shock of distinguished graying hair the coeds just loved him. "Hiya, Pen." Morrissey rumbled from deep in his abdomen, putting elbows to the formica. He sported leather patches at the elbows of a tweedy Norfolk jacket, English country house weekend shooting wear.

"Hiya, David"

"Jesus!" A shout accompanied by a crash of crockery. A tray of dishes and a slippery melt spot on the floor had connected and sent Cousteau flying ass-over-teakettle.

"We've got trouble." Morrissey caught a motion in the corner of his eye and winced, abruptly changing the subject—whatever trouble there was, was private business. Pen brightened considerably at the prospect of trouble. If Morrissey had a worry, things were looking up. Before Maggie the catalog of his life had achieved a stultifying sameness which, when he thought about it, slid him into a brown depression. Trouble, eh? Manageable trouble, the kind talked around by friends at a diner counter? They could handle it. He was ready.

Morrissey winked to announce the arrival of a public nuisance and swung a wide tangent in mid-sentence. "...that here we face the elements unafraid and scratch a living from the unyielding soil by hunting, fishing and trapping small foreign automobiles which, just as in the big cities, we strip for parts. Oh, hiya, Barney. The parts go in the freezer against future need. We are good stewards of the land."

"Hiya, Pen." Barney Tinker, the local redneck. The hunting season was months past, but now as then, Barney was aggressively cruising the tables hoping for a little action. His shooting iron set by, he stalked with but mother wit and guile, exercising the mystique that clings to a moose lottery winner. Barney crept up on wary diners, singling out likely prey, loners, the weak and aged. Suspecting a jibe, Barney gave Morrissey the sugar-frosted, glassy stare that meant David had used more than one subordinate clause in direct address. Last October after his ticket had come up lucky in the moose lottery Barney went everywhere with a Marlin 30.30 in a cloth-suede bag and wearing a blaze orange cap. Life, liberty, and the pursuit of Bambi. Seventy thousand entries, but only one thousand were picked to fill the air with bullets during the one week allotted to plugging the emperor of the woods. Barney was not known for a crack shot and had returned mooseless. There had been an incident with a snowmobile. Barney said the sled had surprised him and he had taken it out by reflex. The occupants survived.

Morrissey bypassed the snub. "How much magic can one man stand? Hiya, Barney."

"Magic, huh? You doing ventriloquism tricks today, Pen?" He didn't get it. He never did. "That dummy next to you is talking and I didn't see your lips move." Barney Tinker taught Drivers Ed. and coached basketball at Willipaq High. An ambitious man, he had his sights on a larger franchise, maybe lunch room monitor.

"Hey, Pen," he interrupted himself, a bad habit formed with captive listeners in Drivers Ed. He forgot what he meant to say and yelled at the proprietor, "Hey, Cousteau, I hear you got some Canadians working over here, that true?"

"Been memorizing license plates again, Barney?" asked David. David turned to Pen to explain. "Barney is exercised about foreigners taking jobs from sons of the native soil. He sees a slippery ladder to tenure as attendant faculty in the lunch room."

Barney continued relentlessly. "You play some real American music on that radio and those Canucks will stop eating here and they'll get the UCLA after you." Barney was a big basketball fan, and they got his drift. He meant The ACLU, the American Civil Liberties Union, not The University of California at Los Angeles.

"Heh. Heh."

Morrissey and Harrington laughed along with Barney, acknowledging his zinger. "It's a free country, Barney, you're welcome to your opinion." The appeal to patriotism worked. He moved on.

"Not bad," said Morrissey, "But he still thinks it's the UCLA." He handed over a clipping. "Get a look at this item. Let this be my entry into the morning's compendium of comfort and joy. Space aliens are after Harry Pease."

The Return of the Orange Virgin

He handed over a quarter column display ad from the Willipaq News, published twice a month.

REWARD

For information leading to the arrest and cooperation in the prosecution of: The Person(s) whose telepathic control and surveillance of my mind, body and home totally deprives me of liberty and does and has subjected me to slavery, peonage, house arrest and imprisonment, mental and physical assaults and injuries and systematic deprivation of my civil, political and human rights: $1000 (one thousand dollars). Serious inquiries about the conditions for payment of this reward will be answered promptly. Letters should include a stamped return envelope. Collect phone calls will not be accepted.

Harry Pease, Esq.

"They said Einstein was crazy and he discovered relativity. And then they said Harry Pease was crazy."

"And, sure enough, Harry was," rumbled Dim Lights.

"Well, I dunno, space aliens living in my teapot would get me a mite distracted, too."

"Harry Profitt Pease is truly one of God's innocents and a good basketball shot to boot. Something is very, very strange with this. More than beer and booze." Morrissey grew pensive. "A finely disorganized mind of Harry's quality would never pull a stunt at this level."

"Well, his sister 'looks in' on him two, three times a week to see if he has frozen or starved to death, or fallen down drunk and let the stove go out. You are arguing that we shouldn't go over and reconnoiter Harry's condition?"

"Hardly. This," Morrissey smoothed the clipping, flattening it out on the countertop, "speaks of serious mental problems. Our Harry has gone over the edge. If he is seeing space aliens or whatever and starts taking potshots with that cannon of his, that's all his sister needs to have him put away. A personal visit is called for." David was not impressed by Pen's assessment of their potential danger. "Could be delirium. Harry gets blind, stinking, falling down drunk when he kills pigs—about a six-pack of half-quart cans per pig. At that rate he can't have enough brain cells left to wind a watch. He needs help, Pen."

"Booze has its own rhythm; when he hits his limit, he passes out. Suppose we go? We burp him, then administer psychotherapy?"

"This," David tapped the clipping, "is a call for help. Drunk or sober, Harry loves company and is amenable to reason."

David smoothed the clipping again, then folded it, halving and quartering it with the edge of his hand, ironing the creases. He flashed Harriet a sign for more coffee. She returned a dazzling toothpaste smile and retreated to the kitchen. Coffee would come in its own good time.

"On a second reading, Harry is nuts."

"Harry is nuts and a friend. This is a problem calling for a creative solution. Are you suggesting we should drop a sack over Sister Elizabeth and let Harry go on his merry way?"

"Harry is nuts but harmless. Even if Libby doesn't see this notice in the paper, her phone will be ringing off the wall. Libby has been trying to get Harry declared incompetent for years, and now her well-wishers will be on the horn to rub her nose in it. Libby is sensitive to public opinion."

"He's an embarrassment and she wants him locked away downstate." Morrissey dropped a donut in his cup and placed a saucer over it, demonstrating incarceration. He tried spearing the donut out with his fork, but it disintegrated.

There were premonitory clatters and rustlings from behind the swinging kitchen doors. With the self-absorbed balance of a whitewater rafter—a forward lean with one shoulder high, a calculated swing of her pelvic girdle that pulled her center of gravity along the line of her forward momentum—Harriet hit the door. Her hips shot forward, a contained writhing, knees slightly flexed. There was a breathless instant with everything on hold, her heavy tray piled with steaming crockery high in the air. The tray as wide as the door glided forward; this was Harriet's moment. Miniature hydraulics buried in the doors wheezed; the laws of physics were in abeyance. A rearward calculated slap with a hip, a forward nudge with a knee, and the swinging doors paused open, just wide enough for Harriet and her tray. The tray moved forward on a perfect horizontal line parallel to the sum of all her motions, never wavering, the acme of precision. With Harriet safe on the other side, the doors swung shut. One defiant, final thrust and she snapped her hips back to catch the closing doors, quieting their return. Harriet shouldered forward with the overfull tray, steaming mounds of pancakes, ham and home fries erupting tiny geysers through the vents of silver domed lids.

"I am a man with a happy home life, but I never tire of watching Harriet." Morrissey leaned forward over the counter and fumbled for the garbage barrel. He dumped his coffee with the wreckage of the donut

---

The Return of the Orange Virgin

into the trash. "From time to time the inner man requires stronger medicine than is served up from an electric wok." He signaled for a refill on the coffee. Harriet caught the sign and nodded. She executed a pirouette and set the tray down at the coffee service to load up for the rest of her trip. Morrissey sighed. "Poetry in motion—stick a strobe on her ass and you'd get perfect lazy-eights."

Pen, too, was appreciative. "Consummate balletic performance, the Roller Derby in sensible shoes."

"Freeze!"

Harriet was on her hands and knees, slapping at the floor.

"Don't anybody move!"

Evoking SWAT teams from prime time TV, even the superb Harriet was captive to the human condition.

"Contact lenses!"

Harriet caught up with her dropped lens and retired to the back to rinse it off.

"We have been witnesses to perfection: flawed and poignant, but perfection, nonetheless. Even the divine Harriet has her vulnerabilities and flaws, but a dropped contact lens doesn't get her into Harry's league. Harry Pease is going for the big time." David helped himself to coffee and spooned in sugar. "This could be serious. This thing in the newspaper will be all Libby needs for hailing Harry into court."

"Are you suggesting that you and I assume a ministry of responsibility to see that Harry remains at large?"

"A committee of two."

"Okeh, we go visiting. First I go home for a shower and a shave. I'm still grubby from the weekend. Meet you back here in an hour?"

"You're on."

Bubbling with news and smelling like a new Spring day, Maggie avalanched into the restaurant. When it was break time and Dim Lights wasn't around, she just turned on the answering machine and closed the office. "You know," said Maggie as she insinuated herself into the booth, eager to share. "You know that Harry Pease has a new pet?"

At Harry's

Pen whistled up Prince, who was slumbering under the sink. The great tail swung into action, banging against the door. Pen picked up the leash and hung it around his neck. "We're going for a ride, boy." Man and dog, the two walked back to Cousteau's where Prince, without preamble, jumped into the back of David's station wagon.

They made it as far as the corner. "Stop here, I'll get us some beer."

"Good thinking. Get a case. Keeping Harry free and at large is a problem requiring lubrication."

"I'll get an extra case of Seadog in case we have to bribe our way in. Or out." The prospect of a confrontation with a madman weighed on Pen as they drove the thirty-odd miles to Harry's.

Pen's abandoned house was across the ledge and cat-a-corner from Harry. "We'll hang out at my place, plan our attack, then walk over casual like. Just visiting on a whim." David cut the engine conspiratorially and they rolled in.

"He's home." Smoke curled up from Harry's metalbestos chimney.

"It's your place, you lead." Morrissey picked up a double handful of beer and eased out of the Volvo.

"Shit!" Pen put a foot through a rotten board on his porch.

"Got the key?" Morrissey set down his two six-packs and hefted a massive and rusted padlock attached to an equally rusted hasp on the front door.

"Don't need one. Here." Pen levered up the sash of a broken front window. He eased himself in and David handed through the beer.

They sat and talked and drank. They talked around the problem, giving it the synoptic scrutiny of a museum viewing of a rare specimen. Clearly, they were messengers of destiny. So many possible permutations were examined, each new avenue opening on yet further complexities, that in an hour they were lost in fine points of logic and more than moderately drunk.

"Time for Harry," said Morrissey, trying to stand. "Perhaps if we viewed the body in its native habitat. Go to the source: get back to basics." He sat abruptly. "Maybe another beer."

The deputation concluded, after some few beers more, that they were in no shape to safely negotiate the quarter mile of wild hedgerows and slippery shale of the windblown bare spots separating Pen's house and Harry's house. They piled into Dim Light's old Volvo and drove next door.

Morrissey pulled his station wagon to the side of the road, half in, half out, wedging Pen's door shut against the rear bumper of Harry's truck. Pen climbed out over the gearshift and stood, beer in hand, as Morrissey's vintage Volvo wound itself down with dilatory sputters after the ignition was turned off. Puffs of oily blue smoke exited the tailpipe, gradually subsiding.

They examined the road for clearance. "Enough room if someone really wants to get by. They can honk, what the hell," David stumbled and caught at the roof rack. Equilibrium restored, he pocketed the key. "Not enough yard to park in and just enough road to get by." Morrissey had parked straddling the ditch.

"Jesus, would you look at that." Harry seemed to be playing basketball. And ignoring them. He had a hoop hung on the side of his house on the side facing the road, bolted through the cedar shakes just under where the weather board met the eaves. Basketball was a posted land for Harry, approaching religion in the winter months. Harry was showing off his stuff. There was that field goal in the state tournament. Folks remembered. The golden boy of high school sports when Ford was president. Once a week the basketball from atop Harry's bureau would get a palpating, a bladder squeeze, perhaps a thoughtful, expert grunt, and he would unclamp the bicycle pump from the Sears 5-speed languishing in the yard with both tires flat, suck the sphincter dimpling the ball's bladder—get it good and wet—and stick in the syringe. A few flys on the pump handle, then into the road: some bounces, a nod of approbation for correct inflation, proper feel, then some basket shooting.

Elapsed time five minutes. The legend was satisfied.

Their breaths effervescent, Pen and Morrissey approached Harry, feeling leading men in one of life's dramas. David leapt ahead to the reason he and Pen had not negotiated the tangles of alders and runaway roses over the ledge to Harry's place, began fumbling out an explanation why they had taken the car, but let it drop. His face was rosy and flushed.

"Harry, we want you to know right off that we are friends, right?" That should set the tone: begin at the beginning, a good start. David breathed easier.

"You are making excuses and you haven't done anything—yet. What's up?" Harry squinted suspiciously. "Morrissey, are you going to tell me that I am a sympathetic character again?" Harry was wise in the ways of

Dim Lights Morrissey. "David, you are a fool. Shut up. Have you been drinking?" This from Harry, who should know. "You sound guilty, give it a rest. Hiya, Pen." Harry was going one-on-one.

"Put down the ball, Harry. We come as friends."

"Pass then, friends, but as a friend I would remind you that in my hands this basketball is a dangerous weapon. One false move and it's stand and deliver. Remember always you are guests in the tents of my people."

"High five, Harry." Pen held both hands out, elbow length, palms up, and got the double slap from Harry. Harry kept the ball under control in the crotch of his right arm, ready in case of hostile action.

"I was wondering if you guys were going to show up," Harry said. "For cronies, pals, you fellas haven't been over too much lately. You have been remiss in exercising your social obligations."

Morrissey said something about how it had been winter. "'Tents of my people.' Harry, have you been watching old movies?"

"Lots of them, David. Hundreds. We've been grinding away at it for a month. The VCR just crapped out." Harry did not look sad over this.

"We?" Pen picked up on the plural pronoun. Spots of high color rose on Harry's cheekbones. "Did they make you Pope, or have you got a girlfriend hidden away? Talk to me, Harry, tell me true; have you finally connected with Alma Nightingale?"

The flush grew deeper. Harry is blushing, thought Pen. A man now sober is having to defend something he did drunk and can't remember, but is convinced he is right all the same.

"Not the Pope. A bishop, maybe a priest. But I didn't know. See, it was all a mistake..." Harry shuffled and mumbled into his beard.

Morrissey pressed the attack. "Harry Pease, you have about as much brains as that basketball under your arm. You have blown your cover and now everyone will think you're nuts. Some of us had reserved judgment. With Libby angling to get you into a strait jacket, you put that damned thing in the paper and signed it."

This was not what Harry had been talking about. He looked puzzled and turned to Pen. "Now, Pen, you know I am not crazy. Libby looks after me; she wouldn't do tha..."

Morrissey handed over the clipping. "Harry, get this straight—the word is out, your sister has seen the lawyers. She wants you to rumba in a rubber room for the rest of your natural life."

The Return of the Orange Virgin

Harry studied the paper closely from all sides, approached the thing warily—a cat stalking in high, dry grass, winterkill. He turned the clipping over, hoping to find enlightenment or at least a coupon on the back. "Sounds like something I'd do drunk. But I didn't." A petulant tone entered his voice. "Party or parties unknown are jamming my reception, could be telepathic powers. My satellite is fucked all to hell, too. Blew me away smack dab in the middle of the NBA playoffs. Could be space people."

Morrissey faced Pen and spoke in a stagy aside, as if Harry weren't there. "Space people. Okeh, I'll let that one pass. Visitations—a working hypothesis. As a phenomenon, 'visitations' is a more user-friendly term. Alright, suppose Harry has visits from space aliens..."

"Space *people*," injected Harry.

"Space people. Fine..." Morrissey continued, ignoring Harry. "Suppose I am a county magistrate and Libby comes before my bench with a brace of suits and depositions averring that her brother is entertaining space people. The conventional wisdom is that, lucid moments notwithstanding, crazy people are crazy all the time. Libby says Harry has fairies at the bottom of his garden—space aliens living in his teapot as you so colorfully put it, Pen. This has lowered her stock at the Daughters of Milo, Eastern Star and the bridge club and she feels—rightly or wrongly, it doesn't matter—that she is the big chuckle at the checkout counter of the Red and White. Add to this the question of Harry's solid waste. Well...! To Libby, Harry is worse than a threat, he is an embarrassment and, short of hiring a Sicilian hit man, packing Harry away downstate is the answer to all her troubles. She seeks the comfort of the law. Exhibit A," Morrissey intoned, waving the clipping under Harry's nose.

"Yep, this could be me," said Harry, studying it again. "'There are strange things done 'neath the midnight sun...' *Shooting of Dan McGrew*, Robert Service. I read a lot in the winter when I'm not so drunk and tied up in knots that putting my socks on is an all day job. But not lately, not drunk, and I don't remember doing it. This went in last week."

A medium-sized spotted pig strolled out from behind a stack of snow tires, paused to sniff a 55 gallon drum that had a rotary crank kerosene pump rusted on, then continued on past an array of stove grates to where they were standing and plumped herself down. The pig looked like she had something to say. "Harry, old muffin, the knotted skein of your sanity or lack of same is only the surface message here. The question before the court will be whether you are fit company for children and pets, running loose on the city streets. Well... hello there." The pig, self-aware in the way country pigs were not, studied a trotter in the center of the triangle of Morrissey, Harry and Pen.

Harry blushed again. *Hmm,* Pen thought, *second time today.* Pen Harrington, smooth talker, was at a loss for words. Harry's got something on the fire. Makes you wonder what's going on between these two—interspecies hanky-panky? "Ah, Harry. Is this your space alien by any chance?"

The pig cocked her head and looked quizzically at Pen. "You, gawky person with the open mouth—yes, I am speaking to you. Are you conscious?" This pig hadn't come to have her ears scratched.

The pig had asked him a question and common politeness called for an answer. "Uh, I guess so." Pen looked around, taking stock. It was nice to know where you were in the last moments before they led you away. Pen had always liked Harry's dooryard. With no effort whatsoever on Harry's part, it blossomed anew each spring with high-stalked lupines, daisy-eyed cosmos, and the spiky bloomstalks of purple-flowered veronica. The flowers were not yet up and Pen stood in a winter-brown slush, slightly drunk and talking to a pig. Morrissey had not moved an inch; he was staring pop-eyed and looking like he would strangle. He turned slightly purple and delivered a sudsy belch.

"I shall interpret your carbonated effulgence as a deferential courtesy. You may call me Morgana, Mister Morrissey." There was a trace of an accent that was hard to pin down. The pig studied a trotter and looked to Harry, as if waiting on the amenities. Harry's fierce flush approached the cheery glow of Harvard beets fresh out of the can. "I can't wait for a proper introduction all day, Harry. You nice men wait right here while I go and powder my nose." She trotted behind the oil drum.

"Harry..." said Morrissey, sounding like a swimmer calling for a rope.

"Now, guys, this isn't at all like it looks."

"I know what it looks like. I want to know what it is."

"So help me Jesus, we are talking to a medium-sized spotted pig with a curly tail."

The pig reappeared after a minute or so and paused to admire herself in a detached bureau mirror that leaned against a stack of tires. She turned her head like a schoolgirl checking her hair in a soda fountain mirror. She trotted back, her tail bobbling and flouncing. She had large ears, way out of proportion. This pig could do a lot of listening, if so inclined.

"Now," she said, "...are any of you," she swiveled to stare at Pen's knees, "the proprietor of a large yellow dog? He broke his chain and followed you here—I had to zap him. I put him under the porch; no one will see him till he wakes up."

"You've killed Pen's dog." Harry sat down with a stunned look, right where he was, folded, sort of. "Mister Harrington here's mighty attached to Prince." He looked to Pen, distancing himself from the deed of murder.

The pig sat down in the dirt in front of Harry and licked his face. She spoke softly, conciliatingly. "I have feelings, too. If some dumb pooch sticking his nose in your ass is your idea of romance, just you try it sometime, Harry Pease."

Harry really does have space aliens living in his teapot, thought Pen Harrington. "Harry, are we really seeing this—the talking pig. I mean, really?"

"You are Mister Harrington," the pig said thoughtfully. "Prince has told me so much about you and Mister Morrissey. He says you quack when you are confused. You are quacking now. Please stop quacking and talk like a normal, sensible human being or I shall be forced to zap you, too. There's lots of room under the porch." The pig had appropriated Harry's left foot, sitting on the toe. A warrior princess prepared to dispense justice.

"Now, Morgana..." Harry started.

Pen had no doubts about his dog being able to handle himself in a scrap. Prince's strategy when attacked was to roll himself into a heavy ball and defy all attempts to budge him. Any medium-sized pig looking for a brawl would have to bring a forklift. "Prince is a lover, not a fighter. Come to think of it, he isn't much of a lover, either."

Her smoky voice grew softer, intimate. "Harry..." she breathed, "Harry, scratch me between the ears. Please."

Harry looked pole-axed. "You killed Pen's dog."

"Oh, Harry, you're such a worrywart. I said I just zapped him. He'll wake up."

"Ohh..." said Harry.

"I can see that it's time for some straight talk," said the pig. "First of all, I am not a space alien and I do not live in a tea pot. I am what you think I am, but you do not yet know what you think. I have been scrutinized and approved by the local fauna." She flipped over and whiffled at the base of her tail. "The fleas love me. With the exception of you three, every being I have thus far met had regarded me as a blood donor, thrown a stick for me to fetch or tried to fuck me. Pardon my French, but this is becoming tedious. Sorry about Prince, Mister Harrington, but I am running with a short fuse."

"You're not from around here," posited Dim Lights.

"Very perceptive, Mister Morrissey. May I call you David?"

"You're not from another world? You didn't land here with your spaceship? No insult intended, but you look a lot like a pig though you don't act like one."

"I am a sentient being: more intelligent, perhaps, than the three of you put together including your dog, Mister Harrington, and the assembled players of Harry's National Basketball Association. It had been a long, cold, lonely spring. One of my aspects has discovered a career in stenography, forgotten who she is and is bumping into things—pathetic. I have had to cut her loose to make her own way. I want to go home and, yes, I put that notice in the paper."

"Lady, Morgana, I didn't for one minute dream you were so desperate. I thought we were having a fine time..." Harry idly rolled the basketball between his palm and the ground.

"You've been a wonderful host, Harry, but life here is so... unfulfilling, if you know what I mean. Here I stumble through a forest I know not."

"You put the ad in the paper," Morrissey said, repeating her words.

"I put it in. Here, I watch old movies. It was fun at first. Then, there is the daily assault by fleas, always a high point."

"But how..." This from Harry.

"Don't fidget, Harry," said the pig. "As charming as our Harry is, I decided I needed help. Harry said you two were always coming over to spend a day, pop a brew and schmooze. But week after week went by and you never came. I had to take measures. Evolution is a continuing process; I understand that to be an article of your faith as well as mine. Unfortunately, I did not have the necessary eons to wait. From the resident victims of natural selection, I chose you."

Harry flagged down a passing dependent clause and sat on it. "You say you are not a pig, but if you were you would be from another world?" His eyes narrowed with the cunning of a born gamesman. "What about the fleas?"

The Return of the Orange Virgin

"I am quite definitely from and of this world albeit exiled to another world, but you are not ready to hear about that. The pig is a, a... disguise. Yes, that does it nicely: a disguise. The fleas are symbolic of a universal brotherhood—the free lunch. They represent an epistemological joy which myself as a pig might share, but frankly, the reality sucks. Hence the ad."

"But how?"

"The phone, Harry dear. I punched in the paper's want ads number and said I was Holly calling for Fletch Davis over at the law office and that it was all right, that this was a genuine legal notice and they should charge it against Fletch's account. This, gentlemen, is a quest, and I have summoned you because you are possessed of the skills to bring my plan to fruition. To wit: a communications specialist and a trained thinker, an academic."

At this point, thought Pen, a contribution is called for from the most level-headed of the assembly. Me, God help us. "What you have got, Miss Piggy, is a broken-down bartender and an adjunct from the State U. Extension. What it looks like is that you are making it up as you go along. You've got our attention and everybody else's. A casualty of which is likely to be Harry's continued at-liberty status."

Pen squatted before the pig, who settled back comfortably on Harry's foot and looked him unflinchingly in the eye. "You look like a nice piggy. Why not make the best of what you have here? Why not settle down and raise many litters of talking pigs? Our immediate concern is Libby—and Harry's elevated profile, thanks to you. Right now any diversion is just a lot of unnecessary bullshit." Pen never finished. "Oops..." He had been waving a finger in the pig's face when he went stiff and toppled forward, his arm sinking elbow deep in the soft mud.

"Mr. Harrington was becoming obstreperous," announced Morgana. "You remaining gentlemen may help put him under the house with Prince, or join him in his condition until all of us are prepared to continue our discussion in a calm, rational manner."

Pen was lying on his face like a toppled statue in some uproarious Balkan coup. His limited field of focus was a blur of mud, brown snow, and melt rivulets. "This doesn't happen in real life..." a small voice, recognizably Harry, whimpered.

"Hmmm, uh, Miss Pig?" Morrissey.

"Morgana. Yes?"

"This 'zapping' you do so well. Can you un-zap also, or must the effects run their course?"

"Ah, the analytical mind at work. The Morrissey magic. I have my magic, you have yours. You were indeed the right choice. I concede a point." Pen blinked, mopped himself off and sat on the ground next to Harry. "This is a gesture of good faith," said the pig, "We will talk, but don't try to bamboozle me. I feel my threshold for trivia shrinking."

They spoke of Libby. As Elizabeth Profitt Pease held the potential for a nearer and more imminent catastrophe than the cessation of the universe at a date yet to be announced, Morgana sat down and listened as they argued around the problem.

❏

You're alone enough; you hear voices whistling through the flue, everyone did. Having to be alert enough to chuck more sticks in the stove every two hours lest you freeze and die was a basic, vestal fellowship with the flame, and the feeder of the fire was pulled into its rhythm. So why not aliens singing in the chimney?

Somehow, somewhere, word that her brother might be entertaining visitors from another planet got back to Libby Pease. That Harry received ETs for tea was privileged information, known only to David and Pen and filtered through the boozy fumes of good fellowship. Whether Harry had actually seen and talked with them was hard to pin down, but on one thing he was adamant: sojourners from the astral planes made Harry's place a regular stopover on their passage from wheresis to whatever. He had seen their spoor: strange messages on the uninhabited channels of his TV, usually in the early morning hours when the decent, Christian stations were turned off.

When he was sober, Harry tended to be less certain about the details. He sometimes laughed them off as hallucinations. Harry's visitations were tolerated because he didn't advertise them; Harry was a private drunk.

Now here was a space alien demanding to go public.

"Your sister has animadversions on the strange, the new, and she will be hostile to you because of me. Well, time to get to work." The pig rose and shook herself.

"Would it be too much to ask you to let us in on your plans?" The pig had an attitude, Pen figured, but there would be time to work on that later. "Just what are you going to have us do?"

The Return of the Orange Virgin

"Why... go to town," she replied, surprised, her head a half turn over her shoulder. "We are going shopping at Walmart. I've seen all the films Harry could find to rent and I have a good grasp on the way things work here. But you two go first and get me a collar and some tags so I'll blend in. Hmmm. Green nylon, I think." She primped at her reflection in a puddle. "Harry and I will stay here tonight. CSI Miami is on and it's a continuing story."

She's casting us as John the Baptists, her advance men to soften up the yahoos, mused Pen. He recalled how the Baptist had finished up his assignment—the patron saint of press agents, the Baptist was beheaded. "Harry, I still have two years left to pay on my car."

"You're a good boy, Pen. Run along now." They were dismissed. "Make that red nylon," called Morgana, "Red I think will go better with my eyes and personality and, yes, Pen, I know I have an attitude problem. We'll work on that later. And don't worry about Libby, I can handle her."

An Infusion of Orrisroot

"Are we communicating a sense of abandonment?" said the pig. Harry's shoulders slumped as he watched David's Volvo become smaller as it wound its way down the hill. He clutched at a loaf of Old Country Rye and a brick of Velveeta he had torn open with his teeth.

"Hmm, fear and hunger predominate. Those we can deal with. Food first. Hungry?" When she spoke he cringed. "Won't listen to reason, eh?" Grasping his ankle with her teeth the pig dragged him to the house. "Harry, I'm still me, you know. You are getting the look of a hunted creature. Believe me, I am no threat." Morgana licked his nose and looked in his eyes.

"Your voice. It reminds me of Lauren Bacall," said Harry.

"Oh, you are just in a fine old state. Have a drink, forget it." She wrinkled her brow and the door of a cabinet of distilled spirits swung open invitingly.

"Well?"

Harry cowered at her voice, protecting his food. Large eyes switched from her to the Velveeta to the liquor.

"You are hardly a fountain of information. Trust me, Harry."

Harry's eyes grew crafty, swiveling between her and the cabinet.

"Suppose I turn my back. Have a drink, then we'll talk. Only one, mind, it's going to have to last. Have a nice party solo, then we'll have one together." Morgana the spotted pig left, bumping the door closed with her hindquarters. On the porch she paused, listening. There were furtive movements and the clink of glass. Satisfied, she nosed the door open and entered. Harry was pacing, glass in hand.

"I am on a quest, Harry, I spoke the truth, but it is not what I thought when I began this adventure."

"What did you think it was?"

"There, that's more like the old you; I won't bite, you know. Your death: immediate and terrible. This is no longer on the menu."

"My... death."

"Well, there, I have let the cat out of the bag; isn't that me all over? The beatitudes of Biff: I have compromised your happy ignorance by countermanding a peril you did not dream existed and then thoughtlessly explaining it all to you. I forget people have feelings, too. Yes, your death, though I had planned something modern and deliciously psychopathic for you, Harry. You should be flattered. Like chopping you in little bits and flushing you out to sea—these are my little ways."

Draining his glass, Harry picked up his basketball where it lay deflated on the bureau and reached for the bicycle pump. "You are not a pig."

"I am not a pig. And you have been in no danger since we first met."

"But you were sent to kill me." He gave a slow fly at the pump handle, listening to the low, slow whoosh of air escaping from the dry valve, and put the ball and pump back.

"And your next question will be, reasonably, who sent me. And the answer, I am only now realizing, is you."

"Me?"

"I sent you and you sent me. We are the guests of inexorable circumstance, simple, two dimensional geometry: I am a line and you are the dot which defines the line."

"Sounds dumb to me. Like a TV preacher."

"Religion does enter in to it, and you must know who I am. I am being taught something and it would be helpful if I could find out what it is. I was coming with sword and cleansing fire to avenge a wrong. You were something else ever the closer I got, a slippery definition perpetually redefining itself, like driving in your fog. You are a simple,

The Return of the Orange Virgin

straightforward man, deviousness is not in you. There is a lesson here for us to discover; the goddess and her victim shall have ended up playing pattycake. Well..." Morgana nudged the door open and eased out into Harry's dooryard. She paused to run her nose down a stalk of lupine, and then proceeded to the side of the truck. "These are modern times. We will be lovers, I promised you that. I want you to know me as I am and that will take some doing. Fire up the chariot, we are going to the Red and White."

"For..."

"For raspberry jam for two—the family size. Now we are going to have a party, just we two."

Later that afternoon, Libby and Maggie arrived intent on checking in on Harry. They found him face down in a pot of raspberry compote. The pig was nowhere to be found and there was no liquor in evidence. By the glowing wood stove a pile of old quilts was still warm with the impression of a medium-sized spotted pig.

❑

"Hulloaloaloalo..." The Fata Morgana, still the medium-sized spotted pig, tested the echo reverberating through the landscape of the raspberry sending. Long stone passageways intersected at odd angles—the minds of their long-dead makers preserved in an arithmetic of design. "An interesting effect. Well, since somebody built these, they must go somewhere. Time on my hands, or trotters, and I am wandering the halls of an echoey edifice." The pig popped her head into a vaulted arch to discover a parallel gallery running alongside the one she was traversing. Her hall was featureless but the new one boasted doorways at regular intervals. "Hmmm. The express and local tracks."

She tried a doorknob with her teeth. It turned easily, inviting inspection. Inside the same polished stone walls as in the hall but with a high, hipped roof done in timber. "The Lady's chambers: mine, I wot." The walls were hung with silk brocade and tapestries depicting scenes of the chase. Two jarring notes. A computer terminus with an associated gimcrackery of flashing lights and a pulsing display that covered an entire wall filled the far end of a deep niche. Filling the remainder of the niche was a creature whose head appeared to be on fire.

The pig—the White Sow of Naxos, for indeed, it was she—walked over and struck up a conversation. "Hi there, nice tail." She began with a compliment for the part that protruded into room proper. "Nobody who looks as strange as you could be all bad."

The creature jumped up, startled and, trying to turn, wedged himself sideways in the niche.

"Sorry about that. Need a hand?"

The creature relaxed, breathing a deep sigh that smelled of unwashed ashtray. There was some theatrical business as he removed a smoldering cheroot from his face. Holding it aloft, he ducked his head, a ruff of businesslike quills rasping along the floor as he reversed his body and turned to face her. "Nice tail yourself."

"You must be a manticore."

"It's you, the pig. You have heard of me?"

"Of course, silly, I named you. But you are also an archetype."

"Then there are others like me..." He came closer with a clacking of quills and scales. "If you are who I think you are, you already have all the answers; I don't get out much. You are the White Sow of Naxos whose coming has been foretold? Or are you the Queen of Heaven?"

"Both, I fear. I am not here; this is a dream sending, Manticore. Where is Biff Bangtree?"

"Dream? I am not asleep."

"Are you sure?"

Sparks flew as he puffed at his stogie. "Real enough. This would suggest it is you who are ephemeral." The tip of his scorpion tail thrashed about and dripped venom.

The pig backed off two and a half meters, sat and groomed herself. "If I were you, I'd get a handle on that. I can tell you are new to this."

The Manticore looked up to see a pearlescent drop forming at the end of his sting. It grew shimmering and amorphous, like a soap bubble in the sun. The cigar fell from his mouth and a spasm of panic rippled down the length of his body. His first thought was to get away, but the tail followed.

Agitated and intrigued at the possibilities of thronging fellow mantichorae, it was stopped by a porcine smile of many teeth and a throaty growl. "Ah, ah, ah, ah. That's far enough. Don't get all worked up; your poison is as lethal to you as anyone." The pig busied herself at the base of her tail.

The crystal pearl, rounded and firmed, detached and flew in a perfect arc to splat on the computer terminal. It drilled a precise nine millimeter hole

The Return of the Orange Virgin

through the apparatus, hit the floor and dissipated, leaving a small cloud of vapor. The screen was blank.

"Oops!"

There was a squeak of plastic wheels as a tall, lean form appeared, dollying himself about in front of another monitor screen quite like the one just fried by the Manticore's venom.

"Whoa, hey, this is great, a flight simulator like in Tailspin Tommy or Smilin' Jack. Why don't you try..." Biff Bangtree, golem, was fading in and out along with his phantom computer screen. He was manipulating a joystick. He noticed the Manticore had company. "Oh, hello there, it's you with the funny pig. I'm just getting the hang of this..." Then disappeared.

"Obviously, he is not getting the hang of it," Morgana observed. "How long has this foolishness been going on? I trust you have an explanation for this apparition, Manticore. Alas, we have established you are real. Can you see him, too? And I recommend you do better than 'It's a bad day for reception from the spirit world.'"

"Since you left. There was the duck, of course..."

"Of course." The pig trotted over to the computer. "Can't say I didn't warn you. I said stay calm. I suppose this means our Biff is stuck in the great wherever. Can't say that I feel deprived; you are much more interesting. Your maladroitness could be an asset. You have botched the babysitting, but I have another errand for you; besides, you are all I have right now."

❑

A dream within a dream. Lying spent, half awake and heavy-lidded in happy fatigue, Harry had a fleeting vision of glinting bronze and red tapestries in a many pillared hall. Tight-thighed, lean and rangy, Harry Pease was good at knots and could pilot the Narrows. And he was twenty-four years old again. He smiled dreamily and reached to pull up the sheet to cover himself.

He smelled burning butter and twine—a tallow candle. It was afternoon; they had burned no candles. He heard a sigh, a giggle, and felt a touch—a curious finger tracing the line of his backbone tenderly to the cleft at his hams. Turning onto his side, he found himself face to face with a golden-haired boy, mediterranean-looking, his tight curls clasped to his head with a circlet of silver. He reached to pull the sheets over himself but Morgana pulled them back down.

"Not just yet, my love. Don't cover yourself. I've invited some friends in for a peek. We don't have anything quite like you at home."

The boy handed Harry a steaming pottery cup and faded to transparency. He could see through him to the far wall of what seemed to be a windowless, low-ceilinged murky hall lit by many lamps and hung with cloth of gold. The boy's eyes appeared huge—they had been heavily outlined in black. Gold pearls glistened at the ends of his lashes and the eyes themselves were large-pupiled and shone with belladonna. He gave Harry a knowing smile and, fluttering eyelids that had been oiled and dusted with mica or flakes of gold, blew a kiss into the cup. Harry blinked and accepted the offered cup. The boy vanished.

"Young Glaucon finds you attractive, my love. The cup is an infusion of orrisroot. It will give you stamina. Drink up and we shall have at it again."

Harry swung his legs over the side of the bed and sat up. He drank and blinked again. A taste of licorice, not bad. The boy had vanished but the hall remained. His lover was most definitely not just a summer person.

"Nor am I your everyday enchantress," said Morgana. She gestured to the tapestry-hung wall. "My friends find you fascinating, and I... Well, I trust you have noticed my feelings for you are not ambivalent."

There was a processional rustling and a dozen or so people filed in and seated themselves on cushioned stone benches along the wall. One of them, a pretty girl with bare breasts, bare feet and a bell-shaped hoop skirt, stood, ran forward to the center of the hall, looked back at the men and women seated behind her for encouragement, and extending her arms performed a bow that was a grand flourish. It was a full curtsey, a theatrical curtain call, bow and genuflection all rolled into one. Harry noticed she wore gold rings on her toes and her eyes, like Glaucon's, were heavily mascaraed.

"Thank you, Philomena," said Morgana. The girl ran giggling back to her seat. "They like you, Harry. They think you worthy of me." The hall faded as the watchers waved cheerily from their bench. "Thank you, my friends, Mister Pease and I have more wonders to perform and it were better you not be seen."

They had performed for an audience. Harry, who should have been thunderstruck, dumfounded, outraged, or at the very least embarrassed, found he was feeling quite pleased with himself. These people were co-celebrants, not common voyeurs, though they had given to understand that the spectacle of Morgana's rollicking ride pleased them immensely.

Looking down, Harry discovered that the orrisroot, along with Morgana's naked beauty, had inspired him again.

Harry woke to discover Philomena seated by his head; now it was she held the steaming cup. A delicate girl smell of lavender and a recent bath filled his nostrils. He drowsily reached out and his hand went right through her.

"Take the cup. She is not for you—not yet." Philomena looked adoringly at Morgana and held the cup to his lips. It was real enough. Licorice tea, steaming and hot. The girl stroked his hair but he felt nothing.

The Orange Virgin leaned forward across her lover's body to fetch a pillow from the head of the bed. She felt a stirring. She leaned forward once more. "Mmm, what a tasty soup we make, you and I, my love." Harry trembled and groaned, happy.

"But enough is enough; and for now, my pet, that is all we have time for. If I receipted my moments of ecstasy against a future audit, you would be high in the ledger." Philomena giggled and kissed him on the mouth. The kiss, like the cup, was real.

Settling herself in a yogic posture, Morgana retrieved the pillow and plumped it between her thighs. "There, that should keep our juices off the sheets. I have a satisfaction at improvising, even in the wilderness. I appreciate the laundromat is a twenty-mile drive around the island." She gave Harry a farewell squeeze and swung her legs over the side of his bunk. The hall with its watchers had faded to tenuousness, but remained visible.

Philomena gurgled and was quiet; her fists shot to her mouth. There was something beyond Harry, thus out of the field of vision she occupied. She chewed at her knuckles and backed gasping to the bench along the wall, the partygoers having emptied it in a mad scramble for the exits. There was immediate seating. The ledge caught her behind the knees and she sat, pressing herself against the wall. The reason for her horror could not be seen, but as Philomena's small, thin keenings of fear rose and descended, it spoke.

"Would you look at that," said the Manticore. "The child is trying to screw herself into the wall. Believe me, my dear, I've been there and you don't want it." The girl's eyes were very big as she inched along the marble. A cloud of blue cigar smoke entered from field left.

"Ha, gotcha! Stay with us; join the party. As a bearer of tidings I would have expected you to at least withhold your criticism until I have had my say. That is the Orange Virgin in there...? It is! Hiya Morgana, hope I'm not interrupting anything."

"It's alright, Philomena. He poses no threat. Unless my ears deceive me, it is my old confidante the Manticore, loosed upon the world. Come, show yourself, fellow. How came you thus and without my leave?"

There was a concatenation of sistrum and dijareedoo, a musical rattling of quills, scales and feathers at the junctures of his attributes as the man-dragon shambled into the picture. He removed his cigar and peered nearsightedly into the mists.

Harry Pease had armed himself with an aluminum softball bat and was standing naked, ready to give as good as he got.

"Calm yourself Harry, there is no threat. This implausible catawampus is a pet of mine." Morgana swung her legs to the floor and stood, stretching languorously. "We had just finished. Your timing is excellent if not your manners, Manticore." The Manticore's tail arched threateningly over his head as he puffed his cigar to a glowing cherry red. "I am sorry old friend, I did not intend to patronize you. Both of you, your noble gestures are appreciated, but stop waving those things about."

The Manticore looked up and blanched. He carefully laid his tail flat on the floor. Harry set down his bat.

"Ahh, simultaneity. Thank you, Harry. Thank you, Manticore. We have brought you, the Caballo Apocalíptico, the Moose of Circumstance, over piggyback on a dream sending. It was a chancy endeavor, but the raspberry was my last available resort. Glad to have you here. You might not have made it; these are the small details you did not need to know. Harry, my love, here is a jolly playfellow to torment your waking hours when I am away. You, Manticore—here you are running loose. Believe me, freedom is overrated. How will you eat? Here you are almost in the real world and you can't even open a can." She reached to stroke Harry's behind as he put on his trousers. "Harry, my wistful dalliance, the dancing magic of your thighs has given me an hour of innocent merriment, but now I must go."

She turned to the sepia-toned incorporeality of the Manticore. "Come and let me scratch your ears." He rattled and clacked happily in the direction of Morgana and out of the picture.

"Oops, sorry. I forgot. I am here and you are there. Life among the primitives. You will have to go around. Enter from the exquisites' bench. Philomena, my dear, do take your fist from your mouth." She gave Harry a tender swat of dismissal. He sat and looked perplexed. "Too bad, my darling, that's just the way things are. You must excuse my blunt ways."

Her hand lingered on Harry's thigh as the Manticore scuttled in past the empty bench to lay his head on her knee. "I will be the moose..." The Manticore studied his cigar, which had gone out. "What is a moose?"

"Oh, only one of those dotty pronouncements dear to the hearts of Sybils and Pythonesses. I do wish I had been more careful. Now it has the force of law and we are stuck with it."

The Manticore caught up with an earlier statement. "Open a can? You spoke of cans. I would hear more of cans, please. These cans are good to 'eat'? I recall something about this eating from the masters who made me. The Dancing Lords who made me and the castle were forever singing songs of 'eating.' They were ever telling tales of pulling down a stag after a merry chase. These stags had cans with 'food' about on them, then."

The onlookers of the bench had returned. By fits and starts they filed in as they realized the new arrival was a playfellow of the queen and immediate dismemberment unlikely. Morgana gestured them back to their seats, giving quiet assurances that all was well.

A medium-sized pig walked into the picture from a filmy border zone. She hopped into Philomena's lap and addressed Morgana. "Huh! So this is the best you can do. Ho-hum, just deserts and all that." She turned and licked Philomena's face.

"Well... our little hitchhiker."

The pig inspected the gilded courtiers arrayed on the bench. "What a clever person you are, Morgana, bringing us here and all. Or almost all. Couldn't pull it off, eh? The manifestation."

"This is not entirely true, pig. You are there and we are here. And thank you for not jibing at my sharing your sundered state."

The White Sow of Naxos ignored the apology. "And your Dapper Dans here—happiness doesn't seem to be of a high order among your renters. Slow getting the heat up this winter? Are you tardy when they bang the pipes—plumbing repairs a low priority? Just what I'd guess for a place this age. Or has my friend got them spooked? Y'know," she said, poking her nose against Philomena's and assuming a conspiratorial tone, "He's been in the cellar all along." She turned back to Morgana. "Guess you don't send them down for marmalade too often."

The Manticore stepped between the two. He anticipated a withering blast of queenly wrath. "You will have to excuse my friend, she is distraught."

"She is me and she is preaching to the sycophants. This is a dream, fool. She is in no danger."

The spotted pig lolled a pink tongue and cocked her head to the side, a portrait of adorableness. "You and I are but dry peas rattling in the cavernous intelligence of the eidolons, Queen."

"Your acerbity is not lost on me, little pilgrim. I would that things had happened differently, but as they have not, why should we not cooperate?"

"I am all ears," said the spotted pig, the White Sow of Naxos, and curled up in Philomena's lap. The wraiths relaxed at the collegial talk, but still kept their distance.

The Orange Virgin again prodded her pillow, pondering. "You, Manticore, the litany of survival has changed since your makers sang, and, obviously, since they are no longer with us, their advice is suspect."

"You say I am 'a moose,' and is a moose like a stag?"

"Wild cattle, vegetarian warhorses. An icon of the mind symbolizing all that is wild and free. These are knots tied in your head, forget them. These are words they use here."

"I am now a moose..." The Manticore seemed pleased. "Lady, I pledge you a compact." He gave a courtly flourish with his tail and the bench cleared once more. "You are the you to whom I am true." The felicity brought a quill-haloed grin.

"Listen to me, Manticore, I will probably prevail..." The Orange Virgin toyed with a plait of her hair. "I have till now. If I do not..." She articulated a meandering shrug, "...you chance being abandoned to wander the earth, a twilight legend and the only one of your kind—riddled with parasites, hungry and scrofulous, your quills falling out in clumps. A scary story for country wives to threaten ill-behaved children." The Orange Virgin stood and shook herself, letting loose a blizzard of goose feathers; her pillow had burst. Harry reached for her and she blew him a kiss as she skipped away from his reach to the center of the room trailing flurries of down. She danced through the tableau with the courtiers, the Manticore and the pig twisting to follow her with their eyes as she moved through them to the other side of the manifestation.

___

The Return of the Orange Virgin

She reflected on Harry, naked and forlorn, the dimming watchers. "Since my lot has been cast with these creatures, I suppose I should be about doing something to make them like me." She shook out the few remaining feathers from the pillow case. "Something heart-warming. I will study on it."

To the onlookers she was fading as a fog wraith in the sunlight. "I shall strip the moonsign from my priestess Linda. She has discovered redeeming features in being a mortal woman, the more fool she." As the watchers dematerialized, she danced through the assemblage and plumped herself in Harry's lap. "In the meantime duty calls and I have been prodigal in my loving embraces." She put her arms around Harry's neck and gave a deep, lingering kiss. "I trust this has been as educational for you as it has been pleasant for me."

The Poet

Tom Winkelman came to in a haystack. A square-faced man with laugh lines at his eyes and a bristly black mustache was handing him a flask. On the world Tom had left behind molecules rushed in to fill the space so recently occupied by him, one third of a kitchen table and a laptop computer that had been sitting on the table. In the now vacant Winkelman apartment there was a small thump that no one heard. The computer dropped gently onto the hay. The table, now standing on one leg, fell over.

"Here, try this. New arrivals are always disoriented. It helps."

Tom took a swallow and gagged.

"Corn whiskey—make it myself. God only knows what the proof is." The speaker picked up Tom's laptop, studied it, gave a shrug and tossed it away over a shoulder; it hit a paving stone and shattered. The man was dressed in a black turtleneck and blue cashmere blazer with a crested insignia pricked out with gold thread over the breast pocket. He reached over for the flask and recorked it. "Blackburn. Paul Blackburn. I admit to being a poet. You speak any Spanish?"

Tom nodded through his spasms.

"Bueno, that will be of some help. I should have rightly asked if you knew any Catalan, but nobody does these days, so I don't ask. Spanish is better than French for getting by, though French is better than nothing. The lingo here is Occitan, Old Provençal. At least as far as the middle of yon wheat field. After that the Fata Morgana deals as she pleases."

"Fata Morgana..." The name the poet mentioned brought with it an evocation of tarot decks, bayberry candles and juniper tea. And tonight he was planning gourmet boil-in-a-bag Szechuan dumplings, one of Linda's favorites.

A ripple echoed through the corridors of eternity. This was the thump felt by no one in the empty apartment left behind by Tom Winkelman, likewise the earthquake felt in the 7th Avenue cellars of the Hotel Taft. Our universe bulged while all others down the line wobbled as each in turn balanced the books by commandeering one-hundred-sixty-five pounds of anything. This caused alarm among the overseers of the arithmetic of creation. Though vast, the number theory of infinity is a biography of finite numbers: sooner or later the ripple cascading thoughtlessly and undiminished, carrying with it all the destructive power of a rampaging laptop computer and one-third of a kitchen table would arrive back where it had started, metamorphosed by the journey into the invisible incongruity that is a not-black hole—too small to notice, the singularity that flattens even eidolons and Szechuan dumplings.

"We are hostages of compassion here," said the poet. "We are expected to have a jolly good time while awaiting her pleasure, just lay about and decorate the landscape. We are all going nowhere. This is a storage area, and we are none of us ever to leave. And I'll bet you have to pee, too. That's the second thing new arrivals have on their minds."

"I had made plans," said Tom.

"Plans," said the poet. "Ah yes, of course you have them. All our arrivals do. Usually the first thing out of their mouths. There are plans, indeed, but you're not in them and that is why you are here."

Tom shakily stood and, catching himself patting his legs in a search for broken bones, felt foolish.

"Plans..." The poet smiled faintly. "You are writing a book or waxing the car. Many of our arrivals say that, too. You are a layabout, then. House-husbanding, the latest excuse for getting nothing done; you cook and clean. Me, I drank a lot and chased women."

Tom started to answer but the poet was walking away, indicating features of the wobbly medieval cottages, the landscape. "This village was translated entire from the fourteenth century," said the poet. "Our plumbing, too, is medieval; there is a squnchiness about your eyes that says you've been holding it a while, scrivener Tom. I'll turn my back if you would be more comfortable. Peeing, that is. It's an opportunity too

The Return of the Orange Virgin

good to miss—being here, not peeing, though that is likewise important. Just let fly; shows us we are alive, eh? House husbanding! No. You are writing a book, perhaps. A waxer of cars and polisher of linoleum will find scant to do in these parts. You are a writer manqué, then, a treasure too rare to be spent all at once. I'm transcribing troubadour ballads—you know, poems. You can give me a hand, scrivener Tom."

The poet stopped before a ramshackle structure of wattle-and-daub. Looking about, he assured himself there was nobody watching and reached into a niche in the whitewashed half-beaming. Tom expected that he might be removing a book of poems. It was a bottle.

"If language studies are not your métier, hang around a while; have a rest. We'll get you placed somewhere. Should you decide to strike off by yourself, there is a traveler's rest some twenty leagues off." Placing the flask in a jacket pocket, the poet wandered off singing wordlessly to himself. Tom had been dismissed. He curled up in a comfortable corner of Paul Blackburn's haystack and waited on events.

When he awoke it was night and it was raining. "Paul. Paul Blackburn!" There was no answer. He peered in the direction the poet had taken hoping to see a light, some evidence of human habitation. There was none.

He started at a cough out on the in the rain-darkened stubble of last year's pasturage. The cough was answered by a rising wail of alarm. A cat. A few yards distant was a fox homeward bound with a dead rat twitching in its jaws. A yellow striped tomcat stood motionless where it had blundered across the fox's path, its tail the size of a softball bat, a low glottal warning in its throat. The fox dropped its prey and coughed again, its tail up and bristling. The cat continued its stream of consonants, retreated perhaps a foot and settled itself, conceding enough for safety but holding honor intact. The fox picked up the rat and continued to its earth. Tom breathed again.

A harvest moon appeared from behind a cluster of high wind driven clouds. Tom hitched his pack and struck out on foot.

❑

There was a cawing of far off crows, nothing special, just afternoon bird talk. The afternoon had settled in, hot, close and heavy. Despite the feeling of impending rain, the sky was a clear, piercing blue and except for a pair of high fluffy storm riders, cloudless. The buzzing of passing insects was intense in the pollen-laden air. A path worn by use rather than design wound down the hill from a step-stile through a blue haze that hung about the valley floor. A thread of smoke rose from just inside some trees at the edge of a cultivated area; in the air was a sweet unfamiliar smell of burning. The traveler's rest the poet had promised with its peat fire. Tom Winkelman swung a leg over the stile and started down the hill. It was a long way down through waist-high undulations of grass gone to early brown with heavy seed heads. He followed the path and although the incline was easy work, he was soon sweating in the close, heavy air. It felt like there was a thunderstorm brewing. A trick of distance—from the top of the hill, the blue mist thinned out the closer down the valley floor he came. A small river wound among occasional cattle, a hopeful, reassuring presence. Near the bottom he paused to catch his breath where clusters of trees, outriders from the approaching forest, offered shade. Past a line of broad-beamed black spruce, their lacy needles a filigree of dripping moisture, a thicket of larch and honey locust framed a house. It looked good. Tom realized he was thirsty and very hungry.

There was a crack like a rifle hot and he jumped. "Shoo, boss. Shoo, boss... Scat!" Another crack! A thin blonde young woman was chasing cows out of a garden patch, shouting and popping their haunches with the business end of a rolled-up wet towel. Crack! The cows—two of them, eyes wide and white, udders flying—went galloping up the hill Tom had just come down. Victorious and flushed, the young woman walked over. She wore cut-off jeans and had her hair up in a red spotted kerchief. "Hi, I'm Val, Valerie Hatt, and my cows have a taste for asparagus." She extended a hand. "You must be Tom. We've been expecting you." She looked after the departed cows. Being chased was something they were used to; they had stopped to browse the hillside a few yards farther up. When the towel had stopped, so had they. Val sighed, "Onion grass up there, we'll have onion-flavored milk for a week. The kids won't drink it but it makes a great cheese."

As they shook hands Tom said, "Expecting me? Things happen fast here. I didn't know I was coming until a few hours ago. A man, a poet..." Had there even been a poet? "A treasure too rare to be spent all at once..." the poet's words played as if he actually had heard them, a reassuring voice—his mother tending his childhood sickbed with platters of ice cream with honey and crushed walnuts over the top, a favorite. "Excuse me; I don't seem able to remember. I was at home, at work... then I was not."

"That's the Fata Morgana—she doesn't miss a trick. Come on, I'll show you around. You'll be happy here."

"Oh?" As with the poet, there was permanence implicit in Val's easy statement that Tom found disturbing. Furthermore the girl's face had a haunting familiarity. He started to ask but was interrupted with the words half formed.

"We have a room all ready for you. Here, let me help you with your stuff."

He shook his head to clear it. His vision had the fish-eye distortion of a fever dream. "Stuff? Uh, that's all right, I don't have anything except what I'm standing up in. I left rather suddenly."

❑

This is an arrival and a departure, for it is important to know that Tom has come to no harm, for death is relative. The haystack, the poet, the whole place, has the smell of wild raspberries from a thermos of abandoned tea flushed out with clear spring water. Dumped and forgotten is not the way of the Fata Morgana with her stray pets. The poet is important also, but in his time, not here. Suffice it that Tom Winkelman could have prospered in Languedoc and thriven under the poet's tutelage. Tom has catapulted into the clear air of a Europe untouched by Huns, plague or industrial revolution to land in a haystack, a happy splat in the Lady's back yard.

In another tale, Tom might live on in place to a wise and fruitful dotage, fathering many crackling-eyed, black-haired babies. The fourteenth century was like that and, after all, he now is the poet's assistant, a place not without honor. Tom might do many good works while corrupting the language and culture hereabouts; he might coach Little League and bring his Morgantowners to first place in many championship seasons. But that *is* another tale.

A Vine-covered Cottage

The house had a storybook air to it—a short ground floor and a steeply thatched roof—wattle-and-daub, clay, sand, animal dung and straw with an occasional fieldstone for accent with framed dormers peeking through the straw upstairs. Tom remembered seeing something like it in brochures for picturesque vacations; all destinations looked alike in the travel folders.

Valerie Hatt picked up a wicker portmanteau Tom had not noticed at his feet. "Like you said, things happen fast; but we try to keep on top of them. You came without stuff... now you have stuff." Hefting the bag, she turned her back and headed for the house. "See? Easy." Explanations were through. Tom followed.

Valerie dumped the case inside the door and threw herself into a kitchen chair. "Hot work, chasing cows. Want a beer, some soda? We've got plenty in the fridge." So saying, she was up again and back with a can of 7-Up and two glasses. Moisture beaded invitingly on the can.

It was cool inside the rough plastered walls. A small fire smoked in a brick and iron stove opposite the door. "You were expecting me."

"Plagiation, kidnapery. A snatch. It's the same old story. Lots of our boarders get here that way. Highhanded if you ask me, but nobody ever does." A breezy, lighthearted laugh.

"Pardon me, but haven't we met before?" Tom remembered the face. It had belonged to a thin blonde girl in hip-huggers with a flaccid belly. Just a memory with no background sketched in. He had seen her, somewhere. The unconscious mind surveys a street scene, fitting made-up histories to passing faces and shapes—the family groupings that spread out untidily across the landscape of an idle mind.

"Probably, on the Other Side. Finite personalities, infinite universe, if you go for that stuff. Anyway, it's an explanation. There are all sorts of familiar faces here. We are true to type, you and I. People tend to repeat." Valerie poured the 7-Up, tongue showing between her lips, her brow wrinkling. "They're mounting some kind of an operation over there and we—you and I—are but two of the casualties. Well, maybe 'casualties' is not the best word. Tim and I have got it pretty good here. Let's see, we've been here for, hmmm..." She searched the ceiling for an answer.

Tom took the glass from her hand and waited. Her eyes had a vague, faraway look. The pause stretched on. Then, after several minutes, she snapped-to and gave him a wide, welcoming smile of many well cared for teeth.

"Two years seems about right. Of course, that's subjective time—local time as we see it right here. Time moves faster at the village 'cause they've been here longer." She added an emphasis, "Much longer." She swung around a kitchen chair and straddled it, looking at Tom, her arms draped over the back. "That's just the way things are here. We do some farming, keep this guest house; and for the kids—well! it's just great. But..."

She looked wistfully to another room where boings, explosions and hyperactive giggles told of children's play in progress. "It's like living in New Zealand. You know, a place that is nice, really great, where you get letters from relatives but nobody ever comes back from. Like dying but

The Return of the Orange Virgin

with regular mail service." Valerie got the faraway vacant look again. And again, it went on for many minutes. The reference to New Zealand must mean all and any options had been closed. By someone. She returned with the same disingenuous smile, a smile that suggested that, for her, their conversation was rolling right along. "We don't want to leave, not really. It would be nice to know we could whenever we wanted to, but we don't, if you know what I mean..."

There was a cry of offended territoriality from the next room. "Ma..."

"And right on cue." Valerie rose, in no great hurry, her glass of 7-Up swinging loosely between two fingers. "There's all sorts of room for them to play; they're learning the language—they speak it like they were born here. And they get along fine with the kids from the village. No fights aside from the normal dustups." By the time they reached the children, the problem had solved itself and been forgotten, the two boys seated silently in front of a television screen. Valerie made a self-conscious gesture, tucking a stray lock back under her kerchief. "Beats the city all to hell for raising kids; they don't even remember any other life."

Tom and Val joined the children on the sofa. The younger sucked his thumb. Timmy and Skipper squirmed apart on their behinds, creating two grownup-sized availabilities before the family shrine. "The TV, it's a touch of home. We get all the latest shows on DVDs. Movies, too. No news—nothing happens." There was a blare of music signaling completeness, then the screen went blank. A click from the video player as with a whirring mechanical sound from within a flashing red light appeared on its front panel. The finale. "Ejection time. And time you two got out and into the sun. Your daddy's haying down by the South Fork; go and shag those cows to a proper piece of grass." Tow-headed, bright-eyed and animated, the two tussled, then obeyed and headed after their daddy. An idealized family. However long they had been here, they were country kids now. There was none of the spattered, non-directed energy of cramped quarters. "You should see them in the winter—they're a handful. But the winters are short and mild..." Valerie's hand pursued the wayward strand of hair again. Giving up on it, she removed her bandana and shook her hair free. It was thick and irregularly sun-bleached. "We've become regular frontiersmen. Plowing, sowing, reaping, doctoring ourselves and the animals. I teach the kids and Tim wrestles with keeping the generator up and running. The coal for the boiler comes from the same place the videos do—wherever. We don't ask."

"You said the children were learning the language. Everybody I've met so far has been speaking English."

"Right. But the local lingo is a kind of medieval French. There's a Provençal village five kilometers upstream and through the woods. Or leagues, versts, miles. Depends on who's walking. We settled on metric as a friendly trade-off. Weights and measures are pretty unpredictable here."

"A whole village? From the way you talk, I gather everyone here came from someplace else. How did you get here, like me?"

Valerie held both hands up, palms out. "We don't talk about that. Neither do they, the folks in the village. The parish priest runs a little school; no frills—reading, writing and some arithmetic. Adaptable folks, these French. They look on being here as a divine dispensation—no wars, no taxes, and business as usual. They have nothing to do with why you and I are here. They popped through six hundred years ago real time, so they've done a lot of settling in. And if I read your body language right, you are about to ask where we are. Don't ask, we're just where we were before we came. The way I make it is we—you and I—are still where we were, and where we are now came around to meet us. You know—like a stage play where the actors stand still and the scenery rotates to meet them. That's kind of dumb sounding, but we have a video."

Valerie retrieved Tom's soda and a DVD from the kitchen. She carried a serious-looking weapon that hung by a sling from her shoulder. "This is the orientation program for new arrivals. We're supposed to show it to you. This is a new one and I haven't seen it yet. Let me know if it's any good. I have to catch up with the kids and my husband; he tends to wander." She winked at Tom and patted her gun. "There's beer and jalapeño dip in the fridge; help yourself to the chips." Valerie inserted the orientation program into the DVD player. "All ready to go. Just punch 'play.' Seeya."

Tom sat quietly for some minutes, glad of the time to himself. The tanned and confident young woman who had left to chase cows was no product of an overnight makeover, but he could swear she had seen her, thin and listless, dragging a gooey-faced toddler in town just the week before. Thinking, Well, what the hell, he leaned forward to the control panel and pressed the 'play' button.

The screen remained blank. A piece of nondescript mood music welled up, suggesting majestic panoramas. Pastoral scenes appeared—mountain valleys awash with morning mists, grazing deer, sun-dappled rippling pools where trout rose to passing flies, and a time-lapse sequence of flowers opening. There was a dissolve to an empty stage, its only furniture a work light on a stand. A man sauntered to stage center. "And so, dear traveler, after many a weary mile, you have at last arrived at this, your destination. You probably have some questions. Well, if you play ball with us, we are prepared to play ball with you.

"Think of the universe as your basic Mom and Pop store. They never have what you want, but since you took the trouble to show up, you make some accommodation and accept something you really don't want but is probably just as good. It's all give and take. Ahh, yes... you want answers. Well, that feathery looking tree in the yard is a mimosa. Yep, that's right, mimosa, just like the drink, but this is a tree—the real thing, too. And around the door? That is honeysuckle. And there is a wisteria bower out back if you'd care to have a look after the showowowooo..." A trap door opened under him and he fell through the floor. This scene must have been shot on a cutaway set, for the camera followed him down, revealing the framing between levels, and caught up with him dressed in a coarsely woven, hooded garment, seated on a slatted bed that hung from the wall by a chain.

The presenter had picked up several days growth of beard and his eyes were made-up to suggest hollowness. Cotton-candy cobwebs had been spun about the set. There was a sound of water dripping in a cavern. "Well, just about the time they yanked the chain on me, you were wondering when I was going to stop the bullshit and get around to business. Well, pardner," here he threw back the hood, replacing it with a cowboy hat, "...the terrible, the awful, the unspeakable truth is, you are in the calabozo, the slammer, the gray-bar hotel, up the river, in durance vile and here you are going to stay until it pleases us to let you out."

A mechanical rat, a big key in its back unwinding as it ran, scurried across the screen at his feet. Reaching under the monk's robe, the narrator drew forth a six-shooter the size of a jackhammer and blew it to pieces with a single shot. It was a bang of nuclear proportions. There was a rain of gears—springs and artificial fur flew past the camera, considerably more than could have reasonably been inside the mechanical rat. He blew across the barrel of the smoking pistol, making the sound of a tugboat whistle. He replaced the gun under his robe, rearranged its folds and sat with hands folded. He looked out from the screen. "'Whoa!' you're saying... 'I didn't do anything.' Well, we never said you did. The truth is, you were a potential embarrassment where you were and instead of blowing you to smithereens, we put you here. Neat, huh?"

There was a 'pop' and the screen went blank. A sound effect of wind faded up, suggesting bleakness. It went on that way for perhaps a minute.

The wind faded down and he spoke with heavy echo, "You could have been HERE."

Tom felt a chill down his back. After wading through all his prefatory remarks, the narrator was finally getting to the point. Tom knew he was not going to be happy hearing what the actor had to say from here on in.

"All your dreams, hopes and aspirations have been swept aside because you were standing where the Caballo Apocalíptico was going to put its foot. I'm sorry if you had made plans, but we have canceled them for you. Your clothes will languish uncalled for at the cleaners; your date will be royally pissed off when you don't show up, be heartbroken and then finally forget you, marry and move to the burbs, have two point seven children and spend weekends passing hotdogs hand to hand at baseball games. Depressing, isn't it? But that's life and you see, you were in the way." The actor relaxed, leaning casually on the pulpit, and thrust his free hand in his coast pocket. The hand came out of the pocket. In it were a half dozen mothballs. He considered the mothballs for a moment then, letting them dribble out onto the floor, leaned forward into the camera. An expansive gesture was called for at this point.

Tom had had enough; this was getting silly. The jalapeño with chips made him thirsty and his can was empty. He got up for another beer. In the kitchen he heard the video talking louder, as though it realized it was losing its audience and had better do something soon or be playing to an empty tent. "But enough about me," bellowed the announcer from the parlor, "Let's talk about you." Then there was silence.

Tom returned with an extra beer, more dip and a dish of carrot sticks and celery hearts. The music swelled to a climax and a voice which was not the narrator's took over—impersonal, molassesy and transparent—an institutional voice of the species most often heard on commercials for financial services. Tom drowsily stretched out his legs and reached for a beer. Having waited, the video continued, a new announcer talking gibberish with the moist, sincere tone of cultural uplift. "Once upon a time there was the smallest ever imaginable piece of silver foil, part of the factory wrapped cocoonage that accompanied each and every stick of peppermint clove chewing gum on its voyage into the world. That's just the way things are..." Tom fumbled about on the tabouret by the couch looking for the remote control. He found it and lifted it, poised to zap the set; then remembered there were no other channels. 'Off' was the desirable compromise. He pressed 'Eject.' There was a whir and the drawer popped out of the deck. The irritating voice was gone. The picture, however, did not fade, and the music went plugging doggedly along, as it documented the miracle of peppermint clove chewing gum.

The Return of the Orange Virgin

He must have fallen asleep, soothed by the wordless drama. For how long? Tom woke up with a snap, spilling some beer, but catching the bowl of jalapeño dip between his knees, to find himself gliding precipitously to the floor. He was settling back again when he felt a glowing against his chest. A glowing and an itch. Setting his beer on the tabouret, he reached inside his shirtfront to scratch. The glowing was not an uncomfortable feeling, but it was spreading. He scratched under an arm. Itchy pits were a summertime annoyance, like bugs or heat rash. And it was getting worse. He scratched liberally, accompanied by the music from nowhere. The music played along as endless sticks of gum cascaded down a conveyor belt. The glow had now spread from his belly to his groin and the itching covered both thighs. Tom jumped to his feet and shucked off his shirt. There was a 'plop,' as something fell to the floor. Just as abruptly the itching stopped and the glow faded.

"Ahem." It was from the TV. A cartoon duck paced back and forth across the screen. The duck was looking out at him. "Well, I hope you have had a safe and pleasant trip. By freeing my moonsign, you have uttered one of the secret, immutable names of Myself, the Rider on the Storm." Tom struggled back into his clothes and sat on the couch, buttoning his shirt. "I am unfortunately, uh... detained. So I fear My plans for you are likewise on hold."

"You are a duck. Where is the peppermint gum? It at least was educational."

"Somewhere on this time line, there has been a tampering. The Fata Morgana, I fear, is at some point in the near future going to try to free you from my sign. We have beat her to the punch." An effect of a page turning across the screen tried to establish itself, but the duck held it off, pecking at the upper corner of the page he occupied. "Ah alas, no more chocolate and peppermint. But My messenger comes and they have served their purpose."

There was a presence, a hand on his thigh, and Valerie slid onto the couch beside him. Her breath was warm and moist in his ear. She let out a long, close sigh, setting up eddies of appreciative yearning across his body. "Sorry I'm late. Got held up." Her voice was close and clove scented like the gum in the video. The duck blew a kiss and disappeared diagonally.

"The video. It thinks that I am a messenger." Tom turned accusingly to Valerie Hatt. "Then I am not the one you were expecting."

"No, you're not. But we never know whom to expect. I am as surprised as you are. And you're very nice, Tom Winkelman."

He was being tested, that was it. He had died after all and this was the portal to the afterlife where the wheat was to be separated from the chaff, the wanted from the unwanted. He touched his chest. His hand came away sticky and chocolate coated. There was a minty odor.

Shootout at EAT

David made a U-turn in the parking lot of the duty-free store across the street from Cousteau's diner and insinuated the Volvo into an open curbside slot in front of the Home Theater. The winter schedule slung askew across both glass doors hanging from a string looped over a suction cup: Features 7 and 9 PM Fri Sat Sun. G Show matinee Sat 2 PM.

There was a medium-sized spotted pig seated on the pavement, looking like a promotion piece for the "G" show. "But how...?"

"Please, no questions. I'm here and that should be enough; I am a goddess, not a technician. Actually, I hitched a ride with the Happy Time Bread man. I didn't talk and he didn't ask. I just hopped in, he scratched my ears, and here we are." She eyed the paper bag Pen carried. "You got the collar? Red?"

Affirmative.

"Good, come along and let's get something to eat. I'm famished."

The pig trotted next door to EAT, stood before the Salada Tea screen door, and waited for it to be opened. Pen held the door and Morrissey and the pig filed in.

Harriet Hopwood was the waitress on duty. Cousteau had rules. "Seeing-eye pig?" Harriet had rules, too, number one being Cousteau's rules seldom applied.

"Of course."

"Nice piggy." Harriet reached down to scratch the Fata Morgana's ears. Pen winced, bracing himself to catch Harriet as she fell. But no, golden goddess eyes looked adoringly up at Harriet and a pink tongue lolled. The woman and the pig scratched on in a rapport of mutual joy.

Pen cleared his throat and Harriet straightened, radiating a dopey post-coital glow. She rubbed her eyes and was all business again. "She's just lovely, but you had better take a booth."

They took a booth. The pig hopped up onto the bench beside Pen. "Tell me the time, Pen. I love it when you tell me the time."

"I have never knowingly told you the time in all our short acquaintance." He flourished a $20 K-Mart digital watch into play.

"No, Pen. Not digital time. Talk analog to me, I'm that kind of girl." She directed her nose at the Telechron plug-in rotary clock hanging over the cigarette machine at the cash register. She jumped to the other bench and snuggled Dim Light's tweed and leather patches. "I know they sound the same when you say the times, but to my mind analog has more panache. Plus what you see is what you get... like me."

Dinner with the ingénue.

Enter the heavy, looking confused, like a refugee from a natural disaster straight out of the eleven o'clock news, all the possessions he could scoop up gathered in his arms. A rumpled day pack dangled from a nylon shoulder strap. It was stuffed so full he hadn't been able to zip it shut and one sock and most of a very soiled sweater, machine knitted with a nordic reindeer design, dangled to the floor. His other possession was a boxy-looking machine pistol with a shoulder-mount extension which he carried at port arms. He looked very unsure about what he was doing toting this appliance. Armed and confused, a dangerous combination. The muzzle of his weapon swept back and forth across the room in nervous arcs. He shrugged off the day pack and let it fall.

"I am a refugee. I claim political asylum. Could you show me the way to the men's room please?" he said in a monotone straight off a Berlitz instruction tape. He had almost got it right, but for an international desperado he lacked the gritty competitive edge.

Harriet threw her arms around the young man's neck and gave him a long, lingering kiss. "Hello there and welcome to America," said Harriet Hopwood, rising to the occasion. "It's in the back."

Their eyes met and held, a charged moment—electricity, right out of True Romances. Harriet was a not unattractive woman in her mid-thirties—and when she used her always spontaneous #5 waitress smile even the Mounties melted. She turned it on. The kid turned his on. He nuzzled her neck and muttered in a language of many rolling glottal stops and galloping Rs.

Morrissey turned to Pen and raised his eyebrows. "Provençal, medieval French, something."

"I know it's something. Where the hell is he from?"

The pig hopped up on the table. "He is from Languedoc, a little village there. His name is Timothy Hatt. He should not be here. This is a mistake. He and his wife are caretakers of a certain property I... Ahh, this is a long story. Suffice it to say the young man should not be here, but since he is, he is under my protection. There has been a displacement. Someone else has taken up the position he formerly occupied on the space-time continuum. Nasty business."

Pen figured Timothy was maybe 20-25, olive-skinned with a bridgeless aquiline nose, and red-haired with a hint of freckles—a blending of transoceanic bloodlines. He and Harriet made a charming, everyday couple. A lovely tableau except for the gun. And he was in a hurry. No one had spoken or moved in the seconds since he had come in the door. He was in a sweat—somebody was after him. Eye contact with Harriet and the brakes were applied.

Let's see, thought Pen, *he is young, on the run packing a piece I have only seen in the movies. You didn't have to be a good shot with one of those things; they were strictly anti-personnel weapons—just push the button and you wash the car. Commando stuff, Al Qaeda, CIA black ops, drug smugglers.*

Harriet's lower lip was trembling. Oh, my God, she's going to hold out her hand to him and say, "Here, let me show you where the men's room is, you poor boy. Need a hand with your zipper?" or words to that effect.

"Harriet Hopwood," said Harriet, holding out her hand.

Jesus, he's going to blow us all to hell and back, thought Pen.

"Tim Hatt," replied the kid. He left off his port-arms death grip on the machine gun, cradled it on his left forearm and kissed Harriet's extended hand, never taking his eyes away from hers all the while. The tension in the diner eased.

At the counter were Champion and Everlast, two Mounties Pen recognized from the gym. He had never learned their names but they wore those brands of sweatpants. They put in time jogging on the treadmill during the winter. They sat with Tim Quigley, a Maine state trooper, evidently catching a fraternal cup of coffee on their way from a workout. They were in civilian clothes, their gym bags piled at their feet, no guns in evidence. These guys may not be the brightest bulbs on the tree, but they were, at least, the home team. Things were definitely looking up.

"You are very beautiful, Harriet, where is the men's room?" The kid asked again; he looked anxious.

"Down the hall along the wall and past the kitchen. Here, I'll show you," and she pulled him toward her. Pen heard a ragged whistle; it was the assembled clientele taking a breath. They had been holding it for all the time of the exchange between Tim Hatt and Harriet Hopwood.

"Well it seems that we are still alive," contributed Dim Lights Morrissey, himself again breathing. "Our visitor from the planet Xenon has been unwontedly quiet..."

"Oh, this is so exciting—young love *and* action," said the spotted pig. "Just like in the movies."

"Until now," said Morrissey.

"Ahhh, this is even better than Harry's movies, no flicker, no digitizing or roll-over." She paused. "How gloriously psychotic... life imitating art."

Some of Cousteau's more alert habitués were leaving piles of loose money on the tables and just plain getting the hell out of there. Two chatty family groups and a solitary diner reading the evening paper hadn't noticed anything and continued shoveling in salmon croquettes, canned peas and foil-wrapped baked potatoes from the steam table. There had been no raised voices; no rowdy cadences marked the exchange between Tim and Harriet. The three off-duty law enforcement officers at the counter had however unobtrusively vacated their stools. The state trooper was speaking quietly but urgently into the phone near the cash register while the Mounties pooled their pocket change and fussed with Canadian and U.S. currencies to make the tab with no one at the register. They shrugged and slipped out the door, trying not to break into a run. Even the RCMP didn't always have the right change. The Mounties were three blocks off their turf, a quarter of a mile into a friendly but foreign jurisdiction and unarmed. The trooper was most likely calling for backup.

The Mounties were officially welcome when in hot pursuit. Unofficially, they would wait outside in the street and move in when the backup arrived to get in on the credit for the bust. They'd do the same for the feds on the Canadian side. On the surface all that had transpired was the display of an automatic weapon in a public eating place. This was indeed illegal, and sufficient to call for help from the local police. However, young Tim did fit a profile—terrorist, drug smuggler, crazy guy with a shootin' iron.

"Ah, Miss Morgana," Morrissey addressed the pig.

"Speak to me, David Lewis Morrissey." A perfunctory nod as the Queen recognized a humble petitioner.

"At Harry's house you demonstrated certain powers that could have been useful in this circumstance, and I was wondering..."

Pen broke in, "What we are wondering is why the hell didn't you warn us about the kid with the gun? You could have zapped the sucker. There's lots of room left under Harry's porch."

"Your human mental furniture is strangely arranged. You and Prince are my only living subjects; I have been busy learning. My entire education of your culture has come from cable TV and the video movies Harry rented. This 'zapping' requires practice, like playing the mandolin. Much as a tattoo, when you've got it, it's there for good. Except that the mandolins will wash off later." She paused, admiring her use of the idiom, turning it, finding it good. "That this 'gun' might be an offensive weapon had simply not occurred to me. I'm getting better at it, but you fade in and out. However, we do have more company coming and she is a fighter, as well as a lover. I feel you should tell that young man on the telephone to lie down on the floor very soon. He has talked enough."

"Quigley, DOWN!" yelled Morrissey and with not a second to spare. The cigarette machine and cash register exploded in a hail of bullets.

A woman strolled in through the shredded remains of Cousteau's Salada Tea screen door; her introductory burst of automatic weaponry showed no respect for cooperative advertising. She was packing more firepower than the National Guard and looked very much like a wronged woman on a tear. "The absent wife," said Pen.

"Valerie is her name," said the pig, her snout in his ear. "Timothy is her husband; he was late for supper and she is harboring suspicious thoughts." All three dived under the table.

A man, slightly drunk, was next. He sauntered through the wreckage of Cousteau's door wearing a blue blazer and a large black moustache. His eyes swam in an astigmatic soup; he looked lost and was seeking a focus. He was toting heavy heat: a machine pistol. Morrissey spoke, a hoarse whisper, "Well, if you are reading our Valerie's mind, could you perhaps zap him like you did Pen's dog?"

"Sorry, but I've tried and the power won't work right now. I'm too upset."

"Ah, I have your attention. Bueno. Ladies and gentlemen, you may call me Val," said Val, cradling her weapon on one arm. "My associate is Mr. Paul Blackburn. You will please notice that he is armed and, while my

The Return of the Orange Virgin

attention may waver during our chat, his does not. I thus sincerely caution you against any abrupt motions, which Mr. Blackburn may misconstrue. He is a poet by nature and is a sloppy shot. You will help us to apprehend our missing associate who has, alas, absconded with an item of great sentimental value to me... my trust and affection. He is a runaway husband. Do not be shy. You. Please come out and join us, and bring your pet with you. Nice piggy."

That meant them. The two men and the pig struggled out from under the table.

"Stay seated and with your hands and/or trotters on the table, and no sudden moves, please." She spoke in unaccented, but syntactically bizarre English. "We hope to inconvenience you for only a brief time."

"This is possible," she went on, "for we have a helicopter waiting."

Uh-oh, thought Pen, *our Valerie views her listeners as superfluous, candidates for an imminent mass rubout.* Did she really have a helicopter coming for their getaway, or had the constant imbibing of cocaine and absinthe make her think it would be nice if some magic transport arrived from somewhere to get her airborne after she had massacred everything in sight? Or perhaps she has a wealthy patron with limitless resources who really does have a helicopter waiting to whisk herself and the gun-totin' poet away to a nearby landing strip from whence a private jet will fly them into the sunset and history.

Morgana hopped up on the bench next to Morrissey again. "The former," said the pig. "El is making believe He is me." She cocked her head toward Valerie in eager attention. The base of Pen's spine was numb as he struggled against a rising panic.

While Valerie Hatt held the stage all to herself, Pen noticed Paul Blackburn had found a focus. He was intently studying a small wall poster announcing a spring retreat weekend by the local chapter of an evangelical women's group. A nonsense song started running through his head.

Armageddon to know you,
Armageddon to know all about you...

Well, it took his mind off things.

Across the table, the Fata Morgana was giving him a strange look, her head cocked to one side, one ear up the other flopped over. In the face of death violent and sudden, his racing mind framed a want ad—adorable pet free to a good home, plays well with others. Both pointy pink ears flattened and she gave a low, throaty rumble, the kind that means trouble.

The powers were back. Perhaps they would live through this day after all. She nodded her head and lolled a pink tongue telling him yes. Nice piggy.

Val rattled on; she finished elaborating a fine point at the end of a forensic string that only a fellow wronged woman could have followed. About her kids and her cows getting into an onion patch and her husband being displaced by an arrival from a parallel world, another dimension. One of those things. She paused for audience reaction. There was none.

The pig hopped off the bench. "Pardon me, I have to powder my nose." With the aplomb of a Park Avenue debutante she passed through the shards of the screen door, now dangling by one top hinge. Val followed the retreating curly tail with the terribly steady muzzle of her machine gun and Pen and David shared a vision of spattered blood and bristles plastered to the floor. Morgana daintily squatted in the street outside.

Morrissey kicked Pen under the table and jerked his head toward the rear. There was Harriet Hopwood, back from her tryst with Tim Hatt, fugitive husband. As soon as Val turned around her number was up. They were all going to get it. Harriet took in the tableau, started blinking rapidly, and then went all glassy-eyed. She held her hand against the wall as though lost, steadying herself.

"Freeze!" cried Harriet and, throwing herself to the floor, started slapping the linoleum. "Don't anybody move!"

God bless her contact lenses.

"Jesus Christ!" Val spun around and emptied her clip of bullets into the air where Harriet had been standing, chewing up Cousteau's ornamental frieze. A Greek motif dinner plate and a genuine oil painting of a bait shack and gnarled fishermen fell to the floor.

"Shit!" Val was having trouble fitting another clip into the pistol's magazine. She had caught the toss of the cosmic dice.

Trooper Quigley scooped a heavy glass sugar cellar from the counter top and, charging to where Paul Blackburn, frozen in a museum-quality pose struggled with his gun's mechanism, fetched him a needless roundhouse slam alongside the ear. The poet went down. Quigley snatched the gun and turned his attention to Val. Val likewise hadn't moved through all the ruckus. Quigley pried Val's thumb away from the stock and gingerly withdrew her index finger from the trigger guard. Valerie was motionless but for one tear that trickled down her cheek.

"Damnedest thing I ever saw." Quigley shrugged, popped the clip and bent to manacle Valerie Hatt. Champion and Everlast, the Mounties, stormed through the door as the city cruiser pulled up on the sidewalk, lights flashing. The hot pursuit clause was satisfied and just in time for pictures. There was a pop of a strobe flash as the bureau chief from the Bangor Daily News limbered her camera.

The Happy Time Bread man had missed the big one. His gun rolled tight in its cartridge belt, chambers empty, Deputy Bob Sawyer was stocking muffins at the Red and White where Libby Pease shopped. That afternoon she would buy two loaves of cracked wheat.

On the Downtown Local

It seemed too easy. Linda's captor had hustled her into a service elevator and hence to the main floor where he propelled her across the lobby.

"You are letting me go? For a while there I thought I'd be stuck here with you till the end of time."

"Hush! Speak no ill of what you cannot understand."

"I understand that you and your confederates are a bunch of certifiable nuts."

"Yesterday's dingy dungeon, today's five star hotel. With doorman service." The Rider on the Storm swept His hand across a burgeoning belly to give a flip to the braided gold cords that hung from His epaulets. "I have decided you are of no further use to Me. Don't take it personally. It's a godhead thingy. Have a nice day." He shoved her out into the street. A moment later, the revolving doors swung open again as he pushed her Bean totes through with his foot.

Linda stood outside the Hotel Taft. It must be almost freezing out, she thought. The thought of reclining in a hot tub with a Kahlúa and brandy close to hand gave her the strength to carry on. Linda bent double from a searing pain behind her eyes. "Whoa, hey! This is going to be one hell of a migraine."

As the heavy brass and glass door snicked shut behind her she turned to give her captor one last look. A nondescript Everyman smiled and waved reassuringly from the security station. He was now wearing the familiar tattered blue of the building's rent-a-cops. All would be well. She just had to get home.

The cold blast of wet air in the street came as a relief. Her sweater was starting to itch through her cotton sleeves. Her rolled umbrella, trendy with a shoulder strap, was slipping. Linda opened it and held it against the sleet, rain, and now snow mixture. A barbered, manicured red-faced man in a camel's hair coat beat her out for a cab. As the door slammed he looked sleekly regretful. Linda felt the sweat trickling down from her armpits.

She decided on the downtown local. As she charged on underground the saturated humidity hit her. She assumed a crouch for the run to the turnstiles. Catatonic passengers whizzed past through the station—noses flattened out against the glass, coats and scarves and bags caught between doors the conductor didn't bother opening. The subway never inspired fear before—loathing, disgust, but never fear. Now it did. That close, breathing one another's castoff air, riding the train was communion beyond intimacy. "Crammed butt to butt and always someone copping a feel and you can never tell who it is."

She positioned her token over the slot and slapped it through a residue of chewing gum with the flat of her palm and advanced, sliding her stuffed totes over the turret with its three metal bars. There was a comforting clunk as she hit the pipe with her hip. Better get a move on.

The next bar popped into place, pushing her through. The machine had found her offering acceptable. She reached the concourse. Her mouth was dry, dry. This was like exercise in a rubber suit. Oh, shit! Her bra strap had just given up the ghost, its elastic sodden and limp. For this day's work, Tom had better take her out for one last dinner, not the usual boil-in-a-bag frozen gourmet treats.

An uptown shoo-wop group shuffled and bopped from the far end of the platform. Downtown locals run all night, doo-dah, doo-dah. Linda fumbled in her coat and came up with a five-dollar bill to drop in their basket. Whatever else the crazy guy was, he hadn't picked her pocket.

Next, the ramps. Down three stories to the trains and right on time. I can make it.

"Hold the doors! Hold the doors!" Linda ran as fast as her skirt would allow. Legs pumping, teeth clenched, she impacted the wall of cramped commuters all ready on board—Oof! She looked around defiantly, claiming her space. The doors slid shut with a pneumatic whoosh that caught her bag outside as the train started to move. One quick, hard jerk and the bag was free and inside. The doors' floppy safety edges met—the caress of rubber lips on her thigh. Huh. Make something of that. The headache was now a pressure of remembered pain, sore to the touch if she could touch that place deep behind her eyes. Linda waited for the agony to resume.

❏

Everything in the Village was stippled aquatint in shades of gray. A patch of wintery sky widened above as Linda dragged her gym tote, umbrella and weary, failing body up the steps of the Christopher Street stop at Sheridan Square. As she neared the top steps she peered out at sidewalk level through the railings.

A tow-headed pre-schooler hip-hopped alongside his baby brother's stroller as a family walked past through the long shadows of early evening. The sleet had become a freezing rain; they ignored it. He knocked her up and left school at sixteen to pump gas, for this was the code, thought Linda. This stringy young mom would always be yesteryear's prom date. Last year the toddler was in the stroller. They were on their way to the bodega for Coke and Twinkies.

Linda felt the world tilt and teeter. Apocalypse, yes, but not now. Her vision blurred as she tried to catch up with the galloping subtitles of her own special movie. Buildings peeled away and Seventh Avenue writhed. This is the Big One and happening to me. She dropped her gym tote and rummaged through its pockets. Didn't she have a bottle of Midol somewhere? The yellow letters were at a peculiar angle she had not seen in any other movie. Acetate shredded and tore; a crevasse zigzagged across the screen to a welling of pink noise from theater speakers. Spooling motors sought equilibrium and ran wild, their logic circuitry sending home a homing signal there was nobody left at home to answer. The film parted and flew off the screen, leaving only a blinding white glare. An uncapped projection lamp brought a Hiroshima sunrise to Greenwich Village. Tornado winds howled and midtown, on West 46th Street, the sun stood still above Times Square.

The family grouping was returning. Each held a plastic wrapped glass pint of Classic Coke. The young mom steered the stroller, a big brown paper bag full of chips and sugary treats wrapped around the bar under her hands. The young mom's stooped shoulders leaned wearily into a long gray march of duty.

I could have been her, thought Linda.

It was the year of her own junior prom. She should have gone with the boy—Eddie? But Mom had said no. Unprotected, rapturous sex in Eddie's car instead. Eddie was now pumping gas.

Linda felt a deep melancholy; to be sucked into oblivion by a cerebral thrombosis—equipment failure—was so tacky. *I wish I had gotten knocked up in high school. Pregnants didn't have to go to the prom. All those yellow subtitles wasted, and just when I had everything all worked out.*

Tonight is the night Tom thaws Szechwan dumplings, too. The memory gave Linda a case of the giggles. When he isn't fucking me, Tom is rinsing the rice cooker. He calls this house husbanding. He waters the plants and stares out the window. These were the little things that made up a life. Tom cleaned house.

The idea of missing out on Tom's dumplings made her disproportionately cheery at her impending death. Linda was suffused with something akin to a runner's aerobic high. She had found a new religion, and it would not be denied—a faith of joy and, well... faith. She grasped at the nearest railing to steady herself. There was the shadowless Hiroshima sunrise, now behind her eyes. A stroke, something cerebral. There had been sidebars on the TV news.

The sleet now carried ice crystals that bit the skin as the driving sideways winds from Jersey picked up. The young parents and their children ran for cover. A freezer bag of Stouffer's Broccoli Au Gratin, a Tom specialty, slid into a pot of boiling water that filled the sky, then faded. Eight years of friendly, non-combative, often passionate marriage and Tom survived only as a name with no face. Then that, too, was gone. A cobwebby gauze covered her eyes as the world blurred. Her knees and elbows warmed and dream filaments twined about her feet as she swooned backwards onto a welcoming pile of eiderdown where she gently bounced in slow motion, again, and again, and again.

"Linda?"

Her bouncing took a pause.

"Yes. That is you."

"Yes, me. You have been invited to join me for Thesmophoria. Won't that be nice?" The voice was Norma Jean leFay from work. "Everything is clove scented. You noticed?"

"I noticed."

"So glad you found the time to visit. I got your favorite cookies from Gristede's—the oatmeal stuffed date?"

"With lemonade?"

"With lemonade," said the goddess.

Linda Winkelman was born the year they invented frozen lemonade. It was the year they added the Bullwinkle balloon to the Macy's parade.

The Return of the Orange Virgin

A Dream of Dancing

Quigley was spinning a Canadian dollar coin, absently tracking it through a coffee spill. Eleven-sided, anodized aureate bronze minted on a nickel blank, it had the shine of new gold. The many flats of its edges made it great for spinning. Elizabeth Regina on the one side. On the obverse, or reverse, depending on your feelings about the British North America Act, a duck. But the duck is not a duck, it is a loon, the lonesome augur of misted mornings, a shivery cry clinging low on the waters of the inland lakes, below the mists calling the fish to rise. The Canadians call this coin a 'Loonie' when they think about it, which is seldom. The Americans never think about it. Hardly the stuff of magic.

There had to be money—lots of it. Somewhere. Following the shootout at EAT, the forces of the Law were left with one confused couple, each maintaining fiercely in broken English that he/she was not married to—had never before seen—the other. English as a second language, the weaponry in evidence, all pointed to an international drug conspiracy. They swore that they were native English speakers but had been out of practice for a number of years they couldn't quite pin down and in a place they couldn't find on any map.

The pistol-packing poet insisted that he was an in-house editor for the Encyclopedia Britannica. They didn't bother to check; he was locked away downstate in the suite sister Libby had hoped to set aside for brother Harry Profitt Pease. The woman, Valerie, disappeared from her cell, leaving only a chocolate mint patty on the pillow. Tim Hatt walked free on a writ of habeas corpus.

"Who says nothing ever happens in Willipaq," Quigley stared at the formica countertop. Nothing had happened for Quigley, Champion and Everlast. It had started for them with the first sirens of spring. Now it was almost fall and with the wisdom that hindsight gives, April had been their cruelest month. The world then had taken on a glossy finish as the prospect of pinning down vagrant dollars shone brighter than the polyurethane on the alleys at the Border Duckpin Lanes.

Dreams of glory followed by months of thankless work ate away at the lawmen's free time. They broke up with girlfriends and were hollow-eyed and snappish on the job. They were frozen in a holding pattern. It was the same old shit day after day. But the three had made a commitment to the golden quest—filling ninety-eight cent notebooks with doodles. Plus a heavy investment in time and effort. None wanted to be the first to quit, besides there had developed that attachment between the keepers and the kept. Tim Hatt knew who they were and what they were doing and was playing the game with them—a sure admission of culpability.

Their tail on Tim had made the three the world's leading authorities on the unendurable tedium of his regular, predictable, and enviably respectable life. Eat, sleep, fuck and study—his English was now flawless. He even recycled and composted. Twice a week he spaded coffee grounds and lettucey salad residue into Harriet's tiny garden. Alternate Thursday mornings he separated glass and aluminum and drove to the redemption center. Tim Hatt had sought no gainful employment. He seemed to live, love, read and mulch. He was sailing through life on a plastic surfboard, sustained frugally with a modest credit ceiling on a MasterCard and a Visa, miraculously refreshed. A tireless routine, and legitimate; they had checked on his plastic. The accounts were supported by a stipend, which he never over-drew, of a blind trust administered by a reputable old-line law firm. It was the bequest of an unnamed relative who had squirreled away some insurance policies in his name. After the first flurry of elated activity, they were no further along the road to success. Their chimaera of career advancement had flown the coop, and with its elopement taken the dreams of chevrons and pensions.

"Doesn't that just burn me up," said Quigley, expressionless, under control. "I am just really cooked, boiled, burned and plain old pissed-off and bummed-out."

Favorite expressions. Quigley saw himself on the short end of the administrative stick. He was in a rotten mood. Actually, the Phoenix, the weather bird of ancient iconography, was the bird who burned, while Chimaeras have reportedly flown coops. The Phoenix, who aside from this paragraph makes no appearance in this story, was another airborne analog of the ancients who should have known better. Because of living on the Greek isles and all, they were close to nature and blessed with discretionary time for seeing animal shapes in the stars. Despite this, the ancients acquired a reputation for wisdom that persists to this day. It was a healthy outdoor life. Full of pride in their Mediterranean location and sparkling beaches, they played with new gods and imported others. The old gods slept.

The new gods danced.

Phoenixes burned and coops were flown—living the good life. But that was then and that was there and that was all long ago. With his hands busy toying with a shining coin and nightmares of an empty coop, Quigley was here, and nowhere careerwise. If you're keeping score, the

Phoenix and Quigley burned and the Chimaera eloped with their hopes, taking with it the Ladder of Success, which the boys had left leaning on the eaves of their edifice of advancement.

"There was a northeaster flattened most of the waterfront where we are now sitting." Champion was trying to be helpful, changing the subject. After six years with the RCMP, he was a constable. He had been posted to an out-of-the-way community at the far end of the Willipaq Ferry. Champion once enjoyed high hopes. What had gone wrong? It worked for other recruits. He had seen them rise. Why, just being nearby when the big busts happened, the glory rubbed off and up the ladder they went. They had gone and he had stayed, checking visas and administering breathalyzer tests. And he had been there, in the thick of it at the celebrated shootout at Cousteau's Diner, but no stripes.

Good publicity for the corps meant preferment all around. Champion had even had his picture in the national press. He had figured to generate countless column-inches of newspaper stories with the high profile investigations at a busy border crossing. But here he was staring at a tiny circle of sky from the bottom of a well of oblivion, an unperson.

Quigley knew Champion was right. There had been no perceptible forward motion since the first few weeks of their concentrated tailing of 'the Kid.' They had almost had him that night at EAT he was sure. Since then it had become a ritualized pursuit.

There is power in a glance, the power that if your eyes linger overlong on another dancer's partner this will require him to forget his timing, drop rhythm, to break the truce. Both preoccupied they spin on woodenly—dancing about the floor around an object of which they must never speak, whose existence must never be acknowledged but for their presence at the dance. Her long blonde hair bound in a stylish coil, picture hat and gauzy dress, a patrician beauty dances open-mouthed, taking short frequent breaths—more, surely, than are demanded by the exertions of the waltz—her eyes rolled back to the whites in a stylized gesture of sexual anticipation which her escort must notice. The escort notices, but he is busy just now covering his back. *We have pretended we are here for the dance; we have broken the fragile protocols that bind together the keepers and the kept.*

Champion had seen something just like this. In a dance piece on the Canadian Broadcasting Corporation's television service, the toughs had been strutting, but out of mutual fear and the respect fear engenders, not allowing their glances to rest overlong on the beauty, transcendent, a prize dancing beneath her social class, the other's beautiful woman. Over the months past the dancers invaded his dreams and, while dreaming, invited him to join them. This he had not confided to his partners. Though he spoke of the show, the dream of dancing was his not to share.

"You watch too much TV, Ed. Straight guys don't go to the ballet, even on the CBC. Pass me down the sugar would you?" said Quigley. "Spare me the cultural uplift, television is turning your brains to shit."

"Careful, Quig, you'll hurt my feelings."

"You're a Canadian; you don't have feelings."

"You gringo white-eyes were happy enough to see our money when the exchange rate was 33 percent." Champion stirred his steaming coffee with his little finger, the way he had seen lumberjacks do in the movies. "Ouch! It's the human condition."

"Ed, your problem is reverse hibernation. Hockey deprivation is showing." Quigley spun the coin. The trick was to get it spinning in place, standing still and spinning.

"There was this ballet on the CBC." Champion slid the sugar past the loonie. Disturbed by the breeze, it wobbled and fell, doing lop-sided figure eights as it settled onto the face of the Queen.

"French television, Ed. You should know better."

"Hockey and ballet. I only get the one channel."

"Hockey is almost over. Try baseball. I have to listen to ballet?"

"This is interesting. It bears on our situation now."

"You think we should wear tights and a codpiece. We go into the woods and find the pot of money under a toadstool. He comes to us and confesses all. Magnetic. Great."

Champion, Everlast and Quigley had become close during the weeks of their partnerless gavotte. Their faith that the fugitives and their mountain of money really existed, gone to earth somewhere on their backwoods patrols, had transformed their lives, given them a quest. They broke up with girlfriends and were hollow-eyed and snappish on the job. But there had been no perceptible forward motion.

"There were these gangsters, see... On TV?" Surreal dance hall bravos—cinch-waisted, spatted, tattersalled and starched with checkered waistcoats and gartered sleeves—swirled with their molls through an eternal Edwardian demimonde.

Watching, alone in his room, Champion had been struck by the parallels between the dance and his life. The beautiful feminine women and beautiful feminine men in a ballet of thugs walked out the designs he had observed forming in their own affair of Tim and the money. For after all, but for the money what were they all doing here? The kid had been a model citizen over all the months of free-time surveillance, happily living off the charity of an unnamed rich relation and his own plastic umbrella. They knew Tim was their man. He had to be a drug smuggler of some stripe or the other with a cash flow to rival the gross national products of many third world nations. Yet there he was, popular as hell, bouncing around town with the irrepressible energy of a boxcar load of ping-pong balls. Tim's rusty English was coming back swimmingly. Old people, children and small dogs just loved him. And the money, the evidence, through some legerdemain known only to Timothy Hatt was probably in an offshore account.

King Stilt-walker and the Queen

Balances were balancing... poise, then counterpoise. Tensions delicately held together what all good sense said should fly apart. The Fata Morgana stared into the rising sun as an incoming tide rippled loose fronds of kelp and bladderweed between the pilings below. She watched the flight of a bird, a bird freighted with a tiny cargo—one soul. She inhaled deeply—through her nostrils, retrieving a melody—and lightly hummed a ditty from one of the pentatonic modes. She snuffed out a cigarette with the heel of her hiking boot.

"Times and places change, not faces. Here I have accomplished something so stupendous, touching the unborn for millennia to come, and there is nobody left on stage but me who knows just what happened. Some congratulations are in order. So I shall congratulate myself. Thank you, Queen of Heaven. 'Oh, it was nothing,' I reply, self-effacing as ever."

A wry smile wrinkled her nose. "And the tyranny the living exercise over the non-living will continue and be called 'History.'"

A blue heron flew in, settled below on the freshly exposed mud, whiffling about for his dinner.

"What about you, King Stilt-walker?" She asked of the bird. "Are you not impressed with this good morning's good work?" Eager after little things, the bird strutted on the mud, long spindly legs and knobbly knees, wings folded in a floorwalker posture, and ignored the Queen of Heaven. "Correct as always, Blue Walker, business as usual. Your reply falls not short of the mark. You are accurate if not deferential."

Sitting on her heels, the Queen of Heaven removed a pebble from where it had wedged in the welt at the tip of a boot, setting it beside her on the chemical green decking. Behind her, and inside the diner called EAT, the disappointed lawmen sat at the counter. "What fools these mortals be," she quoted Puck, the Comics Weekly man, letting fall some few forensic tears to her checkered flannel vest.

Champion and Everlast were constables of the Royal Canadian Mounted Police, the Gendarmerie Royale du Canada, yellow-stripers. Their mothers called them Ed Hurley and Etienne Cyr, and it was as Ed Hurley and Etienne Cyr they were recognized by Canada Post, who brought them Christmas cards and catalogs and carried away their income taxes.

Quigley, the Maine state trooper, was spinning the same Canadian dollar coin. "You Canadians make pretty money."

"We spend it here," said Everlast. "And don't forget hockey."

"Ohhh, shit!" Quigley groaned and pounded his fist on the counter.

"Faretheewell, my little ones," was her whispered investiture to the departed tears. Her evocation carried an allusion not lost upon the tiny falling pearls, thence to evaporate into the world of foolish men. Lifting one diminished teardrop by the tip of a perfect finger, Morgana traced a pattern among the yellow strawflowers of the restaurant's wallpaper. Bright paint, bright wallpaper, bright colors, a song of joy to the eyes, she thought and was pleased. All through the bleak, unrelenting monochromal sameness of winter, they celebrate me with the colors of spring. "You little sisters are the last I shall weep for men on this world of mine," was her valediction to the departed tear, a farewell to one crystal pearl of compassion. "Midsummer Night's Dream, my dainty droplets. Am I not indeed a Shakespeare quoter, quotha?" Morgana giggled. "Or perhaps a spearshaker, a wagglestaffer, a buxom enchantress who knows not poppycock from floppycock. Ohhh! How ribald I have become! Go girls—make your sacrifice—and hurry to join your sisters in the River of the World."

Picking up the phrase as it nudged affectionately at his mind, Champion gestured expansively. "That ocean out there," he expostulated, "Is the River of the World."

"Oh Jesus, not you, too," said Quigley, giving the dollar coin with the bird on its backside an extra hard flick, propelling it over the edge of the counter. All motion ceased, everywhere—the rush of blood through capillaries, the bell clapper hung frozen in mid-stroke, or an assassin's bullet flattened out against a well of onrushing air.

 The Queen of Heaven strode to the edge of a mooring on posts above the bay, and reached out to retrieve the loonie in mid-flight. Life began anew "Oh Womb of the Universe, give me strength that this throw be true." Pulling the pins from her coiled hair, she shook loose the nine three-stranded braids to fall free below her waist. Deity does not have bad hair days. Nonetheless, this had been a day to rattle the attics of infinity—a very bad hair day all round.

"Gaia, take this sucker out of the park!" cried the goddess. With a twist of her shoulders, elbow high and lined with her ear, hip and elbow snapped together, her whole body a catapult, in the best form of the international fast pitch softball leagues. "Oh bird of men, castoff of these grim ganymedes, fly for me. Fly now, oh shining loon. Fly and confuse the eidolons, and by your flight, oh bird of circumstance, save for me this green world where I have shed so many tears."

Through the filtered light and long shadows, the Orange Virgin kicked off her hiking boots and, peeling down wooly socks, wiggled her toes over the edge. Red checked plaid, she worried a king size filter single-handed from her pack as she undid long coils of braid. She flicked her fingers, the cigarette glowed. I am satisfied, but I feel no joy. She sat thus long silent minutes in the shortening shadows. Then, stubbing out her smoke, she rose and smiled a knowing smile. A trick of the light surely, the years fell from her as she shook the weight of grey and auburn from its loosely woven caul.

On the shore, a beautiful child stood above the retreating tide, likewise shaking loose long hair to fall free to her waist. Distant crows rattled at the heightening dawn and reminded the Fata Morgana of home. *And where is that?* she thought. There was a clattering of implements and the child struggled out the catwalk to the end of the quay. The girl, lugging cleaning gear, looked up, smiled and hurried over radiating a look of guileless innocence.

"Hail, sister. Passing through?"

"I fancy so, sister, if you will let me pass. Are you helping or hindering?"

"I am helping myself, sister, if it please you."

The child was carrying a vacuum cleaner, a mop and bucket. "I say, you certainly had the staff scared off. I'm doing a bit of neatening—the new regime and all that."

"If you mean you are the Orange Virgin now, there's no need to be shy; I do not grudge you that. You might have simply wished the dust elsewhere."

The Wise Child shrugged and set the vacuum down. "Not bloody likely. It takes all the concentration I can muster simply to keep hanging on. And how fares it then with you, sister?" The child turned and stooped to set an armload of hose attachments next to the vacuum canister. A big, ugly black and blue contusion bulged around one eye. "We are not proof to collateral abuse, you nor I." The side of her face that had been turned away carried the souvenir of a fierce blow: a bloom of flushed, swollen skin shot with prominent veins crept out around an impromptu bandage seeped through with yellowish fluid. The bandage covered whatever damage had been done to an ear. The Fata Morgana let out a gasp. This was unexpected.

"Colorful, isn't it?" said the Wise Child. "Would you believe I ran into a door?" A glimmer of humor shone past an eyelid all but swollen shut.

"Who dared do this to you?"

The Wise Child lifted her thin shoulders. "One much as you—a promising hegemon who, like you, underestimated me. I turned a stormy trick. Oh, you should see the other guy. And that is where we're off to."

The Morgana touched the child's shoulder with her hand, allowing it to rest there, gently, then withdrawing it.

The child touched her mother's forehead and peered deeply into her golden eyes. "There is no bitterness there."

"No. Becoming mortal at this time has much to recommend it. You are in place, strong and vital. The only way to find out if my assessment of events is correct was to weaken myself to the point of no return. I am resigned to that path. Also because it is the only available path." The shadow Morgana smoothed the child's hair on her unwounded side. "This 'New Regime' of yours—the phrase has the ring of a museum docent. Might you be accepting day-trippers to defray upkeep?"

The Wise Child grinned broadly and picked up the vacuum cleaner.

The Fata Morgana smoked quietly, reflectively, treasuring her time alone in the quiet. "So this is victory—a moment to myself then business as usual for me too, hi-de-ho." She was regretful for Linda, her priestess. But with the advent of the scattered bits and pieces of Linda's soul known as Maggie in the life of Pen Harrington, it had been her time; two Linda Winkelmans were too many. She had to make room for there was a new arrival and the world—this particular tiny piece of creation—wanted room. Humans, so shackled by time, remember only the past and had no memory of things yet to come. Linda's husband would have been done with his apprenticeship by now—whenever now was. "I wonder what he might make of Lamprey and Tawse. And the Manticore. I shall have to rearrange things to find out."

"Harry Pease." A sigh as she exhaled a single stream of blue smoke into the light. The light of a dawn that almost wasn't thought Morgana. Well, I deserve something nice, too. Harry could keep the recollections of forgotten Cleon company. Cleon, old King Cleon. We had some times together, he and I. Not a bad sort, really. She paused to stare down through the decking at the mud flats thirty feet below. A mosaic of bottle caps spun off by the supple wrists of summer picnickers regarded her in turn.

There was something important missing from the scene. Heavy flower stalks of blue and pink. Lupines—where are the lupines? With a setting in New England I would have just naturally supposed... But now it was too late in the season. No lupines, no daffodils.

Darkness defied the dawn and a silent presence made her start.

"Must you creep about like that? You startled me. Now I have lost my train." A rift opened in the night and a good-humored grin exposed rows of perfect opalescent teeth. From behind his back he produced a pot of daffodils.

"Flowers for remembrance, Morgana?"

"Have you been there all this time?"

Wide of shoulder, lean of hip, glistening blackness made an obligation, a deep salaam. "My Lady?"

"El. Sky demon, sometimes you piss me off with your sneakings-about. Next time make some noise—clear your throat or something. And allow me to compliment you on your fine shiner."

The demiurge touched his forehead and winced. It bore the imprint of a mop handle. "It is my pleasure to serve the Queen of Heaven, Lady."

"Your punctilio is appreciated" Dark as forgetfulness, the godling of the new dispensation waited attentively, suggesting unfinished business. White sow of Naxos, was she that easily read? "'...and the calabash of these human lives will yet spill...' oh spare me your hyperbole, Prime Mover immovable, albeit dented. We have lost some, but it is the living who must be served. I have cried for the innocents and they live again, although by rights their passings should have been of no more consequence than tame fish in an aquarium."

"And the Mountie who dreamed of dancing—he, too is dead? You will excuse me for I have been away."

"No, the Canadian policeman is inside, holding with the rest his frozen moment for our need. After this day's work, for him there will be no dancing. But he dreamed, and for some that will have to be enough."

"And what of the husband of your priestess? Will he be happy?"

"Happy happy happy happy. Is that all you can say?"

"Your Marvellousness is as ever a stickler after details. What about the golem, your child of chaos made from the clay of another world?"

"Slice me no circuitous obloquies, either bright prince. The golem's apron would tie nicely round your divine girth as well. The child, Biff Bangtree, will be well." She smiled a secret smile. "I have things, ahh... arranged. Peel me some fact from your roll of rhetoric. Simple declarative sentences, please."

"Well, Lady, we have saved the world. I was curious, is all."

"And that, O Rider on the Storm, will be enough, for now it is ours, together—a mutual glory, and we are stuck with it."

"You were endearing as a pig, you know..."

As Morgana and the demiurge turned to go inside, more coffee and second breakfasts in the forefront of their preoccupations, she willed a hillside of blooming blue lupines and was pleased. Let them wonder.

L'envoi

David Morrissey came boiling around the corner all arms and legs, caromed off the doorpost and skidded to a stop in front of Harry Profitt Pease. He produced a cigar.

"Guess what." Harry was lifted off the floor and swung in a bear hug.

"Guess uhnnn," Harry repeated as the breath was squeezed from his lungs.

"It's an embryo. I mean Maija and I just, well not we so much as she... we never thought at our age and all; but the doctor says its perfectly normal and mother and child are outrageously healthy and we had an amniocentesis, and... and..." He thrust the cigar, cellophane and all into Harry's mouth. "Second trimester."

Harry found speech difficult with his arms pinioned and his mouth full. When he could remove the cigar, he spoke. "This is important to you."

"It means the world, we never dreamed."

"And the tests show it will be a boy."

"Correct."

"Call him Biff, you can make up the rest as you go along."

"Biff? We thought maybe George—Mister Amberson?—Maija's father..."

"Biff." Harry peeled the cellophane wrapper and lit up. "He'll tell you all about it when he grows up."

In the days of old the gods had the whole earth distributed among them by allotment. There was no quarrelling; for you cannot rightly suppose that the gods did not know what was proper for each of them to have, or, knowing this, that they would seek to procure for themselves by contention that which more properly belonged to others.

CRITIAS—Plato, 360 BC, translated by Benjamin Jowett

How the Orange Virgin came to be

"wotthehell toujours gai I always say, there's life in the old girl yet."
—Don Marquis' *Archy and Mehitabel*

When I began *The Return of the Orange Virgin* almost 30 years ago, I had an all-over queasy feeling that the damned thing would move in and take over my life. So it did. Fast forward to 1993, and a typescript that weighed in at twelve pounds and 800+ pages. I figured it was time to go back to the beginning and actually read the thing. Yuck. Thereafter followed a year of rewrite and editing. "Not bad," I said, full with the flush of first-time authordom, and promptly sent the shortened albeit (even I felt) incoherent manuscript off to respected Sci-Fi imprint DAW Books, where my old college roommate, Pete Stampfel, was a fiction editor. To his everlasting credit he actually read it and sent back a detailed critique. Yep—incoherent all right. But there was 'good stuff,' said Pete. Go work on it. I pecked away but after a few tries Orange Virgin went into the drawer.

In the meantime, in-between time, Pete had vetted a series of my tales involving a Georges Simenon Inspector Maigret-style detective. Inspector Pingold was, however, a weasel with a habit of gnawing at his tail when deep in thought. Endearing, I thought. This is how we learn. The series—adult themes with kiddie characters—came back from a blind review tagged, "If we wanted animals in suits we'd be doing *Wind in the Willows*." Sigh.

Forward to the year 2007. Whaddya know, The Orange Virgin *did* have good parts. Mirable dictu! Maybe I'd give it another try. In spite of being made unpublishable by my swiping great globs of the tale for other stories, I thought The Return of the Orange Virgin might have traveled well. Had it matured like fine wine while no one was looking? I went back to check the MS. Nope—still cottage cheese, not cordon bleu. Thus began a rewrite into monthly installments for the website onetinleg.com.

Forward again and the year 2010. The inconsistencies, logical absurdities and plain-out wrong-headedness demonstrated by the author have been lessened, expunged and/or excised as The Orange Virgin was conflated to fit inside the covers of the volume you have in your hands. Have fun reading the Return of the Orange Virgin. Think of it as a hypertext puzzle box.

Rob Hunter
Pembroke, Maine 2010

Orange Virgin Dramatis Personae

The Fata Morgana, Orange Virgin, Lady of the Wild Things, etc., etc. – bitchy, quirky, a goddess.

El – a quasi-divine meddler, an anthem to himself, busy about his own self-worth. He and the Orange Virgin had a disagreement many years before our story. They are both answerable to a higher power.

Biff Bangtree – a golem, Morgana's plaything—the scapegoat, a paraclete, Jesus as Pinocchio. Biff's teacher and companion, the Manticore—a beast with the face of a man, porcupine quills, lion's body and the tail of a scorpion—is stuck in the wall of a castle cellar.

Harry Profitt Pease – the Priest of the Fata Morgana. Nearing 60, he was once the star center on the state champion basketball team.

Penfield Harrington – a lover of night nurses and truck-stop waitresses, he is redeemed by Linda Winkelman.

Linda Winkelman – the Priestess of the Fata Morgana. A knowledgeable competitor in the world of advertising. An attractive woman approaching 40, she could have had the Pork-A-Dillos account.

Tom Winkelman – Eight years of friendly, non-combative, often passionate marriage and Tom survives only as a name with no face. Then that, too, is gone

Supporting Cast

Jack Lamprey and Alf Tawse – elder dwellers, the earth-spirits of Morgana's world of exile. They are immortal but keep busy.

Cousteau McClonaghy – restaurateur, he owns EAT, the diner where Harriet Hopwood slings hash.

Joyce Gladstone (Mrs.) – librarian at the Valiant Memorial Library of Moose City at which establishment **Rev. Murtry** shows slides of the Holy Land and other elevating subjects on Friday nights in season. **Twizzle** is the Rev.'s dog, a weimaraner.

David (Dim Lights) Morrissey – Pen Harrington's pal.

Prince – a big yellow dog, likewise Pen Harrington's pal. Not a weimaraner.

Harriet Hopwood – waitress at EAT. A tightly knit woman, broad of beam and small-breasted, she has the supple lower back and slim waist of a devoted rider of horses. Harriet had played the Innkeeper's Wife in the ecumenical Christmas pageant.

Tim and Valerie Hatt – A pair of fugitive orphans, they pop up in various guises in the narrative. **Harriet** catches the toss of the cosmic dice and falls for **Tim** whilst **Tom Winkelman** has eyes for **Val**.

Paul Blackburn – a poet. Paul is a real person. He is dead and his books are out of print. An expert on Provençal troubadour ballads.

Alma Nightingale – she brightens and defines Harry Pease. A childhood sweetheart, she is friends with

Sarabande – a nymph and Superintendent of the Plantings.

The Manticore – he is Biff Bangtree's cicerone, Morgana's messenger and confidante.

The Moose of Circumstance – the wild cattle of Eternity, a herbivore. A symbol of forgiveness.

The Goat and the Cow – allegorical figures cut from stone, they remain in the cellar where they dream of walking under the sky.

Elizabeth Profitt Pease – Harry's sister. She thinks his eccentricities foreshadow future embarrassments and wants to pack him away downstate as a nut case.

Bob Sawyer – a county deputy.

Cap'n Dan – Pen Harrington's employer. Dan isn't choosy and is elated to have come up with a grownup who can speak and hear, drunk or sober. The high school kids are making 25 cents an hour more at McDonald's than he is paying and don't listen to his radio station anyway.

Champion, Everlast, Quigley – minions of the Law. Two Mounties and a State Trooper.

The Wise Child – an aspect of the Fata Morgana in her dream-sendings.

The Destroyer – another aspect of the Fata Morgana.

Fraxifrage – giant horse of the Wise Child.

A mother and daughter watching the night sky.

A castle child with a finger in his nose. A toddler – the nose is runny and what better place for a finger?

The pig, who started it all, an innocent by-stander.

Pork-A-Dillos, tasty little curls of fried pork rind, a low cholesterol consumer item, dietary peccadillos.

The Dancing Lords – proud of their manicured lawns and arboriculture—quite conducive to creative reflection. At a remove, the screams of the tormented ring from their torture pits. The Dancing Lords have disappeared at the time of our story—no problem.

George Amberson – exists as a mention in the Epilogue. George is the father-in-law of **Dim Lights Morrissey**, father of **Maija**, Mrs. Morrissey, and the putative grandfather and perhaps namesake of the reborn **Biff**.

A brief history of the author

"Hell's Angels wear leather because chiffon wrinkles too easily..."
—Paul Lynde on Hollywood Squares, 35 years ago.

With the onset of late middle age Rob Hunter is the sole support of a 1999 Ford Escort and the despair of his young wife. He does dishes, mows the lawn and keeps their coastal Maine cottage spotless by moving as little as possible.

In a former life [1] he was a newspaper copy boy, railroad telegraph operator, recording engineer and film editor. He spent the 70s and 80s as a Top-40 disc jockey. He won a plaque once, for production excellence, from the Maine Association of Broadcasters. The boss kept it. One of Rob's engineering projects [2] won Senator William Proxmire's (D-Wisconsin) Golden Fleece Award. 100 Years of Air Power was an Air Force recruiting multimedia presentation shot in PanaVision with 70mm slides, quad stereo, the works. It toured in a trailer that sat four.

Rob's wife, Bonnie, is the secretary at a nearby rural elementary school. She is a gifted quilter who beguiled her new husband with the kaleidoscope of patchwork geometry. The nearest town to the Hunters that anybody is likely to have ever heard of—because of Stephen King's The Langoliers—is Bangor, Maine where there are real parking meters and a traffic light. They drive down every six months or so to watch the light change and see the trains come in.

[1] The Milwaukee Journal; Chicago, Milwaukee, St. Paul and Pacific RR Co.; WINS-NYC, WBT-Charlotte; WJAR-Providence; WIVY-Jacksonville; WNEW-NYC; WBAI-Pacifica; WQDY-Calais, Maine

[2] Rob's long-time client at Random House Audiobooks, Sherry Huber, wangled them a 1987 Spoken Arts Grammy nomination. They didn't win. The nomination was for *The Short Stories of Ray Bradbury*.

robhunter@onetinleg.com

Acknowledgements

The Francher was first published in the March 2009 issue of *Aphelion* (www.aphelion-webzine.com).

Mark Twain in Milan was first published as an online serial in *Bewildering Stories,* fall 2010, Don Webb, managing editor.

Platterland was first published in *On the Premises,* the November 2007 issue, Tarl Roger Kudrick, editor.

McMuckle Makes a MInyan was first published in the December 2007 *Ranfurly Review*, Colin Galbraith, editor

Chimaera Constant was first published in the October 2008 *Farrago's Wainscot*, Darin Bradley, fiction editor.

Daphne Longhandle's Last Flight was first published was first published in *The Aputamkon Review II*, Fall 2008, Sarah Dalton Phillips, editor.

The Tirewoman Gabriel was first published in the February 2010 *Necrology Shorts*, John Ferguson, editor.

The Death of James A. Garfield was first published in the July 2008 *A Fly in Amber*—Shelly Jackson, fiction editor.

The Return of the Orange Virgin was first published online as a serial novel on the author's website, www.onetinleg.com. One chapter a month—this sounds easy, however you are invited to browse the work's history, "How the Orange Virgin came to be..." on page 358.

That elegant descriptive for psychic disorder, "running madly off in all directions," is attributable to Stephen Leacock (*Gertrude the Governess*, 1911), and used here in *The Return of the Orange Virgin*, Chapter 5.

The cover image is "Two of Swords," the work of antipodean artist and banjo player Anna Wilkenfeld, and is used with permission. From her home base of Sydney, NSW, Australia she works "...more or less full time at a cartooning company by day, cobbling together a few works for exhibitions by night, and plying my trade as a party cartoonist on the weekends."

The original photograph for the onetinleg.com website logo, "They All Look at Another Side," is the work of María de la Puente Bernardos and is used with permission.

About this Title

This work is licensed under a Creative Commons copyright which reserves some rights for the reader, too. Creative Commons is a non-profit consortium that offers an alternative to full copyright. Offering work under a Creative Commons license does not mean giving up copyright. All rights are reserved by the author but with some exceptions.

Check them out at http://creativecommons.org/licenses/by-nc-nd/3.0/

No creatures real or imagined were injured in the making of Platterland.

Platterland—More Forays into the Fantastic
by Rob Hunter
First published October 2010
ISBN:978-0-578-06803-9

Podcasting and MP3 Audio

You are invited to browse onetinleg.com's Free Reads section. These MP3 downloads are released under a Creative Commons license. They're free. Copy the files as much as you want, pass 'em around. All I ask is that you don't alter the file or sell it. To download—right click "Download" and select "Save Target As" or "Save Link As" depending on your browser. To preview a story just click "stream." The audio versions of the tales from Onetinleg.com will be appearing there as studio time allows.

You can stay ahead of the curve by clicking the RSS symbol to initiate a podcast. A podcast downloads audio files to your MP3 player through your computer. You use a free application (see page 103) to "subscribe" to onetinleg.com's feed, the application checks the site regularly and starts a download whenever it finds something new. If you like what you hear, tell your friends. I'm glad to have you as a listener. Enjoy!

Also by Rob Hunter

Lost in Willipaq
Magnetic Betty
The Quilter Who went To Hell
Midwife in the Tire Swing